everything in between

ARIA HARDING

Editing: Lacey Braziel at Lacey Braziel Edits (www.laceybedits.com)

Formatting and Proofreading: Cassie Weaver at Weaver Way Author Services

Cover Design: Marge Turingan

Ebook ISBN: 9798990264625

Paperback ISBN: 9798990264632

For my Indie Queens.
I had the time of my life writing stories with you.

ONE

jersey

FRIDAY, SEPTEMBER 6

"Thank you, Milwaukee. You've given me a night to remember!"

Adrenaline courses through me with a familiar and exhilarating hum. The last few moments are here. I hit my mark, right where the lift is located. I take another huge bow before standing up tall and waving my arm high above my head. As I descend beneath the stage, confetti falls from the roof and the colorful lights twirl in circles. I catch the last final glimpses of my fans waving back at me before I'm lowered out of view.

The roar of the crowd echoes in my ears, and as soon as the lift stops below the stage, the exhaustion of the pressure from the show hits me light a freight train. My knees wobble and my shoulders ache but even that's not enough to deter the gratitude filling me. I'm so thankful to be the one up there performing, making memories for my fans and putting on a show for them to remember. Even though the night is finished, I'll hold these memories close for many nights to come.

Blinking away the emotions from those last few moments of the show, I center myself again, taking a few deep breaths and counting down from fifteen. Before I make it to one, I am bombarded with the whirlwind of the after-show processes. My tech managers reach for my earpieces and my microphone, stowing them away safely until our next show. Beside me, my dancers chatter excitedly, hugging each other and sharing high-fives at another show successfully finished.

Eyes trailing over the crew that surrounds us, I search for the familiar blue eyes belonging to my personal assistant-slash-best friend.

"Jersey!" I snap my head around at the sound of Bethany's voice only to find her right behind me, a proud smile on her face. "Congratulations!"

She hurries in and wraps her arm around my shoulders. "There you are," I say, sagging against her in relief. Arm tightening around me, she hurries me away from the backstage craziness and into the green rooms. "I was starting to get worried you wouldn't come to my rescue."

Bethany pats my shoulder affectionately. "You know I'll always have your back."

The stillness of the green room wraps me up like a warm hug and I feel like I can finally breathe. There's nothing I love more than being up on stage and performing my heart out, but the energy required to do so wears on me. Once she shuts the door, I fall into the plush sofa that travels with us when we're on the road and take a big breath that hurts my lungs. My muscles are screaming at me and my skin prickles with the adrenaline crash.

Bethany stands by the door with her hands on her hips. "You look exhausted."

I fight out a laugh. "Gee, thanks. Every pop star dreams of

hearing that once she's finished her twenty-fifth show on her cross-country stadium tour."

"You're killing it out there. But I'm worried about you. I don't want you to burn yourself out," she says, and I catch onto her concern.

I exhale and give her as big a smile as I can muster. "Thank you. Going from one extreme to another definitely wipes me out."

"Get a little whiplash going from the highs of performing on stage to the chaos of being handled backstage?"

I chuckle and nod. "Exactly that."

"You really need to take actual time for yourself. I'm talking about no work whatsoever."

I frown, picturing my calendar in my head and the lack of wiggle room. "I'm not sure I would even know what that looks like. And really, that's not up to me." A bitter taste floods my mouth with that statement. "Callum's mentioned booking recording studio time for the rest of the year to finish the next album, so he's definitely not open to offering me time off."

Bethany purses her lips off to the side at the mention of my manager. The room falls quiet between us. My admission is a heavy reminder that I'm a pawn in the grand scheme of things.

"Speaking of, Cal is going to be pissed at you for that little stunt you pulled tonight," Bethany says.

"Oh, no doubt I'll get an ear full at some point. I need to gear myself up for the scolding," I mutter and then sigh, "but I'm going to get out of these clothes."

Bethany reaches for my post-show bag full of my comfiest clothes and hands it to me. I disappear into the adjacent bathroom and get out of the sparkly body suit. My skin is a little damp still from the dancing and the warm lights, but after rinsing and toweling off the sweat from the show, I feel good as new. I pull on my pair of sweatpants, an oversized shirt, and my fuzzy boots—my secret ingredient to feeling more comfortable. Digging through my bag of toiletries, I find my face wash and hairbrush. Once the makeup is off, my face is clean, and my hair brushed through, I can finally relax.

After gathering up the show items for the costume department to put away, I step out of the bathroom to see Bethany standing there holding my favorite post-show snack with a cheeky grin on her face.

"Figured you'd be starving by now." She hands the packages over and takes the clothes from me.

"You're my favorite," I announce, unscrewing the lid of peanut butter and scooping some out with an Oreo. The combination of chocolate and peanut butter explodes against my tastebuds.

"You're my favorite too." Bethany hangs up the bodysuit on the rack next to the rest of my costumes. "Plus, we've been doing this a long time. I know when you're in need of comfort food."

"That you do. And I *love it*!" I sing as I help myself to another hearty serving of peanut butter and moan at the absolute delight this treat brings me. It's the best after-show snack when I'm a little woozy from the lights and the physical exertion of dancing on stage for two and a half hours.

I take out a few more cookies, following the same routine. Bethany even helps herself to one or two. When my post-show sugar craving has been met, I relax into the cushions and close my eyes. In a little less than an hour, I'll be shuttled away from the stadium to the airstrip where I'll fly back to LA on my private jet. Come Monday, I'll be back at the studio ready to work. The turnaround while on tour can be grueling.

"Have you decided on what you're wearing for the VMAs next week?" Bethany asks, reaching for her phone. "I need to let

Kelsey and the rest of the PR team know which designer you've settled on."

Over the last few weeks, I'd been sent multiple dresses in exactly my size that I was encouraged to sport on the red carpet at the VMAs. I'm projected to win Song of the Year again for the third year straight, and I'll be presenting the Best Hip-Hop award. All the up-and-coming designers want their names plastered across every fashion news outlet as I present myself at the award show.

Already, I'm exhausted by the idea. I'm thankful for the opportunity and the fans' enthusiasm for the music I've released this year, but there's nothing I'd like more than to watch the show from the comfort of my home, and thankful that's exactly what I was able to do last year because I was rehearsing for shows. But this year, with my third nomination and invitation to present, Callum insisted I make an appearance.

"This is the big leagues now, cupcake," he said when I voiced my desire to sit this one out too. "There's no time to sit on the sidelines."

"I think I'm going to go with the Agnelli," I say absentmindedly, going for another Oreo and a large scoop of peanut butter as a comfort. A hint of anxiety pokes its head out of the shadows of my mind when I think about using up the last reserves of my social battery at the award show next week. "She's the sweetest and least aggressive of the bunch we've gotten this year."

"I agree," Bethany says, tapping on her phone screen to note my decision.

This was a personal choice I made in the last few years, only choosing to wear up-and-coming designer pieces. Even all of my stage costumes are designed by smaller name designers. Not a single high-end named piece is on my set list. It would be easy for me to get my hands on a Versace or an Oscar de la Renta, but I wanted to give smaller designers a chance at the limelight. Cal was not the biggest fan of the idea when I brought it to the table, but after arguing about it and going back and forth, he finally relented. I can count on one hand the number of times I've bested him in an argument over the years we've worked together. He would love me to be in the pieces designed by the bigger names, but I held firm on my request, not budging until he agreed.

In my opinion, the smaller designers deserved to have someone take a chance on them, like the label did for me all those years ago. Even Cal can't argue with that sentiment.

Unfortunately, my small win with Cal was short-lived. He's been even more of a pain ever since then. As if I need the daily reminder from him that he pulls the strings of my career.

The door to the green room flies open, revealing my twin brother standing there with outstretched arms. "Jersey Matthews, you've done it again!"

I roll my eyes and laugh as he takes the seat to my left, falling into the couch cushions with an audible *oof*. Roman has always been one of my biggest fans. He's an on-screen heartbreaker, landing all the big roles recently in Hollywood. His schedule is as grueling as mine, but he does his best to attend as many of my shows as possible. He's recently finished filming next year's summer rom-com, so his schedule has freed up for a little while.

"How's Hollywood treating you these days, Roman?" Bethany asks.

"Great, actually. My agent is trying to land me a deal for a regular TV show. That would mean I'd be in LA for longer periods of time."

I turn to him, surprised at this news. "You'd like that?"

He gives me an affectionate nudge. "Of course."

Bethany swivels between the two of us in amusement. "The Matthews twins, taking LA by storm. Once again."

I laugh and reach for another Oreo, offering one to my brother too.

"Did you know Hayes Vogt was in attendance tonight?" my brother asks, absentmindedly flicking through his phone and opening a social media app while polishing off the cookie.

I run my hands through my messy hair and ask, *"Who?"*

Roman looks at me like he can't believe the question. "What do you mean, *who?* He's only the greatest quarterback in the league right now." I side-eye Roman like he's equally insane for thinking I'd have any interest in this. He balks again. "Quarterback for the Milwaukee Majestics."

I tilt my head at my brother as if to say, *And?*

He rolls his eyes. "Oh, for Pete's sake. He made a cameo in J-Money's music video and almost broke the internet."

"Oh, yeah. I do remember that, actually. Which one was he?" I ask, thinking back to when the rapper released the video. I do somewhat remember the guy in the cameo—Hayes Vogt, apparently—catching my eye. Roman doesn't need to know that, though. He was handsome and fit, but most of all, he looked like he was having the time of his life. His energy and enthusiasm made the entire video. It's no wonder J-Money got a nomination. It was all anyone could talk about at the label for weeks.

He raises an eyebrow at me, unimpressed, showing me his screen as if I needed the proof. "He did a livestream right as he arrived at the stadium, trying to get your label's notice to bring him backstage so he could meet you."

"Why didn't he DM me on Instagram?" I ask absentmindedly. "We bring celebs and athletes back all the time. Even internet celebrities. It wouldn't have been a big deal."

My brother shrugs. "Maybe he wanted the attention of more people. You know how athletes can be."

I don't know, actually. Having never been into sports, I'd have no basis for knowing their mannerisms or anything about them. I shrug, playing off my naivete, and stare down at my screen as a text from Callum comes in.

CALLUM

WE NEED TO TALK.

His message has anxiety plummeting through me like an avalanche. It's never a good sign when Cal texts me right after a show—in all caps, much less—and Bethany's comment from earlier rings in my ears. Typically, he'd give me the night to rest my voice and come down from the high of performing before hitting me with any business matters, but given I publicly rebelled tonight, there's no doubt in my mind that he's got steam blowing out of his ears.

Within moments, my phone vibrates with his call.

I push myself off the couch, mumbling to no one in particular. "Here we go."

Swiping my finger across the screen, I put it to my ear. I don't get a chance to speak a word before Callum is screaming in my ear. Wincing, I pull the phone away from my eardrum and let him spout his nonsense. When the call has quieted down, I put the call back to my ear. "Are you done?"

"We had an agreement, Jersey," he growls on the other line. "You stick to the set list that's was crafted for you, no variations."

"I was going with the vibes," I tell him, aware of how flighty that makes me sound. "It felt right tonight, Cal."

"I don't give two flying fucks about what felt right," he says, sarcasm dripping off his words. "We pay a lot of money for people to come up with the set list. We practice it, we sound check it. We do not pay you to make last-minute changes. It's not your decision."

"But it's my show," I argue. "People pay hundreds, if not more, to come see me. I should be able to make changes where I see fit and not have my head bitten off for it."

He falls silent and my anxiety ramps up tenfold.

"We have had this conversation a *thousand* times, Jersey, so I'm not sure what you're not getting here. You are a Silver Shadows artist; you *belong* to us. We pay you the big bucks, so you don't have to worry your pretty little head with pointless things like set lists and choreography. All you have to worry about is staying fit and looking good on stage."

My skin crawls with his words, and I bite my tongue. Bile wells up in my throat with an irritated burn.

"I don't want to hear anything like this happening again. Are we clear?" His voice is firm, leaving no room for argument.

"Crystal," I growl between clenched teeth.

"Good." The change in his demeanor makes my head hurt. He continues with a lighter tone, as if he didn't just rip me a new one. "I'll see you soon. We have some more things to go over before we start recording the next album. Rest up, cupcake."

He clicks off the call without another word.

The weight of Bethany's worried eyes land on me, and I clear my throat, hoping my voice doesn't waver when I say. "I'm gonna use the bathroom."

I hurry away before they can stop me, closing the door and resting my hands on the sink counter. I bow my head and focus on my breathing—counting down from fifty this time— wondering how everything went so sideways. It happened without me even realizing it. I was too young, at twenty-one, to fully understand what some of the finer details in my contract meant—that by signing my name, I'd sign my autonomy away to the label as well. I'd perform songs they chose and put out albums they pieced together, with little to no say of my own.

At the time, I only had stars in my eyes, realizing this was my big break. I agreed easily and with little contest.

Now, the weight of the shackles that I so willingly allowed to be fastened around my wrists reminds me I'm a prisoner at their mercy.

Unfortunately, I can picture the keys to my freedom, but they're still out of reach. As far as Silver Shadows is concerned, I'm nothing but their property, their cash cow. It's not every day they stumble across a nobody who is soon selling out stadiums across the country.

All I can do is grin and bear it and wait until my contract ends in three years. They don't know yet that I don't plan to sign another three-year extension. I regret signing the current extension last year, but after coming off the high of a successful album, I had thought *hey, why not*? But now, in some ways, I feel like I'm at the bottom of a mountain, staring up helplessly at the prize at the top.

When my pulse has leveled out, I step out of the bathroom and head back over to the couch. Bethany gives me a sympathetic smile, knowing exactly how that conversation went and that I needed a moment to stew in the aftermath by myself.

"Hayes Vogt said on his stream that he'll be at the VMAs next week since J-Money is nominated," Roman says, eyes glued to his phone as he scrolls through his social media feed, completely unaware of the verbal beating I just received.

"Oh, that's cool," I mutter noncommittally, head still reeling from my conversation with Cal to show any more enthusiasm.

"Maybe you'll run into him. He seemed pretty bummed he didn't get to meet you tonight."

"Why?" I ask, though I'm sure my brother doesn't have the answer either. "I've never even heard of him before you brought him up."

Roman shrugs. "Well, he's clearly heard of you. He must like your music if he's coming to your concerts."

It's an interesting thought. That the quarterback making cameos in J-Money's video would be a fan of my style of music, but crazier things have happened.

"If you do run into him at the show, see if you can get an autograph for me," Roman continues.

I lean back on the cushions of the couch, pushing my wounded pride to the back of my mind. I have too much on my plate between the label, the tour, the album, and thinking about everything on my to-do list before that award show. There are far too many things that need to be addressed. I don't have the time or the energy to care about some football player that I've never heard about—I don't even like football. But seeing Roman so excited about the prospect of me seeing this specific athlete has me muffling a chuckle. My brother is famous in his own right, but that doesn't stop him from appreciating others' fame too. Especially when it comes to sports names.

So despite myself, I agree. "I'll see what I can do."

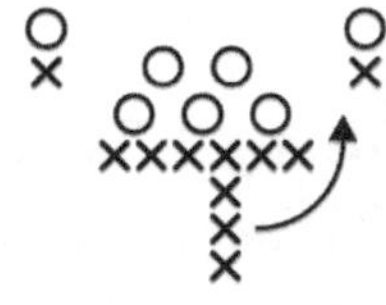

TWO

hayes

FRIDAY, SEPTEMBER 6

ANY OTHER NIGHT, my little sister's relentless bouncing would grate on my nerves. But tonight, I can make an exception.

She's practically buzzing with adrenaline, as if she were the one on stage doing all that crazy choreography.

"Did you see the way she came to the stage right at the beginning? That look on her face that made you feel like she was performing just for you?" Riley gushes. Her blue eyes are alight and glittering with unadulterated enthusiasm.

"I did."

"She owned that whole stadium," Riley says, awe sweeping through her. "And did you see how she strutted across that stage in those high-heeled boots? She made it look easy—which, let me tell you, it is most definitely *not*."

"I believe you," I say, nodding to my sister. How could I not have noticed?

"I don't know how she does that," Riley continues. "Those heels looked dangerous. I'd probably break an ankle."

"She must do a lot of training and practicing to be able to do that." I can recognize a fellow athlete when I see them, even if one of them is wearing thick heeled go-go boots. Suddenly, I'm curious about the rehearsal schedule for a world-famous pop star.

"Oh, she absolutely does," Riley says confidently. I find it amusing that my sister is so knowledgeable on this matter, as if she is a part of the inner workings of the singer's training schedule. She throws her hands up in the air, letting the excitement get to her once again. "Ugh, I love her. Her voice is like an angel's."

I shrug, nodding again. I can't disagree. I did notice that her voice—even with running and dancing across the stage—remained steady, unwavering, as she seemed to hit every note perfectly. Not that I would know if she hadn't. I really wasn't familiar with much of her music until tonight, aside from what I'd heard secondhand from Riley.

"So, what did you think?" my sister asks, breathless. The Uber driver glances into the rearview mirror, as if waiting to hear my opinion as well.

I swallow thickly but opt for the truth. "It was incredible."

Riley reaches over and punches my shoulder a little too hard. "*See*, I *told* you she was more than just . . . what did you call her?"

Embarrassment fills me as I admit, "An overrated pop princess."

"Exactly!" She throws another punch, but I dodge it, not needing another bruise on my deltoid.

"Would you cut it out? I've gotta throw a football this weekend. I need to have a working arm." I'm sure Coach will be super thrilled to learn I can't throw properly in the next game due to my *sister*.

Her eyes glint, and she raises her fist, gearing up to toss another punch.

"All right, all right," I concede, laughing and holding my hands up in surrender. "I was wrong."

"You were so wrong," she teases me before sitting back in her seat, mollified by my admission. She lets out a heavy sigh. "Gosh, that was a great show. And to think you were dreading coming along with me."

"I wasn't sure what to expect when you asked me to come with you. I thought I'd be surrounded by fangirls and bored out of my mind."

Riley smirks. "You should've seen your face when her opening sequence started. I should've recorded your expression."

I narrow my eyes. "She knows how to put on a show, that's for sure."

"Doesn't she? Ugh, she's amazing."

I fight off a smile at the way my sister talks about Jersey Matthews as if she's a friend. I mean, she's been listening to her music nonstop for the last eight years. I can see why she'd feel like she knows her personally.

A thought in the back of my mind comes forward with a vengeance—*Wouldn't it be something to know her?*

I had tried to pull strings for my sister and get her backstage to officially meet Jersey. After all, she was playing in *my* home stadium. It would make sense that we'd be given special treatment. But Jersey's security was rock solid, not budging even as I flexed my name a bit.

It isn't every day a Super Bowl titled quarterback asks to meet a pop princess, but I have no shame when it is for my little sister's sake. I'd do anything for that twerp. Even put my name out there and make a show of wanting to meet the most famous woman in the world. Unfortunately, I came up empty-handed. We were banished to my family's suite to watch the show. To be honest, I think that might've been the best seat in the house.

I couldn't even deny it. Aside from the magnetism she exuded on stage, the number of songs I didn't know but found incredibly endearing was off the charts. God, what would the guys on the team think seeing me at a concert like this surrounded by the crowd singing every word and coming away a Jersey Matthews fan myself?

My sister bounces up and down in her seat, still jiving from the highs of the concert. Glancing over at her every few minutes, I smile to myself.

Riley has brought my family nothing but joy her entire life, and I'd do anything to make her happy. Even go to Jersey Matthews concerts. Hell, I'd go to a Justin Bieber concert if she asked me.

When the car pulls up to my front door, Riley is quick to slide out. I hang back, sliding our driver an extra cash tip and patting him on his shoulder in thanks. Riley is typing her passcode into my front door. Once the door clicks open, I follow her inside. She beelines straight for the kitchen, opening the fridge and grabbing the leftover pasta we had for lunch. In record time, she's got the container open and attacks it with a fork, not bothering to heat it up.

She peers up at me sheepishly with a mouthful of spaghetti. "I'm so hungry," she mutters, mouth still full.

I shake my head and don't bother fighting off the amused twitch of my lips. "Help yourself but make sure to hit the lights when you're done. I'm going upstairs to shower."

She gives me a halfhearted wave as I disappear around the corner, climbing the stairs and going straight to my room. As soon as I walk in, I go straight to the dog bed by my dresser, leaning down and giving my little dog, Periwinkle, a few scratches behind her ears. She looks up at me with round dark eyes and gives a pleased snort.

After saying hello to my furry companion, I close my bedroom door and lock it—a habit I developed when I was a teenager with a little sister—wander into my en suite bathroom and strip out of my jeans and polo shirt.

My home in Milwaukee is on the lower end of luxury. With my salary, I could afford to buy something nicer, but I've chosen to invest my money in other places, donating way more than necessary to some of my favorite charitable organizations, contributing to my own personal interests, business ventures, and stocks, and sliding some into an account to pay for the rest of Riley's college since my parents don't really have the means for that.

But with that being said, I live comfortably.

My walk-in shower steams up in less than no time and I step in, closing the stall door behind me and immersing myself under the hot stream. I close my eyes, immediately hit with the onslaught of memories from the show tonight.

It ended only an hour ago and I'm itching to see her perform again. How could I not? She was made for the stage, made for the limelight.

I shower quickly, washing my hair and scrubbing down with my pine-scented body wash. When I get out, I towel myself off and find my favorite pair of sweatpants before settling in bed. I reach for my phone and start scrolling, searching for some recaps from tonight's show, itching for a chance to relive it once more.

Some of the headlines fly in my face:

Jersey Matthews slays at Majestics home stadium

Jersey Matthews holds everyone under her spell, and here's why

Want to know everything about Jersey Matthews? Click here

I know it's clickbait, but I tap the last link with little hesitation. I don't know much about the pop princess, but after tonight's show, I need to know more.

The article is a quick overview of Jersey's career, relationships, and how she rose to fame and brought her twin brother with her. I'm surprised to see Roman Hendrix standing next to her in the picture that labels them twins. I recently watched a movie he starred in, and I wouldn't have guessed he was her twin. But now that I see them standing side-by-side, I see it. He has the same dark hair as her, the same facial features. Though, her eyes glitter with unmatched energy and spirit, even through the picture.

There are a few other candid pictures of her performing on stage, recording in the studio, and a few fan-taken photos from meet-and-greets. There're a few paragraphs mentioning her recent split from her longtime boyfriend, Corey Shrader—accompanied by another headline:

The juicy details behind Matthews-Shrader messy breakup.

I find myself curious about what she's like in real life, away from the prestige and the stage lights. Is she as friendly as she appears with fans she meets on the streets? Does she appreciate all the words and the stories about what her work means to them?

I know for me, when I run into fans, my favorite part is getting to know them and how they came to be fans in the first place. Especially when I find out they used to be fans of different teams but then switched their loyalties to the Majestics. Nothing makes my heart soar like knowing that I've contributed to building a fan base. By the look on her face in the pictures with her fans, I can deduce that she appreciates them greatly.

Something I noticed at the show tonight too. There was something alluring about the way her face lit up as she waved at her fans in the crowd as if they were long-lost friends. I wonder what it would be like to be the recipient of that kind of attention from her.

Scrolling through pictures of Jersey from the show tonight and some of her other shows from her cross-country tour, I somehow stumble onto one of the music videos from her most recent album. I click on it, tilting my phone so it's in landscape view to see the video better.

This song was the opening act she played at her concert tonight, and I find myself humming along with the melody. I don't know the words yet, but the tune is easy to follow. In the back of my mind, I can picture her stage set up, and certain aspects of her choreography as she greeted everyone and kicked off the show.

When the video ends, I scroll down to the comments reading what some of her fans have to say about her. There's the usual praise, but also many comments saying she deserves to win Song of the Year.

I blink a few times and run a hand over the stubble on my jaw, all the while registering what that means. Then, a quick Google search later, I find out that Jersey Matthews will be attending the VMAs next week.

What a fortunate turn of events, I think to myself.

Anticipation bubbles in my chest, knowing that we'll be in each other's vicinity again soon. I can't explain it, but I need to meet her, talk to her, tell her how much I admire her.

It's stupid, reckless, a distraction when all I should do is focus on the upcoming season and prep my new team for another successful year. But even with all that in mind, the urgency is becoming too much to push to the side.

It's late, but I don't hesitate to reach out to my personal assistant to see if she's awake and available to chat. She sends me a quick message back. I waste no time and press the call button.

"Hey, I need you to get me a new suit, and make sure it really makes a statement."

I had already planned on wearing a traditional black coat and tie, but suddenly, I have the sense that I need to up my game. If Jersey Matthews will be at the VMAs, I want to look my best. A deep-seated eagerness amplifies this, convincing me that this might be the only opportunity I get to talk to her. I'm not about to waste it.

THREE

jersey

TUESDAY, SEPTEMBER 10

"Wait, wait, wait!" Kelsey screeching has me pausing midstep before I set foot on the red carpet. I spin around to see her hurrying toward me, looking alarmed.

"What is it?"

She scuttles next to me and adjusts the neckline of the luxurious silver Agnelli dress I'm wearing before dropping into a squat and fixing the skirts, fluffing them out in the right way.

Kelsey Hurst, my publicist and professional perfectionist. She's been with me for about three years and is personally responsible for every stunning red carpet photo and every dodged media scandal since, including the recent messy breakup with my ex. She fusses over my hair and blots at my makeup to remove the shine before giving me a satisfied once over. "Okay, you're perfect."

I shoot her a blinding smile, one I've been saving especially for tonight. I can hear the cameras clicking already, and though I'm swept up in the craze and the flashing cameras, I glue that exact smile in place and start the grueling process of the red carpet walk.

"Jersey!"

"Jersey, this way!"

"Jersey, give me a smile!"

The paparazzi are relentless with their orders, telling me to turn this way and that, and to give them a special pose that they'll be able to sell to the tabloids. Their goal is to get the best shot tonight, and my job on the red carpet is to give it to them. It's not my favorite thing to do, but it's part of the deal.

I'm on the carpet for about thirty minutes before Kelsey ushers me off into the safety of the venue. As soon as I'm sheltered from the cameras, I let my posture fall a bit, no longer needing to meet those high expectations. I inhale through my nose and close my eyes as I roll out my tight shoulders, trying to drown out the noises of the cameras and the paparazzi from the echoes of my mind.

Bethany is beside me, straightening my dress and hair as Kelsey reads off the order of operations for tonight. *PEMDAS, right?* I'm presenting an award and nominated for another. Tonight will be a busy night, not a leisurely one.

Thankfully, I'm presenting the Best Hip-Hop award, which is closer to the beginning of the show, and the one I'm nominated for, Song of the Year, is near the end. I'll be able to sit and watch a few of my friends—or as close of friends as one can get to the cutthroats in the industry—perform and receive awards of their own.

"Okay, so we're told they want you backstage about ten minutes before you're presenting, then you can go to your seat for the rest of the show." Kelsey reads off her card. "So, we'll show you to your table and get you situated. That way, the cameras can get shots of you reacting to the opening of the show. Then Bethany will let you know when they're ready for you backstage and I'll be back there to meet you and get you into position. Did you memorize your speech? Or do you want to run through it again?"

"I'm good," I assure her. "I've read it a thousand times. I think I could do it backward if I had to."

She gives me an affirmative nod. "That's exactly what I want to hear. And if worse comes to worst, it will be on the teleprompter for you, too. All right, let's go find your table."

I follow closely behind Kelsey. Along the way, I stop to say hello to some of the other artists in attendance tonight, giving hugs and snapping selfies. Some of them I haven't seen since I attended the VMAs two years ago, and I'm thrilled to get the opportunity to check in with them and congratulate them on their accomplishments and nominations.

All the while, my security watches me with eyes like a hawk. Though there are plenty of celebrities here, and just as many security guards to match, they are vigilant in making sure no one who isn't welcome gets too close.

I've been fortunate not to have had to deal with extreme stalkers or fans who take things a little too far—but still, one can never be too careful. I take my security with me everywhere I go when I'm out in public. With my luck, the one time I don't is when something bad will happen and I'll regret it for the rest of my life.

I don't take any chances.

When I make it to my assigned table, I eye my seat and set my clutch down before looking at the other people who have been assigned to my table.

"Kira!" I say excitedly when I see the young pop artist's face across from me. "I haven't seen you in ages!" I hurry around the table with my arms outstretched.

Kira stands from her seat and hugs me back. "I know. It feels like forever ago."

I pull away and hold her at arm's length, taking in the lovely vintage ballgown she's wearing for tonight. "You look incredible."

"So do you," she says, glowing at me. "As always."

"How's everything going?" I ask her, and she launches into it.

"Can you believe it's already been two years since my first album released?" Her eyes take on a wide, awestruck glint.

"Time flies, doesn't it? But it's done so well. I'm always so happy when I hear your songs come on the radio."

"I couldn't have done it without you," she says earnestly, reaching to play with a strand of her blonde hair. "You played such a huge role in helping me throughout that whole process. Without your help, I think I would've gone crazy."

I hug her again, holding her close. "It was my pleasure. And I'm always here for you. Any time."

"We'll need to get together sometime soon. I have a few ideas that I'd love to run by you."

"Absolutely," I agree. "You let me know when and I'll be there."

"You're the best, Jersey. Really."

"I agree," Roy Stevens adds. He's a producer who worked with Kira on her last album and has contributed to my songs in the past, too. "Not everyone would make an effort to come play at a thirteen-year-old's birthday party."

"Or donate to my charity auction," his wife, Iris, says, nodding.

Roy raises his glass. "To Jersey, a class act."

My cheeks flush but I raise my glass, taking a small sip, being mindful that I'll be up on stage shortly. "Thank you, guys, so much. That's so kind of you."

I'm forever thankful for the friends I've made on this crazy adventure. There's something to be said about fame feeling lonely, but that is much less when there are people around you in the same boat. As much as I love putting energy into my own career, I equally enjoy helping others in the industry too.

Taking my seat, I make small talk with some of the other celebrities at the table, catching up and filling them in on some of my upcoming events—without giving too much away, of course. *Cal would* love *that.*

An hour or so into the show, Bethany appears at my shoulder. "You're on deck," she whispers. "They've got two categories to go before yours, but they're ready for you backstage."

I excuse myself from the table and follow Bethany, where I meet Kelsey backstage. She shows me where I'm supposed to wait until I'm announced. When my name is called, the audience cheers loudly and I walk onto the stage. I give smiles and little waves as I go to my mark, trying to ignore the anxious flutters in my belly. You'd think at this point I'd be used to being up in front of audiences like this, and I am, but this is being broadcasted on *live television,* and who knows the number of people watching me give my very first award tonight.

Taking a deep breath, my eyes find the teleprompter in front of me—*just in case*—and I start my short speech about the award I'm presenting this evening, hoping my voice comes out level and not shaky.

"Every year, we gather to celebrate some of the biggest and most successful names in our industry. It's an honor to have been invited to award the Best Hip-Hop music video of the year." I pause to take a breath while the nominees are announced on the big screens behind me.

The spotlight falls on me again and the entire auditorium falls silent as I hold up the white envelope in my hand.

"It takes a lot of dedication, creativity, and motivation to create music that embodies the genre and can be appreciated for generations to come, which is why the winner of this award should be celebrated as a master of their craft. So, the winner of the Best Hip-Hop award is"—with a mega-watt smile, I look up and announce the winner into the microphone—"J-Money, *Tell Me I'm Wrong.*"

The place erupts in cheers.

Music plays in the background as J-Money and a group of other people join him on the stage. The attendant on stage passes me the award for the category that I hand to J-Money when he walks up to me. He accepts it and surprises me by wrapping me up in a tight hug. I laugh, a little awkwardly, and pat him on the back before he lets me go and turns toward the group of people behind him, holding it high. His people all cheer and whoop, celebrating their success.

J- Money turns back to the microphone and addresses his fans. He has every pair of eyes on him—except mine. Every ounce of my attention is on the tallest and broadest man of the group.

And as luck would have it, his entire focus is on me, too.

FOUR

jersey

TUESDAY, SEPTEMBER 10

I FEEL like I've seen him before, but I can't locate his name in my brain. It's impossible not to notice the confidence of his presence. He's a beast of a man, but he holds his tall frame so elegantly, like it's nothing that he's towering over the other men on stage with him. I blink a few times, appreciating the way his broad shoulders fill out the shape of his jacket, which holds no sign of a wrinkle. His hands are delicately placed in the pockets of his dark navy slacks, which are hugging the contours of his muscular thighs. His physique stands out against most of the other men around him. He's handsome, that's for damn sure. Intimidating, athletic, stunning.

His eyes are raking me from top to bottom, leaving a trail of tingly *awareness* over every inch of me. The heat in his eyes makes me feel desired, sexy. My whole body lights up, and suddenly, I worry I might self combust up here. My palms turn clammy, and my chest rises as I take a deep breath, trying to cool myself off as this man tilts my world on its axis.

I cannot faint up here on stage under the weight of his attention.

He's just a man.

An attractive man, absolutely. But just a man.

Glancing away, I focus on the crowd, plastering on a smile and hoping I don't appear as frazzled as I feel. The moment—though lasting only milliseconds—seems to stop time and I'll admit I forget myself for a moment. I'm thankful the moment has broken because I can't fathom the world catching onto whatever passed between us and dissecting every little detail.

Suddenly, I'm ushered off stage and back to my table. As soon as I'm seated, I reach for my water glass and take a big gulp. Bethany disappears, and a few minutes later, stands in front of me handing over a drink in a martini glass.

"What is this?" I ask her, peering at the raspberry-colored liquid.

"Cosmo," she replies simply before disappearing again.

I take a sip. The sweet flavored alcoholic drink hits the spot and eases some of my frazzled nerves.

Finally, after what feels like forever, it's time to announce the winner for Song of the Year. The prestigious category I'm nominated for.

While I'm hopeful all my hard work will pay off in another award to stick up on a shelf, I can't help but think that the other nominees deserve the same recognition. Every one of us in this category have worked our asses off.

The person presenting the award stands back as the screen behind them lists off the nominees. I squeeze my friends' hands when my name soars across the screen, and a second later, they play a clip from my song up for nomination—*Good Times Roll.*

To be perfectly honest, if it had been up to me, this song wouldn't have been the lead single on my latest album, but

Callum and the rest of the production crew were dead set that this was the one, confident it would get me the win for the third year in a row. I had no choice but to go along with it. The song had been an item of dispute between me and the label since I first recorded it, and while I like the lyrics, I think the production of it is all wrong.

Good Times Roll is a song that, if given the proper attention, could have been a ballad for the books. But as per usual, Callum and his eccentric tastes took it a little too far. His goal with the sound made it too poppy and synthesized for my liking. And to be fair, it worked in his favor. The song was an immediate hit, topping the charts within that first week of release. Every time I hear it or have to perform it, I can't help but think that if I had been in control, I would have taken a more somber route, while still giving respect to the genre that I belong to.

But again, it wasn't my choice.

Nothing ever is.

The presenter steps back up to the microphone and holds onto the envelope containing the name of the winner.

"And the winner, for the Song of the Year goes to . . ."

My breath catches in my throat, and I squeeze the hands of my friends. My heartbeat thrums in my ears and my chest tightens with anticipation. The room falls silent, and I count my breaths, waiting to hear the verdict.

"Meghan Connelly, *Summer Lovers!*"

The venue erupts in cheers and the video on the big screen pans to Meghan, who is a few tables down. She stands, looking absolutely shocked.

I release my friends' hands and clap, standing up and plastering on that big smile, showing support for her. Meanwhile, my stomach threatens to jump up into my throat as it constricts with a weird mix of disappointment and satisfaction.

I didn't win? I didn't win!

I swallow, forcing my apprehension down and making sure my face has the mask of excitement, knowing cameras will be on me to catch any hint of ill wishes. Inside, I'm starting to work through the consequences that will trickle my way from this loss, and how my management at Silver Shadows will respond to me not clinching the win this year.

While I'm surprised and a little disappointed, I'm truly happy for Meghan. She's newer to the game, this only being her second album, and although she's been caught on camera saying that I'm old and washed out, and I need to step down to let newer artists achieve the same attention, I don't hold any ill wishes toward her. She deserves it, just as much as the rest of the nominees would if their names had been called.

From what I know about her, she spends hours writing and perfecting her own songs, piecing them together in a perfect blend to create a masterful album. She has more creative liberties than I do, so of course she should win the award over me.

She's what I would consider a real artist, while I am simply a chess piece on the board that is Silver Shadows Records.

When the excitement from the award dies down, I sit back in my seat and get comfortable, ignoring the way my ears ring at a pitch that makes my head spin. Already I can hear Callum grumbling about what we need to do better to secure the win for next year. He'll pace back and forth, wearing a hole in the carpet of his office. He'll say *bigger, better, stronger.*

And I'll be at his mercy.

The conversation hasn't even happened yet, but I'm already dreading the aftermath.

I have three years left on this extension. Three years of *bigger, better, stronger.*

I tell myself over and over again that I can do *anything* for three years, right?

That may be so, but it's still a depressing thought.

After the ceremony ends, everyone seems to get up all at once. Not me. I stay right where I am, letting the hustle and bustle around me settle before I venture out.

The rest of my group waits for my lead, staying in their seats until I push up and turn to them. I give them what I hope is an encouraging smile, fighting off their looks of pity at the loss.

"Well guys, better luck next year. I guess."

Bethany gives me a sympathetic smile and Kelsey presses her lips together. She knows Callum is going to have a conniption.

Together, we leave our seats and head back to the main floor where everyone seems to be gathering.

On my way down, Bethany steps close to me and points across the venue. I follow her direction to see what—or *who*—she's pointing out. My eyes fall on the man who was up on stage with J-Money for the award. He's talking to the R&B singer who won Best New Artist this year. She's tiny, and he's gigantic—she barely clears his chest, but he's leaning down to hear her better, listening raptly to whatever she's saying, giving her his full attention.

"There's Hayes Vogt," Bethany whispers. "The football player your brother was talking about the other day."

Hayes. I knew I recognized him when he was up on stage with me.

Before I can mention that I have any interest in talking to him, or ask him for his autograph for my brother, I hear my name being called across the insanity of the crowd.

"Jersey!"

For a second, everything falls silent. My attention is still on Hayes Vogt, who glances up at the sound of my name. His piercing gaze locks on me but softens when he takes me in, eyes flickering up and down by body. His strong jaw ticks and then he takes half a step in my direction, apparently done with the conversation he'd been having. Something flutters in my chest at the sight of him moving toward me, a determined expression forming on his face and a smile forming on mine.

Against my better judgment, I spin away, deciding I can get his autograph after finding out who has called me. I'm surprised to see Meghan Connelly standing a few feet away from me.

She embraces me in a hug before I can wrap my head around what's happening. Cameras click and flash all around us, trying to catch the moment as it's occurring.

I hug her back, trying to hide the confusion on my face when she pulls me back and holds me at arm's length. She gives me a warm smile which doesn't quite meet her eyes and has me wondering if it's all that genuine. She sounds like she's reading off a script when she says, "Oh, Jersey, it's such an honor to have been nominated right next to you for the Song of the Year."

"Thank you," I tell her, keeping my voice level. "Congratulations on your win. It was well deserved."

She bats her hand, as if to brush off the compliment. "Truly, it should have been yours. Your song was everywhere last year. I didn't even think mine stood a chance."

Despite my suspicion she's fishing for compliments, I give her a little smile. "Your song was great." I hope she can hear how sincere I am. "You deserved that award."

"Ugh, you're the sweetest. I'm sure you'll take it again next year."

I give her a half smile. "We'll see. You might be on a winning streak."

She laughs, and I want to cover my ears with how shrill it is. "Only time will tell. It was lovely to see you." She leans forward and air kisses either side of my face. Waving to the reporters and the paparazzi lingering nearby, she disappears as quickly as she came.

I watch her go and take a deep breath, trying not to let the obvious photo-op get to me. I can't wait to be home in bed with some Oreos and a jar of peanut butter. This may be the last awards show I attend in person for a while. The games everyone plays is tiresome.

"Come on, your car is waiting," Kelsey murmurs, placing her hand on my shoulder and steering me away.

I go willingly with her, but pause when again, the same awareness I felt up on stage tickles the back of my neck, urging me to turn around. Pausing, I scan the room. My breath catches when my gaze falls on a pair of amber eyes a few yards away from me.

Hayes Vogt.

I step toward him, urged by a magnetism I attribute to my brother's request for an autograph.

Surely that's all it is.

Kelsey grumbles in annoyance at the interruption, and she says to Bethany, "I hate these events."

However, I ignore her mutterings, loving watching the way Hayes notices my focus on him and maneuvers around the people between us. A few people call his name, drawing his attention from me, but he doesn't let them get in his way, saying a few words to them before turning his eyes back to mine.

"Jersey, come on. We've got to go," Kelsey admonishes me directly.

My eyes are glued to the broad shoulders and determined

stare of the man who's making a valiant effort to get to me. An urging sensation deep in my bones forces me to stop.

"But—"

Kelsey's arm around my shoulders steers me in the opposite direction of where I want to go. Against my better judgment—and I *know* I'll be getting an earful about this later—I spin out of her grasp and take two wide strides until I'm standing in front of Hayes, meeting him halfway.

Earlier when I saw him on stage, I could tell he was tall, but now I'm struck by how much bigger he is compared to me. Even in my tall, strappy heels, I have to crane my neck to stare at him. We're close—maybe too close—but I can't seem to find the urgency to step back. His aftershave, or his cologne, or *something,* tickles my nose with its spicy scent and I want to lean a little closer to pick up the notes hidden within the blend.

"Hi," I whisper, breathless.

"Hi." His voice is deep and raspy, and it sends a cascade of goosebumps down my arms.

Hayes has a strong jaw covered in light brown scruff but groomed neatly. The muscles in his face split into a wide grin as he regards me with kind eyes. Butterflies erupt in my belly in a way that makes me pause. It's a strange sensation I haven't experienced in what feels like a lifetime.

I encounter people all the time, but I never seem to have this kind of reaction on a first encounter. They're always excited to meet Jersey Matthews, the pop star, but somehow, by the glint in his eye, I know this man is excited to meet *me*—Jersey Matthews, the woman.

What an intriguing phenomenon. I feel delightfully dizzy with that realization.

"I don't have much time—" I hurry out, glancing over my shoulder to see Kelsey glaring at me with her hands on her hips.

My cheeks feel warm when I turn back to him and I press one palm against the side of my face, needing to cool down. "This is so embarrassing, but my brother made me promise to get your autograph if I saw you tonight."

Something unidentifiable crosses his face, and his lips curve up in the corners. He reaches into the pocket of his suit coat and pulls out a blue Post-it pad and a pen, which he uses to scribble his autograph.

"Here," he says, pulling the top one off and handing it to me before scribbling on the next one and giving it to me, too. When he hands me this second Post-it, our fingers brush and a buzzing sensation travels up my hand. I jerk my hand away as if I've been burned and look down to see a series of numbers scrawled in almost illegible handwriting and his name. "Autograph for your brother. My phone number for you. Text me when you're free. Which . . . is a long shot, but hopefully you'll find a few minutes sometime."

I tilt my head up again, raising my eyebrows in surprise, wondering if this moment is real or if I'm dreaming.

I'm met with the intensity of his amber eyes, like warm sunlight or autumn honey. As they flicker over every feature of my face, I find I can't help but love being the subject of his attention. He's looking at me as if I'm the most valuable trophy he's ever seen. A subtle heat sizzles between us, threatening to rise if we linger too long.

Grasping the notes in my hand, I raise it and nod. "I'll text you."

A smile breaks out across his face, revealing perfectly straight white teeth. His whole face seems to light up with that one smile and another current of excitement travels through me. "I'll be waiting."

jersey

MONDAY, SEPTEMBER 16

"I HOPE you're proud of yourself. You look like you don't know what you're doing up there." Callum clicks the remote, turning off the video of me dancing up on stage to ad-libbed choreography from my most recent show.

"What do you mean? The fans have been loving the switch. I've even seen videos of the dance online." My fingers twist together in my lap. Many of my songs have built-in dance breaks, which have become a fan-favorite tradition of my tours. I should've known going off script with the choreography would've landed me a scolding from the higher-ups, but I couldn't help myself. It felt right in that moment.

"It's not what you rehearsed, and it's definitely not what we agreed on." His tone is flat as he levels me with a steady stare, taunting me to disagree. Which I do, of course.

"I don't understand what the big deal is. It's only choreography."

"The *big deal*, Jersey, is that you explicitly went against what we asked of you. *Again*. The *big deal* is that we are your label." I sink further into my chair with the passive aggressive animosity, like a child being scolded. "What we've put into this show has cost us a lot of money. What do you think your choreographer would think of you changing up her meticulously thought-out routine?"

"Honestly? I don't think she'd mind," I say, and that's true. I can recall many times, off the top of my head, where she'd ask me if I had any other ideas as we were going through the routine. "She was always supportive of my suggestions during rehearsals. And you know, as well as I do, that we had a *lot* of rehearsals."

"You're missing the point," Cal grumbles again.

"No, I don't think I am."

"Listen, I don't want to get into this with you today," he says, waving me off. "We have a lot of things we need to discuss, starting with the schedule for your next album."

"I'm all ears." *Anything to stop the scolding.*

Cal switches into business mode, sitting down behind his desk—because of course—flipping his planner open, then steepling his fingers, and giving me a hard glare. I clench my jaw at the way he's glaring down his nose at me. If I could melt into this chair and disappear, I think I would, but I doubt Cal would permit that.

"We have you slotted for the next few months to go in and start recording. It will probably feel like a lot, but it's important that we ride the coattails of this tour's success and get your next album out while you're still on everyone's mind. The last thing we need is for this energy to fizzle out without milking it as much as possible."

"At least you're admitting it," I say under my breath, not

loving the idea of having the need for my career to be milked to within an inch of its life.

Callum's attention snaps back to me and he glowers. "What was that?"

"Nothing. Go on."

He blinks at me a few times, suspiciously studying me to figure out if I'm up to no good. Finally, he continues. "I'll have my assistant send Bethany an outline of the recording schedule so you can have it. I don't expect you'll have any issues keeping to the assigned slots."

"I'll do my best. I have nothing coming up that I'm aware of."

"Good. It's an aggressive schedule, Jersey, so you'll have to be diligent. We have no time for distractions or detours. Do you understand? This next album is going to be bigger and better than anything you've done before. If we can pull this off, you may be able to claim Song of the Year next year."

"When have I ever been distracted?" I ask him. Of course, I knew he'd already be planning on how to win the coveted Song of the Year again. *Bigger, better, stronger.*

"Well, the VMAs, for one," he says, snidely.

"What are you talking about?" I ask him, already feeling the exhaustion seep into me from this conversation. Surreptitiously, I glance down at the watch on my wrist to determine whether I've been here long enough to consider it a successful meeting.

"Your security agent told me you purposefully ignored Kelsey's request to leave so you could go meet up with one of J-Money's extras." Callum says this as if he's accusing me of a crime.

"He's not an extra. He's a football player in the NFL." I inadvertently defend Hayes Vogt. I blink a few times, surprised at myself. Why am I defending him when I barely know him in the first place? Cal arches a suspicious eyebrow, likely wondering the same thing. I quickly spin the topic around on him. "And why is my security guard tattling on me?"

"He works for us. Just like you do. And *ohh*, an NFL player. Is that supposed to make this better?" Callum asks. "Either way, you didn't do what was required of you. To the extreme shock of *no one*."

I let his sarcasm roll off me, doing my best to not let it affect me and give him an innocent shrug. "I don't know. Again, I don't see why this is a big deal. I didn't have anywhere else to be after the show, so I don't see the issue."

"Kelsey had explicit instructions to keep you on task, moving you through the events of the night. How is she supposed to do her job when you don't follow her directions?" Cal questions. "After everything I've done for you, you'd think you'd trust me by now."

"Cal, I was there to network and promote. To meet people and maintain relationships. As you've mentioned, my schedule is tight. That usually doesn't give me a chance to keep those relationships going. Award shows are perfect for that exact reason. What if I wanted to do a collaboration with someone in the future? I'd need to have a good relationship for them to be open to that."

He narrows his eyes and leans toward me over his desk. "No. Your *label* would have to have a good relationship for them to be open to that, and you'd have to have the financial backing to make that worth their while."

"Not everything is about money, Cal." My chest feels tight seeing the direction this conversation is going. I should've known. Most of my conversations with him end up veering past the point of no return.

His voice turns dangerously low and his eyes narrow. "Sorry to disappoint you, Jersey, but I assure you, it is. Your success is because of me. Don't forget that I'm the one with the muscle pushing you forward."

"Are we finished here? I'm supposed to be meeting someone for lunch." I raise my wrist to read the time. The golden watch glints in the refraction of Cal's overhead lights as I read the time, hitting my manager in the forehead.

"Fine." He reclines back in his chair and looks away from me. "Bethany will have the schedule by the end of the day. If you have any pressing issues, please have her call me."

"You got it, boss."

Officially done with this conversation, I push out of my chair and reach for my bag. Inside, I grab my phone and then peer at him sideways. Already I can feel the burn behind my eyes, and I'm breathless, like I had the wind got knocked out of me.

Before I have the chance to walk out, Callum feels the need to leave me with one last parting gift. "Oh, and Jersey? Don't forget, you are what I've made you. Without me, there would be no Jersey Matthews. There would be no album, and there would be no tour." I look over my shoulder at him, my heart sinking into my stomach. He gives me a saccharine smile before he dips his chin, officially dismissing me. "Have a nice day."

I LEAVE Cal's office without another word, letting the door close roughly behind me, the sting of his brutal words seeing me out. There's a metallic taste left in my mouth from biting my tongue, the sting reminding me I have almost nothing to show for the small acts of standing up for myself.

Bethany is waiting downstairs in the lobby. Her eyes squint at the screen of her tablet, hardly reacting as I approach her.

"Hey. What have you got there?"

She frowns. "Callum's assistant just sent over a crazy long email with Cal's insane schedule attached."

I pause for a second. "That was fast. I was there a few minutes ago."

"They must have had it queued up and ready to go." She shakes her head.

"Must've hit send before I even walked out of the door," I say blandly.

"You are their prized pig." She gives me a little smile. "They can't ever seem to let you have any downtime."

"Cal said it's because they have to continue to *ride the coattails* of my tour's success before people's interest in me fizzles out." The sentiment still leaves a bitter taste in my mouth.

"We can ask him to change it," Bethany suggests, but I shake my head.

"You know as well as I do that the only reason he'll change the schedule is if I'm dying or dead. And even then, I bet he'd expect me to finish recording the lead single."

Bethany laughs ruefully. "You're probably right on that one, but you never know."

I shrug, still feeling a little down. "He'd only remind me that fame is fickle and the only way to combat that is to continue to work. All it would take would be one person to turn on me and everyone else follows like a herd of sheep."

"I do know. The thousands of fans at every sold-out show and platinum albums tell me that. You have nothing to worry about." I appreciate Bethany's confidence. I wish I could have even a little bit of that when it comes to relations and communications with my label.

"Not according to Cal. He has no problem telling me that the only reason I'm successful is because of the label's backing."

"You know that's not true."

"Sometimes I wonder if he's right, though." Before Bethany can do her best to convince me otherwise, I shrug. "You ready to head to my place?"

She gathers up her stuff and pops up from her seat. "Yeah, let's go."

On our way out of the lobby, I wave at Louisa, who sits at the main desk on the weekdays. "Bye, Lou!"

With a bright expression, she wiggles her fingers back at me before pushing her glasses up her nose. "Have a good day, Jersey!"

When we walk inside my condo, Roman pops his head up over the back of the couch and gives me a wide, infectious smile before he gets up and walks toward me, arms stretched out wide. The corners of my lips tip up against my will at the sight of my brother. He doesn't usually come over, even though he has his own code and key to get in, so it's always a nice surprise to see him.

"There's my favorite little sister. And my favorite sister's friend!" Roman wraps his arms around me in a big hug.

"Fancy meeting you here," I tease him, patting his back.

"I definitely had no idea you'd be returning to your home at the end of the day. No idea." He plays along. As soon as he lets me go from the hug, he gives my friend a little finger wave. "Hey, Beth."

"Hi there, Roman. You staying out of trouble?" Bethany asks.

"Not at all." He shoots her a wink and then turns back to me. "What have you two been up to?"

"The usual," I say, right as Bethany rats me out at the same time. "I was trying to convince Jersey that she's worth much more than what Callum leads her to believe." Bethany directs her attention at Roman and tilts her head toward me.

"Oh, we need to convince her of that? I thought she already knew." Roman nudges me with his shoulder, looking down at me fondly. I appreciate his faith in me, but even my brother isn't totally privy to my struggles with the label.

"In theory. But it's hard to believe it when all Cal does is remind me that everything comes back to him and the label. He was particularly adamant that I do not have any distractions," I explain, heading over to the couch and collapsing into the cushions, dropping my bag on the table next to me.

"Please, when are you ever distracted?" Bethany asks, as though the idea is absurd.

I let out a long sigh and grab a pillow to hold on my lap. "Apparently at the VMAs, when I ignored Kelsey to ask Hayes for his autograph. Oh, which reminds me. Here you go." Reaching into my bag, I pull out my wallet and find the Post-it note with Hayes Vogt's autograph on it. I've been keeping it safe right next to my Post-it with his number on it.

Roman reaches for the sticky note and stares down at it, mouth agape. He falls onto the couch as if he's in shock. "You actually got it? Sick. I'm gonna have this framed."

"Not only that, but she got his *number*, too," Bethany says, giving me a secret smile. My cheeks heat at her sharing this knowledge with my *brother*, of all people.

"Traitor," I mouth.

"You're kidding, really? Have you texted him yet?" Roman turns his wide brown eyes to me.

My chest feels tight, and I shake my head maybe a little too quickly. "No. And I don't know if I should. Especially not now."

Roman arches a brow. "Why not now?"

"*Because*, I just told you, Cal's on my case about distractions. I really don't need to bring a football player—who is probably a player on and off the field—into the mix, you know?"

"Actually, I don't know if Hayes Vogt is really the dating type," he says, looking thoughtful. "I see stuff about other players all the time, but I'm not sure if I've ever seen anything about him or the people he's dating. From what I've heard and seen, he's a decent guy. Always giving to charity and really focused on keeping his head in the game. There's a reason he's one of the greatest in the league."

I move the pillow on my lap to my chest and hold it tightly, letting it act as my symbolic shield. "You mean he hasn't been involved in a recent romantic scandal that hit the tabloids and made the entire music industry lose their minds?"

Roman barks a laugh. "No. I guess not."

"I can't relate," I tease and shrug it off while anxiety gnaws at my gut.

"Still a sore spot, huh?" Roman asks me, all hints of jest gone.

Glancing away from him, I say, "It's whatever. It is what it is. It's been six months. I've moved on." I can feel Bethany's eyes on me, but I don't look over to her to confirm my suspicions. Instead, I pick at a loose thread on the pillow. Then I ask Roman, "What are you doing here, anyway?"

"Thought I'd come see what you were up to, but then you weren't here." He glances down at his watch. "But I do have to get going. I've got a meeting with my agent."

"Did you hear back about the TV show?"

"Yeah. Unfortunately, they had someone else in mind, so my agent's searching for other opportunities. We're meeting to go over some options."

"Good luck. The right role will come around."

"It always does," he says, yanking me into a side hug. When he lets me go, he gives Bethany a high five. "Catch you ladies later." He salutes us both, leaving us chuckling as he walks out the door.

SIX

jersey

MONDAY, SEPTEMBER 16

"Oh, what a day," I announce as soon as Roman's gone, letting my forehead fall into the fluffy pillow on my lap.

"*So . . .?*" Her mischievous tone of voice has me peeking at her through my eye lashes only to see her Cheshire Cat grin.

"So, what?"

"Why haven't you texted Hayes?" she asks. When I stare at her with wide eyes she laughs. "Did you really think I'd let it go as easy as Roman did?"

I cover my face with my hands and groan. "No, but I was hoping you would."

She chuckles and scoots closer to me, her blue eyes sparking playfully. "Well? Do you think you're going to?"

"I don't know. Probably not."

She turns thoughtful for a moment and then blurts, "I think you should."

Her response startles me and I raise an eyebrow. "Why?"

She reaches for my hand. "Jersey, you have worked your *ass*

47

off these last few months, and I can see the toll it's taking on you."

"I'm fine," I assure her.

"That may be true, but are you *happy*?"

Her question pierces me like a knife, and I swallow thickly, hoping my voice comes out level when I answer her. "I am happy. I love my life. Tons of young aspiring artists would kill for this life."

She gives me a careful smile which tells me she absolutely does not believe me. To be honest, I sometimes don't know if *I* even believe myself. "Do you think that what happened with Corey is still holding you back?"

"Corey?" My ex-boyfriend and I broke up six months ago, so I wouldn't think he'd have any effect on my life anymore.

"Yes, Corey. I know you had a lot of plans for what you wanted your life to look like with him. Which made it hurt so much more when he told you he didn't want any of that with you, right? I can understand why it might be hard to move on, both professionally and otherwise. Why it might be hard to find joy in something you both shared after being betrayed."

"When did you get a degree in relationship psychology?" I tease her. When she doesn't laugh at my weak joke, my eyes fall to my lap. I pick at my thumbnail, doing my best not to clam up at the mention of my ex. "No . . . maybe. I don't know. It's hard for me to think about still."

The only time I *can* think about it is when the words force their way out of me in the form of a tortured cadence of lyrics. I jot them down safely in my notebook, giving them the space to exist without having to deal with the fallout.

"What if, in reaction to that, you went the complete opposite way? I'm worried that after Corey shut you out, you've been too quick to accept what your life is supposed to look like instead of chasing your dreams."

I turn to her and wait for her to continue with her explanation.

"Ever since your breakup with Corey, you've kept your head down and done what is expected of you, putting your entire heart and soul into your work. But what if it's time to put all of that energy back into yourself? I'm worried if you keep going forward like this, Cal is going to crush you—more than he already has. Three years is a long time that you're stuck with him and the label, and I'd hate to see you miserable that entire time."

"You think me texting Hayes will fix all of that?" I ask her, going back to the topic that brought all this to fruition. Texting Hayes couldn't have such an effect, nor should it.

"No, but I think it might be something fun, give you something to look forward to outside of work, outside of the label. Maybe it's time to move past whatever's been keeping you back. You shouldn't have to settle."

Panic floods me. "You think I'm settling?"

"I think that the pressure from Cal and the heartbreak from Corey had you putting up your defenses, and so you did what you had to do to survive and get through that. And Cal has a track record of beating you when you're already down," Bethany says. "But all men are not like Corey or Cal. They're not all going to look at your relationship like a competition or see you as a stepping stone. Somewhere there's someone out there who will see you for *you* and convince you that you never have to settle for anything in your life. That you can achieve any greatness you set your mind to."

"So you think texting Hayes Vogt is a good idea and I should put myself out there?"

She shrugs. "What have you got to lose?" I level her with a

quiet look that says *a lot*. Her blue eyes sparkle, challenging me right back. "Okay, well, why don't we make a pros and cons list? You love those."

She has me there; I *do* love those. I adjust myself on the couch and reach for my notebook, opening it to an empty page and grabbing a pen. "Fine. Con: I may get hurt again."

"Pro," Bethany redirects, pointing at me, "he might make you happier than you've been in a long time."

I scribble down her note. "Con: he's an athlete, and I don't do sports."

"Pro: he's not in the music industry, so you don't have to worry about any conflict of interest."

Tapping my lips with the pen, I say, "That's actually a good one."

"See?" Beth rolls her shoulders back triumphantly.

"Being in the same industry was a major point of contention for me and Corey," I mutter while I write it down in the pro column. "I've never dated someone outside of the music scene. I have no idea what that would be like or where to even start."

"Probably with a text message." Bethany nudges me again.

I shake my head. "There's not enough to sway me either way."

"Oh, come on, Jersey. Are we really going to nickel and dime this? I say shoot him a text, say 'hey,' and see where it goes. Like I said earlier, what have you got to lose?" I roll my lips between my lips and she sighs. "At the very least, what harm could come from it?"

I think about it. "I guess not much. But what about time commitment? Cal still has me on that tight schedule. I don't know if I even have the time to be talking to someone else."

"You don't have time to text him? It takes approximately two seconds to send a text message."

"You know what I mean. What if it turns into something more?"

She shrugs. "What if it does? That's down the road. All we're talking about here is opening that line of communication."

I bite my lip, knowing full well that she's choosing to ignore the obvious. A singular text could turn into a much more time-consuming relationship. That could divert my focus and make things so much more difficult with Callum. "I'm not sure if that's the right thing for me to be doing right now."

"I disagree, but continue." She points at the list. "Pro: Roman likes football, so he can help you understand the rules and such. Pro: he says Hayes is generally not involved in drama—don't lie, I know that is appealing to you."

I roll my eyes. "It is."

"Pro: he may help you stop beating yourself up over what happened with Corey. Help you move on and find joy in your life again."

"I have moved on," I protest. "And I have joy."

"Sure, in most ways. But I know you, Jersey. I know there are times when you catch yourself falling into the *what ifs*. And I can see how down you get after receiving a verbal beating from Cal. You may be stuck in this contract for the next three years, but that doesn't mean that you have to suffer through those years too."

"You know me too well," I tell my friend.

"Or maybe I just know you well enough. At least I hope I would after eight years of working with you. And holding the position as your best friend for much longer than that." She winks at me and then glances down at the watch on her wrist. "I should probably get going, though. I've got a few errands to run before heading home."

We both hop off the couch and she grabs her items. I walk with her to the door and wrap my arms around myself while she finds her keys in her bag.

"I really don't know what I'd do without you, Beth," I say softly.

"I don't know what I'd do without you, either. I love being a part of your crazy life. Think about the Hayes thing, okay? There are more pros than cons—the list doesn't lie."

I nod. "I will think about it."

"Promise?"

"I *promise*." I fight off a smile when she hugs me tightly.

"Okay, well keep me posted." She pulls away and holds me at arm's length. "I'll see you tomorrow."

I see her out, closing the door behind her and leaning my head back against the paneling. As soon as the apartment is empty, I run myself a hot bath to decompress from the day and mull over everything we talked about, returning to the topic of texting Hayes Vogt over and over again. Even when I try to focus on something else, *anything* else, my thoughts circle back to the damn pros and cons list sitting on my coffee table.

Getting out of the tub, I towel myself off and pad back out to the living room, finding the list and studying it begrudgingly.

After mulling it all over, I realize Bethany was right. The pros do significantly outnumber the cons. Or at the very least, they're a little louder and more prominent in my mind as I consider everything. I managed to add two more cons to the list, but even I can recognize they're weak excuses.

Taking the leap, I type out a message to the phone number he scrawled over the extra Post-it note and hit send before I can erase it.

JERSEY

Hey. It's Jersey.

53

SEVEN

jersey

MONDAY, SEPTEMBER 16

THE FINGERNAIL polish cracks on my thumb as my teeth nibble nervously at my cuticle. I pull my hand away and glare down at my finger. There's now a huge chunk of the polish missing from the nail. *Damn it.*

I worry at the dead skin on my lip with my teeth, my nerves getting the better of me as I wait for a response.

Hayes Vogt is a busy man, with a million things on his plate. He's got a game this Sunday—I may or may not have looked up the schedule for the Milwaukee Majestics while waiting for his reply—and he has a goal of leading his team to victory. Which were his exact words in the interview I watched of him from last week, also while I've been waiting.

He's probably asleep already. Maybe he'll respond in the morning when he sees it.

That's what I tell myself, as I settle back into the couch cushions and close my eyes.

My phone vibrates on the coffee table a moment later, and I

nearly jump out of my skin. I reach for it, and a bubble of excitement and trepidation blooms in my belly.

HAYES

Oh hey, Jersey Matthews. Bout time I heard from you 😏

I grin like a schoolgirl at my phone and catch myself nibbling on my thumbnail again. I don't know why, but I'm surprised by him setting the flirty tone of our conversation right out of the gate. It's refreshing, and mentally, I dust off my flirt game, hoping I still have what it takes to keep up. Pressing my lips together, I type a quick response out.

JERSEY

I know, I know.

HAYES

I was wondering if I would ever hear from you…

That was a valid fear for him to have. Until I sent that text message, *I* was wondering the same. Panic settles in my chest, and I mull over what I'm going to say to him next. Flirting is equal parts exciting and nerve-racking. It's been a while since I've done this—years, even. My relationship with Corey was significantly lacking in the flirt game, both from him and from me, so I'm way out of practice.

My fingers fly over the screen and I hit send.

JERSEY

Honestly, me too.

Hayes responds right away with a laughing face emoji. His response time has me smiling down at the phone already, some of the panic easing.

HAYES

Brutal. I like it.

How was your day? Plan out any more
world stopping tours?

I'm grateful Hayes has taken the lead and started up a real conversation.

JERSEY

It was okay. My life isn't nearly as glamorous
as the tabloids make it out to be. A lot more
toeing the line than daydreaming these
days.

HAYES

I can believe that. Want to talk about it?

I consider his question, and I'm surprised to find that, yes, I really do want to talk to him about it all. Maybe it's the fact that he *is* a complete stranger that makes him safe. He's not a part of my world, aside from his brief visit with his involvement in that music video, so he's entirely unjaded and unaware of most of the goings-on in this realm.

JERSEY

My manager and I got into it again today. I
always feel like I can never win with him. Or
any of them.

HAYES

Why do you feel like that?

I sigh to myself, wondering where in the world to begin.

JERSEY

The contract I'm under with my label sometimes feels suffocating.

HAYES

How so?

JERSEY

My manager is very controlling about most of my career, with everything from album titles to song choices. He even has things to critique on my choreography when he's the one who hired the choreographer. To be fair, I switched things up at my Milwaukee show, so he and I got into a giant argument about it right after. But still. It's the principle of the matter.

HAYES

Hey, I was at that show! I thought everything was perfect. You have no complaints from me about any of your dancing. I loved it all, and I really mean that.

My face breaks into a huge smile as I read his text.

JERSEY

Thank you. I wish my label felt that way too.

HAYES

I'll be honest, when my sister asked me to go with her to your concert, I wasn't really sure I'd like it. I'm much more of a country or a rap kinda guy.

JERSEY

I can respect that. Is that why you were in J-Money's music video?

HAYES

Did you watch it??

JERSEY

I may or may not have.

HAYES

I had a blast. Never done anything like that before. I've always been into that kind of music more than anything. But then I went to your concert…

JERSEY

And?

After I send the text, I get off the couch and trek over to the fridge, grabbing a bottle of water before heading into my bedroom. He's responded by the time I toss myself onto my mattress.

HAYES

And I was completely wowed. By the show. By you. One of the most pivotal nights of my life. You're extraordinary. Your label is full of fools if they don't see that, too.

I take a moment to think about how to respond to such praise. He texts again before I can reply right away.

HAYES

And my sister loved it too. She couldn't stop gushing about you on the ride home.

JERSEY

What's your sister's name?

HAYES

Riley. She's twenty, younger than me by about thirteen years. She lives back home with my parents in Bowling Green, but she came up to see me when you were in town for your show.

I guess I never thought to have questioned how old he is or where he came from, but I'm thankful he gave me that information even though I could have easily Googled it too.

JERSEY
That's quite an age gap.

HAYES
She's been a handful her whole life, but we love her even more for it. You have a brother, right?

JERSEY
I do. My twin, Roman.

HAYES
Who's older?

JERSEY
He is, and he never lets me forget it.

HAYES
Ha. I bet not. What does he do?

I pause at the question, rolling my lips together and fighting off a smirk. I have no doubt that if Hayes has looked me up, he's seen the connection to my Hollywood heartthrob brother, but still, he's waiting for me to share this part of my life with him personally.

JERSEY
He's an actor. Roman Hendrix. He uses his middle name as his stage name.

HAYES
The Matthews twins, taking the entertainment industry by storm.

JERSEY

Something like that 😖

HAYES

I've seen his movies. He's good. Not as good as you… of course.

I bite my lower lip, choosing to change the direction of the conversation away from my brother.

JERSEY

How was your day?

HAYES

Honestly, not too bad. Had a workout with my friend, Beckett. He's one of the tight ends on the team. Then we watched some tape for the game coming up this weekend. Typical Wednesday.

JERSEY

What is tape? I know nothing.

HAYES

I have access to watch past games. That way I can study defensive plays and get a feel for what we may be up against in the upcoming games. There's a lot of strategy that goes into being a quarterback.

JERSEY

So Beckett is one of your friends on your team? You said he's a tight end? I'm trying to keep my mind out of the gutter.

HAYES

LOL. Tight end is a position on the offensive team in football. He can tackle as a lineman or he can catch the ball as a receiver. Kind of a jack-of-all-trades.

I'm in way over my head. I'm a complete newbie when it comes to football—or anything sports related.

JERSEY

I see. Are you pretty close with everyone on the team?

HAYES

As much as I'd love to be, that is hard to accomplish. The team is huge, way bigger than just the guys you see on the field. But I'm closest with three guys. Beckett, who is my most reliable tight end. Xaden is a fast as fuck running back. And Quentin is my center.

JERSEY

Now it's my turn to be honest… I don't really know much about football, if you haven't guessed that already. So all those words you just sent… mean nothing to me, lol.

There's a slight pause in his response, and for a moment, I'm worried he's rethinking this whole thing based on my ignorance.

HAYES

Don't worry. I can teach you everything you need to know 😊 I kind of like it. Maybe we'll even get you out to a game one of these days.

JERSEY

I'd really like that. After I master all the football things so I can keep up with what's happening.

The idea of going into this with Hayes—whatever *this* is—completely blind sends a cascade of apprehension down my spine. While I wait for his next text to come through, I reach for my tablet on my nightstand, opening a browser and typing into the search bar, *football for beginners.*

I nibble on the edge of my thumbnail again as my eyes fly over the screen, seeing lots of results pop up from my simple search and I decide I'll have to start doing some homework, so I don't come across as a complete dummy when it comes to Hayes's whole profession. I click on the first one titled "Football 101" and scan the words, starting with the positions that he mentioned until my phone buzzes again.

HAYES

If I can learn a Jersey Matthews album front to back, you can learn football. I have faith in you.

I laugh and stare down at my phone. There's *no* way he's been listening to my music, is there?

JERSEY

You've listened to my album?

HAYES

Like I said… I was wowed.

The grin that takes over my face should be illegal.

As I snuggle into my bed with my tablet, I start my self-study on football, texting Hayes when I have questions. My eyes start to get heavy as the night ticks away.

JERSEY

Hate to be a downer, but I'm getting sleepy, and I've got an early day tomorrow at the studio. I'll talk to you tomorrow!

HAYES

Sweet dreams, Jersey.

Something foreign flutters in my chest—a sense of anticipation for what this might become. For the first time in a long time, I fall asleep, not worried about what tomorrow might bring.

<hr>

I KNOW it's going to be a bad day when I'm summoned to Cal's office as soon as I walk inside the studio. Sure enough, Cal is waiting for me with his arms crossed and jaw set.

"Did you have time to review the song choices?" he asks me, not bothering with pleasantries before diving right into business.

"I did. Did you get my email back?" He gives me a blank look, which tells me everything I need to know. "Why didn't you read it?"

"Because, like I said *yesterday*, we have the final say on which songs end up on the album. You know this. There was no reason for me to read your email when I've already decided."

I set my jaw before firing back, "And I'm telling you, I don't *like* those songs. I don't want them attached to my brand."

"Your brand is *my* brand. At the end of the day, you have no say. You show up, sing the songs, do the publicity, and go on tour. Leave all the big kid decisions to someone who's been in the industry for as long as you've been alive. You're out of your league here, Jersey. Trust me."

Trust is a funny concept for me when it comes to Cal. I trust him about as far as I can throw him.

The familiar frustration and annoyance rear their ugly heads again, but instead of backing down like I usually do, I remember what Hayes said to me last night.

You're extraordinary. Your label is full of fools if they don't see that, too.

Somehow, I find bravery deep inside myself and stand up straighter. "At least meet me halfway. I don't want 'Half the Woman I Am' or 'Silly Little Girl' on the album. Pick different songs, whatever, but I don't want those songs. They're not good enough."

Callum narrows his eyes as he weighs my offer. He drops his arms and seats himself at his desk, grabbing a pen and scribbling himself a note. "Fine. We'll pick different ones. But the rest stay."

I breathe a deep sigh of relief, thankful that Cal didn't make a big fuss about my suggestion. "Thank you."

He turns to me again and scowls. "You didn't win here, Jersey. Don't get any ideas. At the end of the day, I still own you. You'll do well to remember that."

I bite my tongue, choosing silence over getting into an argument with him again. Our last conversation still lingers, like a heavy cloud of smoke. His words echo in my ears, and I do my best to tune them out.

Cal steeples his fingers together. I recognize the power move, and I tilt my nose up, trying to assure him he doesn't affect me. But both parties in this room know that's not true.

"Are you ready to get to work?" he asks, his voice condescending.

I bite back the irritation in my voice, so when I respond, it's professional and level-headed. "Yes, let's get started."

"Excellent. You can go ahead and head down to the studio. I've got it blocked for the morning." He waves me off before opening his laptop and burying his face in the screen.

My eyes burn, and my stomach roils, making me want to vomit, but I do what he says, seeing myself out.

Bethany is waiting for me outside his office, her face etched with concern. "Are you okay?"

I shake my head and hurry to the bathroom, Bethany hot on my heels. I brace my hands against the sinks and squeeze my eyes shut, willing myself not to cry. But it's pointless when my best friend's gentle hand rests on my shoulder. A few tears leak out of the corners of my eyes, and I wipe them away quickly, hoping she doesn't notice.

"I hate him."

She rubs my back. "I know. I wish there was more I could do."

With her strength helping me, I find my own strength to stand up straight and stare down my reflection. I fix my hair, wipe away my tears, and force myself to look put together, reminding myself over and over that Cal might control my career, he might own my brand—for now—but despite what he says, he *doesn't* own *me*.

"I have to go down and start recording now. He let me take off two songs, but I'm sure he'll find some just as terrible to replace them with," I grumble.

"I'm sorry," Bethany says, sympathetically. She knows how badly I want to have more say in my work, but she has also read the contract and knows the restrictions I've locked myself into.

"It's fine." She and I both know that's a lie. "I have to get it over with. Three more years."

"Three more years." She nods sagely, reminding me I'm not in this alone.

Even with her support, echoes of his snide manipulation echo in my mind.

You are what I've made you. Without me, there would be no Jersey Matthews. There would be no album, and there would be no tour.

I can't deny that those words stung yesterday like a slap to the face given all the hard work I've put into my career. But over the last few years, I've made peace with the fact that Callum Strong is nothing but a bully.

Unfortunately, a bully that I am tied to by a legal contract.

How rewarding would it be if I could find the gall to stand up to the people above me, put my foot down, and say that it's *my* career and I want to be the one in charge of the decisions? But every time I try, he squashes me like a bug, putting me in my place and reminding me he's the one who holds the power.

All I have to do is play his game and get through the end of this contract, and then I can walk away and never have to deal with him again.

That's it. Easy, right?

When I've regained control of myself and trust that I'm not going to break down again, we leave the bathroom and go to the recording studio. My phone chimes with a new text message. Hope springs to life in my chest as I read Hayes's name on my screen.

HAYES

Have fun today, Jersey. Do what you do best. Give them hell.

I am emboldened by Hayes, even though he's thousands of miles from me. His support makes me stronger even if it's only over a text message. The knowledge he's got my back gives me that sense of vigor that I've been missing. He hardly knows me aside from one night of texting back and forth, yet he believes in me.

If Hayes can believe in me, maybe I can muster the ability to believe in myself, too.

Before I go into the sound room, I text Hayes back.

JERSEY

You too, QB.

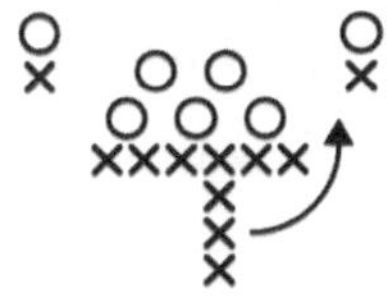

EIGHT

hayes

FRIDAY, SEPTEMBER 20

"Dude, get your head out of your phone." Beckett's voice echoes through the locker room right before a towel snaps and sends a sting across the back of my neck.

"What the fuck?" I shoot back at him, glowering as he gives me a shit-eating grin.

Sunday is our game against the Detroit Blue Devils. At this point, I've done everything in my power to make sure we come out ahead. The team has worked tirelessly to memorize the plays and study the defense so we know what we're up against. Only time will tell if we take home the win.

Beckett points to the phone in my hand as if that's explanation enough. "Who are you even texting?"

"No one," I say way too quickly. Yeah, so I've been texting Jersey practically nonstop . . . what's the big deal?

"You're never on your phone. Now, suddenly, your nose is buried in it." Beckett narrows his eyes suspiciously at me, and then, before I can take a breath, he's lunging at me, and snatches the phone right out of my hands.

"Hey! Beckett, cut it out," I growl. He evades me as I reach for my phone again. A few of the other guys have paused their conversations, now giving us their full attention. They're used to some level of shenanigans between me and Beckett, but even I can admit this is excessive.

"Well, well," my supposed best friend says, looking at my phone screen. "Who do we have here? *Jersey*? Is that a code name or something?"

"Beckett," I warn, but the fucker doesn't listen.

"Are you talking about Jersey Matthews?" Xaden chimes in. "She's like the world's biggest pop star right now. Every time I turn on the radio, it's one of her songs playing."

I stand stone still as Beckett processes that information. Quentin turns around and joins the conversation, shock on his face as he easily reads my reaction. "You're shitting me. *Jersey Matthews?*"

"It's no big deal," I say quickly, swiping my phone back from him. As those words hit my tongue, they leave the bitter taste of a bald-faced lie. "We've been talking here and there."

"*Riight,*" Beckett drawls. "Which is why you haven't been seen apart from your phone for days now. Talking, my ass."

"Beckett," I say my friend's name again, hoping he'll pick up on the hint that I'm not interested in playing these games. There's too much shit on my mind right now to find any humor in his teasing.

Beckett holds up his hands in mock surrender. He still has that sideways smirk on his face, telling me he's up to no good. "Hey, don't be mad at me. I think it's great. Be careful, though. I heard her breakup with her last boyfriend was pretty messy. You don't have time to get caught up in anything like that this season. But maybe hooking up with the *world's most famous pop star* will do you some good, give you a chance to unwind a bit."

"I don't need to *unwind*," I bristle.

He gives me a look that says, *really?*

I roll my eyes and don't respond.

Whatever is blooming between Jersey and me feels too delicate, too precious. I don't want Beckett to simply chalk it up to me needing an outlet. And I especially can't risk the idea that I'm only pursuing her for one thing getting back to her. I'm man enough to recognize the privilege it is for her to welcome me into her thoughts and share her troubles and worries with me.

After we started talking, some online investigating revealed that Jersey ended a long-term relationship about six months ago, and not exactly on amicable terms if the gossip headlines were anything to go by. The tabloids and the headlines can only portray one narrative of the story, which is so rarely the truth. I'd like to ask her about it and get her side of the story, but to do that, she has to open up that conversation herself. We're not even close to where I could outright ask her to spill the dirty details of her breakup.

While I may be interested in knowing her past, it doesn't change what I know about her in the present. I'm confident she'd be open to answer any questions I have, eventually, but I want to wait for the right moment. I don't want to ambush her with my curiosity when she's barely been in my world.

This version of her that she's sharing with me now is all that matters. Everything else can wait. While I haven't figured out what we're dealing with, I know that it's more than a measly hook up.

Hell. I haven't even seen her in person since the VMAs.

We've been texting nonstop since the beginning of the week,

but that's the extent of it. With every little layer she reveals, I find myself falling into a full-blown crush on Jersey Matthews, instinctively reaching for my phone whenever I hear it go off, hoping it's her. I appreciate her willingness to take a chance on me. The fact that she opened up to me right away was encouraging, and I hope her trust and vulnerability are something she'll continue to share with me.

And right on time, a message from Jersey zips across my screen.

JERSEY

I'm in the mood for something sweet.

I nearly groan. I know she's talking about getting herself some Oreos and peanut butter—her favorite snack I've recently learned. Her timing with that message couldn't have been more inconvenient.

Beckett stands behind me, no doubt reading over my shoulder. This fact is confirmed when he snickers to himself.

I set my jaw and walk over to my locker, typing out a response as I go. Fuck Beckett and his stupid games. It doesn't matter what he thinks. He may be my best friend, but right now, Jersey is all mine.

HAYES

Me too 😉

JERSEY

Anything in particular?

My mouth goes dry with her innuendo, and I laugh huskily. Our text messages *have* been getting flirtier, and I like this playful side of her.

HAYES

Depends on who's asking.

JERSEY

Oh, just some girl who can't seem to get you off her mind.

HAYES

Well, in that case...

I'm dying to have you all to myself.

JERSEY

Same here.

I can't help but wonder if she'd be this flirty and playful in person, or if this is a persona she portrays through the safety of the phone. I have so much to learn about her and so many things I want to ask her. I love this lighthearted side, but I don't want to scare her off. So instead of taking things further, I play it safe.

HAYES

How'd recording go today?

JERSEY

About as you'd expect. I got into another fight with Cal, but thankfully, not as brutal as the last one. He wants to go in a different direction on the song that is more "mainstream" than I think the song warrants.

HAYES

I'm sorry. I'm sure it will still be a great song. Everything you put out is amazing.

JERSEY

Oh, stop it. It's mediocre at best. I have an incredibly loyal fanbase who boosts everything to the top 100 as soon as it goes live.

I shake my head. I appreciate her modesty, but she's one of the most famous artists in the world. And, given that I now know she only puts out what her label expects of her, I can't help but wonder how unstoppable she'd be if they set her loose.

JERSEY

How was your day? Are you ready for the game on Sunday?

HAYES

As ready as I'll ever be. You going to tune in?

JERSEY

I wouldn't miss it, MVP. I've been studying up on my football terms all week using my homemade flash cards. Remind me again, how many home runs do you need to win?

I laugh out loud. She's funny. Now that we're all finished for the day, I pack the rest of my stuff into my bag and sling it over my shoulder. I sense Beckett watching me. I turn to him with a questioning glance. He's leaning against his locker with his large arms crossed over his chest, an amused expression on his face.

"What?" I ask him. Even I can recognize I sound tired of his shenanigans.

He pauses a second and then pushes off so he's standing up straight. "Nothing. I'm happy for you. Haven't seen you this happy in"—he shakes his head—"a *long* time."

I exhale, letting my shoulders fall. Beckett was around to remember my last serious relationship back in college. He saw first-hand the range of emotions I went through, the joy at the height of the relationship and the devastation it brought when it ended. Since then, I've been hesitant to engage in anything more serious than a few casual dates. "There's really nothing to be happy for yet."

Something glints in his eye, but I can't place it. "Keep telling yourself that. I've known you a long time, brother. I've never seen you get bent out of shape over a girl you've only been *texting*." He chuckles and claps me on the shoulder when I try to protest. "I'm just saying I get the feeling that this one is different. Special. I was only giving you a hard time. You know I want the best for you."

I roll my neck. "Yeah, I do. Same for you."

"Promise me you won't let this get in the way of football. You know I love you, and I want you to be happy, but I want another Super Bowl ring just as much as the other guys on the team do."

Something tightens in my chest at his comment—excitement? Dread? Acid reflux?

I'm not sure, but regardless, I nod and then head out of the locker room toward the team parking lot, waving goodbye to Xaden and Quentin as they head toward their cars. As soon as I'm settled in my vehicle, I pull out my phone, staring at the last text Jersey sent me, unable to keep the amusement off my face.

Home runs.

HAYES

However many it takes to make it to the World Cup.

JERSEY

Full disclosure: I had to look that up. But you're funny 😆

HAYES

You started it.

On my drive home, I listen to a talk show on the radio make their predictions for Sunday's prime-time game—Detroit at Milwaukee. Who will take home the win?

I tune out their opinions and hot takes and begin running through some of the specialty offensive plays we concocted for this game in my head. I've been working on them so much this week I could name them backward and forward.

There have been games in the past where I've been worried about mixing up the plays or saying the wrong one—many times, the random words we assign to different plays can get confusing. This game, though, I have no worries. I can't.

I have to be on my A game on Sunday. There is no other option.

When I get home, the house is dark and quiet, as it always is on a Friday night. In the distance, I hear the familiar jingle of Periwinkle's dog tags as she moves around her fluffy bed. I set my practice stuff by the front door and head into the kitchen, flipping on the overhead lights.

My phone dings as soon as I do.

JERSEY

Are you done with practice?

I tap out a quick response.

HAYES

Yup, just finished.

As soon as I've hit send, I walk around the kitchen toward Peri's little bed on the other side of the fridge. The small dog squints up at me with a disdainful grimace, and I fight off a smile. Tomorrow night I'll be with the team at our usual hotel we stay in before home games and my housekeeper will take care of Peri for the evening. I'm sure when I get home on Sunday night after the game, Peri will be on the clingy side.

I scratch behind her ears and under the collar of her purple chevron sweater and wait expectantly for Jersey's text to come through. The three little dots appear on the screen, telling me she's typing out a reply. Then they disappear, without anything coming through. I narrow my eyes at the screen when they pop up again.

Finally, after the same thing happens two more times, she finally sends the text.

JERSEY

Would you want to talk tonight?

I can't fight off the grin that appears on my face.

HAYES

Like a phone call?

JERSEY

Yeah, if that's okay…

Hell yes, it's okay.

I don't hesitate, tapping her contact information and starting up a call as I continue to rub behind Peri's ears. From her position on her fluffy bed, she starts making a sound I attribute to purring—never thought Shih Tzus purred until Peri came into my life. The call rings twice before Jersey answers.

"Hayes?" Her voice is a bit timid like she's scared of who will be on the other end of the call.

"The one and only, honey," I tease her, still grinning from ear to ear.

I can practically hear her audible sigh of relief. "It's nice to actually talk to you."

"You too, though I have been enjoying texting you this week. Nice to know you're real," I tease.

Her laugh is a light twinkling sound that reminds me of Fourth of July sparklers. "So, what did you do today at practice? What terms do I need to write down to study later?"

"Oh, you know, the usual. I ran some drills and did some agility training. Coach had a few new plays that he wanted us to run today. All in the name of getting ready for that big game on Sunday."

"Are you ready?"

I sit down on my kitchen floor so I can continue to pet Peri, lest I stop and she throws a fit. Leaning against the fridge, I get a bit more comfortable. "For better or for worse. All I can do is my job. I can't control everyone else."

Jersey hums, thoughtfully. "I guess that's true. I'd be stressing about everyone else, for sure."

I chuckle. "I did at first, but then those sleepless nights start to catch up to you when your job is as physically taxing as mine. I had to relinquish some of the control, or I wouldn't have made it as far as I have."

"I'd love to live a day in your life, I think."

Leaning my head back on the fridge, I smile up at the ceiling. "You say that, but when you get sacked ten times in one game, it's not so fun anymore."

"Ugh, I was watching some of your replays on YouTube the other day, and I can't believe how hard you get hit sometimes."

My grin widens. Pride swells in my chest at those words. "You looked me up?"

She pauses, and I have to fight off a laugh. I *love* that she looked me up. I looked *her* up, so it's only fair.

"I may have done a few Google searches . . ." She trails off. "I'm still working on building my sportsball knowledge, okay? And I want to be able to watch your games and know what's going on."

"I love that you cared enough to look me up, Jersey." Football is everything to me, so it's hard for me to remember that there are people who have never had the beautiful game up on their screens or joined the rowdy crowds at the stadium for home games.

"You do?" Her voice sounds small, and I hate that. Especially knowing how bold and confident she can be on stage. I hate that she'd feel anything but that way for any reason.

"Yeah." I grin into the phone, hoping she can somehow hear it. The fact that Jersey is wedging her foot in the door to this sport that is my very reason for breathing means so much more than I could ever put into words, and knowing she's doing so for me? That makes it even better. I have a lot of people in my world who care for me, but it's been a while since someone's gone out of their way to do something so meaningful for me. "I want you to know everything about me, and everything about my game. And give me another week or so and I'll be singing your songs from memory. If you want me to learn your dance moves too, all you gotta do is say the word."

Jersey finally laughs into the phone, and I close my eyes, listening to the delightful sound. I can't wait for the opportunity to hear her laugh in person, to see how her face lights up when she laughs like this.

I run my hand over my face and shake my head at myself. *I'm so screwed.*

Down beside me, Peri must sense that I'm giving her less than a hundred percent of my attention because she yips, pulling me out of my daydreams of Jersey's laugh and back to the present.

"Do you have a dog?"

I chuckle. "I have a gremlin."

"What does that mean?"

"I'll show you." I switch the call to speakerphone so I can snap a picture of Peri and send it through to Jersey.

She responds a moment later. "Oh my gosh, she's so cute!" she exclaims. "And her sweater? Stop it."

"Her name is Peri," I explain. "Short for Periwinkle."

"What kind of dog is she?"

"Shih Tzu," I say, looking down at Peri fondly. "She's a good dog, if not a bit of a drama queen."

"I've never had a dog," Jersey admits.

"Well, anytime you want to borrow her, you can."

"What does she do when you're traveling for games?"

"My housekeeper takes care of her when I'm gone. Peri sleeps ninety hours a day, so all she needs is some food and plenty of water. She's really low maintenance."

"I love that. Maybe I'll get to meet her one day."

At Jersey's suggestion, my heart clenches, and I find myself smiling up at the ceiling again. Hopefully, this is the first of many, many conversations with her—this could be the start of something that will change both of our lives.

"I hope you will." I breathe.

NINE

jersey

SUNDAY, SEPTEMBER 22

"LET'S FUCKING GO!" I jump up from my couch and shout at my massive TV as Hayes throws the ball to one of the players right in the points area—or *end zone*, as I'm learning. This makes his fourth touchdown of the game, and we're only in the second quarter. As the time has ticked down on the screen, Hayes's drive has seemed to amp up even more on the field.

Bethany laughs from her position on my couch. I spin around to find her and Kelsey watching me in amusement. I place my hands on my hips, but I can't fight off the smile.

"What?"

Bethany chuckles. "Nothing. I never knew you were into football."

"Well—" I say, brushing a few stray hairs out of my face. "It's kind of a new thing."

Bethany and Kelsey share a look. "Apparently," Bethany says.

Kelsey points at the TV. "That Hayes Vogt is an impressive player. Is he the one you were talking with at the VMAs?"

"He is," I coyly agree, leaving it at that.

I sit back down on my couch, resting against the plush cushions, and reach for my drink on the table. I'm sticking with a classic tonight, the old vodka tonic.

"Bethany says you've been talking to him some," Kelsey pries. When I turn to her, she's wearing a soft smile on her face, hinting that she already knows what's up, but she wants to hear it from my perspective.

"A little," I lie. There have been more texts shared between me and Hayes this last week than there were with my ex throughout the entire last year of our relationship.

"And you like him?" Bethany asks.

My cheeks heat and I take another sip of my drink. How do I even begin to answer this? How can I when Hayes and I have only ever been face-to-face once before? I sent him a selfie tonight, but that hardly counts. He probably won't even see it until after the game.

"I think I do," I admit, to both my friends and myself.

"Just be careful, Jersey," Kelsey says. "I remember how brokenhearted you were when it didn't work out with Corey. I'm always reading tabloids about athletes breaking hearts. You and him have the potential to be a PR disaster."

"I think this one is different, Kelsey," I say, trusting my words wholeheartedly. "I think *he's* different. I can't explain it, but everything in me is telling me to run toward him, not away from him."

"Sounds like puppy love," she says softly.

I know she's trying to be gentle with me. Both Kelsey and Bethany were there, helping me through the hardest days of my life when Corey and I ended. Both of them were there to reassure me when I felt like I wasn't good enough or worthy of a future in the industry. Even as Kelsey voices her concerns, I can't help but think she's wrong.

On the TV, the Majestics leave the field for halftime. When the camera zeros in on Hayes, my belly flip-flops. He's got his helmet off as the team goes ahead of him down the tunnel to their locker room. His blond hair is sweaty at the top and whatever he painted underneath his eyes is beginning to melt down his cheeks. It looks like black watercolor paint as it drips down his face and mixes with the perspiration on his skin. He has a few smudges trailing from his cheek to his ear from where he must have wiped his face at some point.

He's a mess, but I love it.

My body heats and I fight the desire to know what it would feel like to have him all sweaty like that, but in a different setting, preferably in a comfy bed. And without the uniform and pads in our way. I clear my throat and swallow thickly, ignoring the way my mouth has gone dry at the direction of my thoughts.

The TV cuts to a commercial, breaking the spell.

"Anyone need a refill?" I ask, reaching for my drink and Bethany's, which is also empty.

Kelsey declines and stays on the couch, scrolling through her phone as I head into the kitchen to work on the drinks. Bethany follows me and leans against the kitchen island as I refill our cups with vodka and mixers.

"Why are you looking at me like that?" I ask her.

"Like what?" she questions back, her lips quirking to the side.

"Like you're already planning my wedding." I stick my tongue out.

"Can you blame me?" Bethany sticks her tongue out, too. "Even Kelsey is catching onto whatever you two have brewing between you."

"Don't get ahead of yourself. Hayes and I haven't even met up officially yet. We're still only talking. I mean, we've texted and called a few times, but that's the extent of it."

"What are you waiting for, Jersey? You were just saying you feel like everything is pushing you toward him. I'm sure all it would take would be for you to say you want to see him and he'll be booking the flights. If the way he sought you out at the VMAs is any indication, that man knows what he wants, and that's *you*."

"I'm not sure we're at that point yet," I explain, feeling the lack of confidence lurking in the back of my mind.

"Okay, I hear you." Bethany nods. "Maybe start smaller. Have you two FaceTimed yet?"

I shake my head. "Do you think that would be the next step? It's been a while since I've been in this stage of a relationship. I sometimes feel like I'm going in blind."

"Follow your heart," Bethany says and then cringes at the cliché. "I know, I know. But really, though. I think Hayes has the capacity to help you rebuild everything that Corey destroyed in his wake. You might have to take a few leaps of faith. Get out of your comfort zone."

"You're probably right. I'll try." In the living room, I hear the TV switch back to the game and I tilt my head in that direction. Bethany follows me back into the living room and we settle in to watch the next half.

Any other train of thought derails as Hayes walks out to the offensive line. His stride is so confident, so sure, I can't help but get excited for this next play. With his broad shoulders, he points at a few players on the line as he shouts things to his other teammates.

Then he takes a step back, situating himself where he needs to be, and crouches into position. The ball is snapped, and he's bouncing around on the field, pivoting this way and that, searching for an opening.

I clutch my hands tightly together as I watch the screen, scanning the field myself, waiting for one of Hayes's teammates to open themselves up to receive the pass.

But it doesn't come.

The Detroit defense work their way around the players protecting Hayes and they tackle him to the ground with a sickening crunch.

"Oh!" one of the girls screams.

"And he's sacked. Blue Devils have taken down Hayes Vogt for the first time this game. Vogt is one of the least sacked quarterbacks this season, so you know they'll be applauding Rife for that one after the game."

I frown as the announcers commentate on the events which recently took place. "Come on, get up," I mutter, eyes still glued to the screen as the players climb off Hayes. He stays on the ground for a moment and then pops up, seemingly unfazed by the whole thing. He shakes his arms out, throws the ball to the referee, and then calls the team together in a huddle before taking the line again.

I let out a long breath I didn't know I was holding and reach for my drink again, ignoring the pointed stares of Kelsey and Bethany.

"He's fine," I announce, though I guess I didn't have to.

Bethany and Kelsey now share another knowing glance, but they gratefully don't say a thing.

Hayes evaded any further violent sacks throughout the rest of the game and managed a few more clean passes, which resulted in two more touchdowns to bring home the win for the Majestics.

I sit and watch the reporters question the players and

coaches after the game, waiting for Hayes to appear. When he does, my chest aches with anticipation in hearing him speak. My lips part and I lean my elbows on my knees, eyes wide as I trace every little detail of his handsome face on my screen.

Throughout the flurry of excitement on the field, the reporter asks him a question. I'm sure he gives a well-practiced, PR-approved answer, but honestly, I'm not listening. Instead, I'm taking the chance to study his face, to watch how his amber eyes fixate on the reporter, giving her his full attention despite the chaos happening around them. I'm listening to the delicious timbre of his voice and the gruffness of his laugh and noting that just like the very first time I heard him speak, goosebumps appear on my forearms. Something about his deep voice itches that exact perfect spot in my brain. It's like music to my ears.

Far too quickly, the reporter is thanking him for his time and he's disappearing from the camera to shake hands with some of his teammates and opponents.

"Gotta say," Kelsey starts. "You picked a looker. That man is somethin' else."

My cheeks flame and my jaw falls open. "Kelsey!"

"What? It's not like he doesn't know he's fine. And those pants." She makes the sign of the cross over herself and then fans her neck.

I cover my face with my hands and groan. This is only the beginning of the relentless teasing that always comes with the start of a new relationship. I had been saved from the heckling during the five-year-span of my relationship with Corey, but now that I'm in the midst of something new, it's clearly open season.

"Our ride is downstairs," Bethany says after a while. "Kelsey, are you ready to go?"

Kelsey nods and turns to me. "Thanks for the invite. I don't usually like football, but I definitely had a great time watching you swoon over your boyfriend."

My cheeks heat and I roll my eyes. "He's not my boyfriend, and I was not swooning."

Kelsey nudges my shoulder. "Whatever you've got to tell yourself. You're still planning to be at my family's gala next weekend, right? I'll see you there?"

I nod. A few years back, Kelsey asked me to go to her family's annual gala to raise money for the impoverished and homeless, and I've made sure to have it on my calendar every year since. This year I donated a few tickets and backstage passes to my upcoming shows to be auctioned off. "I'm looking forward to it."

"You're the best, Jersey." Kelsey gives me a hug.

"Thanks for having us over! Have fun with that quarterback of yours. He's one hell of a catch." Bethany waves at me by the door. I stand up and walk over with them to see them out. As they head down the hallway from my condo, I realize I have a love-hate relationship with the two most important women in my life. I love them to death, and I hate that they know me so damn well.

Once everything is cleaned up, I go in search of my phone, finding a message from Hayes waiting for me.

HAYES

What did you think? Thanks for that selfie, btw. You're stunning.

I flush and do a little happy dance to myself.
Wonder what Cal would think of that *choreography.*

JERSEY

That was amazing. You were meant to be a quarterback. You make it look so easy!

HAYES

Thank you. Nothing but a whole lot of work behind the scenes and an incredible team helping me pull it all off.

JERSEY

It's so impressive how you can read the players on the field and find exactly the right place to throw the ball. Even when you got tackled, you made it look like it was nothing. Did it hurt?

HAYES

Well… it didn't feel great. I'll leave it at that. Comes with the territory. But that's why there are a lot of rules in place to protect the quarterback. Even still, we take heavy hits sometimes.

JERSEY

Have you ever been hurt before?

HAYES

Yeah, plenty of times. It's not a football game if I'm not walking away without some aches or injuries. I have a full recovery schedule lined up throughout the week. Massages, chiropractors, ice-baths, red light therapy. You name it.

JERSEY

What kind of injuries have you had?

HAYES

A lot of sprained ribs, a twisted ankle or two.
Tweaked shoulder. All nuisances more than
anything. Usually means I have to focus
more on rehab and recovery that week. By
offseason, my body is ready for some rest.

I nibble on my lower lip, not loving the way Hayes is describing the physical toll the game takes on his body. How does he do this every week? Touring is physical for me too, and my training is regimented so I can have enough strength to dance up on stage for hours at a time, but I'm not getting two-hundred pounds thrown full speed at me at any given moment. I can't imagine what that feels like for him.

JERSEY

I loved watching you play. I never wanted it
to end, even when they kept running into
you. Congratulations on the win. I knew you
could do it.

HAYES

There was something so satisfying knowing
you were watching. I feel like I put on the
performance of my life trying to impress
you.

JERSEY

Well, color me impressed, #18. Really.

He shoots me a hand hearts emoji and I smile like a dork down at my screen. I swear if anyone could see me now, they'd suspect I was some high school girl in love rather than a twenty-eight-year-old woman. I am ecstatic, high on the thrill of talking with such an enigmatic man.

Nibbling on my thumbnail, I decide to be brave and take the leap of faith Bethany mentioned.

JERSEY

Do you want to FaceTime?

Hayes wastes no time, sending me a response quickly.

HAYES

Do I ever! Let me get home and I'll call you.

My stomach twists in a blend of nerves and excitement. Bethany's words from last week echo in my mind from earlier.

See where it goes. What have you got to lose?

I can do that.

The next hour seems to tick by at a snail's pace, but finally my phone vibrates with his call. My finger hovers over the *accept* button. I take a deep breath, count down from three, and press my thumb to the screen.

Here goes nothing.

jersey

SUNDAY, SEPTEMBER 22

SECONDS LATER, Hayes's face appears on my screen and my stomach flips. I bite into my lower lip, my eyes scanning his features and memorizing how he looks right now.

He's *so handsome.*

Even after pushing himself to the physical brink to claim the win tonight, he's as good-looking as ever. His amber eyes are alight with happiness as they flicker over my face. The only evidence I can make out that he might be slightly worn out is the way his eyes are crinkled in the corners, like he's pushing the exhaustion to the back of his mind for now so he can focus on me.

"Hi," I whisper first, breaking the silence.

His mouth pulls into a crooked smirk, and again, my chest flutters. "Hey there."

His voice is gruff, tired, and I ache to know what his voice would sound like late at night or first thing in the morning.

What would the sound of his gravelly tone whispering my name into the darkness do to me?

Hayes is lounging in his bed, comfortable against some fluffy pillows, and I briefly have a mental image of me using *him* as a pillow. Would those muscular pecs be comfortable to lie on? Or his built shoulders?

"Congratulations on the win," I say with a grin. Padding through the house, I make my way to my bedroom and fall onto the mattress. "Are you too tired to talk?"

Hayes stretches an arm above his head, his biceps flexing with the movement. My mouth goes dry, seeing the strong bulge of his muscular form. He's not wearing a shirt, his broad shoulders and chest bare. The dormant, sexual side of me slowly awakens and I find myself feeling a bit more confident. What would it feel like to have those massive biceps circle around me and hold me close?

"I'm never too tired to talk to you," Hayes says, then is overtaken by a yawn. I laugh and he gives me a sheepish look. "How was your day?"

I'm lying on my belly on top of my bed, and I bend my knees, crossing my ankles together in the air. Hayes's eyes track my movement, darting away from my face for a second before returning to me. I fight off a sly smile.

"It was great, actually. I got to watch one of the best quarterbacks in the league do his thing." He rolls his eyes but doesn't hide the pride that appears on his face. He's so dang handsome I can't stand it. "*And* seeing you out there on the field in that uniform had me feeling some type of way."

Hayes catches on quickly, one brow arching a bit and that smirk of his deepening. "Is that so?"

I bite my lip again and he tracks the movement, eyes darkening. "Oh yeah. Those uniform pants should be illegal."

He laughs and stretches again. "Some type of way, huh?" I nod slowly. "I gotta admit, seeing you in that low cut tank top has *me* feeling some type of way now too."

My eyes fall to the small inset on the FaceTime call reflecting me, where I observe my cleavage on full display for him. Heat blooms through me and my chest flushes bright red. I'm thankful the room has subtle lighting otherwise, I'm sure he would catch onto my embarrassment.

"I guess we're in the same boat then," I tease. "Really though, watching you do your thing out there was incredible. You were meant to command the field like that."

His arm flexes again as he shifts, and my attention goes straight to the bulging muscle, imagining what it would be like to snuggle up against him. His lips pull into a smirk as he tracks my distraction. "Thanks, baby."

My heart skips a beat at the endearment, and I squeeze my thighs together.

"How does one even get pulled up to a professional level football team?" I ask him, meeting his eyes again.

"I was drafted right out of college," he explains. "I've played football my whole life, first with my dad in the backyard, then flag. Then, when I was old enough—and my mom gave the green light—I upgraded to tackle football and made the varsity team in high school. That's when I started making a name for myself, which helped me get to the collegiate level. From there it was simply garnering the interest of the right NFL scouts."

"Have you played on any other teams?"

He shakes his head. "Nope. Majestics pulled me right out of the draft and started me that first season. They needed a new quarterback and drafted me in the first round, starting me out on the field right away, even though I was a rookie. I'm grateful someone in higher management saw the potential in me."

"I think they were right," I muse and he grins. "You seem to be in your element out there. It's like you're making your own kind of music out on the field."

"That's a good way to put it." He nods. "It has been a whirlwind of a career. I'm grateful for the opportunity to do what I love and hone my leadership skills. I have a lot of goals I want to achieve with the Majestics, so I gotta keep my eyes on the prize." Proving his point, his eyes swirl with something and I wonder if he's thinking about what those future games might bring, what plays will make it to the playbook.

"Like what?" I prod him, listening raptly. He's obviously passionate when it comes to football and his team. It's hard not to feed off that energy.

"Another Super Bowl ring," he says with a wide smile. His eyes grow distant, lost in thought, as if he can picture himself holding that trophy in his hands.

"You won . . . last year?" I ask, even though I know. I read that information online during my searches.

"We sure did. The first win for the franchise in twenty years," he says proudly, as he should. "But it wasn't all me. It was a big team win for us. I couldn't have done it without any of them just as much as they couldn't have done it without me."

I bite my lower lip. "I like the idea of having a team dynamic like that."

He tilts his head to the side, appearing a little confused. "Well, you have one too, don't you think? A team is anyone you have in your corner, supporting you through thick and thin. It might look a little different than mine, but you still have one."

I think about Bethany and Kelsey and Roman, how they do exactly that, even when the going gets tough with meeting the schedule or demands of the label. "You're right. I do."

"What about you? How'd you get into singing?" he asks me, pivoting the conversation.

I hum a little, recalling my own origin story. "I've always loved signing. My mom tells me I used to go around the house creating songs as they came to me when I was little. As I got older, it became a dream of mine to make it big, create songs and albums that people could love. But it's damn near impossible to get started in the industry with no connections."

"I bet. I can imagine it would be a crazy grueling process to try and get your name out there," he says. He has no idea. The number of singers who never got their chance to make it to the big leagues is innumerable.

"It is. When I was eighteen, I started performing in dive bars in Northern California where I grew up. I had a fake ID and everything." I laugh and Hayes grins back at me through the phone at the sound. "I just had this dream that someone, *anyone,* would take notice of me and give me a chance to prove that I was worth the time and effort." My voice takes on a tender edge to it. In the back of my mind, I can see a young version of myself, standing at the threshold and staring out into the future with nothing but a heart full of hope and a guitar in my hand.

"Was that hard?" he asks, eager to know every little detail of this time in my life.

"It was a lot of hard work," I agree, sinking further into my pillows. "But it was work I enjoyed doing, and that made all the difference. Eventually, the endless shows with little to no interest from anyone higher than bar management started to wear on me. I was so close to giving up hope."

"I bet," he says, shaking his head.

"After three years of nothing, I was ready to throw in the towel. I told myself to just do one more. One last show, and then I'd call it quits. After that I'd know for sure that this dream was never meant to be." Three years is a long time to stick with the grind with no return on investment. Something I'm reminded of now with three years left on my contract. I'm struck with the coincidental parallel.

"But?"

"But little did I know inside of that dive bar was Lorelai Brown, a recruiter for Silver Shadows. I had no idea she'd take a video of me performing my heart out for something I thought would be my very last opportunity to get up on stage and sing. And I definitely had no idea I'd be called to LA to be onboarded to the Silver Shadows Records roster. I was assigned to Callum, and the rest is history."

"Wow," he says, exhaling a breath. "That's . . . a lot of change in a short amount of time."

"It was. It still makes my head spin when I lay it all out like that. But I'm forever grateful. They took a chance on me, and it ended up changing my entire life." I prop my cheek up on my fist and stare into the screen. Hayes stares right back, studying me.

"But it wasn't all fun and games?" he questions, and I wonder if he's remembering our very first conversation through texts.

I laugh lightly, though really, it's not funny. "No, it wasn't. They rolled out the red carpet for me until I signed the original five-year contract. It was too late by the time I realized Cal had a different idea of what my career was going to look like. And my contract is ironclad, so there's nothing I can do about it, even when I adamantly disagree with the direction he's taking me in."

"I'm sorry," he says, sincerely. "Is there really no way you can change how things are?"

"He keeps me on a tight leash. Occasionally, he'll give into a suggestion, but I think it's merely to keep me compliant. I have three years until my contract is up for renewal again since I recently went through the renewal process. Last time he gave me lots of empty promises to convince me to re-sign. I should've known better, but I fell for it anyway, thinking things would be different this time."

"They keep you on for three years at a time?"

I nod. "My first contract with them was five years, and then they do three-year extensions. That usually allows them to get an album or two out—if they're lucky—with enough time for touring in between."

"Is every label that way?"

"I think every label has a multitude of different deals they can offer artists, either new or returning. I'm not exactly in the *know* about any of that, though. Three years isn't really a long time, but it feels like forever to me sometimes."

"Well, just keep standing up for yourself," he says, eyes on mine. "It's your career. You shouldn't have to bend to the will of someone who doesn't have your best interests at heart."

"I wish it were that easy." I sigh.

Hayes blinks. "If it were easy, anyone would do it, you know? But I think you can do anything you set your mind to, even if that is standing up to your manager."

My heart flutters with the compliment. "Thank you . . . That means a lot to me." His lips quirk up in the corners, but then fall into a massive yawn. I fight off a smile. "I should let you get some sleep. You've had a crazy long day. Do you have to work tomorrow?"

He shakes his head and stretches again before running one of his hands over his face. I track the movement, wondering what it would be like to feel those big hands all over my body. "I don't have to be with the team tomorrow since we won yesterday. I'll probably work on my own, though, get a light workout in, do some rehab, maybe a massage and some cryotherapy to help my muscles heal up. I've got an event out of town on Friday, which I still have to pack and get ready for. Then be be back here by Saturday evening to get to the hotel for curfew before the next game Sunday afternoon."

"Well then, I'll let you go."

"Thanks for suggesting this," he says, eyes gently tracing over my face. "I liked getting to see you this time. You're even more beautiful than I remember."

My cheeks warm a bit. "I liked it too."

"We might need to make this the norm from now on." He yawns again. "All right, well off to bed with you too, then. I'll talk to you later?"

I love the hopefulness which laces his question. "Definitely. Goodnight, Hayes."

ELEVEN

jersey

FRIDAY, SEPTEMBER 27

"Jersey's here!" I hear someone shout as I step out of the limousine and then all the cameras turn my way.

I wave at a few fans who are lingering on the sidelines of the red carpet. Kelsey appears moments later and hurries down the carpet to meet me. She gives me a hug as the cameras flash around us.

"Thank you so much for coming," she says softly to me.

"I wouldn't have missed it." I pull away and grin at her. "You know this is one of my favorite events of the year."

"Ladies over here!" a paparazzi shouts. Kelsey and I turn toward them and pose together.

When they're satisfied with their shots, Kelsey leans in. "Let's get you inside so you can get a drink and sit for a while. Those heels look treacherous."

Inside, Kelsey leads me through the main lobby to the ballroom where the gala is taking place this evening. The space is ornately decorated with beautiful flower arrangements adorning the center of each table with delicately lit candles encircling each piece.

"Oh, Jersey!" a woman calls my name and hurries over to me—Kelsey's mother. "I'm so glad you could make it again this year!"

I hug her back, accepting her air kisses on both sides of my face. "Thank you so much for the invitation again."

"I don't know if you had a chance to meet my son or his wife the last few times you've been in attendance," she says and motions to the couple standing behind her.

"Theo and I met in passing last year, but I'm not sure I've met your wife," I say to Kelsey's brother.

He gives his wife a warm smile when he looks down at her. "This is my wife, Whitney. Whit, this is Jersey Matthews."

"Lovely to meet you." Whitney offers me her hand. "It's such an honor to have you in attendance."

"Really, the honor is all mine," I say, graciously as I accept her handshake.

"Kelsey has spoken very highly of you," Whitney says, beaming at me. "We appreciate your generous donation to the charity auction this year."

"Hopefully, it will raise good money for your organization. I'm always happy to be involved when it's for a charitable cause."

"We'll let you get settled in for the evening," Kelsey's mother says, breaking up the introductions. "I'm glad I got to catch you before everything gets crazy. Kelsey"—she looks to her daughter standing by my side—"will you show Jersey to her table?"

"Sure. We have you at your usual table tonight." Kelsey motions for me to follow her and then wraps her arm through mine.

I wave at her family. "It was a pleasure to see you all."

"Have a great time this evening." Whitney gives me a warm smile.

As Kelsey and I weave our way through the many round tables adorning the ballroom, I say, "This is a good turnout this year. I don't remember there being so many tables the last few years."

She nods in agreement. "This is the largest number of attendees we've had so far. We're very fortunate that so many people are willing to donate and show up."

"I love that." I pat her hand looped through my arm.

Before we make it to the table, there's a commotion by the front doors. "Oh, someone important must've just walked in," Kelsey muses and tilts her head. We take a few steps closer until the new guest comes into view.

"Oh my gosh," I exhale when I catch sight of him. He's unmistakable with his athletic frame, broad shoulders, muscular thighs, and his sharp jaw.

"Is that—"

"You didn't tell me he'd be here," I whisper to Kelsey.

She looks as surprised as I feel as she shakes her head. "I had no idea. My mother handles the guest list."

As if he can feel the weight of my gaze on him, Hayes straightens up, his neck craning to peruse the room. When his eyes land on me, it seems to knock all the breath out of my lungs. My heart jackhammers in my chest when his face splits into a wide grin, eyes gleaming with unabashed delight. His expression beckons to me like a bright light shining among the dim ballroom.

In the weeks we've been talking over text and our FaceTime call, I seemed to have forgotten the sheer impact that being in his presence has.

He wastes no time pushing past the people crowding him and making a beeline toward me.

Kelsey makes an amused sound and then slides her arm out of mine. "I better go see if my mom needs help with anything. I'll leave you to it." With a wink, she leaves my side.

Moments later, Hayes is standing in front of me. He rakes his eyes over my body, and I'm seconds away from spontaneously combusting. His hands twitch at his sides and I wonder if he's going to hug me, take me into his arms, cup my face, *touch* me.

I surprise myself when I realize I want him to.

"Hi, Jersey," he says, his voice low, only for me. His deep timbre sends a delicious shiver down my spine, and I inadvertently take a step closer to him.

"Hi," I say back, my voice barely a whisper.

"You look stunning tonight," Hayes says, the corners of his lips turning up a bit as he takes in my dress, eyes trailing from my face down to my shimmering navy-blue skirt. He's looking handsome in his black tuxedo, too. It fits him seamlessly. "I can't believe you're here."

"You either," I admit. "I keep expecting for someone to walk up and pinch me. Surely, I'll wake up from this dream any second."

"How did you even get involved with this charity?" he asks.

"Kelsey, my publicist. This is her family's event. I've been in attendance the last few years, but this is the first time I donated anything for the auction. What about you?"

He clears his throat and leans forward. "There's a facet of the organization that specifically works with child poverty both in the US and on the global scale. I'm pretty involved in that side of it, and I've done work with them for the last year or so."

Would it be possible for this man to be even more attractive? I love a man involved with charity.

Then something else occurs to me and I blink. "Have you been to the gala before?"

An amused smirk arises on his face. "I have. Not last year, but the year before."

"I can't believe we never crossed paths."

He shrugs a shoulder. "I guess I wasn't looking for you before."

"But you are now?" I ask him, biting my lower lip.

His eyes dart from mine down to my lips and then back up again. "I'm definitely looking now, honey."

I feel breathless. "I like the sound of that." Clearing my throat, I ask, "Are you in New York for the weekend? I can't believe this didn't come up in conversation last week."

"No, just for tonight. I guess that's why I didn't think to mention it."

"Well then, I guess I better make this time count, huh?"

He gives me a crooked smile, and my cheeks flush. I look away, ignoring the fluttering in my belly. "Where are you sitting?" he whispers in my ear, and a shiver runs down my spine.

I point at the table two away from where we are standing. "Right there." Hayes looks determined as he walks over to the table I pointed out, perusing the name cards. I follow him, curiously. "What are you doing?"

He plucks one up and then waves it between his fingers. "Just doing a little rearranging. I don't think anyone will mind."

I catch sight of the name on the place card he grabbed and my heart stutters. *Corey Shrader.*

What the hell?

Kelsey mentioned Corey would be in attendance tonight.

He was always my plus one for the event in years past, so his attendance isn't completely out of the blue, but she conveniently forgot to tell me he'd be seated at my table—right next to me. This must have been a mistake her mother didn't catch when she was finalizing the seating chart.

Hayes walks over to the table he's supposed to sit at and picks up his own place card, replacing it with Corey's. Tilting his head toward me, he gives me another coy smile. "Come on, let's sit for a while."

I follow him back to my table where he places his card next to mine, then he pulls out my chair for me and motions for me to sit down. Shortly after I'm settled, a waiter comes by and delivers two flutes of champagne for us.

Hayes holds his up to me. "To unexpected surprises."

My heart skips a beat, and I clink my glass against his. "Cheers." I take a sip, letting the flavor of the bubbles hit my tongue.

"What the hell?" a voice protests and I stiffen, my muscles in my back and my shoulders going rigid. I can't help but think to myself that it's a voice I wouldn't mind ever hearing again.

I look away from Hayes to see Corey scowling down at me. Keeping my face as neutral as possible, I take a deep breath and ask, "Can I help you?"

Hayes easily reads the tension between us and extends his arm across the back of my seat, leaning toward me slightly. The heat from his large frame seeps into me and I find myself inching closer to him too. Corey tracks his movement and glares at Hayes. "You're in my seat, man."

Hayes narrows his eyes and then reaches for his place card, holding it up. "Nope, don't think so. This is my name. Sorry, there must've been a mix up."

"I think you're at table seven," I add, pointing over to the table Hayes *used* to be seated at. I can't fathom why Corey would *assume* we'd be seated next to each other again this year. We've been broken up for months now.

Corey crosses his arm and stares at me. "Real mature, Jersey. This isn't over."

Thankfully, he stalks away and takes his seat at table seven. Hayes turns back to me with an eyebrow raised. "So that was the infamous Corey Shrader, huh?"

"Unfortunately," I acknowledge and shake my head. "I don't want to talk about him. Distract me."

"You're better off without him," Hayes mutters. His expression changes then, and I can physically see him moving on from the thought of anything to do with Corey. "Are you going to bid on anything tonight?"

"I'm not sure. I haven't really had the chance to look at the listings yet."

"Let's go have a look." Hayes sets down his champagne flute and scoots his chair back. Standing up to his full height, he offers his hand to me. I look at it for a second before sliding my fingers against his. He helps me up but doesn't release my hand.

We walk together to the table holding the items listed for auction and peruse them together. He doesn't let go of me the entire time. When I slide my hand away from his, he gently moves his touch to the small of my back, as if he's afraid I might disappear if we lose contact. It makes my head spin, and my heart takes off at record speed.

I must admit, I like being by his side. I like watching him listen to every word that leaves my mouth, interested in anything I have to say. It's such a contrast to what I had become accustomed to at the end of my last relationship. Corey would rather abandon me to hang out at the bar with other A-list attendees than walk with his arm around me. He was always so focused on himself.

As the evening progresses, and I spend more time with Hayes, I somehow find my interest in him increasing to new heights. The magnetism he exudes is inescapable. I, too, seem to find myself leaning in closer to him when he speaks, itching to hear him talk more or tell me another joke.

And when he throws his head back with a laugh, the full, deep sound makes my belly tighten and my face split into an uncontrollable grin.

The joy he brings me is unparalleled. And I could find myself quickly becoming addicted to the way he makes me feel.

For a short time, I forget that I'm Jersey Matthews, the pop star, feeling like any other woman standing at the precipice of a new romantic relationship. The desire to jump headfirst overshadows any other rational thought. It's lovely, it's addicting, it's . . . refreshing.

As much as I want to hold on to these feelings he's evoking in me, I should know better by now that they are always short-lived.

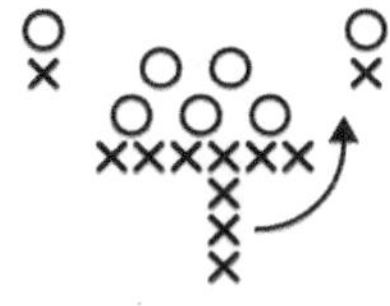

TWELVE

hayes

FRIDAY, SEPTEMBER 27

I DON'T KNOW what lucky star is looking down on me tonight, but I'm eternally grateful that they are. How else could I have managed to run into the one person I was itching to see halfway across the country?

Even in my wildest dreams, I couldn't have imagined I would have gotten to spend tonight with Jersey Matthews. But I'll be damned if I take it for granted.

The more time I've spent with her in person, the more I want to spend with her.

Jersey's expression turns thoughtful and then she's stepping closer to me, wrapping her arms around my waist and hugging me. I'm frozen for a split second before my arms instinctively wrap around her frame. I bend my head, resting my cheek against the side of her hair and closing my eyes as I breathe her in.

She smells . . . intoxicating.

In my periphery, I catch sight of a figure lurking. I glance up surreptitiously to see Corey watching the two of us with his arms crossed and a sneer on his face. I tighten my arms and turn all of my attention back to her.

"I like your perfume," I mutter into her ear.

"It's mine," she says with a small laugh. When she pulls away, she tucks a strand of her dark hair behind her ear. My fingers twitch at my sides, itching to be the one to tuck that hair behind her ear for her. Someday I will.

"Yours?"

"My brand."

"Hmm," I murmur and lean into her again. My hands settle on her waist and I bend my head, running my nose along the length of hers. Her breath hitches and desire crashes through me. "Well, it smells good."

"It does?" she breathes.

"Better than any other perfume," I say, and run my nose along hers again.

Her eyes lift to mine, eyelashes fluttering as she gazes into my eyes. The pull I feel toward her is unbearable, urging me closer to her. Her lips are a breath away. It would be nothing for me to close the distance, to taste her for the first time.

I search her eyes, looking for any indication she doesn't want that. But I find none.

I'm seconds away from taking the leap and crashing my lips to hers when the moment shatters.

In a split second, we're surrounded by journalists and paparazzi. Cameras flash in my face, blinding me with the nonstop light.

"What the f—" I mutter, my grip tightening around Jersey, ready to protect her from the onslaught of intruders. *How did the paparazzi even get entrance to the ballroom?*

"Jersey, is this your new beau?"

"Jersey, what would Corey think about you being caught in such a scandalous position?"

"Jersey, are you trying to make Corey jealous?"

"Go!" Jersey pushes at my shoulders and I snap into action. I wrap my arms around her and push through the paparazzi. She keeps her head down until I find us a quiet alcove, away from the craziness.

Jersey is distraught, her shoulders shaking and her skin clammy. She's muttering to herself, and I try my best to make sense of it all. "I should've known he'd do something stupid like this. That jealous asshole. I had to go and poke the bear, didn't I?"

When I spin her around to look at me, she won't meet my eyes. Again, I cup her cheek and tilt her face up to mine. "Jersey—"

Her expression falls. "Hayes, I'm so sorry."

She turns away from me then, but I catch her wrist. "Sorry for what?"

She shakes her head and tries to pull away from me again. "For all of it. I shouldn't have done that . . ."

"Done *what*?" I urge, pulling her to me again.

She looks horrified. "I almost kissed you . . . and—the paparazzi were there. It's going to be all over the news outlets tomorrow."

"Hey," I say again, raising my hand to cup her jaw. My thumb traces over her cheek and I stare down at her. "It's okay. I don't care about any of that."

"You say that *now*," she whispers, but I get the sense that she doesn't believe me. "I should go. My driver's waiting for me."

"Jersey," I protest, but she's already pulling away from me.

Before she runs out the door, she looks back at me, and her

eyes are glassy. "I had a really nice time with you tonight, Hayes. We'll talk later, okay?"

My shoulders deflate. I don't want her to go, but at least she's not completely running away from me. "Yeah, okay."

"Bye, Hayes."

"Goodnight, Jersey."

When she walks away, my heart seems to go with her.

SCROLLING THROUGH THE HEADLINES, it's one after the other of Jersey and me at the gala last weekend, but they're not flattering remarks.

The next big thing in the football world: Jersey Matthews spotted with her rebound, QB Hayes Vogt

Corey Shrader shocked by Jersey's scandalous outing: "She never used to be this way."

"She's only acting out," says source close to Jersey Matthews

And the worst:

Secret baby on the way? Milwaukee QB captured in a relationship he never wanted

And this from a reputable magazine! Jersey's horrified expression stares up at me from my phone screen. I'm standing right next to her, with my arm wrapped around her protectively, holding my hand in front of the cameras in a weak attempt to shield her from them. My expression is one of pure annoyance and frustration.

Like how I'm feeling right now.

"Bro, look at this one."

Jersey uses star QB to make Corey jealous: "Take me back or else"

Right below the main headline is an interview with her ex. I can't help but notice he's looking awfully smug in the freeze frame.

"Do you think she's using you like this one says?" Beckett asks and I'm not sure if I want to gut punch him for asking or for sounding like he's actually curious.

"I don't think so." I go for diplomacy. "She said they broke up. And you should've seen her. She was definitely annoyed when he showed up and tried to sit next to her."

"Click the video."

"No. I'm not going to *click the video*."

Beckett leans over and presses his finger to my phone screen, clicking another link before I can snatch my hand away from him. I scowl at my friend. I don't need to see this shit.

"You gotta know for sure. You've only been talking to her for a few weeks, not even a month yet. Can you confidently say you know she wouldn't be capable of doing something like this?"

I want to tell him to fuck off, but I don't. Beckett is just looking out for me, like he always does. Grumbling, I look down at the screen, pressing play on the video even though I already know I won't like hearing what he has to say.

"Yeah, I don't know what else to say other than she really let me down," Corey says on the video. "Tonight was supposed to be about us. Getting a chance to be out together, to mend bridges, and rekindle what we had before. I miss her. And I know she misses me, too. She doesn't have to hook up with athletes to try to make me jealous. I'd take her back in a heartbeat."

My irritation increases tenfold and I click out of the video before I can hear him spew any more of his bullshit. The media might be willing to fall for his story, but I'm not.

"Geez," I mutter and run my hand over my hair.

"You're sure you're okay with this?" Beckett asks from where he stands at my side. "This is about to be your life now."

I roll my lips together and glance down at the headline again. I can't lie. I don't love the thought of being the center of the media's attention all the time. Scrolling down the page, I find more photos of me and Jersey at the gala. The two of us are sitting side-by-side at our table. She's leaning one elbow on the table and has her chin propped up against her hand, looking at me as I tell her something. Another captures us perusing the auction items. I'm looking down at her with a look of pure adoration. My hand rests on the small of her back as her body leans into mine.

I felt so fortunate to get to spend that evening with her, even with the paparazzi crashing it at the end of the night, even with Corey Shrader running his big mouth.

"It's going to be different. Take some getting used to," I admit and Beckett nods. "But she's worth it. I know that for sure."

"*How* do you know that for sure?" I know he's looking out for me. Beckett is a skeptic when it comes to love. "How do you know she's not going to get in the way of your goals? *Our* goals?"

"I don't." I shrug. "But if that happens, then we'll deal with it."

"Come on, Hayes."

I slide my phone back in my pocket and walk toward the squat rack to do my final set. "If the other night was any indication, there's something strong between us. I'm not going to let that pass me by without taking a chance on it."

"She's so high profile. This could seriously affect your professional reputation."

"Well then, it affects my reputation," I say a bit too sharply.

"I'm just trying to protect you, man," Beckett defends as he comes over to spot me at the rack.

"I know." I grunt between reps. "And I appreciate it."

"I don't want you to jump in headfirst and risk being the one to get hurt in the end. Tell me you'll think about it. I know she's beautiful, but you've got a lot on the line, too. Like I said, you've barely known her for two seconds and already you're all over the internet in a negative light. You've never been involved in tabloids like this before. Your name means something. To the sport and to the team."

I grit my teeth and do two more reps before racking the bar and sitting up. I swipe my towel over my forehead and sigh. He might be right. Associating myself with Jersey Matthews and all the publicity—good and bad—she brings with her could be detrimental to my career. The career and the name I've worked so hard to build for myself.

Maybe he has a point. I do hardly know her. But I know Beckett, and I know he's only looking out for me.

Begrudgingly, I look up at my best friend and give him a nod. "Fine. I'll think about it."

jersey

MONDAY, SEPTEMBER 30

HAYES

How's it going today?

JERSEY

It's the Monday-est of Mondays. Cal almost had a stroke from yelling at me over the headlines from the gala. And on top of that, nothing I'm recording is to his liking, which means I've had to record the same thing over, and over, and over.

HAYES

That sounds exhausting.

JERSEY

It's not my favorite. I'm so glad to be home. I'm just hoping the final takes we took for today were good enough and I don't have to have a repeat tomorrow.

HAYES

Hoping that for you too. I'm positive it was better than "good enough." And what happened at the gala wasn't your fault. He shouldn't have yelled at you about that.

JERSEY

I'm really sorry about the whole situation.

HAYES

You have nothing to be sorry about. I have no idea how the paparazzi even got in.

I bite my lower lip, dread settling in my stomach.

JERSEY

I think I have an idea...

HAYES

Don't hold back on me now. Tell me.

JERSEY

Bethany was looking through all the photos and a few captured Corey lingering in the background. I wouldn't be surprised if he was the one who let them in.

HAYES

That sounds about right, honestly. I caught him giving me a death glare a few times.

JERSEY

Crazy that all it took was for me not to be interested to garner his attention.

HAYES

His loss. My gain.

I smile down at my phone, my heart singing a happy song to the tune of Hayes Vogt. If I close my eyes, I can still feel his touch lingering on my skin.

HAYES

> I haven't been able to get you off my mind.
> Would you want to meet up again
> sometime?

I don't know why all of a sudden, I'm so nervous. I enjoyed the time I got to spend with him at the gala, but now that he's proposing it—making a meetup purposeful rather than coincidental—I'm wary of putting myself out there so soon and putting him at risk of negative publicity again. I put on my brave face, shoving down any trepidation.

JERSEY

> Are you sure that's a good idea?

HAYES

> I don't see how it would be a bad one.

JERSEY

> Did you see the headlines?

HAYES

> I did. They were hard to miss. Still… my
> question stands.

I don't respond right away, unsure of what to say. Worrying at my lower lip with my teeth, I type out a few responses but delete them all. Thankfully, Hayes beats me to the punch.

HAYES

> I'm going to be in LA next Thursday for a
> game. Then I don't have to be back to
> practice until that following Wednesday. I
> want to spend the weekend with you.
> Paparazzi be damned.

A burst of eagerness and longing course through my body,

starting at the tips of my ears and working its way down to my toes, overshadowing my anxiety about seeing him again.

JERSEY

That's the best thing I've heard all day.

HAYES

Thought you might like that. 😊 I could even try to secure you a VIP ticket to come to the game.

His suggestion should make me excited. Getting the chance to see Hayes do what he does best in person has been something I've been looking forward to. But for some reason it has me pausing. Me showing up at a game shouts "we're in a relationship" loudly, and boldly, to the entire world. That's making a statement—especially being only six months post breakup with Corey. Until now, whatever's been brewing between me and Hayes has really only been mine. Am I ready to share that with the world? Am I ready for the onslaught of opinions from everyone?

JERSEY

Can I call you?

HAYES

Of course.

I count down from fifteen and then tap on his contact information. The phone starts ringing, and he picks up right away.

"Everything okay?"

"Do you want everybody to know we're in a relationship?" I ask him outright.

He pauses for only an extra second and then answers. *"Are we in a relationship?"*

The ball's back in my court. It's a valid question that maybe only I can answer. I pick at my thumbnail. "I think if we're not, I'd like to be."

He exhales a breath on the other end of the call and I can hear his relief when he says, "Me too."

"If I go to your game, everyone will speculate, so we need to be on the same page," I explain. "I don't want there to be any confusion from you or from me on where we stand. Especially after what happened at the gala."

Hayes hesitates again. "Have I confused you in any way? Given you some type of mixed signal? Cause if I have, it wasn't intentional."

"It's not that. It's just—"

"What?" he whispers, urging me to tell him what's on my mind.

I wrap my arms around my legs and close my eyes, breathing in through my nose and out through my mouth for two beats. Hayes must be able to hear the swift change in my demeanor because my phone suddenly chimes, indicating he wants to switch to FaceTime.

When I hit accept, I'm met with the familiar sight of his face, eyes crinkled up at the corners with concern. His gaze rakes over my face and his lips turn down. "Jersey, what's wrong? Talk to me. That's the only way we can move forward."

"You won't be scared off?"

He chuckles. "No, honey, I promise you there's no chance of that."

Taking a deep breath, Bethany's words echo in my ears and I decide it is time that I live a little, without any hesitation. On top of that, his assurance melts through my lingering doubts, so I launch into what's on my mind. "I haven't been seen out with anyone since my last relationship ended and I've *never* been involved in the headlines like this before. Kelsey's been blowing up my phone nonstop about releasing an official statement to the gossip, but then she keeps changing how she wants to approach it. It's just another thing to worry about that no one tells you when you sign up to be a celebrity."

He blinks twice, not expecting that to be the reason. Leaning back in his chair, he gives me his full attention. "Do you want to talk about it?"

I shrug weakly. "I don't know where to start."

"You were together a long time."

"Yeah," I say wistfully. "What a colossal waste of my time. Did you see that too when you looked me up? Or did you hear the gossip through the grapevine, like everyone else has?"

"I did see it, but I didn't read too much into their versions of what happened. I'm aware you dated Corey Shrader, that you broke up, and the media had a heyday with it. That's all I know. I stopped there. I wanted to hear your side of it whenever you were ready to share. Which I'm guessing is now?"

"I guess so." I glance away for a second and then back to his face on the screen.

He bites his lower lip. "What happened?"

I let out a humorless laugh. "That's the question I asked myself right after the breakup, too. I don't really know."

"He's the one who ended it?"

"He was. After I asked him to marry me," I say and watch him closely, gauging his reaction to that bomb. He visibly swallows, his Adam's apple bobbing with the action as his expression hardens.

"Oh yeah?"

"He said 'no,'" I say bluntly, giving another nonchalant shrug.

"Did he say why?"

"He said that if he was going to have a wife, she couldn't be as famous as I was. He's a singer too, so I think my rapidly growing levels of fame were getting to him. He's been in the industry much longer than me, but he's not even close to where I'm at in my career in half the amount of time."

Hayes scowls. "Self-conscious bastard."

"So that was that. A relationship can't sustain a blow like that, so I knew I had to move on. I should've known earlier. I tried to be everything he wanted, but even then, it was never enough. He only seemed to want me on good days, having no interest in being supportive when I was having a bad day.

"Yet at the same time, he always tried to beat me down or diminish my hard work to something like luck, or even giving all the credit to Callum. They were buddies," I add in. Hayes looks confused, so I go on. "The two of them are cut from the same cloth. Which was unfortunate because Cal's input directly set the tone for our relationship. To the point where I suspect the only reason Corey said no to my proposal was because Callum didn't give him the go-ahead. The more I reflect on it, the more I think Callum convinced Corey to date me for the PR."

"Jersey that's—"

"A wild accusation? I know."

"Were they friends before you started dating?" Hayes asks, two lines appearing between his brows as he frowns.

I nod. "Before we started dating, during the whole relationship, and even more so now that we're not together anymore. It's crazy, and I have no proof other than the overjoyed vibe Callum gave off when I told him we had broken up. I had artists texting me I didn't even know had my phone number. My sales skyrocketed because everyone felt bad for me. Instead of ganging up on me, the media was fully in my corner. It was like a dream come true from a PR perspective."

"It sounds more like a nightmare for you, though. I'm sorry you had to go through that," Hayes says. "I promise you, I'd never hurt you like that. Hell, if you asked me to marry you, I think I might say yes."

Despite the weight of the current topic, I laugh. Hayes's face splits into a triumphant grin, successfully breaking the tension. "Don't be ridiculous," I say.

Hayes smirks and shrugs. "All that to say, I'm still okay with going public."

"But what about the media? I'm nervous about what they're going to say about it. Or say about *you*."

"I don't care what they say about me in the slightest. And nothing they say about you could make me feel any different. I'm here for all of you—the good, the bad, and everything in between."

My shoulders relax, feeling lighter after talking this through with him. "I guess I better get myself one of your jerseys then, huh?"

He gives me a heart stopping smile that reaches all the way into his eyes and takes my breath away. "I guess you better."

I never saw Hayes coming, which is maybe part of why I find the idea of being with him so appealing. We're from two different worlds which seems to be a good balance. Knowing he's not with me to use me as a leg up in the world, but because he *wants* to be with me, is comforting and reassuring. That alone gives me the courage to go full throttle into this with him. I'm ready to step into his world and show everyone that he and I are in this together just like he said—the good, the bad, and everything in between.

"Thanks for letting me come over," Kelsey says as she brushes past me into my living room later that night. "We gotta finish drafting this post for Instagram and then we can talk about if you want to do anything further. I loved your idea of shifting the focus away from you and back to the charity, *brilliant!*"

"That's what the focus *should* be on," I say with conviction. "Definitely not on me and my potential dating life."

"I agree," Kelsey says, tucking her knees up underneath her on the other end of the couch and placing a pillow on her lap to act as a desktop for her laptop.

"Kelsey," I start hesitantly. She looks up at me from her screen. "There was something else I wanted to talk to you about. And it's important to me."

Kelsey studies my face for a moment before snapping her laptop closed. "What's wrong?"

"Corey was at the gala," I say. "And he was seated at the same table I was."

"Oh."

"That can't happen again. I want to limit interactions with him as much as possible, and I can't do that if I'm being seated right next to him." I exhale but hold her gaze. "If I'm going to attend any of your family's events in the future, I'm going to need your mother to send Bethany the seating chart for approval. It's nonnegotiable moving forward."

Kelsey nods and swallows. "Of course. I'm really sorry, Jersey. I had no idea she put you next to him or had even invited him again this year."

"It's okay. Just with the storm he managed to stir up in one night, I can't imagine what he'd do with other opportunities."

"Trust me, it won't happen again."

"I do trust you," I say and feel like a weight has lifted off my chest. I hate having to confront my team, especially when they're my friends, but this is a boundary that needed to be set in stone. If I'm going to move on with my life, I need to limit my interactions with Corey.

He's in the past. I'm focused on the future, and I'll do what I can to make sure everyone else around me is as well.

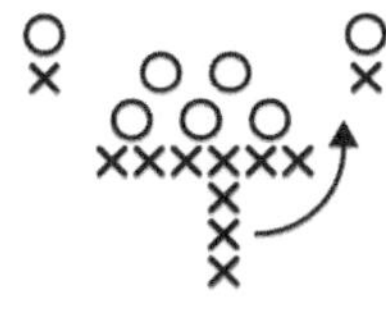

hayes

WEDNESDAY, OCTOBER 9

THE TEAM LANDS in LA Wednesday night before the game where we load up onto a bus to take us to the hotel. The collective energy is palpable, but under control. The whole team knows there's a lot on the line for this game. We have a rivalry with the Los Angeles Lightning going back a few seasons. All eyes will be on me and their QB, watching to see who will lead their team to victory.

My publicity team has made sure that I'm well prepared and equipped to answer any question about the rivalry tossed my way with respect and professionalism. But the QB for the other team is a wildcard. He's talked shit on the Majestics for the last few seasons, throwing slanderous accusations my way about possible cheating or bribing.

Which is enough to make him my least favorite quarterback to go up against.

Aside from the drama with the other team, this will be

Jersey's first game, and I've been a nervous wreck thinking about having her here in person watching me. With the assumed pressure of the game comes an even stronger need to show her what I'm made of. No matter the outcome today, I know Jersey will still be in my corner, cheering me on louder than anyone in this stadium, but I want to win.

For her.

For me.

For the team.

After getting out of the shower in my hotel room, I flip on the TV to a sports station and crawl into bed. Reaching for my phone, I relax against the headboard.

JERSEY

Have you made it?

HAYES

Yeah, we got in a few hours ago. Had a team meeting and then I came up to catch a shower and get some good rest before tomorrow.

JERSEY

So weird to think that we're in the same city again.

HAYES

Fucking finally. I can't wait to see you tomorrow.

JERSEY

Me either. Counting down the minutes. I get to see you sooner though down on that field. Lucky me!

HAYES

Hopefully the game will run in our favor.

JERSEY

Either way, I'll be happy to see you afterward. Looking forward to spending a few days with you too.

HAYES

I'm looking forward to that too.

JERSEY

I have to do a quick interview Monday and then possibly stop by the recording studio to do retakes, but I thought you could come along and we could get some takeout or something afterward, if that's okay.

HAYES

Better than okay. It's only fair that if you get to see me do my thing, I get to see you do yours, too. Maybe I'll be able to provide some background vocals on one of your songs.

JERSEY

I'll be disappointed now if you don't.

HAYES

What kind of boyfriend would I be if I disappointed my girl?

JERSEY

I'm not sure you'd even know how to do such a thing.

HAYES

I do everything in my power to stay oblivious on the matter.

JERSEY

I bet you do!

HAYES

You said Bethany and Roman are coming with you tomorrow?

JERSEY

Yes. Bethany, because she's my best friend, and Roman so he can help me understand what's going on down on the field. My sports ball knowledge is improving, but it will be helpful having him around for the finer details. I want to know everything that happens.

HAYES

I love that you're so invested in the game.

JERSEY

The game… you… tomay-to, tomah-to

I run my tongue along my lower lip, smiling at her little admission. I can't wait to see her and hold her in my arms.

HAYES

Just in case you didn't know… I really like you, Jersey.

JERSEY

I had my suspicions. I really like you too, Hayes Vogt.

HAYES

Fair warning. I'm going to kiss you tomorrow. (As long as you're cool with that.)

My head swirls with the idea of feeling her lips against mine for the first time. I wonder what she tastes like, if she makes little noises when lost in the depth of a kiss. I'm aching to know all these small, intimate details about her.

JERSEY

I'm more than cool with it. I was hoping you would.

HAYES

I don't know if I'd be able to not.

JERSEY

I like the sound of that. But I'll let you go and get some rest. Tomorrow's a big day, but I wanted to check in and make sure you made it.

HAYES

Means a lot. Can't wait to see you tomorrow. 😊

JERSEY

Me either, MVP.

Not seconds later, she sends a picture through of her puckering her lips together as if blowing me a kiss from where she is. Despite the exhaustion from travel and the knowledge that I'll be working my ass off tomorrow, my cock hardens at the sight of her full, pouty lips.

With a tortured groan, I put my phone on the bedside table and roll over in bed. Somehow, I manage to fall into a deep sleep, dreaming about brown-eyed pop stars giving me delicious, soul-stopping kisses all night.

THE CROWD GOES wild as the team takes the field, fully decked out in our uniforms and team gear to do our official warm-ups before the coin toss. Beckett and I and practice some passes while discussing some of the plays we've been working on.

On the other side of the field, Quentin works on some footwork with the rest of the offensive line and Xaden runs a few drills with the backup QB. While I'm with Beckett, I focus my head on the game, running drills and working with my coach for a few last-minute tips. I toss the ball back and forth with Beckett for a while, warming up my arm while he works on his footwork.

When the practice clock hits five minutes, my coach calls it good and lets me head off to the sidelines to stretch. Meanwhile, I scan the VIP boxes along the middle level of the stadium, trying my best to spot Jersey and her friends. When I catch sight of her, my heart stutters and kicks into overdrive. She swings around to face the field as if she can sense me watching her, our eyes meet, and she gives me a little wave.

The grin on my face should be an automatic red-flag ejection.

She's here, and she's wearing my jersey, just like she said she would.

There's something about knowing my name is plastered all over her that has my chest swelling with pride. I fear we're out of crush territory and into the realm of full-on infatuation.

"What are you staring at?" Beckett asks as he saunters up to me. He tilts his head up to where my eyes are still locked. "Holy shit. There she is."

"There she is," I confirm, feeling for once the euphoria of having someone show up for you.

Beckett claps me on the shoulder. "Congrats, man. You deserve it."

"What's going on?" Xaden asks, walking over to the two of us. Beckett points to the VIP box, and Xaden says, "Whoa." He gives Jersey a little wave.

"Hate to break up the little love fest that's going on now, but Coach wants us in the locker room. We can all say *hi* to Vogt's girlfriend later," Quentin teases.

The four of us walk together off the field toward the locker rooms. I make sure to glance up at Jersey once more before ducking into the tunnel, just in time to see her blowing me a kiss. I rub at my chest, unfamiliar with this longing ache.

Coach gathers us in the locker room and reviews some plays we've been perfecting this past week and any last-minute changes. He and I have already discussed these changes ad nauseam, so I allow my thoughts to jump to Jersey for another moment.

Jersey Matthews is wearing my name, my number, and my colors. That number eighteen never looked so good. A sense of possessiveness overtakes me and my heart races knowing she's here for me.

We're playing an away game at the home of one of the top teams in the league. Even with that in the back of my mind, I'm filled with a sense of extreme competitiveness that I can only attribute to my primal need to impress her.

As soon as Coach hands off the pretend mic to me before we leave the locker room, I level my team with a heavy stare and put my fist in the middle of the room. They waste no time, hurrying to meet me in the huddle.

I count the team down. "Three . . . two . . ."

"Dedicated to domination, we stand proud. Majestics Nation!" All together the team shouts our pregame ritual and then we break. My teammates hoot and cheer, clapping loudly as they fire themselves up for the oncoming battle.

Three of my closest friends from the team flank me as we line up in the tunnel to take the field—Beckett to my right,

Xaden to my left, and Quentin, the ultimate powerhouse, right behind me. I swivel from each of my friends and dip my chin. Beckett claps his hands, Quentin pats me on the shoulder, and Xaden gives me a fist bump.

"Let's bring home the win, boys. I gotta show off for my girl."

FIFTEEN

jersey

THURSDAY, OCTOBER 10

"THIS IS *INSANE*!" I shout, my eyes scanning over the field the players are running across following their first possession in the third quarter. After winning the coin flip at the beginning, the Majestics chose to have the ball first in the second half. Hayes has told me he prefers this scenario, giving him a chance to end the game strong. The Lightning quarterback and offense take the field to match up against the Majestics defense. My focus remains on number eighteen.

On the sidelines, Hayes pulls his helmet off and shakes out his sweaty blond hair and looks straight up to my VIP box and points at me, face breaking into a bright grin.

I wave my fingers back, unable to help the bubbly laugh that escapes me. He gives me one last lingering glance before he drops his helmet on the bench and accepts a tablet from his coach to check his upcoming plays before turning around to watch what's happening on the field.

"You all right there, sis?" Roman asks me with a hint of amusement.

"What?" When I turn away from the field, both he and Bethany are watching me with knowing looks. "Yeah, fine." I stumble over my words, my cheeks heating because they caught that quiet moment between me and Hayes. Though the connection between us is now broken, I'm left breathless, excitement brewing.

Bethany glances sideways at Roman and smirks. "Our girl is smitten."

Roman shakes his head, but the amusement doesn't leave his face. "Yeah, no kidding."

"No, I'm not." I make a feeble attempt at defending myself. "I'm just taking in the whole experience. Go football!" I wave my hands up in the air with the forced cheer and immediately feel foolish.

Roman throws his head back in laughter and I sit, forcing myself into time out for a few minutes while LA has the ball. Bethany sits next to me and nudges my shoulder with hers.

"We're giving you a hard time, you know," she whispers. "We are both over the moon to see you so happy."

I sigh. "Me too. It's stupid, but for the first time in a long time, I have something to look forward to."

"Is Hayes staying in town after the game?" Bethany asks before taking a sip of her drink.

I glance at her and nod before looking back at where Hayes is conferring with his coach on the sidelines. "He is, then flying home late Tuesday to pick up practices for their game next weekend.

"What are you guys going to do?"

I roll my lips together, ignoring the way my cheeks heat again. "I'm not sure."

My friend snickers next to me, seeing right through the ruse. "Sure. Is that the new code for hooking up?"

"No!" I say way too quickly. But all I can think about is what Hayes texted me last night. *I'm going to kiss you tomorrow.*

The addictive anticipation has been building ever since.

Bethany rolls her eyes but gratefully doesn't bother me anymore about that topic, leaning close to the edge of the box, to get a closer look at what's going on below.

I'm grateful these two agreed to come with me today. With Hayes playing in Los Angeles, I knew without a doubt I'd be here, but so far, it's shaking up to be much more enjoyable with friends. Surprisingly, Roman hasn't needed to feed me information on the small details related to the game, but it's nice to know he could since he's here. Though I have a baseline understanding of the sport, I know there's a ton of small rules that I have barely brushed the surface in comprehending.

The play has turned over again, and I lean forward, watching as Hayes slides his helmet onto his head and jogs out to the field. His team huddles around him and then they break before getting into position.

"And this is called the line of cribbage?" I ask my brother again, feeling mischievous.

He groans. "The line of *scrimmage.*"

Bethany snickers to herself while I gloat a bit. I can't help but give Roman a hard time. He *is* a Lightning fan, after all.

My attention returns to Hayes and I watch with interest as he hollers something out to the line before positioning himself close to the guy crouching in the middle and leaning forward to catch the ball. The line breaks as the other team struggles to get to him to take him down. My spine straightens and I lean forward to get a better view.

He's nothing short of astounding.

They run a few more plays, until they're right in front of the—

"Where are they on the field?" I ask Roman.

He glances at me quickly before looking out at the players again. "Second and goal. Ten yards from the end zone."

"And that is the area where they score baskets?" I ask, remembering the term from my earlier studies but having too much fun ribbing my brother.

"Yes." He rolls his eyes.

"And that will put them ahead by seven points?" I confirm.

Roman shakes his head. "Six. And then they'll kick for the extra point."

"Oh, right." I bob my head.

"Any more questions?" Roman asks me with an eyebrow raised. "Or can I watch again?"

I laugh and shove his shoulder. "Hey, I'm trying to learn here. You're my designated football guru while Hayes is on the field."

"Lucky me," he teases and rolls his eyes again before zoning back into the game.

Hayes calls his teammates to the huddle one last time before they break and line up once again.

The ball is snapped and Hayes looks left and right, frantically waiting for someone to become available to receive the ball.

What I would give to be inside of Hayes's head right now, to witness the decision-making and the spur-of-the-moment choices.

When no one has an opening, Hayes sees the opportunity and takes it, jumping around one of the defensive linemen charging for him and spinning in a circle. He takes three large steps and launches himself into the end zone.

I jump up out of my seat and raise my hands, cheering wildly for my man. Bethany wraps her arms around my waist and we jump up and down, celebrating Hayes together.

Vaguely, I'm aware the stadium has put me up on the big screen, sharing my celebration with the rest of the Majestics fans in the crowd. People cheer when they see me in the box, totally decked out in Hayes's gear.

The noise in the stadium hits an entirely new decibel.

On the field, Hayes lifts himself up off the ground, tosses the ball to a referee and then flexes his biceps, putting on a show of prowess. Then he points right at me.

I swoon.

There is no other word for it. My pulse echoes in my ears and my hands go clammy, a grin so wide it hurts my cheeks appearing on my face. The crowd cheers even louder, having seen the entire encounter up on the jumbo screen.

The smile doesn't leave my face for the rest of the game.

Hayes leads his team to the win, not letting Los Angeles get ahead at any point of the game. Though LA puts up a valiant effort, the Majestics clinch it with a 35-21 victory.

When the game ends, Roman slides down in his seat, crossing his arms over his chest. I give him a gloating grin. "Fine, whatever. Your boyfriend's good."

"I think good is an understatement."

I am exhilarated inside at the thought of Hayes officially holding the title of my boyfriend. I can't wait to see him to congratulate him on a game well played.

Roman wraps me up in a hug. "All right, little sis, I'm going to head out."

"Do you have a ride lined up?" Bethany asks my brother as she tosses the strap of her cross-body purse over her shoulder.

Roman releases me and nods. "I do. Need a ride?"

"Yes, if you don't mind. I rode with Jersey, but I think she's got plans." Bethany gives me a friendly squeeze on my upper arm. "You don't mind if I head out with Roman, do you?"

I shake my head. "No, go ahead. I'll just wait with my security until Hayes is ready."

Roman glances at his phone. "The car's ready whenever you are, Beth."

"Okay." She turns to give me a hug. "Let me know when you're home."

I hug her back. "Of course. Thank you so much for coming."

"We wouldn't have missed it," she says, beaming at me.

Roman walks over and hugs me, too. "Welcome to the football world, Jersey."

"Thanks for answering all my questions."

His chest rumbles against my cheek as he laughs. "You're welcome. I'm happy to be of service."

Roman and Bethany head out a few minutes later and I wave to them as they walk out of the suite. My security walks with me down through the stadium to wait for Hayes. It takes a while and I offer selfies and autographs to some of the people waiting in the hallways to pass the time. Finally, Hayes leaves the locker room and walks directly toward me, decked out in dark dress pants and a purple button-down shirt. While the Majestics colors are blue and white, Hayes looks regal in this royal purple color. His broad shoulders and confident stature leaves no room for doubt.

It hasn't been that long since Hayes and I have been in the same space, but since then, he has begun to mean so much more to me than I could have ever imagined. I can hardly stand to be apart from him any longer. The butterflies take off in my belly the closer he gets, and I find myself rushing toward him, aching to feel his touch on me again.

Cameras snap around us as soon as I launch myself into his arms, but this time, I don't care. He catches me, hoisting me up against his body and burying his face into my neck. I close my eyes, breathing in the fresh scent of his body wash. Though he smells fresh and clean now, I have a lingering curiosity about what it might be like to hug him immediately after a game, sweaty jersey and all.

I have no doubt Hayes will still be capable of sending my heart racing and my mind spinning, despite the sweat from the gruel of the game.

"You were amazing out there," I tell him, my voice soft so only he can hear it and not the surrounding journalists and paparazzi.

His arms tighten around me, and he makes a satisfied sound in his chest, which sends a shiver of pleasure down my spine. His voice hits that deep, delicious timbre as he says, "I think I might have been showing off a bit."

He drops me back down to the ground and raises his hands to frame my face.

"I'm about to follow through on that promise," he says lowly, just for me, amber eyes darkening with desire as they flicker from my eyes to my lips.

Tilting my chin up, he doesn't hesitate before he crashes his lips to mine. My whole body tingles with need at the first touch of his lips against mine and my fingers find the lapels of his jacket, pulling him into me as I kiss him back eagerly.

For the first time in ages, I feel like I'm exactly where I'm meant to be.

The snapping sounds of the cameras and sounds of surprise fade away and all I can think about is Hayes. *Hayes. Hayes.*

I'm sure I'll worry about the implications of the photos later, but now, all that matters is him.

He finally breaks away and hits me with those heated eyes. "All right, baby. Let's get out of here before we give them too much to talk about tomorrow."

Grabbing my hand, he leads us through the tunnel, our security behind us. I have a car waiting for me right outside of the stadium and we hurry into the back seat, ignoring the shouted questions and requests to stop and chat.

The minute we're safely inside the car, Hayes reaches for me again. I scoot close enough that I'm tucked against his side. His arm wraps around me possessively, making me feel cherished and cared for in a way I haven't felt in a long, long time.

The air in the back of that car grows heavy and intimate, the minimal space between us buzzing with tension. I'm breathless as I lose myself in his eyes, letting myself be overwhelmed by the way he's looking at me right now. It's the kind of look that makes a girl feel like she's the only one in the world.

He leans his head down until his forehead presses against mine and he takes a deep breath in and exhales. "I can't tell you how amazing it felt knowing you were here tonight. Thank you."

"I had so much fun," I tell him, my voice low. The car starts moving, driving us away from the stadium and back toward my condo. "I meant it. You were amazing out there. Color me impressed."

He tilts his head back so he can see me and his eyes grow tender. His thumb strokes my cheek, but he doesn't say anything right away.

Whatever thought process he's lost in finally breaks and his lips twitch up on one side. "I'm one lucky bastard to be sitting here with you."

"Maybe I'm the lucky one."

He leans down and kisses me again, softer and quicker this time. "Good, 'cause you're stuck with me now."

His words stir something inside of me I can't place a finger on. Instead of dwelling on it too long, I settle back against his hold, leaning into his chest and resting my head on his shoulder. He kisses the crown of my head and gets comfortable for the rest of the ride to my place.

It's the sight of Hayes lounging on my couch later that evening when it finally clicks. He opens his arms for me and gives me that heart dropping smile, inviting me to come lay with him and I know without a doubt what he's offering me.

Stability.

Hayes is stable and accountable. He has never given me any reason to doubt him. A stark contrast to my relationship with Corey, where I questioned everything—every little promise or compliment never felt genuine.

When Hayes wraps his arms possessively around my torso and drags me closer to his body, I can't help but reflect that *I am* the lucky one. I'm so lucky to have this man show me what it means to be cherished and cared for.

If this is what it means to be with Hayes, I won't accept anything different.

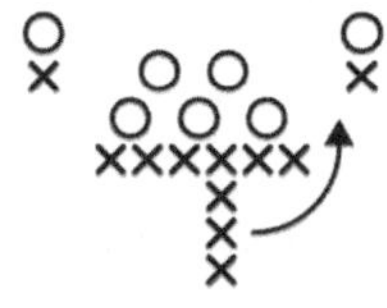

hayes

THURSDAY, OCTOBER 10

"WHAT ARE YOU THINKING ABOUT?" I ask Jersey, gently dragging my finger across her cheek and along the soft skin of her jaw.

Her cheeks are flushed a beautiful rosy color, her brown eyes warm and welcoming as she stares up at me. "Nothing," she says wistfully as her lips curl into a smile. "I'm happy you're here."

"I'm happy I'm here too," I say softly. She runs her hand over the planes of my chest. "I gotta say, I loved having you at the game tonight. I feel like it really pushed me to play my best."

"I don't think you needed me there to do that."

I shrug. "Maybe, maybe not. But it was kind of thrilling knowing you were there watching and cheering me on as I played down on the field."

"I make a pretty good Hayes Vogt cheerleader, if I do say so myself," she says, her voice light.

"And that number eighteen does look good on you," I say low in my throat as I peer down at my number over her chest. I hum to myself, tracing over the white vinyl with one finger. Looking back up at her, I study every feature of her face now that I have the chance to with her so close. Her skin is flawless, a few freckles dotting the bridge of her nose. She has a dimple on her left cheek that appears when she grins at me or laughs a true laugh. "You're so beautiful, Jersey."

She preens under my praise, her eyes widening and her breath hitching. Cupping her cheek, I tilt her jaw up until her rosy lips brush against mine. Our breaths mingle and I can taste the white wine she's been sipping on this evening.

"Hayes—" she whispers against my lips.

"Yeah," I murmur.

My heartbeat hammers in my ears, a touch quicker than normal. Her eyelashes flutter closed, and she sucks in a sharp breath, tilting her lips closer to me, brushing against mine once more.

She opens her eyes again, staring directly into my soul. Her tongue darts out to wet her lips and I groan low in my throat as my eyes track her movement.

"Kiss me," she whispers.

I don't need to be told twice.

My fingers slide from the angle of her jaw above her ear and into her hair. Gently gripping the strands of her thick hair, I pull her toward me, capturing her lips with mine.

The kiss earlier at the stadium was incredible, but this kiss is *life changing*.

I take my time now, getting the chance to be entirely consumed by Jersey Matthews, tasting her, learning her, indulging in her.

My hands circle her waist and I draw her down on the couch until she's laying on her side, facing me where my back is pressed against the cushions. She goes for my mouth again, claiming my lips in a way that sends desire shooting down my spine. My fingers inch up the hem of her shirt where I find the delicate small of her back and the two little indentations there. I trace little circles until I feel goosebumps rise on her smooth skin.

She arches her spine where I'm caressing her and my hand moves from the small of her back up to her rib cage. The pad of my thumb brushes against the edge of her bra and she lets out a little gasp. I pull away from her mouth only to kiss her on the jaw, at the juncture of her neck and her shoulder.

She arches again, wiggling until my hand moves from her side to cup the front of her breast. With a satisfied sigh, she kisses me again, deeply, passionately. My hand squeezes her breast over the thin satin of her bra and she moans into my mouth. Her nipple hardens under my hand through the fabric. Carefully, I swirl my thumb over the hard peak and she makes another delicious little noise against my lips.

I'm dying to discover every minute detail about her. I want to know what she's like first thing in the morning, if she rolls out of bed ready to take on the day or if she lounges lazily, easing into the day. I want to know if she's routine-oriented, or if she does whatever feels right in the moment, switching it up on a whim. More intimately, I want to know what positions are her favorite, how she feels when she's standing right on the precipice of an orgasm. I ache to know what she sounds like when she's seconds away from coming. Or what she looks like as she detonates from the pleasure coursing through her body.

Cupping her breast again in my hand, I resolve that we have all the time in the world to learn and explore every little detail in every capacity. I don't want to rush into sex with her—heaven forbid she thinks that's all I'm interested in with her. I'd rather take my time, ease into whatever this is, let the burn simmer for a while before jumping in. If there's anything I know for certain, it's that I want her heart, I want her mind, and I want her love. We will inevitably blaze like an inferno together, and I want her so badly, but I want her to be comfortable with me. I want to be her place of comfort, her safety net, her biggest fan, as much as I want to be the one to bring her pleasure. There's so much more that I want to explore with her than our brewing physical attraction. This is only the beginning.

Pulling away from her, I peck one more kiss to her swollen lips and then the tip of her nose. She pouts a bit until she can't fight her amusement any longer.

"Why'd you stop?" she teases.

I run my hand over her hair, curling one stray tendril around my pointer finger. "Let's slow things down, baby. We've both had a long day, and you've got another busy day tomorrow. I'm exhausted, and there's nothing that would make me happier than holding you while we fall asleep."

Her eyes grow glassy. "Well, how can I say no to that?"

I kiss the tip of her nose again. "Should we go to bed?"

"To sleep," she confirms, and I don't miss the hint of relief cascading through her mannerisms. It's barely there, but enough to reassure me I made the right decision to call the activities for the night.

"Just to sleep," I agree and then wink at her. "For now."

The brilliant look of adoration she gives me then is an affirmation that I've been waiting for her my whole damn life.

FRIDAY, OCTOBER 11

"Look," Jersey says, holding her phone up for me.

Glancing away from her TV where they're recapping the

game from last night, I take it into my hands and blink a few times. On her screen are the paparazzi photos from last night with the headline:

Love is in the air: Hayes Vogt and Jersey Matthews only have eyes for each other after Lightning game.

"At least they got my good side," I tease, scrolling through the pictures. My chest expands with pride when I get to the one of our first kiss. One of my arms is wrapped around her smaller frame possessively, my other hand holding her chin as my lips are pressed to hers.

The chemistry between us is palpable, even through the photos. Moreso than the ones taken of us at the gala.

I want to get it framed, along with the one of her launching herself into my arms.

"I should've known they'd have those up for the world as soon as possible," Jersey says. There's a hint of something to her tone, and I look at her curiously.

"Are you okay with this?" I ask her. A hint of uncertainty niggles at the back of my mind. I know we talked about this already before she came to the game at all, but I wouldn't blame her if she's a little unsure, seeing the photos in real life.

She meets my eyes and her face splits into a grin. "I am. Are you?"

I slide across the couch, closing the distance between us and kissing her. "More than okay. I want the whole world to know I'm yours and you're mine."

She pulls away and runs her fingers along my jaw. "Andi will probably ask me about the photos in the interview on Monday. What should I say?"

"What do you mean?" I question.

Doubt flickers across her face and she backs away. "It's dumb, forget it."

"Jersey," I press her.

She exhales. "I am your girlfriend, right?"

I swallow, nervous about why she sounds so unsure about her question. I know we discussed the implications of being seen together in public, I thought that the exclusivity was implied. "I'm all in, if you are, Jersey."

"I'm in, too," she says, her features relaxing into a smile. Relief crashes through me.

"Well then . . ." I push myself off her couch.

"What are you doing?" she asks, giggling as I walk across the living room to her balcony.

Sliding the door open, I step outside and walk over to the rail. The city bustles along below me, no one ever the wiser that I'm standing up here. I extend my arms out wide and yell, "Jersey Matthews is my girlfriend!"

"Hayes!" Jersey shouts and then laughs loudly. Her hands press down on my arms and she pulls me around to face her. Her expression is lit up with amusement. "Why did you do that?"

I grin down at her, wrapping my arms around her waist. "We've got nothing to hide, baby. Let the whole world know."

jersey

MONDAY, OCTOBER 14

"So, I've heard some rumors," Andi, host of *Post It and Weep* podcast says. I'm sitting across from her during our exclusive live stream interview, pretty sure where she's taking this. Bethany gave her a list of questions we approved since this is a live event and won't be edited before the public hears it, but I get the feeling she's about to go off script.

Giving a nervous chuckle, I say, "I should've known when I agreed to come on your show you'd want to dish about more than just my upcoming tour."

"You do know me well." She leans toward me, eyeing me across the table like the cat who got the cream. "You'll have to tell us once and for all if they're true."

"That's a lot of pressure," I say, hoping my voice isn't shaking. In my lap, I knot my fingers together and pick at the cuticle on my thumb.

"There's been some rumors and paparazzi photos circling

around of you and a certain quarterback," she teases. My nerves dissipate at the mention of Hayes. "Are you *dating* Hayes Vogt?"

The mental image of Hayes standing on my balcony Friday morning fills my mind, and I fight off a smile. He will be overjoyed with me publicly claiming him on such a broad scale. Which is why I have zero hesitance right now. "Yes, Hayes and I are official. And we've been having the best time."

"Aren't you worried about how this will affect both of your careers?" she asks, without any malicious undertone, simply curiosity. "I know you both have a lot on your plates right now professionally."

I shrug a shoulder. "We do. But we're stronger together. And even in those hard days, we're learning to lean on each other."

"I love that. Do you find it's easy to confide in him, given that he's not 'from your world?'" she asks, using finger quotes. "Or do you find yourself sugarcoating what it's like to be one of the most famous pop stars in the world?"

"Hayes is one of the easiest people to talk to," I acknowledge. "I never have to be anything but myself with him because I know he's there for all of it—the good, the bad, and everything in between. I can't imagine being with a man with a kinder, more genuine heart of gold."

Even as I say it, I know those words to be some of the truest I've ever expressed. Though Hayes originally started the sentiment, it's become something I've held close to my heart since. With each minute and hour that passes, they weave themselves further into my very being, and the more I believe them.

"We're so happy for you here on the show," Andi says, congratulating me. "And you know your fans are eating up every second of this. We live for the outings and the photos. You've got an entire fan base cheering you and Hayes on, both personally and professionally."

"Thank you," I acknowledge. "That means a lot to me, and I know it means a lot to Hayes, too."

Andi levels me with a mischievous smile and I brace myself for her next question. She doesn't disappoint.

"So . . . can we expect to see Hayes in your next music video?"

WHEN I WALK into the studio following my interview, I expect to find a put off Cal, frustrated with my public announcement of my relationship without any prior approval from him.

What I don't expect is to walk into his office to see Corey Shrader sitting in one of the chairs right in front of his desk. He has one ankle crossed over his knee and his hands folded right in his lap—the picture of ease.

I stop dead in my tracks the minute I walk through the door, and immediately the hair on the back of my neck stands straight up, aware that I've walked right into an ambush. Every cell in my body screams at me to turn around and hightail it out of that office, back down to the lobby where Hayes is waiting for me.

I don't get the chance.

"Hey, babe." Corey stands and walks toward me with his arms wide.

I jolt into action, stepping back as he reaches for me to avoid any possible contact with him. The idea of him touching me sends a slither of disgust down my spine. "What are you doing here?"

His arms drop to his side and he slides his hands into his pocket, unfazed by my visceral flinch away from him. "Cal and

I were grabbing lunch to discuss business, and he mentioned you were coming in today. Thought I'd stick around to say hello." Cal is watching this whole interaction from behind his desk.

My spine straightens and I tilt my nose up, eyeing the two of them with suspicion. "That was entirely unnecessary. What kind of business were you discussing?"

Cal opens his mouth to contribute to the conversation when his cellphone starts ringing. He holds it up as evidence. "I gotta take this. You two take your time, work through *whatever* this is, and play nice."

"How convenient," I mutter to myself as Callum steps out of the office, leaving me and Corey alone. "I'm surprised Cal even wants to talk to you after that stunt you pulled at the Hurst Gala. I cannot believe you."

"Me?" he asks incredulously, and I note he doesn't deny the accusation. I must've been spot on with my suspicions that he was behind the paparazzi scheme. "What about *you*? You're riding the coattails of one of your biggest albums yet, but you're out in public at charity events hanging all over your newest boy toy and going on a livestream gushing about him like he's the most important thing you've got going for you."

"I was not *gushing*," I sneer. "She asked me about Hayes, and I answered honestly. And Hayes is important to me. There's nothing wrong with making that fact known. You know what? I'm not doing this with you today—or ever. I'll see myself out."

I turn on my heel and barge through the office doors, striding directly over to the elevators and pressing the button. While I wait for the elevator, I pull out my phone and type out a quick text to Bethany to email Cal to have him call me. I don't know what game he's playing with Corey, or with me for that matter, but I'm not amused. Nor am I surprised when Corey sidles up next to me a few moments later, fully intent on continuing our conversation.

"Come on, babe. Don't let this football guy cloud your judgment. Maybe we should revisit *us* again. Who better to have at your side than someone who's going through the same thing?" Corey pleads. "You know he doesn't understand a single thing about our industry."

"Hayes understands me better than you could possibly imagine. You were never able to understand my struggles because you never had to deal with that before! Your label has a completely different dynamic than mine," I argue back, getting onto the elevator when the doors open.

He narrows his eyes, but follows me into the elevator. "Hey, it's not my fault that I'm not looking to start friction with upper management like you are. I keep to myself and get the job done. When they ask me to go on a podcast to talk about my music, that's what I do. You don't see me bringing the girls I'm seeing into the conversation."

Crossing my arms, I glare at him. "See, you're doing it again. Always dismissing my feelings and writing me off as being the problem. So no, I absolutely will not be revisiting *us* or *you* or anything to do with you ever again."

"Listen, you have a bad habit of reading more into situations than what's there. You know Cal is only trying to help you achieve the most out of your career. Can you blame him for being frustrated when you veer off course at every possible chance?" Corey tries to reason with me.

"No, Callum is always and *only* ever looking out for himself. He doesn't care about my career as much as he cares about how I boost him up." I close my eyes and breath. "You'd know that if you had paid me one ounce of the attention that you always gave to him."

The elevator dings before Corey can say anything else. I'm quick to step off the car, walking directly over to Hayes, who has stood up from his seat at the sight of me. I tuck myself safely against his side, feeling the immediate comfort of his warmth surround me. He wraps his arm around my back, resting his hand possessively on the front of my hip. His commanding presence gives me a chance to breathe, knowing he could likely knock Corey on his ass with minimal effort. All I'd have to do is say the word.

"Everything okay?" Hayes asks me, narrowing his eyes at Corey, who is still not catching the hint.

"As okay as it can get. Are you ready to go?"

"Absolutely," he says and tucks his phone into his back pocket.

I turn to Corey, who's scowling at me and Hayes, eyes zeroing in on Hayes's intimate hand placement. "In the future, please don't invite yourself to my business meetings," I say, my voice hard. "I don't care if you and Cal are friends. Getting involved in *my* career is unprofessional. You have no right to put your nose into anything regarding me or my work. We are not together anymore, Corey, and we're never going to be again."

Thankfully, Hayes can tell I need a few minutes before talking about what went down at the studio. Once home, I head back to my bedroom and do a few of my grounding exercises. I sit on my floor cross-legged, and close my eyes, breathing in through my nose and out through my mouth as I count down from fifty for three repetitions.

When I feel more centered, I join him back in the living

room, right as the food delivery arrives. We plate the Thai food and settle into our seats at the table. Then, Hayes breaks the ice.

"What happened back there?"

I exhale loudly and poke a noodle around on my plate. "Your guess is as good as mine. I *thought* I was going to be doing retakes at the studio, which is why I went up to check with Callum in the first place."

"What the hell was Corey doing there?"

"I wish I knew," I grumble. "As soon as I walked into his office, Corey was there and then Cal conveniently had to 'take a call.'"

"You think he set you up?"

"I don't know." I shake my head. "Possibly. I wouldn't put it past him. I told you he and Corey were buddies. Corey said they had business to discuss over lunch, but I'm guessing Cal must've also had the livestream on, or had someone else watching the livestream for him, and got a little heated at the fact that I outright announced we were in a relationship, so he felt the need to bring Corey into the mess again."

"That's really shitty of him."

I press my lips into a thin line and nod. "Yeah. Nothing terribly out of character for him, though. He can't stand not being the one in control."

"That's awful," Hayes says, his voice low. "I think you need a new manager."

"I wish it were that easy. When I signed on, I was assigned to Cal, and both times my deal was up for extension, the higher-ups refused to rework my contract to assign me to someone else, even though I asked multiple times. I've resigned myself to the fact that I'm stuck with Cal until this extension ends and I can leave the label," I grumble. Hayes frowns and runs his tongue over his lower lip. "I've had about enough of this, though."

"I think you need a vacation," he says gently. "Get some distance from LA and your label."

I nod in agreement, but having no clue where to even start. Then an idea hits me. "Wait . . . what if I come to your place?" I ask.

Whatever Hayes was thinking morphs into surprise. He sets his fork down and then wipes his mouth with the napkin. "You want to come to Milwaukee?"

"I mean . . . only if that's okay," I say, backtracking a bit. "I know you'll be busy with practice, but we could hang out in the evenings and I could have a chance to decompress."

"Nothing would make me happier," he says, his face splitting into a smile. "Do you really think you'll be able to get them to approve it?"

I pull out my phone, opening a text thread with Bethany and typing out a message. "I'll have Bethany work her magic. I've never asked for time off before, so hopefully that will play in my favor."

"Well, count me in. The idea of you in Milwaukee is the best thing I've heard all day."

I grin. If Cal thinks he can pull a fast one on me by bringing Corey back into my life, I'll spring a fast one on him right back and skip town. It's time I stop letting him disrespect me and my feelings.

My phone chimes and I glance down.

BETHANY

Consider it done. Have a nice time 😉

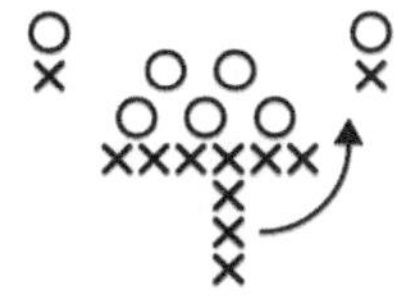

EIGHTEEN

hayes

MONDAY, NOVEMBER 11

RETURNING HOME to Milwaukee after spending a few days with Jersey takes more willpower than I want to admit. When I left Tuesday evening, Jersey still hasn't heard for sure if she'll be able to make it out to Milwaukee the following week or not. I do my best to return to my regular routine once I'm home, though I miss her terribly. I let the focus of the game help drown out the ache that leaving her left deep inside me, giving my all at workouts and team practices leading up to our next game.

Bethany could not, in fact, get it done. Cal pulled out all the stops and made Jersey's life difficult after I left. But she worked her magic—by promising the moon, no doubt—and she's here now. Finally.

As soon as I see her step out of the car, I can't fight off the grin that takes over my face.

There she is.

Fuck, I've missed her.

Jersey peruses her surroundings, scanning my house and

front yard, taking it all in until she finally lands on me. She pauses only a second, then smiles broadly at me as she hurries over to me, launching herself into my arms when she's close enough.

I bury my face in her neck, catching the scent of her shampoo and breathing her in deeply. "I can't believe you're here."

"It truly is a miracle," Jersey agrees, her arms tightening around my neck. Over the last few weeks, Cal had been yanking her back and forth with scheduling. She wasn't certain until a few days ago, and I've been counting down the minutes since.

"Did anything change with Cal's conditions since we last talked?" I ask her, letting her down so I can see her. Her breath comes out in a frustrated puff, swirling between us.

"I had to make a compromise with him. He's big on compromises that work in his favor. I'll have to do a few double sessions, and then he gets to put a few more songs on the album that I had originally vetoed." When I frown at her having to make a concession like that, she adds, "It was worth it. I couldn't stand to be in LA for another day."

Her cheeks are flushed the prettiest pink, making the freckles on her nose stand out more. Her eyes twinkle as she stares up at me. She's average height, but I'm still a good half foot taller than her. I tilt my head down, staring into her eyes and studying every inch of her face for when she's halfway across the country again and all I have is the memory of her here with me.

I trace my hand over her cheek and cup the curve of her neck, my thumb toying with her gold hoop earrings. "I'm sure glad to see you. I hardly slept last night."

"Me either. I was way too excited to see you again and see your place." She shivers as she glances around my broad frame to my house. Her nose is now tipped with a hint of rosy red from the chilly northern air.

"I'm glad you came in today before the snow starts tomorrow," I say, bending down to kiss the tip of her nose.

When I pull away, she's radiating happiness, an excited twinkle gleaming in her brown eyes. "It's going to snow?"

"Tonight into tomorrow. November is normally a little early for heavy snow, but I suppose Wisconsin wanted to pull out all the stops for you while you're here." Reaching for her suitcase, I say, "Let's get you inside."

She wraps her arms around herself, and rubs up and down, warming her skin. "Thanks, I'm not used to this cold weather."

"Me either." I shoot her a wink when she laughs. I love the sound of her laugh.

I open the front door, letting her walk in before following after her with her luggage. She steps into the foyer, taking it all in. "Wow, Hayes. Your home is beautiful."

"Thank you. Here, let me show you around."

Jersey bounds after me as I lead her through the house. We tour the living room and the kitchen, stopping for a moment so Jersey can express her love of the size of the counter space and my stainless-steel appliances. I shake my head in amusement, knowing she has an equally luxurious kitchen at her home, but I let her do her thing, accepting the praise.

We head upstairs to the bedrooms where I show her the guest room and then point down the hall to the closed door.

"This is the guest room, and my room is down the hall," I tell her.

Jersey glances at my bedroom door and then at the guest room, her expression growing thoughtful. She catches herself before I can ask her what's going through her mind and she plasters on a bright smile, taking her suitcase from me and rolling it down the hallway before opening my bedroom door. I follow after her, rolling my lips together to fight off the grin.

Of course, I hoped she'd want to sleep with me in my room, but I didn't want to be presumptuous. I stayed with her in her room while I was in LA, but with this being her first time here, I left the decision up to her. I wouldn't have been offended if she wanted her own space, but watching her waltz right into my bedroom like she's meant to be there means more than I could ever put into words.

She spins in a circle as she looks the room over, then she nods in approval. "This is acceptable."

I fight off a grin and lean against the door frame, crossing my arms over my chest. "I'm glad you think so."

"You have the whole week off?" I confirm, hoping nothing's changed since I last talked to her last night.

"Yup. I'm all yours for the whole week," she says with a wink that sends a tingle of desire through me. I'm seconds away from pulling her into my arms and showing her how comfortable my bed is. "Do you have anywhere I can unpack my clothes?"

I nod and walk to the dresser, pulling open an empty drawer which I haven't claimed yet.

She wheels her suitcase over to the bench by the foot of the bed and hoists it up. I watch her for a moment, letting the fact that she's really *here* settle around me. Jersey seems unfazed that I'm lingering, rather going about her business of unpacking while letting me watch her. She removes her clothes, stuffing them in the drawer, and then grabs a bag, which I assume are her toiletries, and takes it into my en suite bathroom, disappearing from my line of sight.

While she's shuffling around in the bathroom, I turn my attention to the floor, taking a moment to check in with myself. There's something comforting about having Jersey here in my home, in my space. Like she was always meant to be here.

And that thought alone is enough to send my head reeling. I excuse myself downstairs to the living room while she finishes up.

Not too long later, Jersey bounds down the stairs and joins me on the couch, folding her legs under her and tilting her head as she looks at me with doe eyes. I notice she's freshened up her makeup and straightened her hair. She's still wearing the same clothes, cozy in her cream long sleeve sweater and black leggings. Which is fine by me. I have a feeling she'd be sexy as fuck in anything.

"So, what's on the agenda today?"

"Whatever you want, I don't have a whole lot planned. I figured you'd want to get settled and relax after traveling."

She waves her hand through the air. "Oh, traveling is nothing. You know how it is. I'm on a plane so often jetting across the country, or the world, it's just another thing. And LA to Wisconsin isn't too far. I'm ready for anything."

"Well, all right then." I grin, racking my brain to come up with something for us to do this evening. "Are you hungry?"

"Ravenous," she says, placing one of her small hands on her belly.

I waggle my eyebrows and take her hand, leading her into the kitchen. "I've got a surprise for you."

"A surprise?" she asks enthusiastically.

Inside the pantry, I pull out the package of Oreos and family sized jar of peanut butter, placing them on the counter in front of her. Jersey's face takes on an expression of awe and she wastes no time pulling open the cookies and unscrewing the cap off the peanut butter.

"Oh, how do you know me so well?" she gushes, reaching for a cookie and dipping it into the jar of peanut butter.

I follow her lead and give her a wink. "I pay attention."

Jersey makes a satisfying moan, which makes my breath hitch. I glance at her, only to see her eyes closed in delight as she eats her favorite snack. "This is the best thing in the whole wide world."

"It is pretty dang good," I agree, wiping my hands off on the kitchen towel and then wrapping them around her. I bend down to press a kiss to her cheek and then settle back into my place at the counter.

"This is exactly the pick-me-up I needed after traveling today." She nods and peruses the spread. "Good call, MVP."

I chuckle and slide my hands into my pockets, perfectly content to watch her be so happy and carefree here in my kitchen.

My ears sharpen when I hear Jersey humming as she eats her snack. It's not a melody I'm familiar with and I wonder if it's a new song she's working on.

I hate that anyone would be inclined to take advantage of her.

A sense of protectiveness floods over me and before I can stop myself, I'm stepping up to her, placing myself at her back and settling my hand over her hip protectively. I don't know what's come over me, but she doesn't seem to mind.

I clock the exact moment she leans back into my touch, resting against my chest as if it's the most comfortable place in the world. Bending my head down so our cheeks are level, I ask, "What are you humming?"

Her breath hitches, and again she seems to lean into my touch, tilting her head so hers is resting against mine. "Just some melody that's been stuck in my head. There are no words to it yet."

"Yet?"

She nods. "Sometimes the melody hits me before the words. I'll probably figure out the main chorus and the verses before I start in on the lyrics for this one."

"You've never told me much about your own songs."

She sets down the cookies, dusting the crumbs from her fingers on a kitchen towel. "There's not much to tell. The songs I record and put out with the albums are exclusively written by other artists. Callum picks them out, decides they'll match the brand he's trying to create for me, and then I record them."

"What about the ones you write?"

"They never see the light of day," she says sadly. "I still write them because it's therapeutic for me. I have an old notebook I carry around with me full of songs. But I never get to record the ones I write. It's not part of the deal with my label."

"How do you write them?" I ask, leaning toward her as the curiosity builds inside of me.

"Depends on the song." She shrugs and reaches for another Oreo before settling back against me again. "Most of the time it starts with a melody, but other times certain lyrics hit me and then I can't rest until the rest of the lyrics come together."

"Sounds like putting a puzzle together."

She grins and nods. "Exactly like that. In those cases, the melody comes later, once the story is complete with the words."

"You're a diamond in the rough," I murmur, pressing a kiss to her neck. She tilts her head to the side, giving me more access to the delicate curve of her neck.

"I don't know about that." She sounds breathless, which makes me smile against her skin and press another kiss to the divot behind her ear. These sensitive areas of her body are quickly becoming my favorite places to pay extra attention.

"You are. I hate that they are exploiting you for it, not letting you shine to your fullest potential."

"I hate it too," she whispers. Her hand traces up my arm around her middle as she resumes her humming. I rest my chin against her shoulder and close my eyes as I listen to the melodious sound of her voice. I could listen to her sing, or hum, or *anything*, all day long if she'd let me.

Periwinkle trots into the kitchen to investigate what's happening.

"Oh my gosh, is this Peri?"

I step away from her, instantly missing the warmth of her against me. She bends down once Peri comes up to greet her and scratches her behind the ears, running one finger over the hem of her purple sweater. "She's so cute. Look at her little sweater!"

"She's something," I say with a grin, crossing my arms over my chest and leaning my hip against the counter.

"How long have you had her?" Jersey peeks up at me.

"About eight years. She was a puppy when I found her at an adoption day at the pet store."

"Have you always been a small dog person?"

"Not necessarily. But she stole my heart right away. She was all alone in her little cage, shivering relentlessly." I crouch down next to Jersey so I can pet Peri too. "The minute I saw this little smooshed face and holier-than-thou glint in her eyes, I knew she had to be mine."

"That's actually so sweet," she says softly.

"We've been a team ever since." Peri's expression tells me she whole-heartedly agrees with the sentiment, then looks back to Jersey, who's still giving her all the attention.

A warm affection overcomes me as I study this beautiful

woman currently loving on my dog and conclude that I'm in such deep shit when it comes to her. I can't even find it in myself to be concerned about it.

"So, what do you want to do tonight?" I ask her, at a loss for any grand ideas myself. "Do you want me to make a dinner reservation somewhere? Or we can go drive around the city?"

She shrugs and peeks up at me from the floor. "Could we stay in tonight? We can do all that another time. There's no rush."

"Of course." I nod, perfectly happy to get the chance to have her all to myself.

"Maybe we can watch a movie? Order some food in?"

"Truly a much better idea." I open my food delivery app and hand my phone to her. "Here, order whatever you want. I'll feed Peri, then we can figure out what to watch."

Not long later, we have a table full of takeout in front of us and a classic action movie on the TV.

Jersey snuggles right into my side as soon as she's finished with her dinner, making herself at home. Peri stands on her hind legs and places her paws on the cushions. I scoop her up, letting her onto the couch with us before looking back to the TV.

The images move across the screen, but I can't be bothered to follow along. As the minutes tick by, she gets more and more comfortable, resting her head against my shoulder first and then scooting in until she's draped across my chest. I've never been more content than I am with her pressed against me like this. It feels like she was always meant to be here with me.

I don't know when it happens, but the combination of a full travel day and a hearty dinner does her in. Before the movie's halfway through, she's fallen asleep against my chest. Her soft, comfortable snores fill a chasm of my heart that I never knew was empty.

Letting myself bask in the few quiet moments I have with this beautiful girl, I don't disturb her. My hands smooth over her hair, weaving in and out of the silky strands.

Time flies too quickly, and the movie we're watching ends. The screen returns to the home page of the streaming service and I decide it's time to call it a night. Gently, I shake Jersey's elbow, enough to jostle her from her slumber.

"Hayes?" she murmurs against my chest.

"Hmm," I rumble back, still stroking my hand up and down her arm.

"Will you take me to bed?" Her voice is quiet as she asks her question. "I'm sleepy."

My chest aches, and I wrap my arm around her, leaning my head down to kiss the crown of her head. "Yeah, baby. Let's get you to bed."

She makes a soft, snoozy sound in thanks and settles back against me. Not long later, I scoop her into my arms, carrying her up the stairs. I pull back the covers on the side of the bed that's always empty, and I set her down on the edge of the bed. She wastes no time curling up against the pillows and looking at me through thick, dark lashes.

"I should change into my pajamas," she says, eyes darting to the drawer where she unpacked her clothes. "I don't want to sleep in these since I traveled today, but I don't want to get up."

Pausing for a moment, I cross the bed's perimeter, pulling my shirt off, leaving me in only my sweatpants, and hand it to her. She takes it readily, sitting up in the bed and reaching for the hem of her shirt. I avert my gaze, giving her some privacy.

When I hear her own clothes hit the floor, I figure it's safe and look up again. She's nestled in the bedding again, looking up at me with sleepy brown eyes. I was right earlier when I assumed she'd be sexy as fuck in anything—but even I wasn't prepared for the sight of her in my clothes. That does something to a man. Unable to stay away from her any longer, I flip off the lights and crawl under the covers beside her, reaching for her and drawing her close to my body, leaving only a little space between us. Jersey flips around, so she's facing me.

I tenderly stroke the smooth skin of her face with my thumb. "I'm glad you're here," I whisper into the darkness.

"Me too," she whispers back. Her small hand wraps around my wrist. It's such a simple action, but still so intimate. Jersey's eyes study my face, and then she scoots closer to me on the bed until she's flush against me and hikes one leg over my hip.

We're a breath away, but that doesn't faze her. She tilts her chin up, and her lips brush against mine, like a feather.

I can't help the satisfied sigh that leaves my lips, and it seems to spur her on because next, she's pressing her body languidly against mine and locking our lips together.

I respond fervently, dropping my hand from her cheek down to her waist so I can clutch her to me. She arches her pelvis against mine, rubbing her warm center against the length of my steadily hardening cock.

Fuck, she's perfect. She's everything.

My hand traces the curve of her hip, the band of her panties, and then trails up her torso until I'm cupping her breast underneath my shirt she's wearing. The mental image of her in my clothes and the feel of her delicate skin underneath my palm sends primal desire crashing through me and I need her in a way I haven't needed anyone before. I rub my fingers over her breast, flicking my thumb over the nipple until she's quivering beneath me. The small bud hardens under my touch, and Jersey whimpers against my lips.

There's nothing more that I want than to rip the shirt over her head and lap at those pretty nipples. Though we both spent plenty of time learning each other's bodies while I was in LA, we haven't crossed the finish line. I'm yearning to know what it feels like to be buried deep inside of her, but I'm holding back, wanting to make sure she knows that she means more to me than the physical chemistry between us.

Ignoring the raging need I have for her, I pull away, returning my hand to her hip and putting some distance between us so we can both breathe.

"What's wrong?" Jersey whimpers, and then leans her face into my neck, inhaling deeply.

"Nothing." I stroke my hand from her hip up the length of her back to the nape of her neck, where I hold her to me tightly. "You've had a long day. You're exhausted. Just let me hold you tonight."

She exhales and her breath tickles my skin. "I'm so happy I'm here."

"Me too. Goodnight, honey," I say, my voice low.

She nuzzles against me, the tender action tugging on my heartstrings. "Goodnight, MVP."

NINETEEN

jersey

TUESDAY, NOVEMBER 12

MY EYES FLUTTER OPEN, blinking a few times before I stretch out my limbs. I love the way Hayes's soft sheets feel against my skin. Pushing myself up out of the fluffy pillows, I glance around the dark room, all alone in the big bed. A sliver of light peeks through the heavy curtains.

My lips tingle a little, and I brush my fingers down my body, remembering the ferocity with which he kissed me last night. I can still feel the light burn from his stubble scraping against my sensitive skin. My breasts ache with the memory of having his hands on me as he played into my desire for him.

We've both had many opportunities to explore the intimate side of our relationship while still not going all the way with each other. He's taking his time, leisurely becoming a master at commanding my pleasure, skillfully learning every inch of my body and the tender areas which bring me closer to the edge. With every passing moment, the need for him to take me and consume me grows hotter and hotter. I need to know what it feels like to have Hayes make me his. My experience in that department is limited. I can't help but be a little worried that the longer we put it off, I may not live up to the anticipation.

Throwing back the covers, I get out of bed and tiptoe into the hallway. Periwinkle lifts her head up out of her bed, and then goes right back to sleep.

I shake my head and chuckle to myself. *Lazy dog.*

Downstairs, I hear Hayes's deep voice, and it sounds like he's on the phone with someone. Hurrying into bathroom, I brush my teeth and grab my terry robe, wrapping it around myself to keep warm.

On my way down to Hayes, I pass by a window and take in the fluffy snow covering the trees and bushes around his home. Taking a moment to study it, I appreciate the way the outdoors seem so peaceful and quiet. Thick, heavy snowflakes still fall from the sky, swirling around in the wind before landing on the ground.

"Beautiful, isn't it?" Hayes says behind me. His deep voice makes me jump a bit, pulling me out the falling-snow-induced trance.

"I wish we got snow like this in LA Makes me never want to leave."

Hayes wraps his arm around my shoulder and tugs me into him, pressing a kiss against the side of my head. I close my eyes and breathe him in. He smells clean, likely the soap from his shower this morning. The warmth from his bare chest seeps into me and I love being this close to him, letting his strength and his presence consume me.

"You can stay as long as you want," he murmurs against my hair. "Trust me, I won't be complaining."

His statement makes my belly flutter and my cheeks heat. I don't think I'd be complaining either. I'm comfortable here. Part of that, I'm sure, has to do with the fact that I'm here with him. Hayes makes me feel safe, cherished, and protected. These shouldn't be foreign feelings, though now that I'm here with Hayes, I'm suspecting this is what should have been all along. I am beginning to recognize the ache in my heart from their absence.

I turn away from the window. His amber eyes track my movements, pupils dilating when I rise on my toes and lean toward him. He makes a small sound of appreciation when I press my lips against his and it sends a current of need down my spine.

His big hands wrap around my waist, and he draws me closer to him. I circle my arms around his neck and kiss him deeply. I certainly didn't dream up the way my body responds to him.

My skin flushes and I moan against him. Hayes wastes no time and bends down, scooping his arms under my knees and hoisting me up against him. He maneuvers us until my back is pressed against the wall. My breath catches with his display of power, of possessiveness.

Jesus, how am I so attracted to him?

I rock my pelvis against him, searching for friction to ease my pulsing desire. He makes a satisfied noise deep in his throat when he realizes what I'm doing. His hips buck against mine, sending a shock of pleasure rattling through me.

Breaking the kiss, I lean my head back against the wall, gasping for breath. Hayes takes the opportunity to trail his lips along my jaw and down the length of my neck. I gasp when he reaches a sensitive spot, and he zeros in, tongue tracing that area as he kisses me until my head spins.

His hips continue to move against me at the exact tempo that drives me wild.

But it's not enough.

"Hayes," I gasp, goosebumps breaking out against my arms when his tongue dips into the curve of my collarbone.

"Hmm," he murmurs against my skin in response, not letting up on his delicious torture.

"I need you," I tell him, and he groans, the deep sound sending my arousal straight to my core, soaking my boy shorts.

"Don't need to tell me twice," he mutters. His arms tighten around my back and he pulls me off the wall, carrying me down the hall to his bedroom like it's nothing.

I connect my ankles around his middle and giggle when he smacks my butt. Hayes kicks the door closed behind him once we're in his bedroom, even though we're the only two inside the house. I like that, like he still wants to keep these moments private.

He lays me down on the bed and hovers above me. His amber eyes heat as his gaze traces me head to toe, a wicked grin appearing on his lips. He leans over to one side, propping himself up on one elbow as his other hand travels to the knot of my robe. With his one hand, he undoes the tie like a master. He unwraps me, pushing the robe apart and leans down to press a kiss to my sternum over the material of his T-shirt before nuzzling against the side of my breast. The sleeves feel too confining now, and I push at his shoulders before sitting up so I can shrug out of the fluffy material. Fingers grasping the hem of his shirt, I pull it over my head until there's nothing covering my body.

We reach for each other at the same time, and I moan when his bare skin touches mine. "You feel so good," he murmurs against my chest. "Fuck, I've been waiting for this moment to get my hands on you." My nipples harden and I wiggle my hips a little, the thickness of his erection right above my pubic bone, hinting at the pleasure we're about to experience.

Releasing me, Hayes pulls back a bit and reaches for my boy shorts, drawing them down my legs. Once they're gone, I lean back on the mattress and spread my legs, feeling bold and secure enough to do so.

His eyes darken with desire as he takes me in, starting at my face and working his way down my body. His gaze lingers on the center of my thighs and his hands caress the skin on the outside of my knees up the length of my leg. Everywhere he touches leaves a trail of burning hot need.

His tongue darts out and wets his lower lip—something I never knew could be so sexy. His voice is deliciously raspy when he asks, "How is this real life?"

My heart races and I reach for him. He comes willingly, falling into my embrace and kissing the side of my neck.

I wiggle my hips, searching for that delicious friction right where I want it. Hayes groans, his pelvis bucking into mine on instinct. It sends me cascading into pleasure and I dip my fingers into the waistband of his briefs, encouraging them over his hips and tight glutes.

Before I get too far, Hayes stops me, hands wrapping around my own.

My eyes fly up to his only to find him watching me. His pupils are dilated but his jaw is set.

"What are you—"

"Let me make you feel good today, Jersey," he whispers, his voice gruff. "We have plenty of time for all that later, but right now, let me worship you."

How am I supposed to say no to that?

In the back of my mind, I can't help but wonder why he

stopped me. The twinge of worry returns. *Why doesn't he want to have sex with me?*

He takes his time, and those worrisome thoughts dissipate as he slithers down my body with his tongue, tracing every curve and divot, paying special attention to those places that make my breath hitch.

When his tongue finds my center, all thoughts that don't revolve around him leave my brain. All that matters now is Hayes and the way he's working my body. He's a quick study, hitting all the places he knows where best to tease me and draw out the sensations of his masterful ministrations.

Closing my eyes, I let myself be present in this moment, all other coherent thoughts disappearing as Hayes follows through on his promise, worshipping me into oblivion.

AFTER HAYES GIVES me not one but *two* orgasms with his tongue and fingers, he disappears downstairs for a while, letting me bask in my post-orgasmic state. Mere moments pass before he returns with a glass of water and an Oreo covered in peanut butter for *sustenance*.

"Don't you have to be at practice?" I ask him, accepting the Oreo offering.

He shakes his head and settles on the bed next to me. "Tuesdays are typically our off day during the week. I'll still get a workout in, probably review some film." He shoots me a cheeky grin. "Spend some time with my girl."

I beam at him. "I like the sound of that."

"Working out?" he winks.

"*Noo.*" I laugh. "Being your girl."

His amber eyes soften and he leans down, kissing my cheek tenderly. "Me too. More than you can possibly know."

I run my fingers over his face, loving the prick of his stubble against the sensitive pads of my fingers. He sighs and closes his eyes, letting me soothe him. I take the opportunity and thread my fingers through his hair a few times.

"I'll give you ten years to quit that," he says. When he opens his eyes again, they're filled with regret. "But I better get this workout done. There are protein pancakes downstairs my chef made earlier this morning. Help yourself. I shouldn't be too long."

My lower lip juts out in a pout when he pulls himself away from me, and I watch him shuffle around his bedroom, sliding his sweats off and trading them for a pair of gym shorts. He pulls a sweat-wicking shirt over his head, which hugs his muscled chest perfectly. My belly clenches with desire as I take in the muscled greatness that is this man.

Hayes's lips pull into a one-sided smirk. He braces his hands on the mattress and leans over me until his face hovers above mine.

"If you keep looking at me like that, there's no way I'm going to get to work."

"Oh darn," I whisper, leaning up and pressing my lips to his. Those questions from earlier return. *Why doesn't he come back to bed and fuck me?*

He makes a low sound in his throat, and I waste no time wrapping my arms around his neck and pulling him onto me again, hoping he'll give in this time. He kisses me back for another minute before regretfully untangling himself, and I can't hold back any longer.

"Hayes . . ." I begin, feeling embarrassed. He tilts his head, questioning. My cheeks flame and I turn my eyes away from him. "Why don't you want to have sex with me?"

Time stands still for a moment and then Hayes reaches for me again, cupping both of my cheeks and drawing my attention back to him. "There is *nothing* I want more than to be buried deep inside of you and hear you screaming for me." My lower body heats. I like the sound of that. "But this isn't just about me, and I want you to know that you mean more to me than sex and physical intimacy. I want to make sure you're taken care of and comfortable and fully *mine* before I fuck you. We don't have to rush into anything, but don't think for a moment it's because I don't want you. I want you more than anything, and when we do cross that line, it will be mind-blowing."

My lower abdomen tightens, and I gasp right as Hayes leans forward and claims my lips, kissing me with a ferocity that reassures me of everything he shared. When he pulls away, his lips are as swollen as I suspect mine are, his eyes gleaming with arousal. Meanwhile, I'm falling deeper than I ever thought possible, plummeting head over heels into my infatuation with him.

Kissing my nose one last time, he straightens and takes a heavy breath. "You've got me under your spell, Jersey Matthews." His eyes trace over my figure one last time, and then he takes another reluctant step back. "Okay, I actually have to leave now."

"If you insist." I bite my lip as I stretch my arms out over my head, jutting my chest out in a way I know will drive him crazy.

Hayes groans and turns around before he can give in to my temptation. I laugh to myself, loving the way this man makes me feel so powerful. I watch him walk out of the room, straining my ears to hear whatever he's muttering to himself on the way out.

I lay on the bed for a few minutes, considering what he

confessed to me. I can't help but think I've found one of the good ones in him.

Reaching for my phone on the side table, I dial Bethany's number, clicking the option for FaceTime.

"Hey!" Her smiling face greets me. "How's it going?"

I can't fight the matching smile off my face, and Bethany laughs. "Wow, that good, huh? I can't remember the last time I saw you smile like that." She pauses her lips twist into a sly position. "Oh wait, it was exactly three weeks and one day ago, when Hayes was here. Surely that's a coincidence."

"Absolutely a coincidence." I play along, sinking into the pillows again. "Everything going okay there?"

She shrugs. "As well as you can imagine. Cal keeps emailing me with revisions for your new—*compromised*—schedule once you get back. I'm doing my best to keep it as manageable as possible. He's relentless."

"Thank you. I really appreciate you fielding him right now."

"You needed a little break. I'm guessing things with Hayes are going well."

"He's been great. It's weird, but in some ways, it's like he's known me all his life. He's so in tune to everything about me."

Bethany's expression morphs into something soft and hopeful. "I love that for you, Jersey. You really deserve a relationship like that. You deserve a chance to let go and have fun."

Out of all the people in my life, Bethany is the only one who knows the level of struggle I dealt with in my last relationship. She had been on the receiving end of one too many tearful phone calls. I was forever grateful for her friendship during that time, even if there was nothing she could do but listen and be there for me when it felt like I had no one else.

"Thank you," I whisper. "Being here with him feels like a dream I'm going to wake up from at any moment."

"I think Hayes is exactly the kind of man you've been needing," Bethany muses. "Let him be your escape from the craziness of your world."

"I know. He already has become that, I'm afraid." I give her a wary glance. "It almost feels too good to be true."

Bethany shakes her head. "You deserve to have somewhere safe to land. And to be honest, I think Hayes is the best guy for the job. Just live a little. At the very least, you'll get good press for it and some incredible orgasms."

I bite my lip, hoping Bethany doesn't notice the way my cheeks heat up. But it's no use.

"Oh my god." She gasps. "Okay, I'm gonna need you to tell me everything."

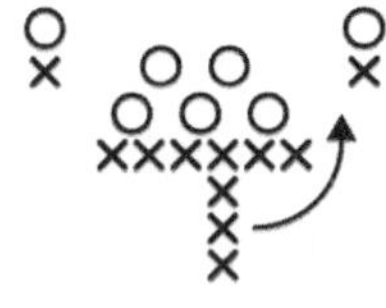

TWENTY

hayes

TUESDAY, NOVEMBER 12

"You want me to sit on *that*"—Jersey points at the sled—"and let you catapult us down the hill?"

I laugh. "Yes, exactly that. It will be fun, I promise."

The world around us goes silent as she mulls it over before glancing at me with a hesitant nod. "Okay, just don't let me die."

"I wouldn't dream of it," I say, feeling victorious as I lean over to kiss her cheek.

After getting in the workout this morning and running through a few hours of tape, I was in desperate need of stress relief. Given that Jersey is a Southern Cali girl, and doesn't get to enjoy snow, I thought it would be fun to go sledding.

I didn't expect her to be absolutely petrified.

She's been a good sport. Eagerly bundling herself up in an extra winter coat, hat, and gloves my sister left here, she was enthusiastic about the whole thing.

Until I situated us right at the top of the hill and told her to get onto the sled.

"Okay, hold on tight."

"Hayes, I don't know about this." Jersey's voice is a little shaky as she grips the handles of the sled for dear life.

I laugh into the side of her neck and wrap my arms around her middle. She's practically shivering in my arms as she stares down the big hill on the back of my property. I have her pressed up against me, my arms banded against her belly and her back tucked comfortably against my chest. It's cozy, for sure, and I'm thinking that sledding with her is going to become one of my favorite winter activities.

It's hard for me to imagine growing up and never having gone sledding before—but I'm happy to be her first.

"Here we go!" I shout and push us off the hill.

The sled crunches against the snow as we inch forward. It's only two heartbeats before we're plummeting down the hill at increasing speed. Jersey holds on tightly to my legs, her arms wrapping around my thighs. I band my arms tighter around her and draw her closer to me so she feels secure as I toss my head back and laugh right alongside her scream.

This is the ideal sledding hill. There are minimal trees I have to watch out for, so we can slide down the slope without worry. By the time we make it to the bottom, Jersey pushes herself away from me and stands up before bending over and bracing her hands on her knees. Her shoulders are shaking, and I eye her with a hint of worry, but then she looks up at me, cheeks flushed and eyes glittering.

"Let's do it again."

Together, we haul the sled back up the hill. Jersey stands with her hands on her hips, staring down the slope once again. She's sucking in deep breaths from the hike, but she turns to me with a devious expression.

"I want to sit in the back."

Wariness settles in my belly, and I shake my head. "I'm not sure that's a good idea."

When I proposed this idea to her, she told me she'd never been sledding before. There's zero chance I'll let her take control of the reins on her second run.

"Come on, buzzkill. I think it's only fair that you get a face full of snow too!"

"It doesn't make much sense for me to sit up front. I'm a lot bigger than you." I land a kiss on the tip of her rosy nose. "If I'm in front, I'll topple the sled without the weight balance from the back. How about we give it a few more goes this way?"

She arches her head toward the sky, annoyed, but even then she's the most beautiful thing I've ever seen. "Fine. Come on!"

Jersey settles into her seat, and I position myself behind her, wrapping my arms around her middle and hauling her back into me again. She wiggles her bottom a bit, getting comfortable, and it sends a flash of desire straight through me.

I clear my throat and tighten my arms around her. Pushing off again, we fly down the hill. Snow flies up around us at every angle. Jersey's twinkling laugh hits me straight in the heartstrings and I decide I could listen to that sound for the rest of my life. I'll do whatever it takes to make sure that Jersey never stops laughing when she's around me.

Finally, when Jersey's teeth are chattering and her nose is bright red from the biting cold, I call it a day. "We should get you inside." I rub my hands up and down her arms. "You're freezing."

Jersey vehemently shakes her head. "One more. And I want to sit in the back. *Please*, Hayes?"

She sticks her plump lower lip out in a pout, and there's no way I'm going to be able to resist her. The girl has me wrapped right around her finger without even realizing it.

"Okay, *fine*. Just one go, all right? Then inside."

She nods and claps her gloved hands excitedly. Groaning internally, I situate myself on the sled first, noting how Jersey slides in behind me and wraps her arms around my broad middle. I know this is a terrible idea, but it's too late now.

Jersey kicks us off the slope and we begin our descent.

We make it barely halfway before we're toppling over in a loud *oof* from me and a slightly surprised yelp from Jersey.

The two of us sprawl in the snow, the sled continuing its slide down the hill without the unbalanced weight limiting its path.

I sit up, wiping the snow out of my face, and search for Jersey, laying on her back in the snow, staring up at the sky and laughing her cute little ass off.

Fighting off the smile, I crawl toward her, crunching through the snow on my hands and knees until I'm looking down at her.

"I told you that was a bad idea," I say with a laugh, unable to fight off the infectious humor that she's experiencing.

"You should've seen your face!" She squeezes her eyes shut, consumed again with the giggles. "Oh my gosh, that was so *fun!*"

Unable to help myself, I lean down and kiss her. Jersey responds by throwing her arms around my neck and tugging me down until most of my weight is resting atop her.

I lick across the seam of her lips, begging her for access. She opens for me like a flower blooming in the spring, her enthusiasm seeping through her kiss. Her arms tighten around my neck and she makes a soft mewling sound in the back of her throat.

Despite the bitter cold, my body heats with a need for her.

But even that's not enough to deter me from some common sense.

I somehow find the strength to pull away from her and scoop her up in my arms and carry her up back toward the house. Her eyes sparkle for a second, her nose still rosy from the cold. Looking over my shoulder, she glances back down the hill.

"What about the sled?"

"Screw the sled," I say firmly before bending down to kiss her again.

As much as I'd like to kiss her the entire way back to the house, I'm worried I'll trip over the uneven, snow-covered terrain. So against my better judgement, I pull away from her and focus on the walk back.

Once we're inside, I disrobe down to my boxers, and Jersey follows my lead until she's in a tank top and her panties. Her nipples are hard, poking through the flimsy material of her top.

Fucking sexy.

After taking a moment to appreciate how irresistible she is, I lead the way to the living room and tend to the fireplace, tossing a few logs on to get it going before grabbing a blanket and a few pillows off the couch.

"Come here and get warm," I instruct Jersey, who's only a few feet away from me, watching the process with interest. She hops over and takes the blanket from me, wrapping it around her shoulders and sitting down on the floor right in front of the fireplace as I situate the pillows around her.

Settling myself next to her, I lean in and kiss her again, needing to feel her against me. She arches languidly against my side, her covered breasts pressing against the bare skin of my chest. When I pull away, her eyes have dilated in such a sexy way with the flames of the fire flickering over her face. "You're so beautiful, Jersey."

She sinks her front teeth into her lower lip—which is a seductive sight, that's for damn sure. Outside, the sun starts to set, and we're basked in the glow of the fireplace and the lingering light from the kitchen around the corner.

"I really had so much fun today," Jersey says, snuggling closer to me. "And this is the perfect way to end a day in the snow."

I shake my head. "I can't believe you've never been sledding."

She shrugs a shoulder. "My parents never had the thought to take us. We've been around snow before, done the snowball fights and snowmen and whatnot when we went to the mountains, but never sledding. I bet Roman would have loved it growing up."

"Well, I'm glad you had a good time. I was a little worried there for a minute."

She laughs. "Me too. I thought I was going to throw up looking down the hill the first time."

"Thank goodness you didn't," I tease her. "I don't think we've hit that milestone in our relationship."

She shakes her head. "Hopefully we'll *never* hit that milestone."

I gently nudge her shoulder. "I want every milestone with you, Jersey Matthews."

Her brown eyes find mine, and they soften in the dim lighting. Unable to keep this distance between us any longer, I lean forward and press my lips to hers in a gentle kiss, once, twice, before pulling away and resting my forehead against hers.

"Are you cold still?" I ask when she shivers again.

She takes a moment to open her eyes again, breathing me in

deeply. "Maybe a little, but I think I know a good way to warm up."

Then, with no further warning, Jersey reaches for the hem of her tank top, pulling it over her head, revealing her perfect naked body to me.

jersey

TUESDAY, NOVEMBER 12

THE WAY HAYES is inspecting me has me feeling like a goddess, sent specifically for him. His gaze travels over me reverently, as if I'm the sky, the moon, and his entire universe.

It makes my head swirl and my need for him skyrocket.

This whole day has felt magical, and all of that is because of *him*. His selfless confession from earlier about intimacy has been running through my mind, and I know, without a doubt, that I want to share this with him.

"Hayes . . ." I say, hoping my voice comes across seductive. His focus moves from my breasts to my eyes where he locks in, studying me and waiting for whatever I'm about to say, an unreadable glimmer in his eye. "Please. I want this with you. I want to be yours."

Hayes apparently comes to terms with whatever is going through his mind because he closes the distance between us again, reaching for me and pulling my body flush against his. The heat of his naked torso against mine sends a pool of desire straight to my center. He kisses me and runs his tongue along the seam of my lips. I open for him, allowing him to kiss me more thoroughly.

From my lips, he moves down my neck, across my collarbone, then to my breasts. Leaning forward, he surrounds one of my nipples with his mouth. His hot tongue flicks across my breast and my pebbled nipple, sending my arousal for him careening out of control. My clit throbs and aches for his attention, my need for him growing with every second. Tossing my head back, I gasp his name, letting myself get lost in the way he's working my body.

One of his large hands traces the curves of my body until he finds the waistband of my panties. He flicks his eyes up to mine, asking me quietly if what he's doing is okay—always letting me set the pace. I nod, rolling onto my back on the floor and languidly wiggling my lower half to encourage him to continue.

He leans down and presses a kiss right below my belly button as his fingers hook into my underwear, pulling them down over the length of my legs. He doesn't remove his lips, and it has me squirming in the best way. I can count on one hand the number of times Corey took the time to pleasure me like this, each time leaving me feeling anxious and self-conscious. Hayes has seen all of me at this point—has tasted all of me—but I still can't get over the intimacy of having him down there and the level of pleasure and satisfaction he can bring me with only his tongue and his fingers.

Even with that vulnerable feeling comes a sense of belonging with him I've never felt before.

And I want more.

I'm desperate to have every piece of Hayes Vogt. I yearn to have him claim me as his. The thought of him moving deep inside of me, thrusting and hitting that spot, sends me spiraling into absolute oblivion.

After tossing my underwear to the side, Hayes spreads my legs and lowers his weight on me, finding my mouth again and kissing me senseless. My hands rove over the muscular planes of his back, dipping into the band of his boxers and pushing them over his hips. He doesn't stop me, raising his pelvis enough for me to help get his underwear off.

With him on his knees like this, I finally have the chance to take in his physique, appreciating the firm planes of his chest and the muscular divots of his abdomen. This man is the definition of fit, and I know he spends countless hours working and training so he can be the best at what he does.

His eyes spark when I reach for him and trace the contour of his pecs. "You could do that forever and I don't think I'd stop you. I love having your hands all over me." His voice is husky, thick with lust. I shiver as his words fall over me. "Close your eyes, Jersey."

I do the opposite. Instead of following his instructions, I raise an eyebrow, asking for more clarification. His lips twitch at the corners and he kisses me once, before saying again, "Close your eyes."

He uses one hand to gently ease my eyes closed. My chest heaves with anticipation as soon as I can't see him. *What is he going to do?*

The blankets shift as he moves his weight off me to one side. My ears tune into every little breath, every rustle of the blanket, every crackle of the logs in the fireplace.

Then his breath is on me, blowing gently across my nipples until they've hardened into tight buds. I start a bit when his tongue presses against one, then the other, warming and suckling them. He gives my breasts equal attention, one with his mouth and the other with his fingers.

I'm soaking wet, my pussy clenching around nothing, the need for him accelerating with every passing second.

Keeping my eyes closed, I whimper. "Hayes, enough teasing."

"Enough?" he rasps. "I don't think it's enough. I barely think we've started."

His hand slides to my center, dipping in and out of the wetness pooling there. I squirm against him, searching for that delicious friction that only he can give me. Without even realizing it, I've spread my legs farther apart, opening myself up for him and inviting him to take me. He makes a satisfied sound in the back of his throat and rewards me by adding a second finger.

I arch my head back against the floor and let him work my body in the way only he knows how.

It's a startling fact, knowing that I have been in serious relationships before and none of those men knew how to bring me pleasure like Hayes.

Part of it, I suspect, has to do with the off-the-charts chemistry we share with each other and his unadulterated dedication for owning my pleasure and my heart. Even a simple glance or a sideways smirk from Hayes has my pulse increasing and need vibrating through my body.

"Hayes," I moan, even just thinking about how this man drives me wild. He murmurs against my lower abdomen where he's raining kisses against my sensitive flesh. I open my eyes and glance down at him. "Enough teasing."

He chuckles and slides his fingers out of me, climbing up my body until his face hovers over mine. He's got a devilish grin on his face, his eyes gleaming with mischief. "Do you need something?"

"Yeah," I nod. "I need you inside of me. Right now."

His smirk grows, and he leans down to kiss me. "Consider it done."

If I thought he was giving me pleasure before, I was sorely mistaken. There's nothing quite like the feel of Hayes's body against mine in this way. He slides up and down my center, getting his cock wet, pausing long enough for his tip to nudge against my clit in a way that amps up my arousal exponentially.

Unable to take the sweet torture any longer, I reach down between my legs and position him right at my entrance. Hayes groans at the sight of me taking control in this way and the sound goes straight to my aching clit. This may be the first time I've ever felt emboldened enough to do something like this, and I like the illusion of power it gives me.

When he's in position, Hayes pauses before pressing forward into me. "I have condoms upstairs."

"I have an IUD," I whisper, arching again when he tongues at my nipple.

He meets my gaze. "Jersey, do *you* want me to wear a condom?"

His question makes me fall for him even harder. "I want you inside me now."

After receiving my full go-ahead, Hayes eases in. The sensation is delectable—it's been a while since I've had sex and the intense pleasure is tinged with a hint of discomfort at the stretch of his thick cock inside of me, but if anything, it adds to my arousal.

I *like* feeling Hayes split me open.

Hayes seems to like it too. He drops his weight on top of me, burying his face in my neck as he eases inside of me. His breath is hot against my skin and his little sounds of ecstasy echo in my ears, sending shivers down my arms and spine.

"*Fuck,* so good," he grits out once he's thrust all the way inside of me. The sound of what I'm doing to him amps up the intimacy of this moment. With other guys, it was always just sex, but with Hayes, this is different.

More meaningful.

He stills for a moment, letting me adjust to his length and his girth. Even the feel of him unmoving, is doing things to my headspace.

I close my eyes and rock my pelvis against him, searching for that friction again.

Hayes obliges me and *finally* starts moving again.

He hits me deep, in just the right place, and I have no doubt that I'm seconds away from exploding. Hayes pushes himself off me, bracing himself on his hands until he hovers over me.

Our eyes lock, and the intimacy of the moment hits me square in the chest. He doesn't look away, taking in the pleasure he's giving me written all over my face. He must see something in my expression because something shifts in his amber eyes and a devilish smirk appears on his lips.

"You're gonna come, aren't you, honey?"

His dirty talk is sinful, enticing. And it brings me closer to the edge.

I fight it, hoping to prolong this moment for a little longer.

Hayes is having none of that, though, and he uses one of his hands to start strumming at my clit, bringing me to the edge and catapulting me over it.

I explode around him, unable to fight it any longer. I catch a glimpse of Hayes's eyes again, fast on mine. There's something behind those eyes that I haven't seen for a long, long time.

Something I'm not sure either of us is willing to put a name to yet.

With those thoughts lingering in the back of my mind, I squeeze my eyes shut and let the wave of pleasure take me under.

Hayes follows shortly after me, slumping his weight against me once again as his orgasm hits. He buries his hands in my hair and holds me close, his lower half gently rocking into me as he rides out the rest of his pleasure.

When he pulls out, I immediately miss the feeling of him and silently wonder to myself how quickly we can do it again.

Hayes hops up and returns a moment later with a wet cloth. Without saying a word, he spreads my legs, using the warm cloth to clean me up. When he's satisfied, he tosses the cloth aside and presses a kiss right below my belly button.

It's such a tender gesture that it makes my heart hurt.

I reach for him, and he settles on the ground next to me, circling me closely against him and tucking the blanket around us. When I settle my head on his biceps, he tangles his fingers in my hair, drawing my head back so he can kiss me deeply. I toss one of my legs over his hip, using my heel to pull his body closer to mine so we can keep this cozy warmth between us.

The fire continues to crackle in the fireplace, and we drift off to sleep with the scent of each other on our skin and the presence of each other in our hearts.

TWENTY-TWO

jersey

SATURDAY, NOVEMBER 16

"Here you go, sweetheart," Hayes says as he rounds the kitchen table to deliver me my coffee refill. He kisses my cheek before taking the seat next to me.

I'm humming lightly to myself, staring down at my notebook and clicking my pen repeatedly. "Thank you."

Hayes props his chin on his fist and leans his elbow against the table, trying to get a closer look at what I'm writing. I cover the paper up with my hands and stick my tongue out with him. "What's this one about?" he asks.

"My dad," I give him the short answer.

Hayes purses his lips. "You haven't really told me much about your dad."

"It can be hard to talk about sometimes." I look back down at my notebook where I have notes scrawled about ideas for some of the lyrics. "He passed away when I was fourteen. Developed an aggressive form of cancer which took him so quickly we hardly had time to process it all."

"I'm sorry, Jersey." Hayes shakes his head. "That's awful to have to go through that at such a young age."

"It was hard, but it gave me a sense of drive. My dad was always one of my biggest fans when it came to wanting a singing career. I think a lot of why I took the risk and started singing at open mic nights was because of him," I explain. "My mom was all for it too, knowing that my dad always believed in me."

"I'm glad you chased after that dream," he says, running the backs of his fingers over my cheek.

I lean into his touch. "Me too."

Hayes goes quiet and then says, "My parents officially adopted me when I was eight. I had been in the foster system until then. I landed with them when I was six, and right away, I knew I had found my home."

His admission catches me off guard, and I glimpse at him with wide eyes. "I didn't realize you were in the foster system."

He smiles ruefully. "I generally don't talk about it. Mostly because I don't remember much from those younger days, but also because my parents are my parents. My life is exactly what it is because of them. There's no reason for me to live in the past. But I thought you should know exactly where I come from."

"Is Riley also adopted?"

"No, she's not." His expression grows lighter thinking about his sister.

"Do you know your biological parents?"

He nods. "I know who they are. But I've never spoken to them. They haven't sought me out and I don't need anything from them to feel validated or fulfilled in my life, so I haven't reached out either."

"I'm sure your parents are proud of everything you've accomplished."

"They are. They're my biggest fans too. Aside from you, of

course." He gives me a heart-stopping grin. I fight off my amusement and roll my eyes.

"Are you going to go see them for Thanksgiving?"

"Yeah, I'll be heading back to Kentucky for a few days. I have a game the week before Christmas, so they're coming for that and then they'll spend the rest of the week here." Hayes grows thoughtful. "What are you doing for the holidays?"

"Well, I'll be back in LA for Thanksgiving—as much as I'd rather stay with you for the next few weeks. Usually Bethany, Roman, and I have a Friendsgiving potluck. Then we watch Christmas movies."

He chuckles. "Sounds like a fun tradition. Sorry I'm missing out. We've got a bye week right after Thanksgiving. I could come see you then."

"I would love that."

"What about Christmas?" he asks.

I hesitate. "I'm not sure what the plans are yet. I think Roman has to leave to film the first week of December and he'll be gone for the rest of the year, probably longer."

"You could come here for Christmas. You could come to the game and meet my parents and then we can all spend the holiday together." His eyes light up at the suggestion and my heart melts.

"That sounds like the perfect idea," I say. "I'll have to double check with the recording schedule to make sure I can get away."

"Even if you can come for the game the week before, we can do Christmas together then. And then you can jet back off to LA before he even knows you're gone."

I laugh. "I think we can figure out a way to make that work."

"What time do you have to be at the airport?" he asks.

Glancing down at the time on my phone I say, "Three o'clock. Still have a few hours before I need to leave. Why?"

His eyes darken and a devilish smirk appears.

Hayes answers by standing up, taking my hand, and leading me to his bedroom, where he proceeds to show me exactly what he had in mind.

TIME PASSES FAR TOO QUICKLY. Hayes has worshipped every inch of me multiple times. I love getting to share this with him. I've become so used to falling asleep next to him and waking up to his handsome face. It's going to be so different going back to living alone. In the few days that I've been here, we've come to have our own little routine, living in the sweet fantasy of sharing our life together.

"I'm going to miss this," he whispers against the crown of my head, reading my thoughts.

"Miss what?"

"You being here. My home feels so much more complete with you in it. It's going to be so lonely once you leave." He tightens his arms around my back.

I close my eyes as I lean against his chest. "I feel the same way." I pull back and stare up into his face. "But I'll be back soon."

We stay in bed together until the very last minute before I have to get ready to leave. Not long later, my bags are packed and the car waits for me outside.

Hayes walks me to the door, and I turn to him with a tearful smile. "I'm going to miss you."

He cups my jaw, running his thumb over my cheek. "I'll miss you too, but it won't be long before we're together again."

"You're right. So why is saying goodbye still so hard?"

"Don't say it then," he says, leaning down to peck my lips.

"We'll still talk plenty. You can FaceTime me when you get back to LA and it will be like you've never left."

I shake my head and laugh, despite feeling like my heart is crumbling to dust. An alarming worry comes out of nowhere and tumbles out of my mouth. "What if this is as good as it gets?"

He studies me for a moment, gaze flickering over my face. "Baby, we've barely begun. The good, the bad and everything in between, right? I want that with you, and *only* you."

The sentiment calms some of the anxiety bubbling through my veins. My eyes burn as I hug him. "I want that too, Hayes. More than I ever thought was possible."

"Then I promise you, I will do everything in my power to make sure we get that. Even if it's through video calls and text conversations for now." He says it with that deep assuredness that captures my heart.

TWENTY-THREE

jersey

FRIDAY, NOVEMBER 29

I HUM to myself as I towel dry my hair from the shower when my phone rings and the sight of Hayes's name on the screen makes me light up. I answer it without hesitation, anticipation pooling in my belly when his face appears on FaceTime. "Hey, I'm so glad you called."

"Hey there, I've missed you too," he says, grinning at me.

"How was shopping with your mom and Riley?"

"Long and exhausting. How was your day? Do any Black Friday shopping yourself?"

"I wish," I say, walking over to the bed and laying on my belly. I prop my cheek on my hand. "Had a long day in the studio and typical Cal wanted to micromanage every little thing. He wants me in the studio Christmas Eve *and* New Year's Eve. Why does he hate me so much?"

"Probably because he's afraid of how successful you could be," Hayes says absentmindedly, stretching his arm behind his head. "That's why he's gotta keep you on your tight leash."

I pause and blink a few times. "Could that be it, though?"

"Be what?"

"You think he's trying to keep me from realizing the full potential of my career?"

Hayes hesitates. "Do you think he's not?"

It's an interesting premise, one that has never actually occurred to me until now. "Cal always seems to care more about my career than he cares about me."

"What *he* wants for your career, though," Hayes points out. "When's the last time you were asked what *you* want for your career?"

"I don't know," I say, my voice small.

Hayes sighs and presses his lips together. Then a thought hits him. "Wait, Christmas Eve? Does that mean you won't be able to spend Christmas Day with me?"

I shake my head forlornly. "No, I don't think so."

"What about the week before Christmas? Are you still planning on coming out to see that game?"

"I am, but I'll have to leave probably Christmas Eve eve."

Disappointment ricochets across his expression, but then he lets it fade. "Casualties of the job, I guess. We'll have many more Christmases to spend together, though."

"I sure hope so," I whisper.

"I can't wait to be with you again next week," Hayes says huskily. "Can't wait to wrap you up in my arms and hold you tight."

His words take my breath away and a wicked idea comes to mind.

"Tell me, Hayes, what would you do if you were here with me right now?"

Something changes in his expression on the screen, and I can tell that already he's enjoying this immensely. His eyes have dilated a bit, but that smirk has remained on his lips.

"Well, if you really want to know. First, I'd lay you down on that bed, flat on your back, and kiss you desperately, until you can't think of anything but me." My breath catches in my throat and my chest tightens. Hayes's eyes fall to my lips and he continues. "Then I'd move from your lips, down to your neck, finding all those small places that take your breath away. Would you like that, Jersey?"

I roll my lips together and nod.

"Are you wet for me right now?"

I squeeze my thighs together and my core clenches. "Maybe," I say lightly. "Might need to work a little harder for it, though, MVP."

His expression turns devious with the challenge. "If I were with you right now, I wouldn't waste any more time. I'd slide that skimpy little tank top over your head. I'd need to get a taste of those perky little tits." He sucks in a breath, eyes darkening again. "Will you do that for me now, baby?"

My stomach swirls with a mix of trepidation and excitement. I've never done anything like this before, but I'm finding that I *want* to. I want to see where he'll take this. He's so easily taken control of this call. I wonder if he'd talk dirty when I see him—maybe if I initiated it.

Propping my phone on some pillows, I rise back on my knees and reach for the hem of my tank, pulling it up over my head and tossing it to the floor. My nipples pebble right away against the cool air.

Hayes groans on the phone, eyes glued to me. "*Fuck*, you're gorgeous."

I fight off a bashful smile. Even through the screen, I love having Hayes's eyes on me and hearing his praise for my body. He makes me feel desirable and sexy.

"Touch them for me, baby. Let me see you play with those pretty nipples."

Still on my knees, I sit back on my haunches, trailing my hands up my thighs, along the curves of my torso, then up to my breasts. I cup them for a moment, closing my eyes and pretending that my hands are Hayes's bigger, rougher hands. When I move to my nipples, Hayes groans on his side of the call as he watches me run my fingers over my sensitive peaks.

I manage to pry my eyes open, searching for his reaction.

The arm that was rested above his head has moved to his side, and his eyes are hooded as he watches me play with myself.

"Are you touching yourself too?" I ask him, surprised when my voice comes out breathy and seductive.

His tongue darts out to wet his lower lip. "How could I not be when you're there looking like *that?*" He nearly growls and it sends need straight to my core. I'm soaking wet for him, and all I can imagine is that tongue sliding across my body.

I reach for my phone and reposition it so I can lie back against my pillows, too. Before I lie down, I shimmy out of my bottoms so I'm completely naked, then fall back on the bed and spread my legs. From the positioning of my phone, Hayes can see *almost* everything. What he can't see on the screen he can use his imagination for—which I have no doubt is fully functioning right now.

"I bet you're wet now, aren't you, baby?"

"Soaked," I admit as I run my fingers through my folds, slickness coating my fingers.

Hayes swears and grunts. "Damn. This is the hottest fucking thing ever. Keep touching yourself, Jersey. Don't stop. But don't come until I say so."

"I kind if like it when you're a little bossy."

"Yeah?" a wicked smirk appears on his face.

I nod and bite my lower lip as I do as he says, sliding my fingers across my pussy and finding my clit. I give it a few determined rubs, desire ricocheting up my spine. My pussy clenches and I need something inside of me.

I wish Hayes were here . . . but my fingers will have to do.

Opening my eyes, I watch Hayes work his body. His attention is rapt on me, eyes never wavering from what I'm doing on the other end of the call. His shoulder rises and falls, rhythmically.

The thought of Hayes touching himself at the sight of me sends my mind whirling. I can't help the moan that escapes my parted lips as I finger myself, searching to ease the ache that's consuming me from the inside out.

"Damn," he mutters and then grunts again.

The sound of Hayes finding pleasure only elevates what I'm feeling inside. I close my eyes again, and picture what it would be like to have him here with me, to feel his thick fingers sliding in and out of my center. I imagine what it would be like to have his lips on my skin—nibbling at my neck, huffing in my ear, sending goosebumps down my arms and my legs.

My pussy clenches around my fingers, and I know I'm close.

"Hayes," I gasp.

"Fuck me. Yeah, baby?"

"I need to—"

"Yeah? What do you need, Jersey? Use your words. Tell me what you need."

"I need to come. Please. Let me come," I beg.

He groans again, the sound spurring me on. "Do it. Come for me. Imagine I'm right there with you fucking that sweet pussy until you can't take it anymore. Come all over for me, Jersey."

The orgasm crests and takes me right to the edge. I cry out, needing a little more to push me over.

"Do it. Now."

The sound of his gruff command does the trick.

I fling myself over the edge of pleasure and clamp around my own fingers, imagining exactly what he told me—that it was him here inside of me instead of fingers.

Distantly, I hear the sound of Hayes gasping, coming down from his own orgasm.

I ride out the wave, lingering a moment longer. Slowly, the world comes back around me and I remove my fingers from my center, wiping them off on the comforter and turning my head to see Hayes on my screen.

He's wearing a sleepy smile on his face, eyes glazed over. "Hey there," he says, repeating his opening phrase. "You alive over there?"

My lips turn up and I breathe in deeply. "Barely. That was—"

"Fucking hot."

"Yeah. It was."

"Can we do this every night?" he teases, sending me a wink.

I laugh and shrug a shoulder noncommittally. "I mean . . . I wouldn't be opposed to it."

He chuckles, his voice still gruff. Aftershocks of the intense orgasm travel through my body. "Me either." He yawns again, and while I know he enjoyed our little rendezvous immensely, I suddenly feel bad knowing how long of a day he's had.

"You should sleep," I whisper.

His eyes find mine and he falls silent, watching me, memorizing me. His gaze flickers over every one of my features, leaving a hot trail of yearning in its wake. "You too," he says softly.

"We'll talk later?" I ask him, a thread of doubt rearing its ugly head.

"Absolutely. You'll be the first thing I think of in the morning."

That statement makes my heart flip. I feel like I'm more than enough for him, like I'm treasured and valued.

"Goodnight, Hayes."

"Goodnight, beautiful."

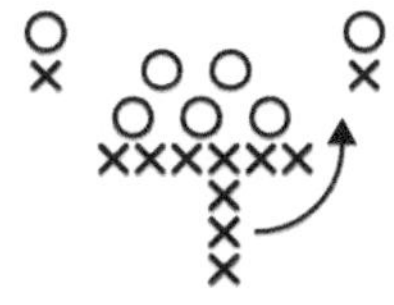

TWENTY-FOUR

hayes

TUESDAY, DECEMBER 3

"Everyone decent in here?" a male voice echoes throughout Jersey's condo.

She groans and rolls out of bed, grabbing her robe off the hanger and flinging it on before leaving the bedroom. "There's Roman. I thought he was joking when he said he'd bring us breakfast this morning." She shakes her head. "Guess not."

I chuckle and pull on my sweatpants and a shirt before following her out of the bedroom. I flew in late last night, desperately counting down the minutes until I got to hold her in my arms again. We barely let each other go throughout the late nighttime hours—the perfect way to start a bye week, if you ask me.

Jersey has her twin in a tight hug and he sways her back and forth, though he releases her when he sees me, wrapping his arm around her neck. "Sorry to interrupt."

I hold up my hands. "No problem here." My eyes fall on the box of bagels he's brought. "Thanks for breakfast." I help myself to an everything bagel and slather on a heaping dose of plain cream cheese.

"I wanted to meet you face-to-face and see my little sis before I leave," Roman says, and Jersey rolls her eyes. "Figured meeting you this morning would be my only shot for a while."

"I'm sure your schedule is about to be super hectic," I say before taking a bite of the bagel.

Roman nods. "It is. I'll be back in a few months, though, and we'll be back to our regularly scheduled shenanigans. Hopefully, by then you'll have another Super Bowl ring, and Jersey will have a fully recorded album."

"Ugh, one can only hope," Jersey says, shooting me a wink as she puts strawberry spread all over her chocolate chip bagel.

"That's for damn sure," I agree.

"I'll get out of your hair. Just wanted to stop by. You're in good hands, Jersey," Roman says. When he releases her, he reaches out and gives me a firm handshake. "It was good to meet you, man. You take care of her, okay? I don't want to have to fight you because I'll probably lose." He sizes me up. He's a few inches shorter than me and not nearly as broad.

"Hopefully, it will never come to that," I reply with a chuckle.

"I have a feeling it won't."

Jersey's eyes glisten as she looks at her brother. That one little comment seems to mean the world to her. Roman gives his sister one last hug and then heads out the door, leaving the two of us to eat our bagels and continue getting ready.

A few hours later, Jersey and I sit side-by-side in a conference room at Silver Shadows. Jersey has an iPad in front of her and her worn-down notebook open to a clean page. She's been humming a few bars over and over to herself, scribbling some words down, toying with them, and then usually scratching them out to start over again.

At her request, we got here early, before her scheduled time in the recording studio. She's got another half-hour before she's due to start.

"What's it like to record an album?" I ask her.

She looks up at me with dazed eyes for a second before she focuses back on the present. "What do you mean?"

I shrug a shoulder. "I'm just wondering if it's like in the movies or TV or anything."

Her lips quirk. "I suppose a little bit. I record vocals either with or without a backing track, and then we play it back to make sure it came out how we want it to. Rinse and repeat." She runs her tongue over her bottom lip, thoughtfully. "Do you want to come in and watch?"

I raise my brows. "Can I?"

Her brown eyes take on a defiant edge to them. "I mean, *technically*, no, but I like the idea of you being in there with me."

Leaning toward her, I cup my hand at the nape of her neck and pull her into me for a kiss. I can't wait to watch her creative process unfold and I can't wait to spend more one-on-one time with her after the fact. She whimpers as I kiss her, making a dissatisfied sound when I break away.

"Let's go out tonight," I suggest, twirling a strand of Jersey's hair around my finger.

Surprise fills her. "Out?"

"Yeah, like out on a date. A real one." I can't fight the grin off my face. Already, I love the idea of walking around downtown with her on my arm, me getting to show her off to the whole world.

"In . . . public?" she squeaks.

Now I arch a brow at her. *"Yeah?"*

She swallows thickly and glances back down at her notebook. "I'm not sure."

"Why? I'll be right next to you the whole time." I lean forward and nuzzle behind her ear with my nose, curious why this side of her is making an appearance today. "I would never let anything happen to you. Besides, everyone knows we've been seeing each other. It's no secret."

She turns thoughtful. "Corey never wanted to go out. Mostly I think it was because my presence would garner more attention than his, and he hated feeling like he always came in second to me."

I give her a heady look. "I don't mind coming in second to you. Not now, not ever."

Her lips turn up in the corners. "He always felt the need to point out that they only liked me because of the music Callum picked out for me. That I wouldn't be where I am if I had used my own songs."

"Somehow, I can't see that being the case. I'm sure your music would garner just as much, if not more, love and accolades."

"I don't know. Maybe he's right." She runs her finger over some words she's written in her notebook, a forlorn expression now on her beautiful features.

"Why would you say that?"

She chuckles. "Because it's true? I'll never be the Christina, or the Taylor, or even the Britney."

"What are you talking about? You already are. Have you not been paying attention to the sold out stadiums or the platinum albums? You're America's sweetheart," I argue.

"What if I don't want to be that anymore?" Her voice is

small, as if she's afraid to say it out loud. Her eyes hold a sense of guardedness as she watches me, waiting for my reaction.

I fall silent as her quiet admission lays heavy between us, giving it the space it needs. Carefully, I ask, "Then what do you want to be?"

"I want to be me. I want to write and sing the songs that I want. And those may be heavier and edgier than what people know me for. I just don't know how that will go over. I've probably written five albums worth of my own songs—though none of them have ever gotten recognition, nor will they if Callum has anything to do with it."

"Let me hear one."

She pauses, her eyes going wide with a sense of alarm. "What?"

"I want to hear one. Play for me." My lips twitch into a smile thinking about getting to hear my own personal Jersey concert. I've been aching to hear her velvety voice again. And to have her sing for me in an intimate setting? I might spontaneously combust.

She studies my face, and for a moment I think she's considering it, but then her shoulders fall. "I can't."

"Why not?" I ask her, disappointment settling in my chest.

"I'll play you one when it's just the two of us sometime. Away from *here*." She nibbles on her lower lip and I wonder what she's not telling me. Her gaze darts to the door again and then falls back on me. "There're a lot of people in this city who only see me as a pawn, and they only give me so much freedom. I've tried to convince them to let me try with my own words and they've laughed in my face. I'm not about to try again. At least not yet. I have to protect that part of me."

I ponder her words, hating that she questions if she has any power when she should have it all. This label should be falling at her feet, begging for her to give them the time of day, but here she is, feeling like a prisoner in her own gold-plated life.

I hate that for her, and I resolve to contribute in whatever way I can to give her back the power of her voice.

"Go out with me tonight," I suggest again. "The only way for you to be the version of yourself that you want to be is to do it. You have to be willing to step into the light, make yourself uncomfortable, and reach for that power that you so desperately want. You've gotta take it yourself."

Her eyes shine as she listens intently to what I'm telling her. "What if I can't?"

"Then I'll be right behind you, showing you that you can."

TWENTY-FIVE

jersey

TUESDAY, DECEMBER 3

"W**HAT IS HE DOING HERE?**" Cal asks dryly when Hayes walks into the recording booth behind me.

I glance at him over my shoulder before turning back to Cal. "I thought Hayes could hang out while we recorded today."

Cal frowns. "No."

"No?" I repeat, confused. "There are always a ton of people in the recording sessions."

"Yeah, *employees*," Cal says to me like I'm stupid, "who have signed NDAs and have been properly vetted by the label."

"Hayes is my boyfriend," I tell him. "He's not going to leak anything."

"No offense, Jersey," Cal sneers. "But if you wanted to have your boyfriend sit in with you while you worked, you might have actually been able to keep your last one around a little longer."

Hayes stiffens behind me and takes a step closer. I blink slowly and run my tongue over my teeth. *All right, then.*

"It's fine, Jersey. I'll wait until you're finished," Hayes says. His presence still looms behind me and already I'm missing it, knowing he'll be on the other side of the studio.

"Good man." Cal dips his chin.

I watch Hayes leave the studio and exhale, frustrated.

"Okay, let's go, people!" Cal's voice booms through the small space of the recording studio and rattles my brain, startling me back to business. "We've only got a few hours to get this perfect. We don't have time to waste. Marco! Take Jersey's stuff and put it off to the side."

Cal's phone rings and he swears under his breath, pulling it out of his pocket, but his face lightens up when he sees the caller ID. He meets my eyes and holds up one finger, accepting the call and placing it to his ear. "Meghan! I was hoping I'd hear back today! Have you given any more thought to my offer?"

"What do you think that's about?" Bethany asks.

I shrug, unconcerned. "Who even knows with Cal."

"You're probably right. Are you ready for this?" Bethany mutters, looking at her watch.

"As much as I'm going to be."

"Write anything good today?" Bethany asks.

I shake my head. "No, I'm still playing with a few melodies and chord progressions. But it's going to have to wait."

"Do you need anything?" Bethany asks. "Hot water or tea?"

"Maybe a tea with some honey in it."

"Coming right up."

The next few hours are spent recording and re-recording, layering and making sure I'm enunciating the lyrics properly. Cal watches and listens to every little detail meticulously, the disapproving expression never leaving his face.

"Again!" he shouts through the mic into the studio. "This time pretend you're Meghan Connelly and hit those notes like she does. She's got the best range. You'd do well to take a chapter out of her book."

I grit my teeth and ignore the gnawing pain in my chest at the comparison. "My range is perfect for the songs I record."

"Do as I say, Jersey. Again!"

When I finally leave the recording studio, I feel like I've been run over by a truck. Hayes is waiting dutifully for me outside of the recording room, and his face lights up when he sees me walking toward him.

"Hey," I say, standing up on my tiptoes and planning to give Hayes a kiss on the cheek. Before my lips land on his skin, he turns his head, capturing my mouth with his.

When he breaks us apart, his eyes glitter. "Hey there."

Already I feel better with him near me. "Sorry you had to wait out here. It probably wasn't as exciting as you thought it would be." I shake my head.

He shrugs. "That's all right. Getting to watch you from out here was . . . enlightening."

She tilts her head. "Why is that?"

"I could see the struggle going on inside of you. You love what you do. I can tell how much giving life to your music and words means to you." He brushes his hand down my cheek and runs his thumb over my lower lip, eyes darkening as a slow smile appears on his face when I suck in a tight breath. "But even I could tell that the words are wrong. I could see you struggling, trying to find the right delivery for those words that aren't yours."

When he drops his hand, I bite into my lower lip. "How can you see me so clearly?"

"Because I'm looking *and* paying attention." His expression is soft as his eyes study my face, proving his point.

I part my lips to say something else but someone else interrupts. "Well, isn't this cozy?"

Hayes turns his head as I stiffen, glowering at the newcomer as he approaches. He's like a parasite I can't get rid of. "What are you doing here?"

The hair on the back of my neck stands up and Hayes snakes his hand around my waist, protectively drawing me closer to him.

"I was supposed to meet with Cal an hour ago, but your recording session went over. I got bored waiting so I thought I'd come up here and watch." He slides his hands into his pockets and gives me a sardonic grin. "You know, like old times."

"You never came to any of my recordings." I narrow my eyes accusingly.

Corey rocks back on his heels and then shifts focus to Hayes. "Hayes Vogt, right? We still haven't had a chance to formally meet each other. I'm Corey Shrader. I'm sure you've heard lots about me."

"Nothing worth repeating."

His lips twitch in an amused smirk. "Good game the other day."

"Thanks," he says brusquely. "If you don't mind, we were kind of in the middle of something."

Corey raises his hands. "My bad. Just figured I'd pop by and say hey. I'm supposed to be going out with Cal for a drink or two later. But I'll leave you two to your *something*. I'll see you later, Jersey."

"Don't count on it."

He snorts a laugh and then turns away, leaving us alone again. I wrap my arms around Hayes, burying her face in his chest. "I *hate* that he's been around so much. I feel like I've seen him more in the last few weeks than I did during our entire relationship."

He runs his hand up and down my back, staring after Corey. "Why do you think he's here?"

"I don't know. But I don't like it."

"Me either. Are you all finished?" he asks, redirecting the topic. I love he's not giving Corey any more energy than absolutely necessary.

"Yup. I just gotta grab my stuff and we can head out."

Hayes bends down and presses his lips to mine, sending all thoughts of Corey or Cal straight out of my mind, too. "Perfect, 'cause I believe you have a hot date, Ms. Matthews."

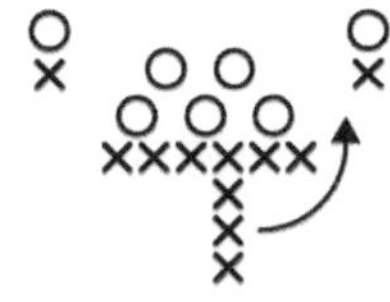

TWENTY-SIX

hayes

TUESDAY, DECEMBER 3

ONCE JERSEY IS CLEARED to leave the studio, we go back to her place to clean up before heading out for dinner. I ask her a few times if she is still up to going out after her long day, but she reassures me each time.

"Yeah. I need a break. And possibly a drink . . . or three." She gives me a smile that doesn't reach her eyes.

I take that as a personal challenge—we're going to end this evening on a high note.

"I'll find us the perfect place then," I assure her, grabbing my phone and reading over the reviews of a few places before settling on one that I'm sure will amp up Jersey's mood.

Not long later, her driver is pulling into the restaurant parking lot.

Jersey peers out the window as the car comes to a stop and then she turns to me in question, one of her dark eyebrows arching on her face. "A bar?"

I smirk at her. "Gotta keep it interesting."

Her eyes go wide with alarm. "I don't think I can go in there. We don't have security."

Running my hand down the back of her hair, I say, "I'll be right next to you the whole time. No one's getting close to you unless you tell me it's okay."

Her eyes trace my face and I see the moment my words soften her. She exhales and tilts her head. "All right, let's go."

Together, we get out of the car and walk up to the front door. I pull it open, letting Jersey walk in first before following closely behind her. As soon as I step into the establishment, I know everything I read about it online was true to its word.

The bar instantly gives me a semblance of home. The warm wood paneling on the walls and ambient lighting are inviting and comfortable. The scent of french fries and smash burgers permeates the air and my stomach rumbles at the prospect of delicious food. At the far end of the dining area, next to the bar seating, is a small stage where a young girl stands, front and center, singing boldly into the microphone while confidently strumming at the guitar around her neck.

I figured Jersey would love a place with an open mic night, which is why I chose this place over all the other popular places here in LA

I suspect I was right.

Jersey gasps a little, her attention zeroing in on the young artist singing her heart out.

While she's distracted, I find us a place to sit. Grabbing her hand, I pull her over to a small two-seater table close to the stage. Her gaze never leaves the singer as we walk past the oblivious barflies. I was also right in taking the chance that Jersey could fly under the radar here. We're far enough away from the main scene—not to mention the general demographic of pub crawlers isn't too into pop princesses—that I knew she'd be safe here.

Otherwise, I wouldn't have taken the chance.

I'd throw myself in front of a bullet for her if I had to. I wouldn't even hesitate sacrificing myself to keep her safe. It means a lot to me to know she trusts I'll always have her back.

Jersey slides into the seat directly facing the stage, her eyes still glued to the young girl. When the singer finishes her set, the bar erupts into cheers and applause.

"Wow," Jersey says.

"She's really good."

Jersey shakes her head as if I don't understand. "She's better than good. You can see that she really *loves* what she's doing up there. She loves singing, she loves playing, she loves it all." She presses her lips together in a tight line and her eyes grow shiny. "I've forgotten what it's like to feel that way."

My heart aches for her and I want to reach across the table to hug her, to take away whatever pain and frustration are eating at her. Instead, I place my hand up on the table, offering it to her. She slides her hand into mine, and I note how small her hand is compared to mine—dainty, delicate, *perfect*.

"You'll get that back. I know you will."

Something flashes behind her eyes, and I suspect it has a lot to do with the man currently steamrolling her career. "I hope so. One day."

The waiter comes by then, giving us a warm smile as he puts down a few cocktail napkins and glasses of water. "Hey guys, what can I get you?" He scans over Jersey first, then me before doing a double take. "Oh shit. Hayes Vogt, right?"

I notice Jersey is trying to fight off a smile at not being the center of attention. Giving the kid a sheepish nod, I acknowledge him. "In the flesh."

"Dude, you *crushed* us this year." He holds out his knuckles and I fist bump him. "You're a living legend."

I laugh, relieved that he's being a good sport about it. "It was a good game across the board. The Lightning really left it all out on the field."

"Yeah, I'll say." The server nods. "Anyway, good to meet you. If you have a minute on your way out, I'd love a picture and an autograph."

"Sure."

"Sick." He fights off a broad smile before schooling his features. "What can I get you to drink tonight?"

I order a beer and Jersey orders herself a vodka tonic. The server hurries off to get our drinks and Jersey levels me with an amused smirk, mindlessly running over the petals of the flowers on the table with her fingers.

"What?" I ask her, feigning innocence as I take a sip of my water.

"Is this why you picked a *dive* bar?" she teases.

"Definitely not. I figured we'd have the best chance of flying under the radar here. And besides, even if I'm recognized, I'm not as big of a deal as you are."

"Hayes," she protests. "That's not true. You're just as important as I am."

"Maybe in the sports world, but my fans won't be as feral as your fans, and you can't even say I'm wrong. I've been to your show, experienced your fans." She rolls her eyes but doesn't disagree. Her attention falls to the flower again, a breezy expression falling over her face.

My phone buzzes on the table and I glance at it, biting back a laugh when I see the picture my housekeeper has sent of Periwinkle. She's made a fort of sorts on the couch and has buried herself under the blankets and pillows. There'd be no way one could know she was under there if not for the two beady black eyes peering out. I flip my phone around and show

Jersey, who fights off a smile and shakes her head at the amusing pup.

The server returns a few minutes later with our drinks and we put in an order for some appetizers—fried pickles and pretzels with beer cheese. When he walks away, another up-and-coming artist takes the open stage and introduces himself.

Jersey props her head up on her hand, leaning forward a little to get as good of a view of the singer as possible. A blissful expression takes over her face the moment the singer starts his first song. She might be entranced by the music, but I am entranced by her. I live for these small moments.

I could watch Jersey like this for hours, days, years, an *eternity*. Her face so clearly displays her love for music and songwriting, and I wish there was a way I could bottle it up and sell it, but I'm grateful I'm the one that gets to see it in real time.

Her love and her passion are priceless.

"He's so good," she says, eyes sparkling as she takes in the person on stage. "Listen to the cadence of his lyrics." And later, as he finished his set and is walking offstage. "He wove that melody together masterfully." She shakes her head in awe. "He's gonna go places."

Even as she enthusiastically explains things I really have no clue about, I listen intently, wanting to understand the things that are so important to her. I want to learn everything about her: her likes, dislikes, and everything in between.

She's lit up with excited energy the entire ride back to her place. "You remind me of how excited Riley was after we saw your concert," I tell her, remembering the night fondly. "She was pretty wound up the whole way home, too."

Jersey beams at me. "Was she?"

"Oh yeah. She's a huge fan of yours. She's going to be so

excited to meet you some day. You two have a lot in common, so I'm sure you'll get along well."

"Will she be at your game before Christmas?" she asks. "She'll be done with school by then, won't she? I can't wait to meet her."

I shake my head. "She'll be done with school, but unfortunately, no. She'll be coming up for Christmas Day, but she won't be there for the game. She's apparently got a new boyfriend she's going to spend some time with." I try not to let my dissatisfaction show at the thought of my sister dating. It will take a lot for someone to be worthy of her in my books.

Jersey's expression falls. "Dang it, I won't get to see her then. *Ugh*." She falls back against the car seat. "Why does Cal have to be such an asshole? I mean, what kind of scrooge wants me to be in the studio on *Christmas*?"

"That is pretty petty of him," I agree and then reach for her hand. "But you'll get through it. *We'll* get through it."

She exhales and squeezes my hand. "You're right. I was looking forward to our first Christmas and getting to meet your parents and Riley, though."

"You'll see my parents at the game and I'm sure if you really want to Riley could be talked into a FaceTime. That would make her day. I'm in this for the long haul, Jersey. We'll have many more Christmases to spend together." Hands still entwined, I tug her closer to me, wrapping my arm around her shoulders. She leans against my side, where she stays for the rest of the ride.

When we walk into her condo and close the door behind us, she launches herself into my arms, taking me a little off guard. Her arms wrap around my neck and she hugs me tightly.

"Thank you so much, Hayes."

"For what?" I murmur into her hair, burying my face against her and breathing her in. She gives the best hugs.

"For everything," she whispers.

When she untangles herself from me, I meet her gaze and my breath catches. Her warm brown eyes are overflowing with emotion and desire. It sends need skyrocketing through my body.

My hand rises to cradle her cheek, and I tilt her jaw up, positioning her so I can kiss her. She sighs happily as soon as my lips are on hers, leaning into the kiss, driving me wild.

Not wanting to break apart, we stumble down the hallway toward her bedroom, each of us having the same want and need on our minds.

Jersey kicks the door closed behind me and then finally breaks away. She gives me a heady stare as she takes a step backward, her hands falling to the hem of her dress before raising it up and over her head, exposing her body to me.

My mouth goes dry as I take in the lacy blue bra and panty set she's wearing. The color stands out against her smooth skin. I reach for her again, unable to bear the thought of not touching her.

"You are everything to me, Jersey," I murmur against her mouth as I kiss her deeply again. She whimpers as she arches into me and the sound goes straight to my dick. I walk her backward until we're right at the edge of her bed.

She falls back against the mattress and I follow closely behind her, pulling my shirt over my head in the process. I lean down to kiss her again, resting some of my weight against her, the heat from her flushed skin seeping into mine.

Fuck, she feels so good against me.

I could die a happy man knowing what it's like to kiss her

and have her body against mine. The need to have her, consume her, to *know* her becomes overwhelming.

As I hover above her, something has me pausing. I stare down at her, memorizing the way she appears right now, exactly in this moment. My heart is hammering in my chest, desire coursing through me at rapid speed, but still, I slow down and take in everything about her right here.

Her pupils are dilated, her already plump lips swollen from the ferocity with which I've been kissing her. She's looking up at me as if she's trying to memorize everything too, commit it to memory.

It's right then that I realize I love her.

Everything else doesn't matter—not the short-span of our relationship or any of the obstacles or potential conflicts standing in our way. Jersey was made for me, and I was made for her. We were always meant to find each other in this life, even if it took longer than we would have hoped.

She's mine, and I'm hers.

That's all there is to it.

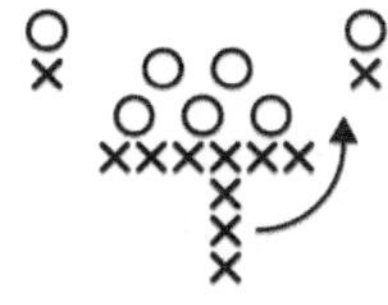

SUNDAY, DECEMBER 22

JERSEY

Good luck today, MVP

Her text comes through right as I'm boarding the team bus to head to the stadium. We've spent the last two weeks apart, but she flew into Milwaukee last night, planning to spend a few days here with me and my parents before having to fly back tomorrow for her recording session on Christmas Eve. I had to stay with the team in our team hotel, as we usually do the night before home games, so I didn't get to see her last night. And I'm missing her, desperately.

HAYES

Cheer loud for me, okay? I wanna hear you down on that field.

JERSEY

You got it, #18.

With one last lingering look at the screen, I power the phone down and focus on my pregame routine, shifting my mindset on the way from the girl of my dreams to the Dallas Rampage—a team known for their impeccable and ruthless defense.

All last week I focused on footwork, perfecting my avoidance skills, knowing their linemen will be out for blood today. We're nearing playoff season, so the stakes are high. I have my eyes set on the number one seed.

That Super Bowl ring will be ours.

By the time the team makes it to the stadium, I'm dead set on giving today my all, even if it kills me.

Beckett meets me at our neighboring cubbies in the locker room and we change out of our suits into our warm-up jerseys. When we hit the field, my focus zeros in on running through drills and getting my muscles and mind prepped for the battle ahead.

We lose the coin toss to the Dallas Rampage, so right from the start, I'm exiled to the sidelines, watching the first play shake out. My blood thrums through my veins as the adrenaline spikes. I'm itching to get out on that field and get that ball between my hands.

While I won't turn down getting first dibs at the ball to start the game, I'm more content with getting the ball first in the second half—in fact, I prefer it. By then, I'll have a feel for the game, a feel for the team. And if we're leading, it allows us to keep that momentum, or if we're trailing, it tells me how much work we have to take lead.

It doesn't always shake out the way I want it, but that's part of the game.

The Rampage came to win today, that's for damn sure. Already, by the end of their first possession, they've scored the first touchdown of the game—a scoring drive with their tight end sneaking past all of our defenses.

I knew going in this would be a tough game, but the pressure amps up as I pull on my helmet to take the field. We've gotta keep up, otherwise they'll stomp all over us.

In the huddle, my offensive lineup looks to me for direction, wondering which play we'll attempt first to give us the best chance to get points on the board.

My brain whirls all over the plays we've been practicing and I finally settle on one I *know* will work. After a quick glance down at the band on my forearm to make sure I read it right, I look up to see my teammates watching me expectantly. The heat of my breath swirls in the chilly air as I call, "Let's go boys, Steer Right, Tether Flex, Flip Zebra, Can 42 Slide on one."

The team breaks and we get into formation. I position myself a few yards behind Quentin, geared up for the pass.

I give the call, and the ball is snapped right into my hands and the play begins. I bound back a few steps, staying on the balls of my feet so I can maneuver around the pocket as Beckett and the rest of the strong side of the offense holds the defense. My eyes track my teammates, waiting for the perfect opportunity for the pass.

While my eyes are down the field, in my periphery, I see someone barreling toward me. I dodge away from them, my footwork paying off as I spin away and gain a few yards down the field.

That was close.

That would have been a nasty hit with how fast he was coming at me, combined with the size of him. A quick burst of relief fills me before I push it away.

My vision tunnels, and finally, I see my chance.

Beckett darts across the field, wide open

When the ball leaves my hands, I know Beckett going to catch it. I get tackled to the ground the minute the ball leaves my hands, but I catch sight of Beckett gaining yards off the pass.

Wilson, Dallas's most notorious defensive lineman, crawls off me and I pop back up, my eyes going to the scoreboard to see the replay.

Instead of the replay, there's a picture of Jersey's face up on the screen and my breath catches in my throat. She's got her hands cupped around her mouth as she cheers.

My lips twitch in the corners and I draw my eyes away, staring at the field so no one can see what I simp I've become at the sight of her.

Beckett runs up next to me and claps me on the shoulder. I glance up to see him giving me a worried look. "What?" I question.

"Head in the game, man." His voice is level. "You know I'm happy for you, but let's finish this."

I clench my jaw. I know he's right. I have to focus on the task at hand. "Right."

It's imperative that we clinch this win to keep our seed in the playoffs, keep our home field advantage, and do our damnedest to get to *the Big Game.*

The first half flies by, and by the time we come back out for the third, we're down one touchdown, the taste of revenge hot on our tongues.

The clock is ticking down, nearing the end of the third quarter, and we waste no time taking the field and huddling up. On our next possession, we take the ball all the way down the field to the fifteen-yard line. I glance at the clock, and a sense of satisfaction washes over me when I see we've got the right amount of time left in the quarter to get one last scoring drive—exactly what I was aiming for. Keeping sight of the clock and running strategic plays to keep us on the field longer and exhaust Dallas's defense.

I wave my teammates forward, choosing to line up right away instead of going for the huddle and allowing Dallas's defense to regroup and rally.

The stadium is going absolutely nuts, willing us to get this next touchdown and tie up the game, but the noise settles as we approach the line of scrimmage. Time to focus.

I confidently stride over to my position at the back of the line. I yell my play, "Charlie 32!"

The ball is snapped, and my eyes dart around for the player I'm searching for.

But he's not open.

The Rampage has double teamed him, seemingly in the know of what our plans were.

Quick to find a new option, I scan the field, but no one's there. I clench my jaw and weigh my options.

I take a step, deciding to run it myself, but it's too late.

A defensive player sneaks away from our offense and comes barreling toward me. I do my best to sidestep him, but his momentum is nothing to be trifled with.

Before I even know what's happening, he's launching himself at me and taking me down.

As I fall to the field, my left leg gets caught in his, and his momentum is still too much to force him to stop or to reposition. When we land, my leg twists at a sickening angle and something deep inside my knee pops.

I swear and fall to the ground, knowing in my soul that I won't be getting up from this one.

TWENTY-EIGHT

jersey

SUNDAY, DECEMBER 22

"GET UP," I whisper, wishing there was a way Hayes could hear me out on that field. "Get up!" Turning to Hayes's mom—Merilee—next to me, I ask, "Why is he not getting up?"

"That was a hard hit," his mother murmurs beside me.

The stadium has fallen into hushed silence as their quarterback lays motionless on the field. The sun shines down on the turf from the open-air stadium, but as the game comes to a halt, the day seems to dim.

The athletic trainers trot out to him, huddling around his body and blocking my view of him. From my position in the box, I stand up on my tiptoes as if that will give me a better view of what's happening down below.

Concern fills me as I wait for him to do something, anything, and I twist my fingers together into a tight knot.

Come on, Hayes, get up.

I step closer to her, wrapping my arm around her shoulders

and hugging her close. As much as Hayes means to me, that's her *son* down there.

"He'll be okay." I try to reassure her, though my voice breaks at the end of the word. "He's gotta be."

Hayes's mom and I stand there holding each other, waiting for any type of signal that he will be okay. Hayes's father squints down at the field with a grim expression, waiting for Hayes to pop back up to his feet, like he always does.

My throat goes dry when an emergency medical cart drives out onto the field. The people attending to Hayes quickly jump into action to get him onto the stretcher and into the vehicle to wheel him off field.

I cover my mouth with my hands with a gasp. "Oh god."

"Come on, Jersey." His mother grabs my hand and drags me out of the VIP box. My heart is pounding in my ears the whole way. I can't seem to stop the incessant anxiety-ridden thoughts from ricocheting through my mind.

He didn't get up. Was he moving? Was he breathing?
Why didn't he get up?
Is he going to be okay? He's gotta be okay.

She leads the way down to the team quarters of the stadium. It's a wonder I walked at all the way my ankles are wobbling in my boots. Time seems to disappear until Hayes's mother stops one of the trainers walking toward the diagnostic room.

"I'm Hayes Vogt's mother," she explains and points to her husband and then to me. "This is his father and Hayes's girlfriend."

The trainer's eyes flash between the three of us, but then she nods. "Hayes is getting his preliminary check right now. He took a hard hit to the knee." I blink rapidly, willing the burning behind my eyes to disappear. Hayes's parents are both cool, calm, and collected, listening intently and nodding as if this is not their first rodeo. It likely isn't with a quarterback for a son. "We're still trying to determine what the next course of action will be. We're discussing transporting him to the hospital so he can get an MRI. That way we'll have a good sense of what we're dealing with, but he's done with this game."

The trainer gives us a grim look before heading back into the diagnostic room, leaving me standing with his parents in the hallway, watching as the doors to the medical room swing shut. Wrapping my hands around my torso, I try not to shiver, but it's no use. It's just as warm down here as it was in the VIP suite, but full body shakes take over.

Hayes's mom wraps her arms around me and leads us to a place where we can sit and wait. A cell phone ringing cuts through the heavy silence and Hayes's dad pulls his phone out of his pocket, glancing at the screen. He locks eyes with his wife and tilts his head toward his phone. "It's Riley."

"We're fine here," his mother says and gives her husband the go-ahead. He walks away, putting his phone to his ear.

"Hey, kiddo . . . Yeah, we're waiting to hear what the diagnosis is," he says gently to his daughter.

My chest feels tight, and I try to take a deep breath, counting down from fifty as I lean against Hayes's mom. "What happens to a quarterback if he busts his knee?" I ask her quietly.

She smooths her hand over my hair and rocks us back and forth. "It depends on what he injured. He may need surgery or he may be able to get by with physical therapy. His doctors will have more answers for us."

"Will he be able to play again?" My voice is shaky as I voice my fear. I hate that I'm feeling so vulnerable, but my worry for her son seems to overshadow anything else right now.

"I hope so, sweetheart," she whispers, holding me close in a way only a mother knows how.

When I finally pull away from his mom a few minutes later, I wipe my face and force out a humorless laugh. "Sorry."

She gives me a kind smile. "It's okay, sweetheart. There's nothing to apologize for." I wipe my nose, embarrassed by the way it's dripping down my face from my tears. His mother politely doesn't comment on that fact. "Would you like to stay here and wait for him? Or go back home?"

Home.

It's not home without him, though.

My throat feels tight. "I'll wait for him."

We sit together for a few more minutes, long enough for Hayes's dad to return from his phone call with Riley. I regain control of my breathing but continue to count down from fifty, starting over each time I make it to zero. Inside, I'm telling myself that Hayes is okay, he's not seriously injured. His trainers and medical team will take care of it.

"You know, I remember the very first time Hayes had an injury on the field," she says. Her voice is level, calm, as if her son isn't in there having medical tests run on him. Turning to her husband, she asks. "Do you remember?"

He nods and leans against the wall. "How could I forget? He was a freshman in high school, starting out on junior varsity."

I turn to her in anticipation. "Yeah? How did you cope?"

She chuckles, her eyes glazing over as she recalls the memory. "He was so excited to be playing, and in his very first game, he got tackled right to the ground and ended up spraining his ankle so bad he had to sit out half the season."

I already know this event probably shaped who Hayes would become as a player for the rest of his career. "What did he do?"

"Oh, he was so upset those first few days," she says, nodding to herself. "But then after that, he seemed to look at things differently. He still attended every game, even on those crutches, and he watched, and he paid attention. When he finally got back into the game himself, he had a broader understanding of what was expected of him in that role."

"Wow."

A fond expression appears on her face as she remembers her son at that age. "That's Hayes. His whole life, he's always been one to look at the glass half full whenever he can, rather than letting circumstances get him down."

"Do you think he's upset about this?" I ask.

"Undoubtedly. But he'll find that silver lining. And I'm sure it will have a lot to do with you being by his side." She leans toward me and nudges my shoulder with her own. "I'm so glad you've found each other. He's been alone for far too long."

I give her a sad smile. "I don't think he's been alone at all. I don't know how he could be with parents like you and Andy. You've raised an amazing man," I tell her, my voice soft. I peer up at his father to see him watching me with glassy eyes. "It's been a privilege to know him."

Merilee gives me a warm smile. "He has said the exact same thing about you, dear."

I can't get over how much they love him.

How much I've grown to love him.

The fluttering in my belly and soul-crushing affection I feel whenever I'm with him only confirms the feelings. I am completely in love with Hayes. Watching him drop to the field and not pop right back up has activated a whole new kind of fear inside of me—the fear of being unable to experience this life without him. Being robbed of sharing the highs, and the lows, and everything in between with *him*. Somehow, this man has finagled his way into the deepest recesses of my heart and set up camp there, with no hope of ever leaving.

Not that I want him to leave. Ever since Hayes has come into my life, I've known nothing but happiness and contentment. I can't picture a version of my life he's not a part of.

Time ceases to exist for a while as I'm lost in my hopeless thoughts of infatuation over him, but finally, I hear that low voice that knows the exact tune of my heart and soul call my name.

"Jersey." As soon as I hear his voice, I straighten my neck, catching sight of Hayes on the stretcher as they wheel him out of the diagnostic room. He stops the EMTs right before they adjust the stretcher to load him into the emergency rig.

In a few long strides, I'm next to him, taking his hand and squeezing it tight. "Hey there, handsome." I curse when one traitorous tear sneaks out of the corner of my right eye and falls down my cheek.

Hayes's amber eyes track the movement, and he squeezes my hand. He plasters on a tight smile and, in a shaky voice, says, "I'll be okay. It's just a scratch."

I laugh through the emotion that's threatening to explode out of me and shake my head. He and I both know this isn't *just a scratch.*

"They're sending me to the hospital for an MRI." His face is pale, missing that usual luster it usually has. I can only imagine that his thoughts are running a mile a minute, thinking about what this injury could mean for the rest of his season. "Will you guys meet me there?"

"Of course we will, sweetheart," his mother answers, stepping up behind me and placing her hand on my shoulder.

Hayes meets my eyes again and I notice his typical glint is gone, replaced by a deep-seated worry. "Jersey, will you take my car? It's still in team parking from yesterday before we were bused to the hotel. The keys are in my bag. That way, we can go straight home whenever they release me."

"Of course."

Hayes nods and then drags my hand closer so he can kiss the back of it before letting me go.

His trainers and the EMTs get him settled in the ambulance and close the doors behind him. His parents wait with me while his trainers collect his bag and personal items from the locker room before handing them to me.

We do a lot more waiting at the hospital in a private waiting area while Hayes is with his doctors. The entire time I seem to hold my breath, my chest aching with the pressure of the unknown. Eventually, a nurse comes out to tell us Hayes has finished all the necessary testing and is ready to go home.

Hayes looks weathered as they wheel him out in a wheelchair, and I can tell he doesn't want to be here right now dealing with this—he wants to be with his team.

I stand up and hurry over to him, wrapping my arms around his neck and kissing the side of his cheek. "Are you okay?" I ask, stepping back and giving his mom the chance to hug him too. His father claps him on the shoulder.

"Yeah," he says, his voice gruff. "As good as I can be, I guess."

"Will you need surgery?" his mom asks, cupping her hands on his cheeks and hitting him with that motherly worry.

He lifts his head again. "Unsure yet. I'm supposed to meet with the orthopedic surgeon tomorrow to go over next steps."

"Well, we'll deal with whatever happens, right?" his mom says, attempting to be optimistic.

He gives her a tight smile. It's not his usual happy expression, hinting at his inner turmoil beneath the mask he's putting on for his mom. "We sure will." He glances between all of us. "Do you know how the game ended?" When no one answers right away, he deflates. "Was it bad?"

Andy grimaces and nods.

Hayes drops his head to his chest and huffs out a long breath. "Damn it." He takes a moment, his jaw muscle ticking. He seems defeated when he turns to me. "Can we go home now?"

My throat tightens and I nod. "Of course."

"Will you drive? They doped me up on some muscle relaxers and pain meds."

We take our time as we make our way to the exit. While we walk, I call the number for the hospital's valet to bring the car around to the front doors. The minute we step out of the hospital's doors, we're swarmed by reporters and cameras. Their questions fly at us, each one sending my nerves on edge.

"Hayes, how are you feeling?"

"Mr. Vogt, do you think you'll be back in the game next week?"

"Hayes, what did your doctors say?"

"Jersey, do you feel guilty for distracting Hayes?"

"Jersey, how is your new album coming along?"

"Jersey, is it true you're dating Corey Shrader again, too?"

I know they're doing their jobs, trying to get the shot of Hayes's current state after such a significant injury, but they're only making a difficult situation harder.

Against my better judgment, I swing around and glower at them. "Don't you all have something better to do? Leave us alone!"

Hayes eyes me with an eyebrow raised and holds out his hand for me. I weave my fingers through his and we focus again on getting to the car, keeping our heads down. The car is waiting for us right outside, so it's not too much of a hassle.

He settles into the passenger seat, and I hop into the driver's side. As I pull out of the parking lot, I scowl at the reporters still snapping photos of our departure. They have no understanding of privacy.

All my irritation disappears once we're on the road, and Hayes quietly says, "I'm glad you were there tonight."

"Me too," I whisper, turning to him.

He exhales and rolls his head along the headrest to give me a somber smile. "I had great plans to bring home a win tonight. Sorry for disappointing."

The emotion that I had discovered, but tucked away for later, comes rearing back at full force and my eyes burn. I will it back, blinking rapidly and focus on the road. Overcome with love for this man who is always so focused and driven, I extend my hand over the console, wanting to ease his hurt in any way I can while still getting us home safely.

He threads his fingers through mine, and I squeeze his hand. With every fiber of my being, I reassure him. "Hayes, you could never disappoint me."

"The good and the bad, right?" he asks, a muted twinkle appearing in his eye.

I nod, my eyes starting to burn again. "And everything in between."

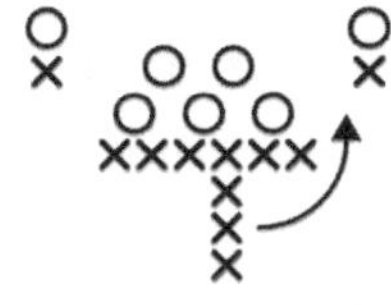

hayes

MONDAY, DECEMBER 23

THE DOCTOR'S grim expression clues me into the severity of what's going on and the set of Coach's jaw really drives it home.

"Well?" I ask, leaning forward and ignoring the shot of pain the movement sends through my injured knee.

"You're gonna need surgery," my doctor confirms. "We're looking at a grade three ACL tear, and we're going to need to reattach it if you want to continue playing long term. Unfortunately, with an injury like this, you've got a long road of recovery ahead of you."

I roll my lips into a tight line. "So, I'm out."

"For the rest of this season, at least. We'll get you into physical therapy and slowly work you back up into the swing of things with your training. Full recovery can take anywhere from eight months to a year, but as long as you keep to your regimen with your trainers, you should be ready to go for preseason in August."

Coach exhales deeply next to me and my stomach churns with annoyance. One bad play and I'm out for the season.

"Okay, so what's next? Surgery? How quickly can we get in there and do that?"

"I'd say let's schedule it right after New Year's. Then that will still give you the full offseason to rehab and start building up strength."

"We have to wait?" I ask him, my frustration growing. "Why can't we get it over and done with?"

He gives me a steady stare. "That's not how it works. We've gotta let some of the inflammation in that knee go down first. We'll get you in some physical therapy starting tomorrow, but the surgery will have to wait a few weeks."

I lean my head back and groan. This is not what I was hoping to hear today. "Okay, fine. Schedule it for January second. Then how long will I be out of commission?"

"You'll have to take it easy for the first week, but then you can start putting weight on it and building up strength shortly thereafter."

I look over to Coach, who's already waiting for my reaction. "This is going to ruin the season," I mutter.

He nods. "That it is, son. But there's always next season." He claps me on the shoulder. "Our focus now should be getting you better as soon as possible so we can come back with a vengeance next year."

"So now it's a waiting game?" I confirm with the doctor and my coach. They both give me pitying looks and nod somberly. Reaching for the crutches that are leaning up on my doctor's desk, I rise from my chair. Extending my hand for a handshake, I thank the doctor and hobble out of the room.

Coach follows closely behind me, and together we walk down the hallway of the performance center and into the office wing of the performance center. I limp in, letting him close the door behind me. I collapse into the chair in front of his desk and bury my face in my hands—a position I've grown fond of in the last twenty-four hours.

To say I'm frustrated with this turn of events would be putting it lightly. I know no one is holding the injury against me except myself—it was an accident. It happened in a split second, with no maneuvering out of the situation.

How many times have I been tackled in my career? Far too many to count. I know the drill by this point, know how to position my body in a split second to protect myself as best I can when I have two-hundred-plus pounds landing on top of me.

We train and train for this, how to land, how to get back up, but even then, sometimes that's not enough.

The guilt eats at me though from the inside out.

I should've seen it coming. I should've had more foresight. I should've gotten out of the way.

The pressure that comes with leading a team at this level is unrelenting.

I couldn't sleep last night, only able to picture the injury in slow motion, allowing me to see every millisecond that went wrong.

The only thing saving me from falling into complete insanity is Jersey. She held me close last night, and whispered that she was proud of me over and over, until I was able to get some rest.

I can't express how grateful I am that she's here to help me through the worst two days of my professional career.

Knowing that she's there, in my corner, ready to support me through this gives me the strength that I need to push through.

I've been putting on a brave face since the injury yesterday, knowing there's not much I can do about this situation. The cracks are starting to appear though, and it's fraying me apart at the seams.

How could I have let this happen?

Will my team ever forgive me?

Will I even *have* a team to come back to?

Of course, I know that even with this injury, I'm still under contract. I know Coach won't give up on me that easily.

It's still so difficult to push down the feelings of failure and see the silver lining when we had such a promising season ahead of us.

The pressure of Coach's hand on my shoulder forces me to bury my feelings down the rest of the way and put on that brave face I know everyone is expecting of me.

"Sorry," I mutter, dejected.

He pats my shoulder and then takes the seat next to me. "We'll work through this, Hayes. We've dealt with worse punches thrown our way."

I force a dry laugh, appreciative of the lie. Sure, the team has dealt with a number of scandals over the years—substance abuse and sexual assault charges—things that Coach and the rest of the administration have a strict no tolerance policy on.

But a bum quarterback?

That's a first for us.

At least since I've been a part of this franchise.

We spend so many hours in the gym, practicing, doing agility work, getting physical training all in the hopes of avoiding an event like this.

Inevitably, it still happens. All season reports are broadcasted about severe injuries to quarterbacks. I mean, that's why we have backup players who run the exact same plays and drills that the primary QBs run.

It's all a failsafe to make sure the team is not completely screwed if something happens to its playmaker.

All this preparation for worst-case scenarios.

Yet I never imagined it would happen to me.

"It will all work out in the end, Hayes," Coach says, eyeing me. "We'll run through the rest of the season, see how far we can take it, and then regroup next year once you're back to one hundred."

Something boils in my chest, frustration, irritation—not at Coach, but at myself. For letting this happen.

"I should probably get to work on this physical therapy," I say. "No better time than the present to keep this knee as strong as possible." My face falls and I'm filled with dread. "Before they cut it open."

It's a scary thought, going under the knife when my entire career rests on my physical ability to perform. What if something goes haywire? What if they sever a nerve and I'm never able to walk right on my leg again?

Of course, I have utmost faith in our medical team here with the organization, but even still, the negative outcomes attack me at an overwhelming speed before I can stop them.

"You're not the first QB to tear an ACL," Coach says, his voice even. "And you won't be the last."

He pats me on the shoulder again and stands up. I'm grateful for the mild *come-to-Jesus* statement. He's right.

I've got to stop feeling sorry for myself and get my head back in the game. Sure, I'm out for the season, but I've got a lot more seasons left in me.

"Thanks, Coach," I tell him. Dropping my eyes and nodding, taking his words to heart.

I hear him take a deep sigh in and let it out in a *whoosh*. "Why don't you head on home? Get some rest tonight and I'll check in with you tomorrow. I'm sure the performance team will have their PT schedule worked out for you by then and I'll have them email it over."

It's weird being dismissed from his office knowing I have no purpose to serve the team other than moral support for the rest of the season.

Standing up, I offer my hand to Coach and he gives me a firm shake, dipping his chin at me. "Don't beat yourself up too much, Hayes. It's out of your hands now."

I exhale sharply. "I know. That might be the part that sucks the most."

Coach presses his lips into a thin line and nods. "Yeah, I can understand that. We'll chat more tomorrow, okay? Go get some rest. Oh, and Hayes, don't read the headlines."

With one last handshake, I leave his office and make my way down to where I'll wait for my driver. During the short drive from the performance center to my house, I do pull up the headlines.

"Pure panic in the Majestics locker room: 'Where do we go from here?'"

"Season-ending injury for Vogt and the Majestics"

"Pop sensation responsible for football star's poor concentration resulting in injury"

My driver pulls up at the front stoop, and I angrily shove my phone into my pocket. Hopefully Jersey hasn't seen these. It's horseshit! Lying fuckers! "Thanks, man. See you soon," I tell my driver as calmly as I can. He doesn't deserve my wrath.

I take a deep breath and make my way inside the house. As I walk into the living room, I hear Jersey in an animated conversation.

"No, I'm telling you, I won't be there . . . I don't know, Cal, but figure it out." She groans. "Hayes's injury is severe. It's not just a sprained ankle. I'm staying here with him, and that's final."

My heart thuds as I peek into the living room to see her with her headphones in, phone in hand, glowering down at her planner in front of her. And all my concerns with the media are forgotten. I can deal with that as it comes.

"I'll be back in the New Year, and we can figure out rescheduling then, or you can email Bethany and she'll take care of it for me. She has my tentative schedule, and she's aware of the situation." She sucks in a breath and turns around, sensing my presence. She holds up one finger, giving me a tight smile. "Cal, for once, *please* don't be such an ass. We'll talk later."

She hangs up and then pulls her earbuds out of her ears, standing up and coming over to see me. "Hey there!" Her voice is lighter than I was expecting, given the nature of her last conversation. "How'd it go with the doc?" she asks as soon as she's in front of me. She runs her hand down the side of my face, her brown eyes searching every inch of me.

An unusual sense of panic runs through me and I'm quick to deflect. "Oh, it was fine." For some reason, telling Jersey that I'm out for the season makes it more real, and I'm not ready to admit that out loud to her yet. "What have you been up to?"

Jersey tilts her head to the side, noting my quick change of subject but apparently choosing not to question me. She glances back toward her phone sitting on the table. "Callum's been calling me relentlessly since he caught wind of your injury. He's pissed that I left—he's under some sort of delusion that since you're injured, I should be high-tailing it back to LA" She closes her eyes, shaking her head as she lets out a heavy, frustrated breath. "Before he called this last time, I was listening to a few demos he sent over for the songs I'll be working on next time I'm in the studio."

I'm much more comfortable talking about Jersey and her career—now that mine is pretty much over for the season. It bothers me that her manager has been on her ass for taking some time off to be with me, but I know there's not much she can do about the situation. I'm thankful that she wants to stick around while I'm recuperating.

"Will you sing them for me?" I ask.

She rolls her eyes and waves me off before walking back into the living room and settling on the couch. I follow after her on my crutches, trying to fight the smirk off my face, already anticipating her answer. "If I sing for you, it's going to be something *I* wrote, not something these big wigs at the studio pieced together. Trust me, it's not really worth hearing until it's all finalized."

I know by now that Jersey is not the biggest fan of what her label provides for her. At the very heart of it, I couldn't care less about the lyrics or the words. I appreciate the sound of her voice.

Leaning my crutches against the arm of the sofa, I fall into the cushions next to her and elevate my busted knee on the table. Opening my arm for her, Jersey wastes no time settling into my side and resting her head on my shoulder. I trace light patterns over the smooth skin of her arm and lean my head back against the back of the couch, closing my eyes and breathing deeply.

I know I have to say it out loud. I have to admit it to Jersey and, more importantly, admit it to myself. "I'm done for the season."

"Are you okay?" she asks softly a few moments later. Her voice is timid, like she's afraid to question me. She hasn't asked this question outright yet, but I've seen it in her eyes ever since we got home last night. She's curious to know how I am, but not confident enough that I'll let her in on the inner workings of my mind.

I will though. Of course, I will. I'd do anything for her.

"I don't know," I admit and a pain rises in my chest. With my free hand not wrapped around Jersey's shoulders, I rub at my sternum, trying to ease the discomfort. "I will be . . . eventually."

Her delicate hand falls on my chest, right over my heart, and I cover it with mine, loving the way her small fingers fit in mine.

"I wish there was something I could do," she whispers.

"You're doing it," I reassure her, turning my head and pressing my lips to her forehead. I mean it. I can't imagine what dark place I'd be in if she weren't here with me. "I'll bounce back. It's just a tough pill to swallow at first. This is the first time I've had to take a step back in my professional career. I'm trying to make peace with that."

She's quiet for a moment, then she says, "Your mom told me about your ankle injury your freshman year of high school."

I chuckle to myself, remembering those days and how important everything felt back then. I never thought I'd be where I am today—dreamed it, sure, but never actually imagined I'd be the lucky one.

"She said you're always a *glass-half-full* kind of guy."

"I try to be," I say.

"But you're allowed to be sad too," Jersey says, pulling back a bit so I can see her eyes. She has this way of staring directly into my soul that sends shivers down my spine. "You're allowed to be sad for now, but then you have to get up and come back even stronger."

I run my hand over her head, tucking a few stray strands behind her ear. "How'd I get so lucky to have you in my life?"

She fights off a smile. "You made the effort. And that means a lot in my book."

Leaning forward, I claim her lips in a gentle kiss, savoring her and thanking every other fool she had in her life for letting her go so she could find her way to me.

jersey

WEDNESDAY, DECEMBER 25

"*JERSEY*," a sing-song voice whispers in my ear, startling me awake. I groan into the soft pillows and stretch. "Wake up, Jersey."

Slowly, I flutter my eyelids open to see Hayes staring down at me, scruffy stubble lining his jaw and his eyes bright with excitement. I stretch again, fighting off the grin at seeing that level of affection in his eyes.

He leans down and presses a kiss to the tip of my nose. "Wakey, wakey."

"Too early," I mumble, still grinning despite the ungodly hour.

"It's ten o'clock." He laughs.

"*Too early.*" My eyes squeeze shut again and I will sleep to overtake me.

"It's Christmas." He runs his nose along my jaw before placing another kiss by the crook of my ear. "And there are cinnamon rolls waiting for you downstairs."

I open one eye and my mouth involuntarily waters at the thought. "Cinnamon rolls?"

Hayes leans back and gives me another shit-eating grin. "Yup, but you gotta get out of bed if you want one."

"Ugh, so mean," I grumble. Despite myself, I toss back the covers and step into the bathroom so I can put in my contacts and wash away the remnants of sleep from my eyes.

When I emerge, Hayes is lounging on the bed, arms tucked behind his head. He eyes me with a smirk on his face.

"What?" I ask him, suspiciously.

"Nothing. Just like the sight of you walking around my bedroom, like it's yours."

My cheeks flush and I pull one of Hayes's shirts out of his dresser as well as a pair of my own underwear from my drawer. His shirt swallows me, acting like a loose-fitting dress, falling past my hips. "So, about these cinnamon rolls?"

Hayes pushes himself off the bed, still limping quite a bit from the knee injury that's only a few days old. He's taken to hobbling around with his crutches and using me as a support whenever necessary—which suspiciously is *all the time*. I tend to think he likes to be touching me at every possible opportunity.

Not that I'm complaining.

Slowly, we make it down to the kitchen, passing by the living room on the way. I nearly stop dead in my tracks when I catch sight of his Christmas tree standing proudly next to the fireplace. It's not the tree that's giving me pause, or even the sight of Periwinkle sitting on the couch in a Santa hat and a red plaid sweater, but rather the presents sitting underneath.

"Hayes," I say, breathlessly. He follows my line of sight and chuckles.

"Some are for my parents and Riley, too. They'll be over later today to exchange gifts," he answers my lingering, silent question. His parents stayed in town after his injury and are staying at a hotel not too far from his house. Riley flew into Milwaukee last night, and I can't wait to meet her.

A sense of relief overcomes me. Hayes and I agreed to exchange Christmas presents this year, even though we've only officially been dating a few months. I definitely didn't go overboard with my gifts, so I would've felt guilty if he had.

"Come on." He tilts his head sideways. "Breakfast first, presents later."

In the kitchen, I find a pan of melty cinnamon rolls waiting for us, along with some coffee. I plate up two of them each and place them on a tray along with mugs of coffee to take back into the living room so we can eat by the light of the glittering Christmas tree.

After Hayes settles in his seat, finding a comfortable position for his knee, we waste no time digging into the cinnamon rolls before they get cold.

"Oh my gosh," I mutter, shooting him an impressed glance. "This is incredible."

He chuckles and then leans forward, wiping his thumb along my bottom lip, collecting the icing that slipped from my bite. I track his movements, watching as he takes his thumb and sticks it in his mouth, licking the frosting off.

"You give me too much credit," he says once he's finished licking the frosting off his finger. "These are just the canned ones."

"Well, they're good anyway," I say with a shrug, taking another bite.

We both polish off our breakfasts in record time, unable to help ourselves from the warm, sweet treat. Once our plates are empty, I collect and take them back into the kitchen. When I come back, I gather up the presents from underneath the tree, carrying them over and placing them on the cushion between us.

Hayes picks up a small box wrapped flawlessly with a shiny silver bow on the top and hands it to me. Once the package is in my hands, I tease, "Did you wrap this?"

He chuckles. "Hell no. My housekeeper helped me out. If I had wrapped them, they would not be nearly as fancy."

Fighting off a smile, I start on the edge, sliding my finger under the paper and opening it up delicately.

"Oh, come on, just rip it," Hayes teases. I blink at him, unsure that I've ever ripped a present open since I was a child. My cheeks warming a bit, I do as he says, clumsily ripping the paper and finding I enjoy it much more this way. Beneath the discarded wrapping paper lies an unmistakable jewelry box.

Carefully, I lift the lid and reveal the present inside. My breath catches in my throat at the sight of it—a gold-plated number eighteen necklace, Hayes's jersey number. Across the front are a multitude of diamonds, or what I suspect are diamonds.

"Are these real?"

Hayes nods, watching me warily to see if I like his gift. I'm speechless really. I can't imagine how much something like this would've cost him. Though I know with Hayes's yearly contract, it's probably a measly drop in the bucket. He doesn't act like he's loaded, but there's no doubt he's living comfortably like the rest of the big name football players in the league.

"Wow," I whisper, studying the necklace again. My fingers run over the beveled edge and the ridges of the diamonds. "This is beautiful."

I hear him swallow next to me. "Do you like it?"

"I love it," I correct him. "Will you put it on me?"

Hayes's eyes go soft. "Of course. Come here."

His instructions send butterflies through my belly, and I hop off the couch to the floor, positioning myself in front of him and handing over the necklace before pulling my hair off my neck.

I hear him fumble with the packaging, trying to get the dainty necklace out of the box using his big hands. Then he's reaching around my head, positioning the necklace and clasping it at the back. When he's done, he leans down and kisses my shoulder next to the strap of my tank top, sending tingles down that entire side of my body.

"Let me see," he says against my skin, his voice husky and low.

I turn around ungracefully on my knees, dropping my hair off to one side. Hayes takes me in, his chin lifting and a proud smile gracing his lips.

"Fuck, honey. I love the sight of my number on your body," he rumbles, eyes glued to the pendant lying on top of my breastbone. His praise sends my head spinning with sensations I don't think I'll ever get over—passion, adoration, longing.

"I like the way it feels on my body," I say, my cheeks heating with the admission.

Hayes seems to like that and his eyes darken. His voice is a low growl when he says, "I'm going to need you to open your next one before I take you right here in front of the Christmas tree."

I laugh to myself, reaching for the second smaller box that he gave me and setting it in my lap. To be honest, I wouldn't mind a little sexy interlude, but with Hayes's injury still so new, I know that is unlikely to happen right now. Hopefully next year we'll be able to make plenty new memories of us making love in front of the Christmas tree.

"Here, it's your turn now." I hand him a box, feeling giddy

at the prospect of him opening his very first Christmas present from me.

"For me?"

"Just for you." I wink. I picked out a watch for him, engraved on the back with our names and the phrase *Everything In Between*.

Hayes runs his thumb over the engraving and looks at me with deep, emotion filled eyes. The intensity of his amber eyes as he stares at me makes me ache for him. Seeming to catch onto this, he leans over and cups my cheek, kissing me deeply.

When he pulls away, I can tell he's thinking about having sex in front of the Christmas tree again. The idea is enthralling, and I lick my lower lip. His eyes have darkened as he tracks the movement. Moments later, he rakes his gaze over me, appreciating every little inch of me.

My heart feels full as I preen under his gaze. Leaning forward, I kiss him again, wishing I could freeze time. I never thought sharing a Christmas with someone could be so intimate, but I should've known Hayes has a way of making everything so much more exhilarating.

"Thank you," he says, focusing on the watch as he slides it on his wrist. "This is great."

"You're welcome," I whisper, loving the way the watch looks on Hayes's wrist. "I was hoping you'd like it."

"It's honestly perfect. I've been needing a new watch, and now I get to carry a piece of you with me when I wear it. Now open your second one."

My heart skips a beat and I suck in a tight breath, dropping my eyes from him—he couldn't possibly know how spot on his words are.

I waste no time ripping apart the packaging and revealing the box inside. I tear through the thin layer of tape and pull out the Styrofoam box. I *hate* Styrofoam, but I manage to put my ick on the back burner and open up the present.

What's inside is even more stunning, even more breathtaking, than the expensive necklace that's now sitting proudly around my neck.

"Oh my god," I say, taking in the small snow globe in my hands. "This is—"

Before I can finish my sentence, I give it a shake, watching as the snow flits around the globe surrounding the couple sledding down a steep hill, arms wrapped tightly around each other.

"That day was really special to me," Hayes says, his voice sounding thick. "I wanted to commemorate it. I hope it's not too cheesy."

"Not at all," I respond, eyes still glued to the pair on the sled. "Honestly, I don't think I've ever gotten something more thoughtful."

To anyone else, it may appear a trinket, a souvenir, to my time spent here in Wisconsin. But to me, it's the immortalization of when I knew what we had was special, and what we could build together could be something magical.

I'll never forget falling asleep that night, tucked warm and safe against Hayes's bare chest in front of the flickering fireplace. The minute I closed my eyes, I could see it all, exactly what he said. The milestones.

The good. The bad. And everything in between.

Now, more than ever, I want that with him. We've barely begun our journey together, but I know without a doubt that it's going to be the journey, the partnership, of a lifetime.

"Your second present isn't really something tangible," I say. His eyes crease a little in suspicion. "It's more of something I want to share with you."

He's been asking me for this, waiting patiently until I was

ready to share this side of me with him. Share the side of me that only those closest get to see.

My skin feels itchy, but I push my discomfort aside, knowing sharing this vulnerable side of myself with him will be worth it. I know I can trust Hayes, and I want him to know this part of me.

He's watching me intently, waiting for me to share what's on my mind. "Okay." His confusion dissipates, and he waits for me to explain myself further.

Setting the snow globe down, I hold up one finger. "One second."

I bound up the stairs, throwing open the door to Hayes's room and rummage around in the closet to find my stashed guitar. Unbuckling the case, I run my fingers over the smooth strings of the instrument and pull it out, hoisting it up into my arms and setting the strap around my shoulders before going back to the living room.

Hayes is waiting patiently. When I round the corner, his eyes widen as he takes in the guitar in my hands.

I brace myself and raise my chin, knowing that this is an important moment for the both of us.

"I want to sing for you. One of my songs."

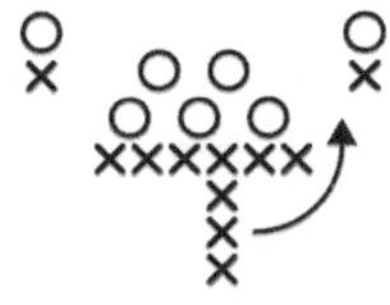

THIRTY-ONE

hayes

WEDNESDAY, DECEMBER 25

MY HEART FEELS like it has jumped into my throat.

"Really?" I ask her gently, worried that if I speak too loudly her offer will disappear into thin air.

Jersey settles back into her spot next to me and wrings her hands in her lap. Her normally full lips are pressed into a tight line and her typically glittering eyes are more reserved.

She gives me a small nod and shies away from my gaze. "I've only ever played my original songs for a few people. It's not something I share easily. Maybe someday I'll be able to share my words with the world, but until then, they're the biggest part of my identity that I still claim for myself."

"This one's called *A Piece of Me*," she says, reverently.

I start a bit, understanding now why she averted her eyes when I said I would carry a piece of her with me a few moments ago.

Her eyes find mine and I still see the trepidation behind them. I clear my throat and give her hand a squeeze. "I hope you know by now how much you mean to me, and that I'd do anything to protect you. I'll do the same for your words. It means the world to me that you're trusting me with something so sacred. I promise I don't take that lightly."

Her gaze softens, and she looks down at the guitar in her lap. Untangling her hands from mine, she places them on the strings and then takes a deep breath, blowing it out and then starting the first chord progression.

I sit back and watch her work her magic.

Her voice echoes through the living room, swirling and taking shape as if it's an entity all its own. Similar to the first time I saw her perform, I find myself falling under her spell. Her words wrap around me and consume my every thought.

As she finishes the first verse and begins the chorus she opened with, I reflect on the meaning. Her words are descriptive, all coming together to tell the story of where she started and ultimately—what I'm assuming—is leading to where she is today.

Her tone grows stronger once she hits the crescendo of her chorus. Her eyes flash to mine and she fights off a smile, clearly appreciating how I'm hanging on her every word.

How could I not? She's an artist, weaving together pieces of the English language to create the most intricate story, highlighting her journey and her struggles.

I'm mesmerized by her, fully and irrevocably entranced.

All that's left
Is a piece of me
A piece of my soul
That's broken and blue
It's one regret, a broken dream
Begging to be true
Leaving behind

Only a piece for you

Jersey's struggle with her creative identity is one I know she's been dealing with for most of her career. She's hinted at the level of despair she has about not being granted any creative freedom, but this song alone shows me that those feelings run far deeper than what she's hinted at.

Jersey transitions into the bridge of the song, taking the melody and changing the key a bit so it stands out. Subconsciously or not, her posture changes as she gets ready to lead into this next section. Her shoulders square, her spine straightens, and the wistful expression she has on her face morphs into one of determination.

They won't stop me
I'll keep trying
I'll keep going
Never backing down
I'll never give up
I'll never stop fighting
Until all that's left are the words
That together create a piece of me

She strums a few more chords and hums along to the melody, her face taking on that wistful expression once again. My pulse is pounding in my ears, mixing with the beat of her song.

Slowly, she finishes out the song and then lets the final note linger a bit longer, dissolving into the silence of the room around us.

Our gazes lock and I suck in a deep breath, unable to put into words what I'm feeling. It's a mix of admiration that I got to listen to a personal concert performed by her, and gratitude that she'd show me the most intimate parts of herself.

Slowly, I reach for her, taking the neck of her guitar and

carefully setting it off to the side. She tracks my every move, watching with interest to see what I'll do next.

When her guitar is safely placed next to her, I wrap my hand around her wrist, urging her closer to me.

"Come here," I murmur. She comes willingly, not needing much coaxing until she's climbing back onto the couch.

I shift a bit, wincing as I find a comfortable angle for my knee. Jersey crawls closer toward me and tucks herself into my side, leaning her head on my shoulder and snuggling into me.

Her breath fans across my lips as I regard her. She traces the angles of my jaw with her thumb, eyes staring soulfully into mine.

"What did you think?" she asks me, her voice a whisper.

"I think you amaze me more and more every day," I tell her honestly.

"I wish everyone at the label felt that way when I sang for them," she tries to joke. I can hear the sadness in her voice and it makes me sad for her. Especially knowing what kind of talent she has, what kind of creative touch she possesses for music.

"There's no question in my mind now that Cal and your label are intimidated by you." She pulls back a little, waiting for me to explain. "Your song is amazing, and your voice is . . . unmatched. Together, you'd be the complete package. Can you imagine what kind of power that would give you?"

She shrugs one shoulder, but I can see she's hanging on my every word.

"You'd have people falling at your feet, traveling across the world to see you, to get a *piece of you*." My voice falls soft. "The power you'd wield would send the entire place into a tailspin. They're only telling you no because they're not willing to let go of their control over your career."

"You think so?"

"Jersey, *I know so*," I say with conviction.

Something shifts in her gaze and she leans forward, closing the distance between us until our chests are pressed together and her nose runs along the length of mine. I guide her to move from my side onto my lap. Once settled, her thighs on either side of mine and her hands resting on my shoulders, she pauses for a moment, letting the tension build between us before she presses her lips to mine, kissing me tentatively.

I can't seem to help myself though, and my hand snakes up from her waist to cup the back of her neck. She makes a mewling sound as she kisses me, wrapping her arms around my neck and arching her back.

My fingers tangle in her hair and I angle her head to the exact position I want her in so I can kiss her deeply. I pour everything that I can't say with words into this kiss, and I hope she can feel it.

I want her to know how awestruck I am by her.

I want her to know that I think she's the most amazing and wonderful woman I've ever met.

I want her to be confident that she can be whatever version of herself she wants to be, even if it seems impossible right now.

There's so much more I wish I could put into words, but they seem to escape me the longer she kisses me—flitting from my brain like a whisper in the wind.

Maybe it's the painkillers doing their magic, or maybe it's her, but I barely feel the ache in my knee, too transfixed by this woman sitting on my lap.

Her nails gently scrape down the length of my arms, and she threads our fingers together.

I'll never tire of Jersey's touch all over my body. Every inch she graces comes alive with desire and yearning for her. I pull away, staring down at her with hooded eyes, and wondering how the fuck I got to be so fortunate to get to have these quiet moments with her.

My life has never felt more complete than it does right now with Jersey in my lap and her hands all over me. God, now that I've experienced what it's like to have her here, I can't imagine a world where she's not.

The mere thought has my heart constricting to painful levels, and to ease some of the ache, I untangle our hands and wrap my arms around her, drawing her closer to me until there're only inches between us.

Finding her lips again, I kiss her tenderly, breathing her in and memorizing her taste. She kisses me back, matching my enthusiasm.

It's all I can do to commit this moment to memory—focusing on how absolutely flawless she is. Her passion and her depth, her thoughtfulness and her dedication. I'm the luckiest man in the world to have the privilege of experiencing the intimate parts of Jersey Matthews—both physical and otherwise.

I wonder if she was meant for me all along, if all these years I've had so many failed relationships, all in the name of finding her someday.

I'm one lucky fool.

"Fuck, you look so hot right now," I mutter, and she preens with the praise. My fingers tow with the curled ends of her hair, twisting the silky strands between the pads of my thumb and forefinger.

"Am I hurting you?" Worry appears in her gaze.

"Absolutely not." I can't imagine the disappointment of her stopping. I appreciate her worry for my post-injured self, but really, she's up high enough on my thighs that her grinding over my cock isn't hurting me at all, in fact, quite the opposite. "There's too many clothes between us still."

She arches a dark brow and she bats her eyelashes at me. "Oh yeah?"

"Yeah." I lean forward and nibble on her earlobe as my fingers reach for the hem of my T-shirt she's wearing. Slowly, I raise it up and over her shoulders and head. "Hmm. That's a little better."

My mouth waters at the sight of her, topless, sitting in my lap in only a pair of black lace panties. The gold necklace around her neck glints in the light of the Christmas tree, accentuating my number across her chest. I don't think I've ever seen anything sexier than her right now. Her nipples harden, under my gaze, begging for my attention.

"Now what?" She's breathless, her cheeks flushed and her eyes wide as she waits for her next instruction. I love this side of her, and I love that I'm the only one who gets to see it.

A wicked smile appears on my face. "Take off your underwear."

THIRTY-TWO

jersey

WEDNESDAY, DECEMBER 25

WHEN HAYES'S doorbell rings not long later—after we've both showered and put on presentable clothes—I pop up from the couch. "I'll get it." I'd be lying if I said I wasn't a little excited to see his mom again and finally have the chance to meet Riley.

A flutter of butterflies takes flight in my stomach, but I chalk it up to anticipation.

Throwing the door open, I'm immediately greeted by a hug from Hayes's mom. "Oh, Jersey! Merry Christmas!"

I wrap my arms around her shoulders and grin from ear to ear. As soon as she lets me go, I'm engulfed by a similar hug from his dad. He pats my back and then lets me go, placing his large hands on my shoulders and holding me at arm's length.

He smiles, his eyes crinkling in the corner. He pats my shoulders again before letting me go. Then he bends down to pick up a large tote bag full of ornately wrapped presents. Eyeing the Christmas tree, Andy heads into the living room to deliver the gifts, like a younger, trimmer, Santa Claus.

Following closely behind him is a young woman, watching me with wide eyes, as if she can't believe that I'm standing there in front of her. I step forward and hold out my hand.

"You must be Riley. I'm Jersey."

She blinks a few times, looking down at my hand before taking it. "Wow, you're shorter than I thought you'd be. Not that you're short . . . but—I'll stop talking now."

I can't help but laugh. "Most people are surprised by that. My show costumes are all paired with either high-heeled boots or tall platform shoes, so I don't look small compared to my backup dancers."

"Uh, how tall are you?" Riley asks, amusement sparkling in her eyes and looking a bit dazed.

"Five-foot six."

"Right, that's not really *that* short. I'm only a few inches taller than you. I get it from my dad," she tells me.

"Riley, stop fangirling over Jersey," Hayes calls from the living room, ribbing his sister.

She drops my hand like it's made of molten lava and her cheeks heat as she glances at me nervously. "I'm not!"

"Don't listen to him," I tell her, conspiratorially. "Maybe *I'm* fangirling over *you*."

Riley rolls her eyes. "Please."

"Come in here, squirt," Hayes calls, wanting to see his sister.

She shakes her head at me as if to say *"brothers"* but walks into the living room, bending over the couch and giving Hayes a big hug.

I can't help but appreciate the small gesture. It's clear they're fond of each other, and it makes me miss my brother. Distantly, I wonder what Roman's doing for Christmas. I know he's on site for a movie shoot, but I have no idea what that looks like while on set.

I decide I'll have to send him a text later, wish the menace a Merry Christmas.

The rest of us follow Riley's lead, moving into the living room to sit by the Christmas tree. It appears Hayes's mom has helped herself to a cup of coffee and she holds it in both hands as she settles down on the couch at the opposite end of Hayes. She catches my eye and pats the seat between her and her son.

My chest flutters and I take her up on her offer, settling into my position. Hayes rests his arm across the back of the couch, opening up his side for me to fit into.

Cheeks heating, I scoot closer to him. Even though I was in a serious relationship before, there were never many personal displays of affection. Not that Hayes is going over the top, but even still, his assumption that I would curl into his side while his family is here speaks volumes.

A warmth settles inside of me once I'm pressed to his side. He meets my eyes and gives me a soft smile and a wink before looking away.

"I'm impressed, Riley," Hayes says.

"With what?" She tilts her head sideways.

"No screaming, no hyperventilating, no nothing? What gives? I thought for sure you'd trip over your words or your feet when you met her." I elbow Hayes in the side, rolling my eyes.

Riley's cheeks flush a little, but she holds her own against her brother. "I'm not *you*. '*Oh please Jersey take my phone number. Please, Jersey, date me.*'" She puts on her best imitation of Hayes, lowering her voice a few octaves.

I cover my mouth with my hand, stifling my laughter. Hayes playfully glowers at her. "That's not what happened. Is it, Jersey?"

"I don't know. Sounds pretty spot on to me."

The group busts into laughter as Riley reaches over to give

me a fist bump. Hayes pretends to look wounded. "I have the feeling you two are going to be ganging up on me from now on."

"You know we will." I wink at him and lean into him more.

We all chat for a while, eating some of the snacks Hayes's chef prepared for us before Riley takes it upon herself to play Santa. She crawls closer to the tree on her knees, reaching under the fluffy branches and pulling out a package. She reads the tag and then hands it to her mom. The process continues until each of us has a small pile of three to four presents in front of us.

I learn the Vogt family are very orderly when it comes to opening presents. In my family, as soon as the presents are divvied out, it's a free for all and everyone opens their gifts at their own pace, tossing out quick *thank you's* before moving onto the next one. I always take my time, unwrapping the gifts leisurely and appreciating the care that went into the wrapping —a habit I inherited from my mother.

With the Vogt family, every person gets a chance to open one, and everyone takes turns. I'm finding I like the orderliness of the Vogts' traditions, despite having grown up with the chaos and appreciating the sentimentality of those memories. Even though they all take turns with their process, they don't waste time on the wrapping paper, ripping right into it just like Hayes had me do earlier.

Hayes's family turns out to be excellent at giving gifts. They don't go over the top, but I can tell all of their gifts have had a lot of thought put into them. From his parents and Riley, I receive a personalized yearly planner that I can customize and a gift basket full of personal spa-day items like bath bombs, candles, and lotions.

My phone chimes with an incoming text. I pull it out of my back pocket and can't fight the smile off my face when I see the most awkward selfie of my twin giving me a thumbs up while wearing a Santa hat. He probably picked up on my curiosity as to what he was doing today via twin telepathy—which we don't have, but often joke that we do.

ROMAN

Merry Christmas, little sis! 🎅

JERSEY

Merry Christmas! Miss you!

Still smiling, I type out a similar message to my mother and hit send. After, I set my phone down on the table and look around the room at Hayes and his family, feeling just as welcomed with them as I would my own. Over the last few years, it's been a rare occurrence that I would be with my family for any major holidays. Even though it was something I requested, more times than not, the schedule got in the way and I was somewhere else, far away from my family, celebrating on my own or with my close friends.

I might not be with my family this year, but Hayes's family easily welcomes me into their circle as if I'm one of their own. Their love fills me to the brim and reminds me exactly what this holiday is all about.

When the presents have been opened and the discarded wrapping paper is cleared away, Hayes's father stands and rubs his hands together. "All right. Onto the next tradition."

I sit up straighter, watching with interest, when Riley hops up from the couch and bolts into the kitchen. Hayes leans forward, grabbing the remote off the coffee table and turns on his TV, opening up a streaming app.

"What's the next tradition?" I ask, not patient enough to wait and see.

"We always watch *The Santa Clause* after opening presents,"

Hayes explains. He finds the movie on the app and clicks on it, hitting pause before it starts playing.

"I've never seen that one," I admit sheepishly, and Hayes turns to me with wide, surprised eyes.

"How?"

I shrug, feeling a little embarrassed. "We're more of a *Christmas Vacation* and *Home Alone* kind of family."

Hayes nods, as if that's permissible. "Also classics. Can't go wrong with either of them. You'll love this one, though."

Riley comes back moments later with more snacks, a bowl of fresh popcorn and a plate of Christmas cookies. "Here, Jersey, you've got to try these Oreo Balls."

"Better grab the peanut butter for her," Hayes says to his sister.

"What?" Riley asks, and I fight off a smile. "Why peanut butter?"

"Don't ask questions, just do it."

Riley groans but does what he asks, returning with the jar of peanut butter. "Okay, weirdo. I got her the peanut butter. Happy?"

"Exceptionally," Hayes says, rubbing his hand over my back affectionately. My cheeks flush, but my heart sings.

That evening, after the movie and a family dinner, his family gathers their things to return to their hotel. After giving everyone big hugs and sending them off, Hayes and I head back to his room. As soon as Hayes is comfortably in the bed, he opens his arms for me and I snuggle right in, closing my eyes and breathing in his scent. There's still a hint of cologne on his skin from this morning, that clean, fresh smell lingering and surrounding me like a warm blanket.

I don't know when or how it happened, but he's become my home.

Pressing my face against his chest, I listen to the steady thump of his heart, letting it quiet my thoughts.

"Did you have a good Christmas?" Hayes whispers into the darkness. I shift a little bit, hoping to get a glimpse of him in the dark.

"I really did. I'll have to convince my family to watch that movie next year too. I loved it."

"I'll be your backup. They can't say no to both of us." He runs his hand over my hair and my heart aches in a tender way, thinking about all the future Christmases we'll have together. I nestle further into him and sigh.

"I think you made my mom's day," he murmurs quietly.

"How so?"

"She was really worried about what to get you. I told her over and over again that you'd be grateful for anything."

"I loved her gifts," I say, and I mean it. "Really, I don't think I've had such a good Christmas in a long, long time."

"It feels right, having you here with my family." Hayes's voice drops into a tender register and he turns his head a bit, nuzzling his nose against my temple.

The words bubble out of me before I can stop them. I tighten my hold around his torso and say with all of my heart, "I love you, Hayes."

He breaths me in, his hand flexing against my hip to hold me close. "I love you too, Jersey. Thank you for letting me be a part of your life."

I close my eyes and focus on the beat of his heart, slightly faster now than it was before. His thumb on my hip rubs smooth circles. It blows my mind a little bit that Hayes is the one thanking me, when really, I should be the one thanking him.

All it took was a Post-it note and a purpose, and now I can't imagine what my life would look like without him. Without me even realizing it, he has woven himself into the center of my being, and I'm not sure who Jersey Matthews is without the support of Hayes Vogt behind her.

With Hayes on my team, I am stronger than I ever have before. With Hayes, I can be unstoppable.

THIRTY-THREE

jersey

THURSDAY, JANUARY 9

"How's it going over there?" I ask Hayes when he grunts in frustration.

He turns his eyes to me and scowls. A few beads of sweat form along his brow from his band exercises. "This shouldn't be that hard. I'm an NFL quarterback for fuck's sake, and I can't even bend my leg."

I give him an encouraging smile. "You'll be back to a hundred percent soon."

"Hopefully," he grumbles. "I feel like these exercises are going to be the death of me."

"It will pay off." I get up and walk over to him, planting a kiss on his cheek before sitting next to him on the bench. "Maybe you need a change of scenery. I'm heading back to LA next week to start prepping for my upcoming shows. And you'll love how much nicer January feels in LA compared to Wisconsin. It's not crazy hot, but warmer than here."

Hayes gives me a sharp look. "I'm not on a vacation, Jersey.

Playoffs are this weekend. On top of that, I have to meet with the coaches and trainers and come up with a schedule to get me back as soon as possible."

"They can't expect you to be there, can they?" I ask him incredulously. They were quick to get Hayes in for his knee surgery the day after New Years, as planned. "You *just* had surgery a week ago."

"Even still, this rehab won't do itself. My doctors said these early weeks are the most important for my overall outcome. I don't have time to jet off to LA"

"You could do your exercises there. Meet with the training staff virtually."

He shakes his head and frowns down at his knee. "I need to be around for the team too. Hopefully I'll be able to sit on the sidelines and cheer them on. There's so many reasons why it would be better for me to stay home and focus right now. I have to be in the best shape for next season."

My shoulders deflate and I twist my hands in my lap. "I understand."

Moments later, Hayes reaches for my hand and threads our fingers together. With a dejected sigh, he says, "I'm sorry. I didn't mean to get snippy with you."

"It's okay," I tell him and meet his eyes. "I'm just sad I won't get to see you for a while. My first show is the first weekend of February. But then maybe I can come back here to watch the Super Bowl with you and spend a few days before I go to Austin for the second one." I pause and then add, "You know, if the team doesn't make it to the Super Bowl."

He's wearing an expression I can't place my finger on, but his eyes have softened from frustration to affection, making me melt inside. "What?" I ask him.

His gaze traces my face, and he raises his hand to cup my

cheek. My breath catches as he leans in and places a gentle kiss over my lips, making me swoon right where I'm sitting.

Finally, he pulls away and his lips curve into a sad smile. "Nothing. I want every second I can have with you. I just—I wish things were a little different right now."

"It's a transition period. You'll be back and better than ever, and all of this will be behind us."

"I hate feeling like I've let people down. The team, my coach, *you*."

"You haven't let me down, Hayes. And you haven't let the team down."

"I hope you know how special you are to me." His voice turns husky. "I don't want you to ever feel like you're not. Even when things like this get in the way."

I lean my forehead against his, loving the way his presence surrounds me. "You're special to me, too."

When I close my eyes, I imagine what the future will bring. I can see each of us fulfilling our dreams, reaching our goals, knowing one is behind the other, supporting and cheering the whole time.

It's everything I could ever want.

Hayes is everything I could have ever wanted.

***

WEDNESDAY, JANUARY 22

The next few weeks in LA are a whirlwind of checking boxes and meeting required deadlines. The next two months contain six shows across the country. All my time is spent in rehearsals, nailing the choreography and set list, or in the studio, finishing the recordings for the next album.

"Jersey!" Cal hollers for me. "We need to re-record these harmonies. Chop, chop, this is our last day in studio for months, so there's no time to waste."

"Okay, coming!" I call from my position on the couch. The recording studio has become my home for the last few days, and I'm grateful Hayes decided to stay in Milwaukee for this period. He would've been bored out of his mind by himself.

I hand my notebook to Kelsey before getting up. "Will you slide this in my bag for me?"

"Of course." Kelsey nods and takes my stuff for me. "Also, before you leave today, we need to discuss scheduling some interviews for before and during your next stretch of shows. I have a few good ones lined up. We just need to find a time that works for your schedule."

"Perfect. I'll find you when I'm done here."

Bethany is tapping away on her phone but looks up when I approach her a few minutes later after doing a few neck and upper back stretches. "Do you need lunch or a coffee or anything?"

"A sandwich and coffee would be great." I look over to where Cal has his head bent as Kelsey hoists her bag over her shoulder. She nods at something he says and glances away from him quickly. She's probably running the press options by him too before we discuss later. "I have a feeling today's going to be a long day."

I'm right on the money. By the time I get home, I'm exhausted. I drop my work bags in the guest room and run myself a hot bath. My muscles ache from rehearsal and I need a chance to unwind before tomorrow.

Half an hour later, when I'm relaxed, I tuck myself into bed, snuggling into the pillows. Reaching for my phone, I click Hayes's contact information and the FaceTime starts ringing.

We haven't spoken much more than a few quick texts over the last few days and I'm missing him something fierce.

He answers shortly, giving me a tired smile once he sees me. "Hey, honey."

"You look like you've had a day like mine."

His raspy laugh confirms my suspicions. "Long day full of exercises that kicked my ass when they shouldn't have."

"You're getting stronger every day," I remind him. "Have you spoken with Beckett since the playoff game?"

Hayes nods forlornly. "He's pretty frustrated about it still."

"Not at you, I hope?" I ask, and he shakes his head now and sighs heavily.

"No. Not at me. More with the overall circumstances. We should've had that game. We should be the ones in the Super Bowl in two weeks."

"Maybe, but even still, the team *did* make it to the Conference Championship. Don't dismiss that accomplishment too quickly."

Hayes averts his eyes. "I should've been there."

"You'll be there next year, and it will be your best season yet. I know it."

His lips quirk up at my strong conviction. "I don't know how I would've gotten through this without you."

"You give me too much credit. All of your resilience is your doing."

"Even still. You played a big role in all of it." His eyes grow soft as he studies me through the screen. "I miss you. It's the worst thing coming home from therapy and not having you snuggled up on the couch. Peri agrees. She misses you too."

"I feel the exact same," I whisper.

"Tell me about your day." He changes the topic.

"Nothing exciting. I was at the studio this morning to get

some last-minute recordings in, more fine-tuning things like harmonies and background vocals that needed adjusting. After today, the album should be pretty well ready to go."

"Can I listen to it?" Hayes asks. "Get some VIP early access?"

"Of course."

"Won't be as good as if it were all your songs," he says, his voice growing more serious. "But I know it's amazing still."

"Maybe someday I'll get the chance to say out loud that my album was fully written and recorded by me."

"You will." The way he sounds so sure when he says this sends my heart soaring. The gruffness and confidence of his low timbre, the perfect ballad to my soul. "So you're all ready for the first show?"

"Mostly. We have rehearsal time scheduled throughout the week and breaks in between, so I can fine tune anything that comes up. But most of it is the same as the shows last year, so it's muscle memory at this point." Our very first show is in ten days in San Diego. The clock is ticking, but I'll be ready, and I know the rest of my team will be, too.

"Still, that's a lot of dance moves to remember." Hayes shakes his head. "I don't think I could do it."

"I mean, you all come up with your touchdown dances. Don't you have one too?"

Hayes laughs. I love the sound of his laugh. "I don't get many touchdowns, so I don't really have one on retainer."

"We'll need to change that," I say, a grin forming on my face. "Once your knee is feeling better, I'll show you some moves."

"Then I'll have to get myself a touchdown to show them off."

"See?" I tease. "A win-win."

"Sounds good to me."

"I miss you so much, Hayes. I can't wait to come home in two weeks." The idea of being able to snuggle up next to Hayes again makes me feel all warm and cozy inside. It will be my first Super Bowl weekend, and there's no one I'd rather spend it with than him.

His lips turn up. "Home, huh?"

I fight off a smile. "Home."

"I do like the sound of that." He sighs. "It's not home anymore without you."

jersey

FRIDAY, MARCH 28

"T-minus twenty-five minutes until show time!" Bethany says, stepping into the room. I glance up just in time to see my crew of six backup dancers crash through the door of the green room behind her.

They all crowd me, sitting next to me on the couch or plopping themselves down on the floor in front of me. I can't help the joyous laughter from taking over.

"How are you feeling, Jersey?" Donovan asks as he settles next to me. Like the others, he has his stage makeup on and an infectious grin already on his face. "Ready for our last show?"

"Yep. It's a little surreal. To be going on the stage for the last time for a while."

"Especially since we're in New Jersey for the last one," Petra adds. "Perfect to finish off in the state you were named after."

"It is perfect, isn't it? Funny how that worked out." I wink at her, knowing she had likely played a big part in confirming the dates and locations for the shows when they scheduled them months ago. "But yes, I'm excited to go back to the regular routine."

"Six weeks of shows isn't too unmanageable, but I bet you'll be ready to go home and get some rest when we're finished." Bethany winks. "You deserve a chance to snuggle up with that quarterback of yours. Spend all of April resting and recovering."

My eyes drop to my lap and I fight off the blush threatening to color my cheeks.

"How's he holding up after his injury?" Marcus questions. "Will he be ready for preseason?"

I nod my head. "Absolutely. Overall, he's doing much better. He's been hitting the physical therapy ever since he had his surgery. Getting stronger every day."

"Well, the Majestics sure missed him. Their Conference Championship game was *rough*." He shakes his head, mouth pulling into a frown.

"Yeah, definitely not what they were hoping for this season, to say the least."

"Can't imagine they would've had such a hard shut down if he had been on the field," Donnovan adds with a shrug. "Did you two watch the Super Bowl?"

"We did. It was a little bittersweet for him. He still loves watching the game, but not as much as he loves being a part of it himself. He's really missed it the last few months. But he'll be back and better than ever next season."

Donovan and Marcus high five each other, Donovan exclaiming, "Next season's gonna be epic! Hayes Vogt comeback, baby!"

I laugh, thankful for how my dancers have dedicated themselves as Hayes Vogt fans. Before I started dating him, I don't think they had much interest in football, but now they've even got their own Majestics apparel.

I hope with everything in me they're right. Hayes has his sights set high, and I have no doubt he'll be able to do everything he aims for.

"Will Hayes be here tonight?" Lola, one of my lead dancers, asks.

My stomach sinks. "No, he won't. He wanted to be, but his physical therapy schedule is pretty grueling. He's putting 110 percent of himself into his rehab so he can be ready to go for next season."

"Oh," Lola says, giving me a pitying smile. "I'm sorry."

I shrug my shoulders, not letting her know I'm bummed too. "I can't hold it against him. He said he'll be tuning into the live stream tonight from home. And I'll see him next weekend once I've got the all clear to head back to Milwaukee."

Petra leans her cheek on her hand and gives me a dreamy expression. "Isn't it crazy that only a few months ago you barely knew his name? You two are the cutest couple ever."

I roll my eyes, ignoring the way my cheeks heat up again. As if on cue, my phone buzzes in my lap and a text message comes through.

HAYES

Good luck tonight! You're going to crush it.
Give that stadium the best show ever!

"He must've known we were talking about him," Petra teases. Lola giggles as she wraps her arms around my neck, giving me a big hug.

I smile halfway, looking down at his name on my screen on top of the selfie of the two of us I have set as my background. My stomach aches, and suddenly, I'm missing him so much more than before.

"Jersey, can I talk to you for a sec?" Bethany asks, pulling me out of my thoughts. She tilts her head off to the side.

Untangling myself from my dancers, I join her on the other side of the room, where we can talk a little more privately. Her blue eyes study my face and she reaches for my hand. "Are you doing okay?"

"Of course." I squeeze her hand. "Why do you ask?"

"You seemed a little disappointed when you mentioned Hayes wouldn't be here."

"Oh." I purse my lips and nod. "Yeah, I mean, of course I'm a little sad. I would've loved to have him see a concert where I know he's present. He hasn't seen a show since the very first one he went to."

"Did you ask him to come?" Bethany asks. When I nod again, her eyebrows draw in. "What did he say?"

"He left it at he couldn't get away from training right now. He looked devastated, honestly. Like a sad puppy dog." I shake my head. "His career is just as important as mine, so it's okay. I can't hold that against him. There will be plenty more shows, more opportunities. I can't expect him to drop everything and hop on the first flight out every time I'm performing."

"I'm sorry, Jersey."

"I mean, he's heard the whole concert with me belting it out on the treadmill at home over the holidays," I say, then laugh, hoping Bethany will buy it that I'm okay. I don't think she does. "I'm still going to perform my heart out because that's all I know how to do. He'd do the exact same if our roles were reversed. It's the only way to move forward."

She squeezes my hand again, but winces. "I have some bad news."

My face pales with nerves. "What is it?"

"Cal just texted and said he'll be arriving midway through

the show. He said he wanted to see the last one before you go on break."

"But he couldn't get here on time to see the beginning?" I ask flatly.

She shrugs. "I've given up trying to figure out the whys or the reasonings of Callum Strong."

I sigh. "Me too. Well, thanks for giving me the heads up."

"He'll probably expect to see you after the show."

"I expect nothing less."

Bethany glances at her phone and nods. "Time to go." She turns to the dancers and waves them over. "All right, everyone, let's do this!"

Me and my group head out of the green room and up to the stage. When we're five minutes from the opening set, my dancers and I stand and gather in a circle. We wrap our hands around each other's shoulders and huddle up. Their eyes all fall to me, expectantly.

"I want to thank each and every one of you for showing up time and time again and for pouring your entire hearts into making our concerts memorable. I appreciate you all and I know our fans do too. Let's go out there and do what we do best. Ready?"

Our pre-show ritual begins. I start the process off and then look to my left to keep the momentum going. "Celebration!"

"Inspiration," Petra announces, turning to Donovan on her left.

"Passion," Donovan says.

"Devotion!" Marcus adds.

"Energetic!" Lola winks.

The last two dancers get louder as they share their goal words.

"Elegance!"

"Motivation."

The circle comes back to me and I bow my head in the middle. They all follow my lead.

My voice is reverent as I close out our routine with the word I always do. "*Gratitude.*"

The group together counts to three and then, out of the huddle, we move into a group hug. My heart is full. I close my eyes and take it all in, thankful to be standing here celebrating our last show with some of the most important people to me.

We release each other and get into position for the opening song. From my mark, I can hear the fans screaming at the top of their lungs. The whole stadium is alive and vibrating with anticipation.

My pulse races, echoing in my ears until my heartbeat drowns out any other thought than the one most important phrase in show business.

No matter what's going on in my personal or professional life, no matter what is happening in the world around me, when I'm on stage, only one thing matters. I repeat it in my head, taking a deep breath and putting the biggest smile on my face before I walk out onto the stage.

The show must go on.

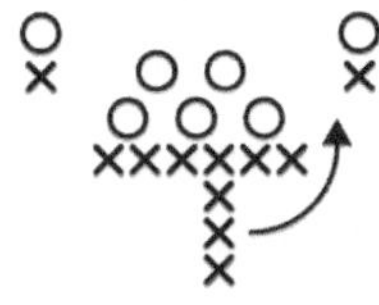

hayes

FRIDAY, MARCH 28

"Good evening, New Jersey!" Jersey says boldly into the microphone before giving the thousands of people in attendance a blinding smile. My chest expands with a sense of pride again like it did when she first stepped onto the stage earlier tonight.

That's my girl up there.

The crowd goes wild and Jersey has to take a step back from the microphone. The camera follows her every move, putting her gorgeous face up on the screen so everyone can see her. Her eyes sparkle with eyeshadow and the overwhelming gratitude she has for the fans cheering her name. Her lips are plump and filled in with a lipstick that I want to kiss right off her, especially when she grins like that. She laughs a few times, shaking her head in awe before she steps back up to the microphone and waits for the noise to die down a bit.

"I am so excited to be here tonight. I've been looking forward to playing this stadium for the entire tour! This state is my namesake, which means tonight's show is extra, *extra* special!"

Jersey waves both her hands to the crowd before spinning on the toe of her sparkly heeled boot, brown silky hair flying across her shoulder as she spots the guitar that's been perfectly placed for her. The stadium lights go dim around her, and then there's one purple spotlight directly on her. She starts strumming a few chords on the guitar and steps up to the microphone for the acoustic section of the concert. Her lips pull into a wide smile as the crowd goes *insane* as she delivers the opening line of her song, "Good Times Roll."

I nod along to the beat, a small smile resting on my lips as I watch Jersey have the time of her life up there on the stage.

"She's really something, isn't she?" Bethany asks next to me.

Turning, I glance her way for a brief second before looking back to the stage, not wanting to miss a second of Jersey doing what she does best. I hadn't realized Bethany had snuck into the VIP box. "She really, really is." Then a thought occurs to me. "I figured you'd be backstage just in case Jersey needs something mid-show."

Bethany shakes her head. "There are too many people backstage, and plenty of people around if she needs assistance. Besides, I love watching her sparkle as much as you do. She's going to lose her mind when she finds out you're here. It's going to make her whole day."

I can't wait to see how excited Jersey will be at my surprise attendance. The anticipation is killing me. "Thank you so much for helping me pull this off last minute. It means a lot to me."

Bethany dips her chin. "Well, Jersey means a lot to me, and I've really loved getting to see her happy since she's been with you. I'll do anything to keep her that way." She pauses and gives me a pointed look. "So don't mess it up, otherwise I'll come for you."

Jersey and her dancers have pulled my attention back to where they are doing a choreo-break as they transition into the next song. "Trust me, I have zero intentions of messing anything up with her."

Bethany purses her lips off to the side, clearly fighting off a smile. She nods sagely. "I'm glad to hear that." Bethany nudges my arm gently. I pry my eyes away from Jersey on the stage. She tilts her head toward the door. "We should probably get down there if you want to surprise her. There're a few songs left, but you're a little slower than you used to be."

Her eyes dart down to my braced knee. I wince. Even though I know she's teasing, the reality still stings. I'm getting stronger every day, but there's still plenty of work to be done until I'm back to full speed.

Jersey has been a big part of my recovery journey. Every day she encourages me to push harder to keep working toward my goal. When she's home, she sits next to me while I do my exercises for my knee, strumming the strings of her guitar and humming quietly to herself. When I pause what I'm doing to watch her, she feels my stare, meets my eyes, and hits me with "Ten more reps, MVP."

I follow Bethany's lead and trail behind her out of the VIP tent and through the crowd on the floor. Thankfully, we go inconspicuously for the most part, aside from a small group of fans who recognize me right off the bat.

They wave me over and Bethany allows me to stop to take a picture with them. I give the camera a big thumbs up and thank them for coming to support Jersey. The girls all share excited glances and say "thank you" to *me*.

Laughing nervously, I wave and continue my trek toward the side of the stage. Jersey is at the other end. She does a twirl and then spins again on her toe, skipping up the stage to where Bethany and I are standing.

As she gets closer, my pulse picks up, like I'm some teenager about to talk to the prettiest girl in school. It doesn't matter that Jersey has practically been living with me for the last few months or that I know her as intimately as one can know another person. All that seems to matter is that she's coming closer to me, and I can't *wait* for her to see me standing here.

Jersey stops down the stage from me. She points out to the crowd, singing boldly into the microphone. The fans in front of her on the floor raise their hands, waving them in the air. The noise from the stadium is deafening with the mix of her loud music, her voice, and the voices of all of her fans singing along to every word.

I've seen a lot of people be the center of attention for a stadium this big, most of them part of a football team or other performers. There's just something about the way Jersey owns the stage when she's up there. It's clear she was born for this. She was born to bring these songs to life and to give these fans something to sing for.

Those thoughts in mind, I'm not surprised when my throat grows a little thick, watching the woman I love smile widely as her attention lands on a young fan right at the edge of the stage. She bends down onto her knees, all her focus on this one person out of thousands. Even from where I am standing, I can tell this young person is living out one of their biggest dreams. I have no doubt that if Jersey could hop down from that stage and wrap them up in a big hug, she would.

That's who Jersey is, I've learned. She's got a big heart for those around her.

Which makes it so much worse that her label takes advantage of her. There's nothing I want more than to see her succeed without the restrictive constraint of the people managing her career. Watching her on stage now, I know she'd be unstoppable if only they'd give her the chance.

The song ends, and Jersey gives the young fan one more enthusiastic wave before pushing herself up to her feet again. She continues to head back to the main stage, strutting in my direction.

My chest grows tighter the closer she gets to me. I'm so damn excited to see her reaction.

Jersey doesn't disappoint.

Mid-stride, Jersey spots me right as she's strutting past. She falters for only a second, her expression going blank as her eyes register with her brain what she's seeing. It takes only another second before that blank expression is morphing into something far more beautiful—gripping enchantment. She smiles so widely I wonder if it's hurting her cheeks and her eyes glisten with unspoken emotion.

My whole world stops at the sight of her. Jersey lifts her microphone to her mouth to sing the next lyric, but doesn't tear her eyes away from mine. I do the same, unable to take my attention off her. Eventually, when she has to look away, I can still see the smile playing on her lips.

For the rest of the song, Jersey's eyes keep drifting my way, making sure I'm still there.

I watch her, raptly, loving that I get to see her do her thing for such a responsive audience. I've played in this stadium before and I don't think the crowd was close to being half as engaged as they are now. She's a sight to behold, and I'm grateful I get to see every moment of her creating her empire.

When the song winds down, Bethany grabs hold of my

elbow and leads me away from the side of the stage around the riggings to the back, where she tells me we'll wait for Jersey to finish.

The echoes from the crowd ring in my ears, and I can picture Jersey standing on the stage, waving at each and every one of them, giving them all one last glimpse of her before she disappears behind the backdrop of the stage.

The lights to the stadium turn on, giving me the hint that Jersey has successfully gotten herself backstage. Still, cheers echo from outside in the stands, but they slowly die down with each second.

"She should be here in just a moment," Bethany tells me offhandedly. I glance at her to see her attention solely on her screen as she types an email.

As if she heard us summoning her, Jersey comes around the corner. She pauses a few feet away from me before taking off into a lopsided sprint. She's still wearing her costume from the last set, and I'm slightly worried about her running in those crazy stiletto boots.

I shouldn't be, though. Completely unfazed by the high heels, she throws herself into my arms and I do my best to catch her while keeping my balance. My knee screams a little at the pressure, but I ignore it, focusing on the woman in my arms. I bury my face in her neck, breathing her in. Her skin is hot and sweaty, but she still smells undeniably like Jersey—sexy.

"You were incredible," I whisper into her ear.

She holds me tighter. "I can't believe you're here."

"I wouldn't have missed it." I pull back and cup her face, tilting her chin so I can lean down and kiss her. When we break apart, her cheeks are flushed for an entirely different reason. "I love you, Jersey. You're magnificent."

Her brown eyes widen and glisten over. She hugs me again

and murmurs, "I love you too. More than you could ever know."

My heart soars at hearing those words leave her pretty mouth. I don't think I'll ever tire of hearing her say those words to me. If I had it my way, I'd be whisking her back home, just so I could keep her all to myself. I'd make love to her all night, worshipping her body in such a way that she'd never doubt how irrevocably obsessed with her I am.

I instantly notice her absence when she pulls out of the hug. Her hands raise to cup my cheeks. Her thumb strokes along the light stubble on my cheekbone.

The world seems to disappear around me, the only person present, the beautiful woman right in front of me. Her brown eyes flutter over my face, as if she's committing this moment to memory—and I'm doing the same. I want to remember everything about this moment here with her.

"All right, you two lovebirds, let's get you into some privacy before everyone watches you two get naked," Bethany interrupts the quiet, intimate moment between us and points behind my shoulder. Jersey follows her finger and I peer back to see too.

The outermost part of the stands are in full view of where Jersey and I are embracing. All of her fans cheer and shout, waving and jumping up with excitement that she's looking their way. Their phones are all aimed directly at us, capturing this moment for all of eternity.

I bark out a laugh, wondering if by some chance I'll get to see it soon on the internet.

Any other man might have an issue with the cameras and the attention, but I don't mind one bit. It comes with the territory of being with Jersey Matthews. Especially being here with her at her concert.

Luckily, I've been trained and briefed on how to interact with the media and rabid pop music fans.

Flashing a wide smile, I raise my hand and wave right back. This only spurs them on and they cheer even louder.

Before I can do anything else to encourage them, Jersey grabs my arm and entwines our fingers together. We walk hand-in-hand down the tunnel and out of the sightline of her fans.

Jersey is shaking her head. Her lips twisted in amusement. Once the sound has died down, she says, "I should've known you'd eat that up."

I chuckle and wrap my arm around her shoulder, dragging her to my side. She leans into me, placing her hand on my chest to stabilize herself. I'm walking a little slower than I would normally, but she doesn't seem to mind, sticking close to me the whole way to her green room.

Once we make it, she lets go of me to get cleaned up. I give her the space, taking a breather on the couch so I can prop my knee on a pillow. The hours of PT paid off tenfold tonight. Even with that, it's starting to ache and I don't want it to swell too much.

Thankfully, Bethany seems to read my mind, and she brings me a bag filled with ice. I suppose it's a perk of performing in a professional athletic facility.

About twenty minutes later, Jersey comes out of the bathroom in a completely different outfit, fresh makeup, and her hair tied back into some kind of twist, which is clipped to the back of her head.

She does a little spin and I give her a slow clap. Her face is alight with energy and if I didn't know any better, I wouldn't have guessed she just performed a two-hour show for thousands of screaming fans.

She settles on the couch next to me, kissing the side of my neck. I wrap my arm around her, cup her cheek, and tilt her chin up so I can kiss her properly again.

When she pulls away, her brown eyes are alight with joy and that alone is worth everything.

THIRTY-SIX

jersey

FRIDAY, MARCH 28

"WELL, DOESN'T THIS LOOK COZY?" a sickeningly familiar voice says to my right, breaking the quiet moment I'm having with Hayes. I turn my head to see Corey Shrader standing in the doorframe of the green room, watching the two of us with snide interest.

"What are you doing here?" I ask tightly, standing up to face him. Of all the nights that Corey had to ruin, he had to pick this one.

Corey looks bored with my question. "Cal invited me."

I cross my arms, almost like a protective barrier between me and my ex.

Hayes stands up from the couch, and I'm keenly aware of his large frame at my back. I can practically picture the unamused glare he's giving Corey right now.

Corey's eyes slide to him and again, he is entirely unbothered. He extends a hand to Hayes. "Hayes, good to see you again."

I roll my eyes and Hayes scoffs, not accepting the handshake. "Actually, not really."

Corey's lips pull into a smirk. He lets his hand hang in the air for a second before he drops it back to his side. "All right, then. She's sure got you whipped."

My shoulders tighten and Hayes makes a dissatisfied sound low in his chest. I wonder if Corey can hear it, and I wonder if he'll heed Hayes's warning.

Hayes is much bigger than Corey, in height, in stature—in every way that matters.

Corey would not fare well going up against Hayes one-on-one.

But of course, I should've already predicted that wouldn't stop him.

"She's pretty good at that. Hopefully, you'll wise up like I did and realize she's only interested in using people who help promote her career."

"Stop it, Corey," I say. Of course, he'd take that angle. In Corey's mind, he probably takes credit for everything I worked so hard for, thinking he gave me a one up.

He didn't. I earned what I have.

"Let's go." I turn to Hayes and reach for his hand.

"What's wrong, princess?" he sneers, using the old nickname he used to call me. It makes my skin crawl that I'd ever thought it was endearing. "Worried I'll scare your new boyfriend off and you'll be all alone again?"

"I think we're done here." Hayes steps in, his tone leaving no room for negotiation. "You can see yourself out."

"What's the matter, Hayes? Feeling threatened? I bet if you asked nicely, Jersey would be open to a little two-on-one action."

Before I know what's happening, Hayes is pushing me behind his body, rearing back and swinging. His punch lands right in the middle of Corey's face. With a sickening *crunch*, Corey falls to the ground and covers his nose, swearing.

"Hayes!" I shout at him, moving back around to his front so I can glare at him.

He's still scowling at Corey on the ground, absentmindedly shaking his fist out.

"Why did you do that?" I question him. Finally, his eyes find mine and he seems confused for a second.

"What do you mean? That dick has had it coming for a long time."

I grab his large hand, flipping it over so I can inspect his knuckles. They look okay for now, but I suspect there will be some bruising later.

Annoyance takes over. "You've already got a busted knee. Do you really want to sit out for another season with a broken hand? I think quarterbacks need to have two working hands."

He blinks, taken aback. "Are you *scolding* me right now? For punching *that guy*?" He points down to Corey. "If you think I'm above punching someone to protect you and your *name*, you better think again. I'll do anything to protect you. No matter the cost."

I cross my hands over my chest and exhale. His words stir a deep affection in my chest, and I'm forever grateful for his protectiveness, but I also need him to understand where I'm coming from.

"What the hell, guys?" Bethany asks, hurrying into the green room. I shrug, unable to give her a better answer right now.

"I agree. What the *hell*?" Cal's menacing voice breaks through.

My skin goes cold. Corey has pushed himself up off the floor and he's wiping away some of the blood from his split lower lip.

He glares at Hayes and then frowns at Cal. "I'm pressing charges, and you can't stop me."

"That won't be necessary." Cal holds up a hand, effectively shutting Corey down. I'm a little surprised to see Corey deflate so easily. "You can go now, Corey."

My ex-boyfriend clenches his jaw but doesn't argue, seeing himself out of the green room. When he's gone, Cal turns to Bethany. "Please get Mr. Vogt out of here, as well. Jersey and I have some important business to discuss."

Irritation gnaws at me as Bethany gives me a helpless look, glancing between me and Cal. I give her a small nod and she sighs. "All right. Let's go, Hayes."

"Try not to punch anyone on your way out," Cal sneers.

Hayes glowers at Cal as he walks by, brushing his shoulder. There are no words passed between the two of them, but there doesn't need to be. The malice is thick enough to cut with a knife.

When Hayes is gone, Cal glowers at me, fire in his cold eyes. My stomach sinks. "We need to talk. Sit," he growls, pointing to the small sofa. I don't put up a fight, sitting on the couch like a child being scolded, even though I have nothing to feel guilty about.

"Are you kidding me with this?" Callum asks me, placing his hands on his hips. "I thought it would be nice to see your last show of this stretch, celebrate afterward, get excited about the album release later this year. But then this football player comes in and puts all that in jeopardy with one well-placed swing!"

I blink twice, watching as Callum's face turns from his normal shade to an angry red with his irritation. He's not the only one who's irritated, though.

Scowling at him, I cross my arms over my chest. "He was

trying to protect me. Corey was making a fool of himself at my expense. Why was he even there in the first place, Cal?"

"Listen," Cal says, pointing his finger at me, totally glossing over my question as if I didn't even ask it. "You know I don't give two fucks about who you're slumming it with on the side. What I do care about is how it's affecting your public image. We've put a lot of time and effort into creating your brand only for you to go and mess it up with some guy who's going to drag you down and get you caught up in a narrative you don't want to be a part of. What do you think the media would do if they found out that your new boyfriend punched your old boyfriend? You don't have time for this."

"Cal, my fans are eating it up. Any time Hayes and I are spotted together, they go insane. My fans are happy for me and Hayes, and that's going to convert to more sales. You should be happy, too."

"Oh, trust me, about that part, I *am* happy. At least you'll chart again with this upcoming album and we'll be able to swing a tour twice as big as this one. But what I'm pissed about is how irresponsible you've been acting, like you're wanting to throw it all away for *some guy*." He waves his hand in the air dismissively. "We've spent all this time and money creating your brand, this *version* of you that people can relate to—and now you're dating a ticking time bomb who could ruin your whole career just like that." He snaps his finger in my face and I flinch. "He *punched* Corey Shrader. Should we have a lawyer on retainer for when the quarterback turns on *you*?"

Callum is right. They have put a lot of time and effort into turning me into this angelic character. The pop princess who keeps to herself and is professionally driven, having no time for relationships or anything other than work. They turned me into the victim when Corey and I broke up, playing on the wounds and the heartbreak of my fans and using that to create this narrative that couldn't be further from what I want for my career, for myself.

I'm their pop princess, and they've locked me up in a tower.

Now that Hayes has rescued me, it's not meshing with the persona they've created.

I stare at him a moment, musing about how skewed his perception is on this matter. Callum is criticizing me like I've floundered myself out to the highest bidder.

I can count on one finger the number of times Corey attended one of my shows. When I try to think of any instance where he showed up for me, I come up completely blank. And we dated for a *long* time. Knowing that Hayes went out of his way, being injured, to support me means more than he could ever know.

It's not as though this was the first time Hayes and I have been seen together out in public—not by a long shot. Our relationship isn't something we were keeping secret. I've been spotted at his games and we've had pictures taken of us when we went out on public dates. Hell, there were headlines blaming me for his injury.

Showing up for me tonight? That was a very big deal. And what he did just now, defending my name and my character? That was an even bigger deal. Even if he did risk injury to his throwing hand.

Callum pinches the bridge of his nose as if this is the scandal of a lifetime rather than what it actually is—a boyfriend showing up for his girlfriend, in private no less. "It will be fine," he says, as if that is something I'm worried about. "Everything will be fine."

"Cal, it's not a big deal." Has Cal officially lost it? Why is he acting like this is something new or different? "It's not breaking news that Hayes would be here to support me."

"It's about the *narrative*, Jersey!" he snaps at me and I take a step back. "If Corey takes this public, it's up to *us* to respond which determines how the public and the media will continue to see you."

"Why don't you simply talk to Corey and ask him not to go public? He's always done what you've asked in the past."

He ignores my counterstrike and goes for the kill, aiming for my heart. "I don't know why I even bother with you. You don't understand any of this, so why don't you stay in your lane and let me handle everything for you like I always do! We'll have to do some damage control, make sure that people and fans know you're truly committed to the album this year. We'll do a few teasers, do a few behind the scenes of you recording."

I bite my tongue. When have I ever given the impression that I *wasn't* committed to the tour and to the album? Callum has clearly made up his mind on the matter, and me telling him that he's wrong won't do any good. There's nothing I want more than to tell him I quit and to shove his suggestions where the sun don't shine. What would I give to do that, to finally be free of him and his stupid agenda?

Of course, I don't, because I *can't*. The memory of the iron-clad contract I'm under weasels its way to the forefront of my mind, and I remind myself I only have a few more years of this. And then, I'll be free to do whatever I want with my career.

So I stay silent.

Still lost in his own thoughts, Callum is suddenly struck with a brilliant idea. His eyes grow wide and he snaps his fingers a few times, bringing that idea to the forefront of his mind.

"We could stage a public breakup," he says, bobbing his head a few times. His eyes are now on me as if he's gauging my reaction. The mere idea of Hayes not being in my life anymore makes my eyes burn.

I freeze and then stand up from my seat, officially done with this conversation. I don't say a word as I walk to the door. I've had enough of Callum and his "brilliant" ideas.

"Jersey, wait, just hear me out!"

I wave a hand at him but don't bother looking back. "No, thanks."

He and I have very different ideas of what it means for my career to be successful. I'm contractually obligated to listen and fall in line with some things, but I will not let him jeopardize my relationship for PR.

Closing the door behind me, I'm finally safe in the empty recesses of the stadium. I take a few deep breaths and close my eyes, leaning against the wall.

When my head has cleared a little and my heart rate has returned to normal, I start walking down the hallway to find Hayes and Bethany, ready to put Cal and Corey out of my head for the rest of the night.

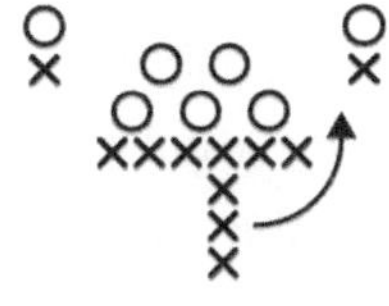

THIRTY-SEVEN

hayes

MONDAY, APRIL 7

"You need to break up," my publicist demands.

I stare at her blankly, then look to Coach, wondering if he is wishing he were anywhere else than here right now—like I am.

Leaning forward, I steeple my fingers against the table. "No."

My publicist sighs. The exhaustion is evident on her face. I know she's been going through it ever since Corey took to the internet, ranting about me punching him at Jersey's show and calling out the league to take action. She's been trying to clean up the narrative for anyone trying to give me bad press about the situation.

"Hayes, please," she says, leveling me with a look that begs to give her a break. "This is not good for you, and it's not good for her. You had your fun, but it's time to get back to work."

"I'm not breaking up with Jersey."

We've been going around in circles for the last thirty minutes on this topic. I keep glancing at my watch, knowing

Jersey is due to land in Milwaukee this morning. Hopefully, we can wrap this meeting up so I can go on vacation with my girl.

My publicist gives Coach an exasperated look, like she's begging him to back her up on this matter.

Little does she know that Coach couldn't give two flying fucks what I do in my personal life, as long as I still show up and give the performance of my life every week.

Which I do during training and rehab and will even more once when we're back for the season.

"I can't believe this," she mutters. "You've already lost a number of sponsorships. You're losing so much money from those deals. You're lucky Corey Shrader isn't pressing charges, otherwise this could be so much worse."

"Listen," I say, deciding that I'm well and over this conversation. "Jersey and I are not breaking up. Not now, not ever. There will be other deals, other promotions. There is only *one* of her. I don't care about the sponsorships. If they're dropping me because I stood up for my girlfriend, then I don't want to work with them anyway. Why don't you get to work finding me better sponsors? Otherwise, I'll have to find a new publicist."

"Really, Hayes?" she asks, unamused. "I've represented you your entire career. You'd throw that professional relationship away for someone you've only known a few months?"

I open my hands and shrug. "Jersey is my future. So, I don't know what to tell you."

She sighs and I know I've won. She can't argue when I lay down the truth like that. "Okay. I'll continue to run damage control where I can. But please, for the love of god, try not to punch anyone else."

I grimace. "I'll see what I can do."

I leave the meeting room, ready to get on with my day. On my drive home, I replay her words.

You need to break up.

It's not good for you, and it's not good for her.

I know that being with her is good for me, but the thought that I could be hurting her? Even in any capacity is enough to set my blood on edge. We're good for each other, aren't we? I think everything we've been through thus far has proven that.

With a sigh, I press my head back against my head rest, thinking it all over. My teeth grit and I shake my head.

I can't fathom the idea of my life without Jersey.

But not as much as I can't bear the idea of being together being bad for her.

My thoughts are still spiraling into uncertainty an hour later when I park at the airport commuter lot to wait for Jersey. My fingers tap along my denim-clad thigh. Glancing over at the clock, I wonder how much longer it will be before I hear from her. She should be landing any moment now, and I'm desperate to see her.

My bags are packed and loaded into the back of my truck with enough clothes to get me through a week—and I can always do laundry if we decide to stay longer. Periwinkle is settled in her little bed in the back seat, waiting patiently for the car ride to be over.

I haven't seen her in a little over a week, but it feels like an eternity. I know Cal has been on her ever since the show in New Jersey, giving her task after task to check off, keeping her swamped with busy work. I've hated not being able to be there for her through it all.

When I suggested she join me for a little getaway a few days ago, I had my fingers crossed she'd say yes. Even when she agreed, I was a little surprised. Jersey is so laser-focused on doing what she needs to for her career. Though I hoped she'd run away with me, I wasn't sure she'd go for it. It seems she is as ready for a break from the madness as I am.

It fills my heart, knowing that she's missing me just as much as I'm missing her.

Jersey arranged for her jet to land at one of the smaller airways so she wouldn't have to deal with the pain of the public.

A text message chimes and my stomach tightens.

JERSEY

I'm here

I shoot her a quick text saying that I'll be around in a minute and then pull out of my spot, heading toward where I need to be to collect her.

Sure enough, she's waiting for me with a suitcase in tow, her security guard standing right behind her, keeping a weather eye on their surroundings. I park the truck and slide out of the driver's seat, rounding the front to her.

Just like in my dreams, Jersey launches herself at me, wrapping her arms around my neck and pressing her torso against mine. I waste no time burying my face in her hair, breathing in her fresh, clean scent and relishing her in my arms. My hands snake around her trim waist and I hoist her up against me, wanting to be closer to her.

"God, I missed you," I mumble.

She makes a cute sound in the back of her throat, a blend between a mewl and a whimper, and tightens her arms around me. "It feels so much longer than a few days."

I let her go and frame her face with my hands, tilting her chin up so I can have access to her mouth. She parts for me immediately, allowing me to kiss her like it's the air I'm needing to survive. When I finally have satiated my fill of her—for now

—I pull away and stare down at her. Her gaze has glassed over and her lips are deliciously swollen.

She blinks a few times and then beams up at me. "That's some hello."

"Gotta make up for lost time," I say with a wink. Glancing back at her suitcases, I grab one and her security takes the others. "Shall we?"

Together, we walk back to my truck. She slides into the front seat while we get her bags settled in the vehicle, leaving her door open.

"All right, looks like you two are all set," Jake, her security guard, says. He closes the hatch in the back and turns to me.

"Are you not coming with?" I ask him.

Jersey pops her head out of the door. "I told him since I'll be with you, I'll be in safe hands." My chest clenches. "Besides, you said we're going to your lake house, right? Will we really even be out and about that much?"

I shrug. "Valid point." A smirk appears on my face and I turn to her, waggling my eyebrows. "You'll be lucky if I even let you out of the bedroom."

Jersey laughs and shakes her head again, this time in amusement. "See? I don't need him around for that."

"I'd rather have you all to myself, anyway."

"I'll take that as my cue to leave," Jake says with a laugh.

I give him a handshake. "Thanks for watching out for her."

He dips his chin. "Right back at you."

I hop into the driver's seat and peer out the rearview window at the security guard walking back to the plane, then down at the girl in my passenger seat. "Ready to go? You've got everything you need?"

"I'm more than ready. I started packing the minute you invited me out here."

"Did you pack your guitar? I didn't see it with you."

Her lips roll into a smile, and she shakes her head conspiratorially. "Nope. I didn't even pack my notebook."

I raise my eyebrows. *"Really?"*

"I didn't. It's still back in my room in my work bag. I haven't touched it since being at the studio last. I am officially on vacation."

"I like the sound of that," I say, proud of her for doing this for herself.

"Me too. I'm so ready to unplug and relax. How far is this lake?"

Plugging in my phone to the charging cord, I get it set up on its stand so I can see it if necessary. Pulling away from the airport, I answer, "Just shy of four hours. It's a bit out of the way."

"Can we stop for coffee first?"

A few minutes later, we're in the drive thru of a small coffee shop. We pull up to the screen to place our orders and Jersey leans over my lap so she can see the menu. While she's draped across me, I run my hand over the back of her head, her silky strands caressing the tips of my fingers.

She fights back a shiver, and I fight back a smile.

"Good morning. Order whenever you're ready," the barista inside says through the speaker.

"I'll have a caramel latte," Jersey says through the window. She turns to me, expectantly.

"I'll do a large black coffee."

"Great, that will be $12.99. Please pull around to the window."

Once Jersey's back in her seat—mostly—I pull the car around the bend of the drive thru and then hand the worker my card when she holds a hand out. She does a double take when she sees me and then bends down to peer in my window. Her jaw drops open.

"Oh my god, are you Jersey Matthews?"

Jersey's reclining over the console now, and she gives the girl a wide smile. "I am."

The girl leans further out of the drive-thru window to see Jersey better. "Wow, I'm such a huge fan. We've seen Hayes around here before," she glances at me and then back to the pop star in my front seat, "but I never thought we'd see you here too!"

"We tend to be a two-for-one deal these days," Jersey responds, giving me a fond pat on the shoulder.

I run my hand through her hair again, not minding one bit that she's the star of the show. That's exactly the way I like it. I'll gladly take a step back to watch her shine.

I get my credit card back and then we're being handed two coffee cups. The girl waves at us both and gives us an air hug. "Thank you so much for stopping by! It was so nice to meet you!"

Jersey waves at her as we pull away. When we're on the road again, she settles back in the passenger seat and smiles down at the coffee in her hands. "She was nice."

"This is Wisconsin. Most people are nice," I say, turning the steering wheel with one hand while I get my coffee situated in the cupholder.

"Well, I like it." She takes a sip of her latte and then makes a happy sound. "I'm so glad to be back. I'm liking LA less and less with each day that passes."

I give her a sideways glance and then run my tongue over my teeth. "You don't have to go back, you know."

She sucks in a surprised breath and falls silent next to me, but I can still hear her breathing. She does her best to level herself out. In and out.

It's a crazy notion. Absolutely bonkers of me to be bringing it up at this point in our relationship. But I'm doing it anyway.

I don't like the idea of her home and my home not being the same place.

"What do you mean?"

I reach over and put my free hand on her thigh, running my thumb over the silky-smooth material of her leggings. "You could stay here, in Milwaukee. This could be your home base in between shows rather than having to go back there."

"But the recording studio is there." Her voice is weak, like even she isn't happy about that fact.

"I'm sure there are places to record here in the city." Then I have another idea. "Or I'll build you a recording studio at the house."

She falls silent again. The air in the cab grows heavy, not in an uncomfortable way, but in a way that feels a bit fragile. I wonder if both of us are afraid to break the delicate balance of this dance I've spun us into.

"You'd do that for me?" she finally asks in a small voice.

I glance over at her and fight off an affectionate smile. "I'd do *anything* for you, Jersey. Something like that is a drop in the bucket. Just say the word and it's done."

She falls quiet again. My attention falls back on the road, and I reach for my coffee, taking a sip.

"Callum tried to persuade me to end our relationship," Jersey whispers.

"He *what*?" While I'm not entirely surprised, I am annoyed. Callum's really got some nerve. But then again, didn't my publicist do the exact same thing to me this morning?

Her lips tighten into a straight line and she nods regretfully.

"Right after the show you came to. I'm sorry I didn't tell you right away. But obviously, I didn't let him convince me. He thinks staying with you is a bad move for my career."

I scoff and shake my head. "Right, like he really cares about your career more than keeping his pockets lined."

Jersey exhales. "I know. I walked out on him. He's been pissed at me ever since and even more moody than usual, but honestly, I don't care. I wish there was a way out of this contract for me."

"Have you talked to your lawyers about it? Is there any loophole?"

"I have, and there isn't," she mumbles. "The contract from the label is airtight."

I reach for her hand and thread our fingers together. "We'll get through it, together. You're not alone anymore, okay?"

She squeezes my hand and gives me a grateful smile. "How could I ever forget?"

"Can I tell you something crazy?"

"What?" She's a bit hesitant, unsure where I'm going with this.

I shoot her a sideways glance, the wave of uncertainty returning. "My publicist told me the same thing this morning."

Her jaw drops. "That we should break up? You're joking."

"Not at all." I grit my teeth again. "She said it wasn't good for either of us. That it was bad for you."

She falls silent, then carefully asks, "What did you say?"

"I told her no. That if she had a problem with it, then I'd find a new publicist."

Jersey's surprise makes it all worth it. One of these days, she may stop being so shocked that I'll keep choosing her. "You didn't!"

"I did, and I meant it. No one is breaking us up if I have

anything to say about it." I swallow thickly and glance at her. "But—Jersey, I don't want to ever hurt you. If you feel like being with me is bad for you, I don't—"

"It's not. Don't ever think that. There's only ever been a few things I've been sure of in my entire life, and one of those things is that you're good for me. You are."

My lips twitch, her words relieving the knot of tension balled up in my chest. "You're good for me too."

When I glance back at her, she's still watching me. Those full lips curved up and her eyes twinkling.

"Why are you looking at me like that?" I ask her.

"Because I love you," she says without hesitation. "I love you a whole lot."

I squeeze her hand again, feeling like the luckiest guy in the world. "I love you a whole lot, too."

THIRTY-EIGHT

jersey

MONDAY, APRIL 7

THE REST of the drive passes uneventfully. Hayes flips on a random playlist on his phone and we play a game where we each take turns guessing the name of the song. Bonus points if we can name the artist too. I hold my own on the pop songs, but Hayes has me beat by a long shot when it comes to the alternative and rock genres.

Some of his guesses on the country songs have me laughing so hard the muscles in my abdomen start to hurt.

Time flies by and soon we're pulling off the highway and driving over the long bridge into the town Hayes tells me is called Minocqua. My stomach rumbles when we drive past the sign, indicating our arrival.

"Hungry?" Hayes asks with a sideways smirk.

"Maybe a little." My cheeks flush.

"I know a place that has crazy good food. It's a hole-in-the-wall. You up to checking it out?" He glances over at me when we've stopped at a red light.

Reaching behind me, I dig around in my bag and pull out a hat. Settling it on my head, I fluff my dark hair around my shoulders and then give Hayes a smile.

"Let's do it."

A few minutes later, Hayes is parking the car in a somewhat empty parking lot, but I suppose it's still early in the day. The neon sign on the outside reads "Red Zone: Sports Bar and Grille."

Hayes scoops up Periwinkle and her little dog bed, ignoring my confusion and giving me a wink. Together we walk into the dimly lit bar and I look around, taking in my surroundings. Right away I'm met with the sight of the long bar, an impressive display of shiny bottles of liquors and spirits lined up in a tier illuminated by a back light.

There's a shorter, heavyset man standing behind the bar who saunters over as soon as we walk in, tipping his chin up at us as we enter. He lays out two small cocktail napkins in front of two empty seats and then braces his hands against the bar.

"Well, as my eyes deceive me, if it isn't our own hometown superstar back to grace us with his presence."

Hayes steps forward and extends his free hand, Peri still relaxing in his other arm. He's holding her like a football, which is endearing. The bartender shakes his hand, a broad grin on his face. "Good to see you, man."

"Good to have you back, Hayes. We've missed you here. And who is this beauty you've brought along? She your lady?"

Hayes's whole face lights up. "She sure is. Jersey, this is Mickey. Mickey, this is my girlfriend, Jersey."

Mickey gives me a speculative stare, one eye narrowing slightly. "She looks a little fancy for our small town, don't ya think?"

I peer down at my clothes, not feeling fancy at all. I've been traveling all day. My leggings have a smear of whip cream on the front of them, my shirt is all rumpled, and underneath my hat, my hair looks like I haven't washed it in a week.

"I think she looks perfect," Hayes says back. "Mind if I let Peri hang out in your office?"

Mickey waves his hand toward the couches by the window. "You can put her over there, she's fine. It's not busy today, anyway."

"Thanks, Mickey." Hayes shoots me another fond wink. The appreciation in his gaze sends a shiver of desire down my spine. If we weren't here in public, I'd kiss him silly.

But I have plenty of time do that.

"This is a great place you have," I say when Hayes walks away, looking around the bar again.

Televisions are mounted everywhere my eyes fall, different sports events playing on the screens. There's the main bar which Mickey is standing behind and then another separate bar against the far back wall. A few sitting areas are established in front of the bigger televisions, L-shaped couches positioned for perfect viewing. Away from the bars and the seating areas there are a handful of high-top tables—plenty of areas to station while watching favorite sports teams dominate on the screens.

"You a big sports fan?" Mickey asks me. He must have grabbed Hayes a drink while I was perusing the bar. He slides the pint glass to Hayes, making sure not to spill any of the foam over the side. "Whatcha drinking, darlin'?"

"I'll do a vodka tonic, please," I respond, then segue back to his first question. Giving Hayes a sideways smirk, I say, "I am now."

Mickey chuckles as he prepares my drink and slides it to me. "She's a keeper."

"Don't I know it." Hayes sets his glass down from taking a sip. "Jersey is a singer."

I raise an eyebrow at him, but he gives me a shrug in response. I glance around the bar again. There're only one or two other patrons here in the whole bar. And given the demographic, I doubt they've *never* heard my name.

"Really?" Mickey says, raising a brow with interest. "Preston and I have talked about maybe starting up a live music night. We might need to get you up on the stage."

"You'd have quite the crowd if you got her in front of a microphone," Hayes says, fighting off the amusement in his voice. "She's part of the big leagues."

Mickey tilts his head and observes me again. "You know I thought you were familiar. What'd you say your name was again?"

"Jersey Matthews."

"Well, I'll be." He turns away from me and puts his hand up to his mouth, cupping around his lips. "Hey, Preston! Come out here for a sec!"

A taller, lankier man pushes his way through a set of heavy black curtains hiding what I assume to be the kitchen from view. He walks over to us with his head tilted curiously, but his expression lightens when he sees Hayes standing there.

"What's up, man?" His voice is deeper than I expect it to be. He goes for a fist bump, which Hayes eagerly returns. "Long time, no see."

"No kidding. How've you been, Pres?"

"Nothing exciting happening over here. You know how it is." Preston shrugs his shoulders jovially. His eyes fall on me and he blinks a few times in surprise. "You're Jersey Matthews."

I laugh. "In the flesh."

Preston holds a hand out for me to shake and I return the

gesture. "My daughter loves you. She's going to lose her mind when she finds out you were here in our bar."

My heart warms and my lips curve into a smile. "What's her name?"

"Chloe," Preston responds, a proud expression on his face. "She's fourteen."

"I'd be happy to sign something for her or take a picture with you."

"We'll be here for a few days," Hayes chimes in, watching me closely as he speaks to Preston. "Maybe you could bring her by to meet Jersey."

I nod at Preston in agreement. "Yes, I would love to meet her."

"Really?" Preston asks, hopefully. "She would be over the moon."

I grin. "Yes, please."

"But we're trying to keep our stay on the down low, guys, you understand?" Hayes asks Mickey and Preston.

The two of them share a look and then nod solemnly. "Say no more. We've got you covered," Mickey says, sliding me a refill of the drink I've polished off. "We'll leave you to it. Let me know if you need anything else. Me and Pres have a bet to settle."

Preston rolls his eyes then explains. "Tonight's our coaster Olympics rematch."

My interest piques. "Coaster Olympics?"

"On slow days, we create some sort of competition with the coasters." Mickey holds up a cardboard coaster with the Red Zone: Bar and Grille logo on it. "Preston's whooped me the last few events, so I've got to get back in the game."

I glance at Hayes, shaking his head in amusement. "Now this is something I think I have to see."

Preston and Mickey share another look and then Mickey

rubs his hands together in front of him. "What's on the docket today, Pres? Got anything we can play with them too?"

Preston smirks and develops a sneaky glint in his eye. "You already know I do."

Preston explains the game and we dive right into competition.

He calls it "vacuum" where the goal of the game is to pass the coaster around using the suction from our lips. Whoever is the last one standing—the only person not to drop the coaster—wins the figurative gold medal.

Not even ten minutes later, I find myself laughing hysterically as Hayes and Preston take their turns trying to pass the coaster from one to another. Hayes is to my left and I have Mickey on my right, Preston positioned across from me in the circle.

I clap my hand over my mouth, giggling as Hayes tries to pass the coaster to Preston. Hayes is currently doing a great job of keeping the coaster suctioned to his lips and Preston is trying to take it from him. He purses his lips and goes in for the hand off.

There's something far too hilarious about the sight of Hayes and Preston mouth-to-mouth with only a coaster between them.

Preston manages to take the coaster and fist pumps the air with both hands victoriously. Two seconds later, he loses his hold on the coaster and it falls to the floor.

He looks at it dismally. "No gold medal for me."

Hayes reigns victorious at the vacuum game, and I manage to best the three men at the flipping game before we decide to call it on the competition.

I can't recall a time I've had this much fun at a bar.

Hayes and I eventually drag ourselves out of the bar a few

hours later after some delicious smash burgers and a few more drinks. I'm still laughing to myself, thinking about how much fun we had with Mickey and Preston, as we make our way to the truck. Hayes has his arm wrapped around my shoulders and he holds me tightly to his side. I'm carrying Peri's fluffy bed in my free hand while she's content to be a football in Hayes's arms again.

"That was *so* much fun. Thank you for bringing me to meet them," I say, leaning into Hayes even more. My heart and my belly both are fully satisfied.

He presses a kiss to my hair and unlocks the truck, opening the passenger side door for me to slide into my seat. After I'm settled, he leans in a bit, kissing me properly on the lips.

When he pulls away, he says, "I'm glad you had a good time. They're never boring, that's for sure."

I lean my head against the headrest and grin. "Can we come back again while we're here? I still need to meet Preston's daughter, too."

"You really wouldn't mind doing that?" Hayes asks. "I know I kind of put you on the spot. If you don't want to open up that kind of attention, you don't have to. Preston will understand."

I shake my head. "No, I don't mind at all. I really do love getting to meet fans. It's when there's a ton of them, that it can get a little crazy. But if it's only Preston's daughter or a few others, it would be totally okay."

Hayes's expression softens. "I'll let him know."

"So, how about you show me this lake house now?"

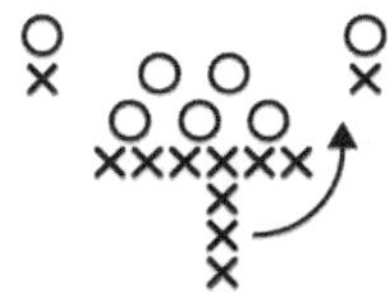

hayes

MONDAY, APRIL 7

"THIS PLACE IS AMAZING," Jersey says, plopping herself down on the couch. She gazes out at the lake through the huge bay windows. "I don't know if I'll ever want to leave."

"I know the feeling," I tell her, settling down next to her. A sense of contentment wells within me when she snuggles up at my side, leaning her head against my shoulder. "I'm happy I get to share this place with you."

"Me too," she agrees, her eyes glistening. "How long have you had this house?"

"A few years now. Most of the time I use it in the offseason. There's some good fishing in the lake," I tell her. "Beckett and the guys will sometimes come up and hang out for Fourth of July. We'll go out on the boat and chill."

"You have a boat?"

I nod. "I do. It's a little too cool still to take it out, but once the weather warms up, we'll come back up and get you out on the lake."

"I'd love that," she says. "This house already feels like another place I could call home."

"Hmm," I murmur, leaning down and pressing a kiss to the top of her head. "I like the sound of that." We fall silent for a while, and then a thought strikes me. "I have an idea."

She laughs but doesn't protest when I scoop her up into my arms. I carry her out of the living room, through the sliding doors, to the porch where the hot tub is located. With her arms around my neck, Jersey looks at me, an eyebrow arched on her forehead.

"What are you up to, Hayes Vogt?" she questions, a sly smile toying on her lips.

"Something dangerously wicked," I tease, leaning down and kissing her deeply before placing her back on her feet. Wasting no time, I pull off the cover to the hot tub and turn to her expectantly. "Well?"

She crosses her arms over her chest. "Well, what?"

I tilt my head toward the hot tub. "You getting in?"

"I don't have my swimsuit on," she says stubbornly. I can tell she's loving every minute of this little game we have going between us.

"You know you don't need a suit."

"What if someone sees?"

"We're the only ones out here, baby. Now take off your clothes and get in the tub," I command.

Her eyes widen and her lips part on a gasp. Her cheeks flush and her thighs press together. A delightful sense of pride lights like a fire at the thought that just my words have her losing her composure.

Somehow, I get the sense that she needs this. She needs a chance to breathe, a chance to restore herself and not worry about what's next. She needs that release, that opportunity to forget for a little bit.

I'm happy to give her that.

Holding my gaze, her lips quirk, and she reaches for the hem of her sweatshirt. It's a bit chilly out tonight, but it's nothing that the heat from the hot tub won't help. Her arms cross in that sexy way as she lifts the material over her head.

My mouth goes dry as she tosses it to the side, revealing her baby blue lace bra. Her eyes hold a challenge as she reaches for the band of her leggings, pushing them around her hips and shimmying her sexy legs out of them. My jeans grow impossibly tight as my eyes rove over her.

She has legs for days, toned and strong from her endless hours of practicing choreography for her concerts. She has delicious curves and luscious breasts, begging for my attention. I trace her figure, appreciating the cinch of her waist and the swell of her hips tapering down to her knees.

Jersey places her hands on those gorgeous hips, hitching off to one side, accentuating her curves.

"Now what?"

My tongue darts out to wet my lips. Jersey's eyes track the movement. Her chest rises and falls with her breath as she waits for her next orders. I trail a finger over her lacy bra and matching panties. "Take these off."

"I think this is a little unfair," she says as she reaches behind her, unclasping her bra and letting it fall. Her nipples pebble instantly from the chilly evening air. "Here I am giving you a strip tease and you're still fully clothed."

"Not for long," I respond, eyes still locked on her. "Don't you worry."

When her panties join her other clothes on the porch, Jersey spins around and crawls into the hot tub, giving me the perfect view of her pert little ass.

Once she's settled in the water, her attention falls on me and she waves her hand expectantly.

I reach behind my shoulder with one hand and pull my T-shirt over my head, flicking it to the ground to land by hers. My jeans and boxer briefs follow shortly thereafter.

Jersey's eyes trail over my body like mine did to hers.

Everywhere her eyes touch heats up, igniting my need for her. Not willing to be apart from her much longer, I climb into the tub, closing the distance and claiming her lips.

Jersey's arms wrap around my neck as she opens to me. My hands caress her body, sliding over her waist and rounding her hips until I can maneuver her onto my lap. I spin us, so my back is to the edge, and she's perched right on top of my lap.

Her center lines up against my cock and her hips glide up and down the length. She braces her palms against my shoulders as she works her body over mine. Even through the water, her heat surrounds me and drives me wild. We fit together perfectly, meant to be together in this way.

"You drive me crazy, Jersey," I mutter, digging my hands into her hips and arching up to kiss her.

She makes a happy sound as she kisses me back, her hips continuing to wiggle over mine. Hot tub sex might be out of the question. There's no way I can maneuver her in the way I want her in such a small space, but that doesn't mean we can't have some fun before going back inside.

Swiping my tongue over the seam of her lips, Jersey opens for me willingly, her hands tightening around me as I deepen the kiss. The hot water sloshes around us, steam rolling off the surface and surrounding us until everything else seems to disappear.

Raising one hand, I cradle her cheek in my palm, tilting her head to the perfect angle so I can plunder her mouth.

When I finally have to come up for breath, I pull away from her, returning my hand to her hip and leaning back against the ledge, watching her work over my lap.

"You look so pretty when you ride me like that."

Her cheeks are flushed from the exertion and the temperature of the tub. Nibbling on her lower lip, she hoods her eyes and sinfully grinds against my cock.

I groan, leaning my head back and closing my eyes.

"All right, I can't take it anymore," I gasp, sitting up from my reclined position a few minutes later. "I have to be inside you."

I move her off my lap and push myself up and out of the hot tub. Jersey watches me, swollen lips parted. When I offer her my hand, she takes it, but asks, "Where are we going?"

"Back inside so I can fuck you properly." I pull her after me, scooping her up into my arms once again. She squeals but doesn't fight me.

Despite the two of us dripping wet, I walk back into the house, not stopping until I've crossed the threshold of our bedroom. I set Jersey down on her feet and then snatch a towel out of the en suite bathroom. Wasting no time, I rub it up and down her body, wiping up every droplet of water before doing the same to myself.

When we're dry, I toss the towel to the side and prowl toward her again, my hungry sights set on my beautiful prey.

Jersey's eyes darken and she takes a few steps backward, bumping into the edge of the bed. She falls against the mattress just in time for me to capture her again, wrapping my arms around her thighs and pulling her to the edge of the bed. Her legs spread, welcoming me. Instead of thrusting home inside of her, I let my hands trail over her curves, down her sides, then up her thighs until I find her heated core.

My finger strums over her clit, my mouth finding hers again and kissing her as I work her body. She arches against me, opening her legs wider and giving me more access.

When she's soaking wet, I position my cock right at her entrance, but before sliding deep inside her, I pause, leaning over her with one hand braced next to her head. My free hand cradles her cheek again and draws her attention to me. She's got so much going on in her world, but right here, right now, all I want her focusing on is me and the perfect way our bodies work together.

"Eyes on me, Jersey." I rub my thumb over her swollen lower lip.

When those gorgeous chocolate eyes land on me, I push the rest of the way into her. I watch every little nuance of her expression—her eyelids flutter a bit, her breath catches, and her cheeks flush.

Exquisite.

I let myself become consumed by every little sound she makes as I bring us closer to the edge. There's nothing else to say other than I absolutely *love* being with her in this manner. Getting to know her on such an intimate level does things to me that I've never experienced in the past.

I want every little moan, every gasp of pleasure, every glance right before she squeezes her eyes shut in ecstasy. I want anything and everything Jersey can give me.

She must feel the same because she wraps those sexy legs around me, hooking her ankles at my lower back and pulling me closer to her.

"Hayes," she gasps as I hit that perfect spot deep inside of her.

"You feel so good, sweetheart," I murmur, leaning my weight against her and burying my face against her neck, breathing her in. "You gonna come for me?"

She groans and bucks her hips against me. I grin against her neck and keep up my pace.

"That's it. Let go for me," I whisper, biting her earlobe. I feel her pussy grip me like a vise, and I grunt, the pleasure building at the base of my spine as we hurtle over the edge of bliss together. With one last thrust, I hold myself deep inside her, letting the wave of pleasure consume me.

Jersey trembles underneath me with her own aftershocks. I rest my weight on her, being careful not to squish her. She runs her fingers through my hair, settling me as my heart rate quiets down.

"I don't think I'll ever get tired of that," she mutters. "Watching you fall to pieces."

"I don't think I'll ever get tired of you," I whisper, wrapping my arms around her body and hugging her tightly. It's the honest truth. "I love you."

Her hands move to my face and she draws me up until I'm looking right down at her. Her lips curve into a sexy smile and she says the words that mean the most to me in the entire world. "I love you too."

FORTY

jersey

WEDNESDAY, APRIL 16

"MORNING," Hayes says, pulling me out of my zone. I've been curled up on the couch for about an hour, sipping my coffee and getting lost in a book. The quiet lake life has really been good for me, and I've loved getting to spend time here. Periwinkle has snuggled in my lap and she turns her head at the sound of Hayes's voice too.

He comes over and scratches at her ears before leaning down toward me. Tilting my chin up to accept his kiss, I greet him back. "Good morning. There's more coffee in the pot if you want it."

Hayes makes a satisfied sound and heads into the kitchen. While he does that, I go back to my book, and a few moments later, Hayes joins me on the couch, moving my feet so he can sit under them and places them in his lap. He takes a hesitant sip of his coffee, testing the temperature.

We sit together in a nice silence for a while. Last night, Hayes pressed kisses over every inch of my body repeatedly until I was an exhausted, satiated mess in the bed. We fell asleep curled around each other, like we have for the last ten days.

This is the first time in I don't know how long that I've been able to sit and enjoy myself, not having to meet deadlines or be present for publicity. It's been nice, and I'm dreading having to return to the grind.

It's inevitable. I know it is, but it's nice for a moment to pretend.

These have been some of the best days of my adult life. It's been a delicious taste of what life could look like with Hayes long term. I'm convinced that everything is better when it's just Hayes and me against the world.

"What are you thinking about?" he asks, twirling a strand of my hair around his finger. He studies my face, as if he's trying to read my innermost thoughts.

"Wondering if I have it in me to ask for things to be different at the label."

Hayes is unfazed. He nods sagely and continues twirling my hair. "No need for you to wonder. I know you do."

Exhaling, I move from my position to his side, curling against him, wishing he could osmosis his strength and confidence into me. Up on stage I might look like I have it all together, but in real life, I question myself at every turn when it comes to professional decisions. I wonder what happened to that bold eighteen-year-old girl who fearlessly and unapologetically went for what she wanted. Is there any way I can get her back?

"Have you ever had to have those hard conversations with your management?" I ask him, curious to know if he's ever been in my shoes.

"Sure," he says, wrapping his arm around me and pulling me in closer to him. "Every time my contract goes back up for negotiation, it's nothing but conversations and give and take."

"You always seem to come out on top, somehow."

"I have a great team who has my best interests at heart. And the Majestics franchise always have my back. They want me on their team, and I want to stay on their team."

"Maybe that's where we're different," I admit. "Cal wants me to stay with Silver Shadows forever, but on his terms. I sometimes wonder if they see me as their prized cash cow. But if it were up to me? If I had to say yes or no right now to stay with them? It'd be a no. A hundred percent."

Hayes runs his hand up and down my arm. "I think you need to talk to your team, see if there's any way they can support you."

"I already have. My only option is to wait it out. After that deadline hits though, I'll be walking. There's no way they're going to stop me."

"I'd kill to be in the room when you stick it to them once and for all," Hayes says with a chuckle.

"Cal has it coming to him, that's for sure." My lips twitch as I think about how red his face will turn when he realizes he has no say in my career anymore. Sure, Silver Shadows will likely always maintain ownership of my past music and much of what I've done in my career thus far. However, Cal won't have ownership of *me* anymore. The music I've created there isn't really me anyway, so losing them is a loss I can deal with for the price of my freedom.

AFTER A QUICK GROCERY RUN, Hayes and I head back to the house. Honestly, I'd be perfectly content never going back to normal. This small town has wormed its way into my heart and I could easily see creating a place for myself in this community. In the back of my mind, I know at some point I'll have to go back to the normal hustle and bustle of my life, and that will be sooner rather than later. I have more shows coming up in a few weeks, and with those come intensive rehearsals to make sure everything goes as smooth as possible.

We're planning to leave in a few days and already, I'm missing this quiet fairytale life we've been living together.

I'm watching the road pass by, appreciating how the pines seem to tower over the road and stretch on for miles. Hayes switches the station and then turns up the volume a smidge when the radio host states she has an exciting announcement. I mildly tune in, still looking out the window at the beautiful Wisconsin scenery, getting lost in the thought of Mickey and Preston being the ring bearers at our wedding.

Or more specifically, getting lost in the thoughts of Hayes's and my wedding.

"You all are in for a treat now. This is Meghan Connelly's brand new single, fresh out of the recording studio. It's called 'A Piece of Me.' Enjoy."

I blink, staring at the radio, a little surprised at the coincidence that her new song is the same name of one I've written in the past. The song starts and as it progresses, my mouth goes dry as I listen to the words.

No. It can't be.

It is *my* song.

But it's not.

Those are my words, but it's not the right melody, or the right beat, or the right *anything*.

But those are undeniably my words.

The exact same words I sang for Hayes on Christmas Day.

I turn to him, and he's watching me with wide eyes and a slack jaw, picking up on what's happening right now, too. Any fluffy, fairytale daydreams I was having quickly turn to ice, cutting through my heart and freezing me from head to toe.

"Hayes," I whisper, unable to hide the betrayal seeping through me. "This is *my* song."

His expression deepens into something less akin to surprise and more like hatred. "I thought those were your lyrics."

I wrap my arms around my middle. He doesn't get it. "Hayes," I say again.

"What?"

"*You* are the *only* person I've played this song for. Ever," I add. I'm going to throw up. The implications of what I'm telling him are too much. He couldn't have. He wouldn't have. There is no version of my life where I can imagine Hayes betraying me like this, but how else could my song have ended up on the radio?

He catches on quickly, and he shakes his head, holding his hands up as we're stopped at a stop sign. "I would never, Jersey. You can't possibly think I would have leaked it. It doesn't even sound the same!"

"You said you wished you would have recorded it," I whisper, helplessness oozing into accusation.

"Yeah, but I didn't!" His voice breaks. "Jersey, I love you. I would never betray you. I swear, on everything, I had nothing to do with this."

I bury my face in my hands, focusing on my breathing.

In through the nose, out through the mouth. Count down from fifty.

All around me, the world is crumbling. My words, my most

prized possession, sung into existence in a way that destroys their depth, the very essence of their meaning. The most intimate parts of me being aired out to dry and then donned by someone else.

I never could have foreseen this happening without my explicit knowledge.

I feel violated and dirty.

Someone stole from me and blasted it across every airwave and every streaming service.

Dizziness consumes me and the whole world tilts in the wrong direction, past the point of no return.

"Stop the car," I mutter before clapping a hand over my mouth.

He does without any hesitation, pulling over to the side of the road. We're only minutes away from the house, but it's too late.

I toss open the door and stumble out of my seat just in time for my lunch to come hurling forward.

On my hands and knees, I retch, the weight of the situation souring in my gut like spoiled milk. My stomach revolts at the idea that someone would do this to me. My head continues to spin, trying to make sense of such a betrayal.

Within seconds, Hayes is next to me, rubbing my back and pulling my loose hair away from my face.

Tears burn in my eyes and I can't help the broken sob that escapes me. It hurts my chest and I feel like I'm about to collapse under the weight of what's happening.

"Hayes," I cry, squeezing my eyes shut and willing this pain to go away.

"I'm here, baby," he whispers. He covers me, his larger frame surrounding mine as if he's trying to protect me from anything hurling my way.

But it's too late.
I'm wounded.
I'm broken.
Where do I go from here?

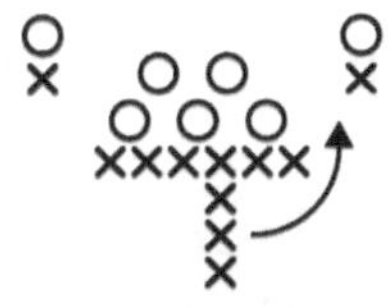

FORTY-ONE

hayes

WEDNESDAY, APRIL 16

JERSEY PACES BACK and forth across the living room floor. I'm slightly concerned she'll wear a hole in the hardwood with how hard she's stomping around, but I'm not about to tell her to stop. I'm not sure she'd listen if I tried.

She's in full crisis mode right now and all I can do is sit by and offer support where I can.

Her phone has been glued to her ear for the better part of the last hour. She's been on and off phone calls with Bethany, her manager and PR team, her mom, Roman, and her lawyer— not necessarily in that order.

Her dark chocolate hair is strewn atop her head, messy from her relentlessly running her fingers through the strands. Though her voice is level, I can pick up on her panic, which rises with every passing minute.

I wish there was something I could do, but I'm completely lost. This all goes way over my head. All I can do is sit here, giving her moral support.

When Jersey hangs up the latest phone call with her lawyer, she runs her hands over her face and groans. Shuffling over to where I'm seated on the couch, she falls down next to me and buries her face in my chest. I wrap my arms around her, my heart hurting for her and frustrated that I can't help her any more than I am already.

"I can't believe this is happening," she whispers. Her shoulders tremble as she drags in a shaky breath. My thoughts flash to the sight of her hunched over on the side of the road, crumbling under the weight of her new reality, and my heart breaks a little more.

My beautiful, strong Jersey. I'd do anything to keep her from feeling this pain ever again.

I smooth my hand over her hair and cup the back of her neck, holding her tightly to me. "What did your lawyer say?"

"She's reviewing the contract to determine whether taking my original song is a violation of my intellectual property rights, or if it would fall under the category of intellectual property they own. It gets a little gray since there has never been any interest in any of my original songs so far."

I admit, I like that her lawyer is searching for loopholes and ways out. No matter what, someone's getting sued over this. It would be an added bonus if Jersey can also escape from the chokehold this contract has her under.

"What do you think happened?"

She shakes her head. "I have no idea. The only way for them to have gotten those words would have been to hear me sing them"—her eyes cut to mine and my blood turns to ice—"or they somehow got a hold of my notebook where they were written." I know she believes me, but it still hurts that I'm a plausible option for her words getting leaked.

That must be how they did it, but it's going to be a matter

of finding out the finer details, and then proving that Jersey had written those words first.

I have no doubt her lawyer will be able to handle the infringement situation. She'll get a large payday—even though it may take time—but I have no idea what will happen next.

"What do we do now?"

"Best-case scenario: I get writing credits on the song and a share of revenue. Meghan's already recorded it," she says ruefully, her shoulders sinking. "And it's already been streamed and downloaded thousands of times by her fans. There's no going back in that aspect. It's her song now. Even if we move forward with legal action, the song is out there. Sure, I may be able to get licenses and credits and compensation, but no one will ever recognize it as mine as much as they do hers."

I remember back to when Jersey sang it for me on Christmas. This song is such an intimate part of her, a clue in to some of her most inner thoughts and feelings. I can't imagine how devastated she must be feeling to have had that part of her displayed for the world to see, without anyone knowing they're her words.

"I wish there was some way I could help," I admit, running my hand up and down her back.

"You are," she says, pressing against me in a hug. "You're helping just by being here. I can't imagine if I had to go through this all alone."

"You're never going to be alone again," I assure her. "You're stuck with me now."

"I love the sound of that," she whispers, tucking herself against me tighter.

We sit together for a while, weathering the storm. Jersey stays glued to my side while she answers text messages and phone calls, constantly seeking that comfort of the connection between us.

The afternoon quickly disappears, the sun lowering beneath the horizon. We've been stuck on this couch all day, only getting up to use the bathroom or to grab a snack before returning.

To be honest, I like this fortress we've built together over the last few hours. I can tell Jersey's feeling a little better, reassured by the endless stream of messages and promises from her team and her lawyers. The color has slowly returned to her cheeks, and she seems more alert and chipper than she was when this news first broke.

That's not to say that she's not still devastated, because she definitely is. But she's being strong, powering through the pain.

Outside, I catch sight of a few snowflakes swirling around the windows. As I run my hands through Jersey's hair, I can't help but feel like the snow is hinting that this might be a new beginning for us. A new, exciting chapter. As much as it sucks right now, at some point the bad will have to end, leading into something that can only be good.

Out of nowhere, the doorbell rings and I groan, burying my face in Jersey's neck. "Maybe they'll go away."

She laughs and taps my shoulder. Putting on emphasis, the doorbell rings again, and again. Swearing under my breath, I push off my girl and storm toward the front door, grumbling the whole way.

"Okay, okay," I say right before swinging the door open. It rings again, right when I open it to reveal a young woman standing on my porch. Her eyes are wide and scared, her shoulders trembling from the chill of the early March air. I can't help but feel like I've seen her before, but I can't place her face. "Can I help you?"

She stands up on her tiptoes, looking around me. I don't like that one bit, so I step closer, letting my broad frame block her view. She appears intimidated and takes a step back.

"I'm here to see Jersey. Can I talk to her?"

I cross my arms over my chest and glower at her. Is she a fan? How'd she find out Jersey was here with me? "Who are you?"

Jersey answers the question for me, peeking around my shoulder to see the visitor. I step aside, letting her past when I realize she recognizes the girl.

"Kelsey?" she asks, stepping forward. "What are you doing here? How'd you know where to find me?"

The girl's eyes fall, and I catch a glisten of what I can only assume are tears. "I'm so sorry. I have your location on my phone. I've just been—I'm so sorry, Jersey."

"Sorry for what?" Jersey takes another step toward her and places her hand on her shoulder.

"Your song," Kelsey says, looking up at my girl now. Her eyes are rimmed red, and a tear streaks down her cheek. "I'm the reason your song got leaked."

Jersey's hand falls from the girl's shoulder and she sucks in a breath. The world around us grows so silent we can hear the snow falling outside.

Oh shit.

I watch Jersey closely, to see what she'll do. She rolls her lips together, studying Kelsey for a moment before she nods her head. What she says surprises me, yet it doesn't. Jersey Matthews is one of the most compassionate people I've ever met, even when faced with someone who has wronged her.

"I think you better come inside."

FORTY-TWO

jersey

WEDNESDAY, APRIL 16

"Can I get you anything to drink?" Hayes offers Kelsey as soon as she settles herself on the living room couch. Hayes stands at the top of the two steps leading down to the living area. He has his arms crossed over his chest and he watches me with hawk eyes as I settle myself next to my publicist and face her.

"Um, I'll take a water if it's not too much trouble."

Hayes nods and takes a few steps into the kitchen where he pulls out three glasses, setting to work filling them up. While he's doing that, I turn back to Kelsey.

"What did you mean? When you said you're the reason my song got leaked?"

When I had spoken with my publicity team earlier today—the team Kelsey is a part of—there had been no mention of this. She had been on that call but had remained silent, letting some of the higher-ups on the team take the lead and work on perfecting the PR statements. At the time, my head was still spinning, and I hadn't thought too much of it, but now that she's here sitting in front of me trembling, I suppose I should have.

Kelsey inhales a shaky breath and turns her tear-filled eyes to mine. "I want to start by saying that I've really loved working for you and getting to be a part of your team."

"Kelsey—" I start, but she shakes her head, cutting me off.

Reaching into her bag, she pulls out my notebook, the exact same notebook I believed to be back in my condo in LA, stuffed among all of my other items I brought with me to my last recording session.

"What . . . how did you get this?" I ask, confused.

"When you were recording your last session in studio a few weeks ago, Callum approached me." I frown. Kelsey is on *my* team, but I sometimes forget that she has ties with Silver Shadows as well. "I didn't really think anything of it, at first. He was talking to me about this and that, trying to get a feel for our current PR ideas and what not. But then he turned things around on me."

"What did he want?"

"He played me." She shakes her head, her tone growing hard, as if she's berating herself inside. "He told me you had discussed a song that you wanted to run by him, and that you told him you'd give him your notebook to review it."

My blood runs cold. So my song *was* stolen right out of my notebook. Hayes comes back to the living room and sets down the glasses of water on the table in front of us before perching on the arm of the couch, hovering above me protectively.

"He told me you probably got sidetracked with recording and forgot to give it to me. I should've been more cognizant, especially when you explicitly asked me to put the notebook in your bag. If you had really meant to share it with him, you would have told me to give it to him, or told him where to find it. Or given it to him personally." Kelsey squeezes her eyes shut. "Things have been so busy, and I've been so overwhelmed that I haven't been sleeping—so I wasn't thinking clearly."

I reach over and grab Kelsey's hand. Despite it all, I'm sympathetic toward her. Kelsey and I have worked together for years now. I have no doubt she wouldn't hurt me with malicious intent.

"You gave him my notebook?" I ask her, even though I know by now that she did.

She looks regretful. "I did. I promise I put it in your bag when you asked me to, but then Callum asked me to give it to him, and so I did. I took it back out of the bag and handed it to him while you were busy talking with Bethany."

I draw in a deep breath and roll my lips together. Kelsey bows her head, ashamed, and picks at her fingernails. The truth falls between us like a barbed wire. Both of us unsure how to move forward now.

Inside, I'm a mess, my head reeling with the implications of what she's saying. *She* took my notebook with my lyrics in it and delivered it to Callum personally. While I was in the *same* room. I should've known it would be someone close to me professionally. My stomach sours and I wonder if I might throw up again, only this time with disgust at myself. Here, I thought Hayes betrayed me like that.

Before I can fall into a full-blown regret spiral, Periwinkle peeks around the edge of the couch.

The Shih Tzu notices Kelsey and saunters up to her, tags jingling with every step. She nudges Kelsey's leg, grabbing her attention. Kelsey reaches down and rubs at her ears. I get up from my seat and go over to Peri, scooping her up and setting her on the couch right next to Kelsey so she can pet her better.

"She's cute," she murmurs, rubbing the little dog, who is eating the attention up and grunting like a guinea pig.

"Let me get this straight," Hayes interrupts. His voice is level, but I catch the hint of annoyance at the situation. I'm sure it's frustrating to him that she's sitting here, petting his dog like she didn't just stab me in the back. "Instead of asking her to confirm Cal's story, while she was right there, you went ahead and went through her things until you found her *private* journal, which she asked you to put in her bag, and then gave it to Callum. Knowing that things between the two of them are what they are."

Kelsey blinks a few times under Hayes's scrutiny. Her eyes well up again with tears, but she fights them back. Her gaze cuts to mine, and she nods, not hiding anymore. "Yes, I'm so, so sorry. Jersey. I had no idea it was because he was planning on stealing from you. I wouldn't have if I had known, I promise."

"I'm not sure what to say," I tell her, truthfully.

"I know there's not much I can do at this point. It's too late. But it was really important to me that you knew what happened. That it was my fault."

I pause for a second, still overthinking everything. I turn to Hayes, only to find his eyes already on me. His eyes narrow a smidge, as if he's trying to read what's going on in my head. When he finds whatever he's looking for, his chin dips slightly in acknowledgment. As much as I want to rage and cry and wreck everything, I can't. Kelsey is a victim here too.

My voice is level as I say, "It was your fault . . . but it was also Cal's. He tricked you, knowing that you respect him and his instructions, and you'd do what he asked without question. He took advantage of you, Kelsey." I take a deep sigh.

"I'll have to tell your bosses," I continue, keeping my voice even. "From that point, it's out of my hands. I don't know what they'll do with the situation from there."

"I understand," she whispers. A tear sneaks out of the corner of her eye and she is quick to wipe it away. "I'm the one to blame. I should be fired for this."

Despite everything, I have nothing but sympathy for Kelsey. Maybe it's seeing how she's sitting in front of me, looking so dejected. I can see the self-loathing rolling off her in waves, and that breaks my heart.

She made a mistake, at my expense, but she is still a good person.

"Come here," I say, reaching for her. Kelsey comes willingly and falls into my arms. I hold her tightly, hugging her and rocking her back and forth.

"I'm so sorry, Jersey. I never wanted to hurt you." Her voice breaks off at the end and her shoulders shudder with a sob that she's trying to control.

I rub my hand up and down her back. "I forgive you, Kelsey."

That seems to do it. Kelsey's whole body sags against mine, the tension leaving her with my forgiveness.

Hayes locks eyes with me again, a softer expression now on his face. "I'm going to go get the guest bedroom ready."

I nod and Kelsey pulls away from me, wiping at her cheeks with both hands and taking in a heavy breath. "No, that's okay. I'll go find a hotel to stay in."

"Kelsey," I admonish. "It's late, you're upset. Stay here tonight. We don't mind at all."

"You're sure?" she asks, glancing from me to Hayes with trepidation.

Hayes is the one to console her worries. "Positive. You can head back tomorrow once you're feeling better."

Kelsey looks down at her hands. "Thank you."

I reach a hand out and put it on her shoulder. "Don't beat yourself up too hard, okay? People make mistakes. That's what it means to be human."

Lord knows I've made plenty of mistakes in my life, too.

"Okay," she says, forcing a nod. I'm not sure how much she believes me right now, but hopefully once the emotional warfare of this moment wears off, she'll find it in her heart to forgive herself.

"I'm going to go see if Hayes needs my help. Just relax here for a little bit."

I push myself off the couch and then head to the guest bedroom where Hayes is laying a freshly folded towel on top of the queen bed. He looks up when I walk in and immediately opens his arms for me.

Burying my face in his T-shirt, I breathe him in, letting the smell of him calm my nerves. He presses his lips to the crown of my head and holds me tightly, knowing that's exactly what I need right now. I let myself bask in him for a few minutes, not saying a word. He lets me, lending me his strength.

After a few minutes, I untangle myself from him and take a deep breath, letting it clear my head as much as possible.

Finally, I whisper, "I'm sorry."

He pauses. "What do you have to be sorry for?"

"I thought you—I should've known you'd never betray me. I'm so sorry for allowing that thought to cross my mind for even a second."

Hayes rests one hand on the angle of my jaw, his thumb stroking over my cheek, eyes tender. "I forgive you. I would've done the same thing, jumped to the same conclusions."

"I still feel terrible about it." My eyes flicker away from his, ashamed.

"Don't." He leans down and pecks me on the lips. "I'm not upset about it, so you shouldn't be either. Let it go, Jersey. We're okay."

I inhale a shaky breath and nod once. "Okay."

With his hand still on my face, he asks, "Do you need anything else from me?"

I shake my head and circle his wrist with my hand. "No, I don't think so."

"I'll wait for you in our room, then." He leans down and gives me another soft kiss, which I return gratefully.

Hayes excuses himself, disappearing down the hall toward the main bedroom. I take another moment to collect myself before going back to find Kelsey. She's wrapped around herself, holding her knees to her chest. She looks up at me with sad eyes when I walk into the room.

I throw a thumb over my shoulder. "I'll show you to your room."

Lithely, she unwraps herself and follows after me down the hallway.

"There's a bathroom right there, with soap and extra toiletries if you need them," I point out. "And here's your room."

"I can't believe you're being so nice to me after everything I told you," she whispers, eyes grazing over the guest room before falling on me. My throat tightens and I turn to her.

"I presume since you came here telling me all of this that you're willing to help make things right?"

"Yes, absolutely."

"Would you be willing to release a statement stating

everything you told me? That Callum stole my song to have Meghan release it?"

Kelsey's eyes shutter for a second, but then she nods her head. Her releasing a public statement highlighting her involvement will solidify her grounds for termination "I will."

I reach for Kelsey again, giving her a big hug. "Thank you. Everything will be okay. It will all work out the way it's supposed to. Whatever happens next, know that I consider you part of my team. I'll have your back for as long as you have mine."

Even as I say those words, I have to convince myself they're true. When it comes to Kelsey, I have two options: I can shut her out and dismiss her for betraying me, or I can forgive her—which I have already—and allow us both to move on.

"Thank *you*, Jersey." Her eyes glisten.

"Goodnight, Kelsey. Try to get some sleep."

"You, too. Goodnight."

I give her a sad smile and leave her to herself.

Inside our bedroom, Hayes is already under the covers and leaning against the headboard, waiting for me. He looks up from his phone when I enter and a sense of calm overtakes me.

After I get ready for bed, Hayes wraps me up in his arms, holding me tightly to his chest.

"I think I need to go back to LA tomorrow," I whisper into the darkness.

His hold on me tightens. "I thought you might say that."

I close my eyes, focusing on his heartbeat. When I tilt my head up, he's already looking down at me. "Will you come with me?"

Relief floods his features, and he leans down to peck my lips. Then he reaches for his phone. "Absolutely. We'll leave tomorrow. I'll have my assistant arrange for a jet."

"Thank you." I snuggle back into his hold and close my eyes again.

The rhythmic sound of his heart thumping in my ear reassures me I'm not alone. Everything *will* be okay. What happened has happened, and now the only way to move forward is to weather the storm.

THURSDAY, APRIL 17

MY MIND RUNS on full cylinders throughout the entire night. Hayes and I get up right at six the following morning and I'm still exhausted. When I stare at my reflection in the mirror, I can see it. My eyes are tinged pink from the lack of sleep, and I have dark circles under my eyes.

I run some cool water and splash it on my face, hoping I'll at least feel a little refreshed from my night of restlessness. As soon as I'm dressed, I start packing, thoughts spiraling this way and that.

In so many ways, I'm helpless, I'm in a transition period waiting to get back to LA so I can work with Bethany and my lawyers to figure out what to do next. I hate feeling helpless, which is why one thought stands out to me more than the others right now. Something that I *can* do next before we leave.

"Hayes."

He pauses at the sound of his name and turns, running a hand through his hair. "Yeah, baby?"

I press my lips into a thin line, wondering how he'll react to my slight change of plans. "I promised Preston I'd say hi to Chloe before we left . . ."

"Don't you think we—"

"Hayes, please," I say, my voice breaking. "I need this."

Hayes stares at me a moment, and then nods once, sliding his phone out of his back pocket, typing on the screen and then putting the phone to his ear. "Hey, it's Hayes. We have an emergency and we're going to need to leave town quickly today. Jersey wanted to say hi to Chloe though before we go. Do you think you could make that happen?"

An hour later, the truck is packed, and we head out. Hayes holds my hand over the console as the lake house disappears behind us.

"Sorry I ruined your vacation," Kelsey says from the backseat where she sits with Periwinkle.

"It is what it is," Hayes mutters, glancing at her in the rearview mirror.

"There will be more vacations," I add, though I'm forlorn about leaving.

The drive is quiet and seems to take an eternity before we pull into the parking lot of Red Zone. Hayes meets me at the front of the truck and offers me his hand, which I readily take. My head still spins with everything that's going on in my world, but as soon as we walk into the bar and I see Chloe beaming at me with stars in her eyes. I put my troubles to the back of my mind, focusing on her.

Even as my world crumbles around me, without fans like Chloe, I'd be nothing. The least I can do is take a few moments to give back to her. Let her excitement remind me that all this will be worth it in the end.

By ten o'clock, the three of us are back on the road. As we

drive away, I stare down at the selfie Chloe and I took, feeling my eyes well up again as everything comes back to hit me.

Hayes reaches for my hand and threads our fingers together. "That really meant a lot to Preston and Chloe. He said that this was a dream come true for her."

"I'm glad I got to see her," I say, my voice thick. I swipe away at a tear that escapes from the corner of my eye. "I told her I would make sure to get her tickets for my next show."

"I bet that made her whole year."

"I hope so." I nod.

He squeezes my hand, and I look out the window, wishing there was a way I could go back to the cabin, lock myself away, and shut the rest of the world out, pretending none of this happened. Unfortunately for me, though, it did, and the list of things that need my personal attention keeps multiplying.

The drive is spent mostly in silence. My nose is glued to my phone where I'm answering text messages and emails and the occasional phone call—mostly from Bethany or my lawyers. I have a meeting with them first thing tomorrow morning to figure out the next moves. Bethany has been texting me with updates on the statement my lawyers released and any new updates from the label or the media. Kelsey is working hard on drafting a statement that she'll release directly to the media.

Hayes is doing everything he can to be supportive. He's almost always touching me in some way, his hand laced through mine or his palm resting on top of my thigh. It's his way of quietly lending me his strength.

As soon as we make it back to Milwaukee, we drop Periwinkle off at home. The little dog gives us a mournful look when we say goodbye, but then she plops down into her bed, perfectly content to sleep until we get back. We meet Kelsey back down in the truck and drive to the airport. The flight from

Wisconsin to California flies by, my mind buzzing with scenarios preventing me from catching an hour or two of much needed rest.

Even that night, back in my condo, as Hayes draws me into his chest and holds me tight, I can't shake the anxiety brewing in my belly. He kisses the top of my head and runs his hand up the length of my back, trying his best to soothe me. It works to an extent, but when morning arrives, I still feel entirely unrested.

My lawyer—Carla—Kelsey, and Bethany arrive first thing in the morning right as Hayes is brewing a pot of coffee. I open the door to welcome them in and they step into the apartment. Carla readily accepts a mug of coffee from Hayes, while Bethany stays back and wraps her arms around me in a tight hug. Kelsey stands right behind her, looking about the same as I'm feeling right now, with dark circles underneath her eyes.

I close my eyes and hug her back, grateful that she's here with me right now.

"I'm so sorry, Jersey," she says. "I can't believe this is happening."

My throat feels thick, and I don't say anything back, for fear of bursting into tears again. I can't cry about this today. The necessity of handling the situation takes priority, but the blatant violation and betrayal is still simmering underneath the surface, and I know at some point I will not be able to hold it back.

"Here, I brought you something," Bethany says before reaching into the canvas bag on her shoulder and pulling out a package of Oreos and a big jar of peanut butter.

I laugh, despite everything, and accept the gift, my heart warming from the small gesture.

"Let's head into the living room so we can get started," I say, taking the cookies and peanut butter. I meet Kelsey's eyes and give her a weak smile. "Thanks for coming."

"I gave my statement yesterday to the press and resigned from my position," she tells me as we make our way to our seats. I haven't had a chance to read her statement, but I don't doubt she did what she had to do. "I've heard from a few of my friends at Silver Shadows. Callum is getting ready to give a counter statement today, so we should probably be ready for the worst-case scenario."

Carla is sitting on the chaise lounge by the coffee table. She takes a sip of her coffee and sets it on the table. "We need to start drafting something for your team to put out, Jersey."

"I can help," Kelsey says, sheepishly. "I may not technically be a part of your publicity team anymore, but I still have those skills."

I nod. "I'm fine with that."

Carla pulls a notepad out of her briefcase along with her laptop. She opens it up and starts typing. Hayes sneaks into the living room and takes a seat next to me, wrapping one large arm around my waist and settling his hand on my hip. I lean against him, letting his warmth ease some of the tension in my body.

"I have Kelsey's statement right here," Bethany says, handing me her tablet so I can read it.

Kelsey Hurst, a publicist for Vantage Personal Relations, is speaking out regarding Meghan Connelly's new song

"I'm making a combined statement for myself and on behalf of Jersey Matthews. It is imperative that people know that the song recently released by Meghan Connelly, produced by Silver Shadows, was taken without consent from Jersey Matthews's private song bank. Callum Strong, the manager for both singers, enlisted me to help him steal from Ms. Matthews, planning to use what he stole to promote Ms. Connelly's career without consent from Ms. Matthews. I am committed to ensuring that Mr. Strong and Silver Shadows are held accountable for this abuse of power within their industry."

I breathe a heavy sigh and look at Kelsey. She's wringing her hands in her lap. "Thank you."

"Is it enough?"

"Yes, it's perfect." I nod my head and hand Bethany her tablet back. "I didn't even know Meghan had signed with Silver Shadows."

"I didn't either, but do you remember when Cal took her call that day you were in studio?" Bethany asks me. I vaguely remember what she's talking about and nod. "I wonder if he was brokering that deal with her then."

"They really didn't waste any time then." Hayes muses next to me.

I agree. "They must've signed her and had her recording pretty quickly."

"Callum always has multiple things going on at once. He even had a big role to play in your relationship with Corey," Kelsey adds, seemingly oblivious to the bomb she just dropped.

I blink a few times and my brain steers in a different direction, intrigued with what this might mean. "How so?"

"Well, he set you two up, and then eventually told Corey to break it off with you," Kelsey says, dismally. "Not that Corey put up much of a fight. It was almost like he was relieved Cal advised him to end things."

"*Really?*" I ask. I can feel Hayes's eyes on me, watching my reaction to this news. If anything, this drives home how lucky I am that things with Corey didn't work out. "If he was so deep in Cal's pocket, that was destined to crash and burn at some point. I'm just glad I got out of that situation when I did." I look to Hayes and can't fight the smile off my lips. "And I'm much better off for it. Cal's utter disdain for my relationship with Hayes has much more clarity now. He couldn't control the narrative how he wanted, and he *hated* that."

He winks at me and leans forward, pressing a kiss to the top of my head.

"None of those details matter now," Carla interrupts, redirecting us to the task at hand. "We need to focus on what our goals will be moving forward, and how we're going to get you there."

Hayes's hand tightens around my hip, but he doesn't say anything. "What do we need to do first?" I ask her, leaning my elbows on my knees.

"We'll need to discuss your terms," Carla says, peering at me over the rims of her glasses. "In my professional opinion, I believe the best course of action would be to move toward termination of the contract. It is going to be difficult to prove that Callum stole from you, especially with you not having a registered copyright of the lyrics."

"But it's my song. Don't I own any type of copyright?"

"You always own intellectual copyright privileges of anything you personally create," she explains. "However, it will be difficult to prove if we proceed that route and this ends up going to court. There is no digital time stamp on a handwritten notebook. There is no way to convince a judge or a jury that you wrote those lyrics first."

I bite my lip but nod. "I understand."

"It would be best to come to an agreement with Silver Shadows that moves toward terminating your contract with them. The only problem is that you have a clause in your contract stating that upon termination, Silver Shadows will maintain the rights and privileges to anything you've created under their label."

My stomach tightens like I got sucker punched, and I draw in a sharp breath. I was hoping there would be a better outcome on that front. Bethany looks at me in concern. "So, they'll still own me."

"Well, not necessarily," Carla says. "They'll own your catalog. You'll still be listed as the artist, but Silver Shadows will retain the rights, so you'll have to have their approval to use any of the songs moving forward. But you'll be free to continue your career as you see fit without the oversight of the label for future albums or tours."

I swallow thickly, and let that really sink in.

Though the thought that all my work will stay behind me when I leave is heartbreaking, it's comforting knowing that even if I stayed with Silver Shadows, I *still* wouldn't have the control over it as I want. That fact alone puts everything into perspective for me. Ultimately, leaving the past me behind so future me can have the freedom to do what I want with my career is a fair trade. I had hoped for something different, but this is the reality, and I'll have to make peace with that.

Bethany told me once that I shouldn't have to settle for anything in my life, but on the flip side of that, there are times where compromise is necessary. Settling would be for me to allow Callum to steal from me and walk away from the transgression scot-free. But I'm not allowing that. I'm going forward and making sure they can never use me to their advantage again. I'm compromising the backlist so I can move forward and reach for the stars and moon myself.

"Okay," I say. Bethany's focus is still on me, watching for any hint of distress, but she won't find any. "Let's move forward with searching for a path to terminate. They can keep everything; I don't care. I just want to be free."

"We'll do that." Carla scribbles something on a notepad and then looks to me with an eyebrow raised. "Callum Strong's lawyer is saying he's requesting a meeting with you present. Would you be comfortable meeting with him face-to-face or would you like me to handle this for you?"

I don't need long to decide. "I want to be there. Cal and I have had a rocky relationship, but he took it too far this time. I want him to look me in the eye and explain to me why he stole from me."

Hayes gives me such a look of pride that makes my heart melt, and Bethany nods her head, her lips curving up a bit.

My lawyer types out a response. "I'll make sure that happens then."

jersey

MONDAY, APRIL 21

HAYES HOLDS my hand in the back seat of the tinted vehicle as we drive to Silver Shadows. My nerves are fried, hands shaking with anxiety and mouth dry as I stare down at my phone.

BETHANY

We're here. Heads up, there're a ton of paparazzi sitting outside the building. Also, Callum did an interview this morning that's already circulating. Here's the link.

I click on the video she's sent and tilt my screen so I can watch.

"What's that?" Hayes asks, leaning toward me to get a better view.

"Callum did an interview earlier today," I mutter, my eyebrows pulling together.

On my screen, Callum is standing in front of Silver Shadows

with a plastered smile on as he points to someone in the crowd. "Yes, your question?"

"Was there a contract or written agreement for the usage of Jersey Matthews's song?" a female reporter off screen asks.

Callum's eyes sharpen, but somehow his fake smile gets wider. "There had been a *verbal* agreement in a private conversation between me and Jersey. She had been worried about the label making a statement about her relationship with Hayes Vogt coming out as a PR move. The song was exchanged for the label's indifference to the matter."

This statement sends the other reporters around in a flurry. More hands raise and questions are shouted at Callum as cameras flash all around him.

I click off my phone and scoff, ignoring the acid taste in my mouth. "How convenient that he'd reference a verbal agreement."

Hayes shakes his head, giving me a look of sympathy. "There's no paper trail with a verbal agreement. Now he won't be expected to produce anything for proof."

"He's always thinking one step ahead," I whisper. It's hard not to feel defeated, but I remind myself that the battle's not over yet.

Hayes gives my hand a squeeze of encouragement. I close my eyes and try to focus on my breathing for the last little bit of the ride—the last little bit of calm I'll have before this shitstorm.

When we arrive at the studio, we're dropped off at the front door and I slide out of the car first, Hayes close behind me. As soon as my foot lands on the concrete, cameras go off, shouts echo around me, and my ears turn red with trepidation.

Paparazzi are everywhere.

Bethany's warning text hadn't prepared me for the sheer *number* of them.

Hayes doesn't hesitate, wrapping his arm around my shoulders, guiding me through the crowd. I hadn't thought to bring along my security team—I usually don't when I'm heading to the recording studio. Especially with Hayes in tow, I felt safe. Given the change of events, I'm extremely grateful to have him here with me.

It's typical practice that Silver Shadows employs security around its premises to avoid this, with how many artists and stars they have coming and going.

However, no one would guess that fact based on how many people are crowding me suddenly. They throw questions at me about Kelsey's statement, and Callum's sad excuse for a counter statement which he released earlier.

"Jersey, would you like to comment on the verbal agreement between you and Silver Shadows?"

"Jersey, will you and Hayes be breaking up now that your PR stunt has been exposed?"

"Hayes, how will this affect your game next season?"

"Jersey, do you think Silver Shadows will keep you on their roster after this scandal?"

He ushers me past the people screaming at us, never once giving them a chance to ask me anything. I keep my head down, allowing him to lead me through.

Once we're inside the building, I feel like I can finally breathe again. Hayes runs his hand through his hair and scowls at the people still outside.

"That was chaotic," he grumbles.

My hands are still trembling. "I should've expected it. I should've brought security with me."

"Now I'm even more glad you asked me to tag along. I would've lost my shit if they did anything to you."

I walk closer to him and lean against his side. He leans over and presses a kiss to the top of my head. "They probably wouldn't have reached for me, but I am glad you were here."

He inhales deeply and wraps his arms around me, holding me tightly to him for a few minutes.

When I let go, he gives me a forlorn look. "Are you ready?"

Shrugging a shoulder, I aim for being nonchalant, but really my intestines are coiling in my belly. "As ready as I'll ever be. My team is up there already waiting for me."

"We should get up there then," he says.

As we pass the front desk, I wave at Louisa, the typical weekday receptionist. "Here to see Cal?"

"Yeah, is he in his office?"

"He told me to tell you to meet him in the bronze conference room on the eighth floor," Louisa says, reading off a notepad.

"Eighth floor, bronze conference room. Thanks, Louisa."

"Of course. And Jersey?" I turn to her before heading to the elevator. She gives me a sympathetic smile as she pushes her glasses up the bridge of her nose. "I'm sorry this is happening to you. No one deserves this. Especially you."

"Thanks, Lou. That means a lot to me."

"Good luck with everything," she says. And I nod, reaching for Hayes hand.

Before we get on the elevator, I pull him back. He turns to me with questioning eyes. "Actually . . . I think I need to do this myself. I'm sorry."

His eyes soften, and he shakes his head. "Don't be sorry about that. You're more than capable of going in there and telling them what's what." He reaches for me again, hugging me to his chest. "I'm so proud of you, Jersey. Don't let them push you around. You're stronger than you think, so give them hell."

With one last kiss on the top of my head, he releases me and steps back. I feel silly, but I wave at him before I get on the elevator. He winks at me and then goes to sit on a comfy chair in the lobby. The doors close, and I'm on my way.

I stop at the floor where Callum's office is and meet up with Bethany, Kelsey, Carla, and a few of her colleagues. All of us ride up to the eighth floor, which seems to be the longest three-floor ride I've ever taken. I take a deep breath, steeling myself for what's about to transpire. As soon as I'm off the elevator, I'm walking down the hallway to the bronze conference room. I garner a few looks and a few whispers from other staff members, but I don't let anyone get to me.

Standing outside the conference room door, I look from Bethany to the others. With a dip of my chin, I say, "Ready for this?"

They acknowledge me and Carla comes to stand next to me. "We don't back down," she says, leaning toward me. "They *stole* from you. Don't let them forget that. After today, you'll be a free woman."

"Free," I whisper.

Bethany puts her hand on my shoulder from her position behind me. I cover her hand with mine and nod. "Okay. Let's do this."

Callum waits for us inside the conference room, arms crossed as he leans back in his chair at the long oak table. A man I can only assume is his lawyer is sitting next to him, a laptop screen illuminating his face.

Callum glares down his nose at me. "Was wondering when you'd show up. We set this meeting for ten minutes ago."

I raise my chin, not letting him get to me. "I was ambushed by paparazzi outside the building. What happened to your airtight security, Cal? Awfully convenient you let that slack on the day we're supposed to meet."

"Let's get this over with," he mutters, not taking the bait.

"We're done, Callum," I say, hoping my voice sounds as firm as I want it to. "I'm pulling out of Silver Shadows once and for all. There's nothing you can do about it. Your days of controlling me and my career are officially over."

Carla steps forward and pulls something out of her briefcase, setting it on the table in front of Cal's lawyer. "Obviously, we can all be in agreement that there was a breach of contract. There's not much else to say other than the fact that your client stole from my client, violating the terms. As of today, my client will no longer be under contract with Silver Shadows Records. This is an agreement of termination of the contract effective immediately and acknowledgment that my client will get proper compensation and credit for her intellectual property. In return, we will not take this to court. I believe we have outlined fair terms that we can all come to agreement on."

Callum rolls his eyes and scoffs. His lawyer shoots him an annoyed glance. Callum doesn't heed the silent admonishment, choosing to let his ego get the best of him.

"This is ridiculous. You have no grounds for termination. The contract specifically states that anything Jersey Matthews creates while under contract is property of the label."

"You coerced Kelsey and had her steal from my personal belongings," I say incredulously. "That's the definition of invasion of privacy and theft, not to mention a blatant abuse of power."

Cal waves his hand, dismissing the notion. "It won't hold up. We'll take you to court, Jersey. You might be successful, but you're nowhere near as resourceful as the label."

"There isn't a judge that would rule in your favor, and you

know it," my lawyer says, glaring at Cal's lawyer behind the desk. He narrows his eyes, but looks away.

Callum watches the exchange with disdain. "Are you serious? You're not going to argue back anything?"

The lawyer exhales. "We've spoken about this, Callum. There is clear professional misconduct here. What did we agree on before this meeting?"

Cal clenches his jaw so tightly I'm worried he might crack his molars. Instead of addressing his lawyer, he turns back to me. "What's your plan now, Jersey? We own your entire career up to this point. You think you'll be able to continue on as if nothing happened? Say goodbye to the tour, say goodbye to the album. If you walk away now, all that goes away. You would be nothing if not for me."

The goal for me is freedom. That's all I care about.

Sharing a look with my lawyer, we seem to communicate silently. She nods.

"I trust you'll review and sign that. You can send it back to my office as soon as it's complete." There's nothing else for me to say, so I turn to leave, but pause . . .

Facing him again, I narrow my eyes. "Just tell me why."

"Jersey," Carla says, urging me to go, but I can't. I have to know.

"What did I *ever* do to you to earn so much contempt from you?"

Cal levels me with a blank stare, folding his hands on the table. "You were signed to Silver Shadows. Against my say. I voted *no*," he says with a humorless laugh. "I said I didn't want you, but they assigned you to me, anyway. I never planned on you turning into an overnight sensation, or for the momentum to increase. My only option then was to ride the wave, but you could be so stubborn, and I wasn't going to allow one of your misguided opinions to wreck everything *I* had built thus far."

"So, you hate me because I was willing to speak up for myself?"

"You needed to learn your place. You needed to be broken. I was the only one who was capable of doing that."

And he had succeeded. The memories flood in, reminding me of all those times I let him walk all over me, make decisions I didn't agree with all for the sake of "keeping the momentum." Keeping the peace. He had broken me, and I had gone along with most of what he said.

"At the end of the day, it didn't matter. I made all the decisions because I knew what was best. After all, *you* work for *me*," he snarls.

I straighten my spine, anger licking up the length of my entire back. Narrowing my gaze on him, I say with the utmost conviction, "Not anymore, I don't."

Turning on my heel, I walk right out of there, holding my head high.

The minute I step through the conference door, a weight lifts off my shoulders. The pressure in my chest dissipates and I can finally breathe again.

My team follows after me, closing the door quickly behind them and giving us privacy.

I don't stop, and walk toward the elevator and clicking the button, once, twice. When it arrives, I step in, my team in tow and crowding around me. I press the button for the ground floor, and when the doors close, I nearly collapse. Bethany and Carla catch me, each of them bracing me under my arms.

Though I'm finally free, the realization seems too much for me to hold right now. Slowly, they lower me to the ground.

I focus on taking deep breaths, trying not to let myself

succumb to the intensity and absolute nightmare of the last few days.

I barely register the elevator stopping, the doors opening, and Bethany calling for Hayes. But soon enough he's there, crouching in front of me and cupping my face with his hands.

"I've got her," he says to the women. He scoops me up into his arms and carries me to one of the seating areas in the main lobby. I rest against his chest, feeling overwhelmed but so, so free.

"I did it," I whisper, just to him. My fingers clench in his T-shirt. Hayes sits down, placing me in his lap and pushing my hair out of my face so he can see me better. The sight of him watching me so tenderly, pride shining in his eyes, makes my heart ache and tears burn behind my lids. "I did it."

"I knew you would," he whispers before pressing a kiss to my lips. "I'm so proud of you, Jersey."

I let out a long-awaited breath, finally cleansing my lungs of the poison I've been breathing. I look around and find Bethany watching me with tears brimming her eyes.

My lawyer is tapping on her phone, but she looks up when she senses my gaze on her. "You did great, Jersey. Cal's lawyer just sent me notification that Cal signed the agreement. You're officially an independent artist."

"Wow," I say with a breath. "It feels a little surreal."

"What's next, then?" Bethany asks.

I turn from her to Hayes, who is still watching me with pride. He strokes his hand over my head again. It's a valid question. I have no idea what's next. The last two days I've been consumed with confronting Callum. That was what was next. But now? Now I have endless possibilities. I don't have to conform to the Silver Shadows schedule anymore. I can do whatever I want, go wherever I want, sing *whatever I want.*

Hayes's amber eyes study mine intently, like he's trying to read my mind. There's no chance he could. My thoughts are swirling around like a cyclone. I keep settling back on one notion, and I know that has to be what happens first.

"I want to sell my condo," I say with conviction. Hayes's lips twitch at the corners. "I'm moving to Milwaukee."

epilogue

JERSEY

ONE YEAR LATER

"WHAT DO YOU THINK?" I ask Hayes when I step into the living room. I do a little spin and my yellow dress swishes around me.

The weight of Hayes's eyes hit me like a freight train, and if I wasn't feeling beautiful before, I sure as hell am now. He gets up from his seat on the couch and saunters over to me, gaze trailing over my dress and landing on my face.

When he's close enough, I see his attention flit down to the red stain on my lips before meeting my eyes again.

"That dress has me thinking that we should probably just stay in tonight." His voice is low, promising something that has my toes curling and nerves tingling.

"You'd have me miss my own release party?" I say, my voice breathy.

"If I get to take that dress off you? Yes, absolutely." I know he's teasing—he'd never want me to put aside such an important event—yet the insinuation is fun and scandalous.

It only made sense to have the release party in my favorite little town on earth, so tonight we're celebrating the album at Red Zone. Preston and Mickey were over the moon when we asked them to host the party at their bar, sharing a quick glance and agreeing within seconds. I made sure Preston knew Chloe was invited too, so he could bring her along. We'll be meeting up with our friends and a few lucky fans who were chosen by my new PR team to be in attendance.

"What if I make you a deal?" I ask him, playing along.

He bends down and nibbles a trail from my shoulder up to my ear, where he whispers, "I'm listening."

"What if—" I pause, sucking in a deep breath when his teeth tug on my earlobe. "We go to the release party, and then you get to take the dress off *after*?"

"Deal," he says without hesitation before capturing my lips in a deep kiss.

When he pulls away, my head is spinning. Crazy, given I haven't even had a single drink yet tonight.

He has my lipstick smudged all over his lips and mouth, just like he always seems to when I put on makeup. It's like he has to mess up the first coat just so I have to reapply a second one.

I reach up and wipe at his mouth a bit, unable to keep the amusement off my face. "You always do this."

His eyes glint mischievously. "Maybe I like the idea of your lipstick smudged all over me. You all over me."

"Your flirt game is strong tonight," I muse.

"I'm just proud of you." His voice has grown soft again, tender. "You've accomplished so much in the last year."

"You have too," I respond, thinking about the replica of the Lombardi Trophy sitting on Hayes's trophy shelf at home. His Super Bowl win last season still goes down in my memory as one of the most unforgettable nights of my life.

"Maybe." He kisses the tip of my nose. "But tonight isn't about me. It's about you—my beautiful, talented, incredible *fiancée*."

I preen under his praise, thinking about the long days and the longer nights piecing this album together.

It was a daunting task, deciding I was ready and willing to put out my first independent album. Without the weight of a big name label behind me, there was every possibility that the album could've flopped and it wouldn't take me anywhere, but with the settlement on top of additional compensation for Meghan's song helped with the production cost. Even without being a part of Silver Shadows, my fan base is devoted and willing to take a chance on me—the real me.

They've *loved* the album.

It shot up to the very top of the ranks, where it has stayed for the last few weeks. Words can't even describe how thankful I am.

Silver Shadows has been working hard to rebuild their reputation in the time since I left. Meghan Connelly—bless her —made a public apology, saying she didn't realize the song had been mine, and she rescinded her offer with Callum, only agreeing to stay with Silver Shadows under different management. Callum resigned after receiving significant backlash from the media and internet and is now officially out of the music industry. Tonight, I'm making a statement. I'm taking this piece of the industry for myself and putting my name back out there.

Jersey Matthews. The *real* Jersey Matthews.

And after tonight, Hayes and I will start planning for our wedding.

We're planning to get married next spring, in the offseason.

I'm not settling for anything short of greatness, for the both of us.

I can't wait to be Hayes's wife. I can't wait to continue to accomplish all of my hopes and dreams with him by my side, and I can't wait to watch him do the very same with all of his goals.

Thinking about all this, I wrap my arms around his waist and hug him. "Thank you for believing in me, Hayes. I really couldn't have done this without you."

He kisses the top of my head and tightens his arms around me. "You could have. I just made it easier."

He's made everything in my life easier. I can't imagine my life without him.

When we make it to Red Zone, I'm awestruck by everything once more. Fans are lined up outside of the bar, waiting for me to arrive. As soon as I step out of the car, they chant and scream my name, holding up photos and vinyl albums for me to sign.

I can't fight the smile off my face, waving at them as I pass, choosing to stop here and there to take photos and thank everyone for coming and supporting the album. Hayes is behind me the whole time and keeps a hand centered on my lower back, letting me know he's close by just in case I need him.

But I don't.

It's like I fit right back into the version of myself who was the world's top charting artist with no hesitation.

Once I saw everyone there, excited to see me, it all came back, like riding a bike.

By the time I make it inside the venue, I'm filled to the brim with gratitude. My hands are shaking, but more from excitement rather than nervousness.

Roman and Bethany meet me not long after I've entered. Bethany hugs me while Roman shakes Hayes's hand.

Bethany holds me at arm's length, taking me in head to toe. "What a knockout dress."

"Thank you," I say, swishing the skirt a bit for good measure.

Mickey and Preston walk up on cue, Chloe standing next to her dad. She gives me a quick hug, and then asks, "So, what do you think?"

The lighting in the bar is lower, creating an ambience. A DJ is stationed at the other end of the building, vibing with all the dancers already out on the floor. Servers walk around carrying trays of champagne and appetizers.

"This is incredible. I can't believe you guys organized all of this."

"You deserve it." Mickey grins and Preston readily agrees.

"And you two helped?" I ask Roman and Bethany, though I know their answer already.

"Moral support." My brother winks.

I laugh and roll my eyes. Same old answer, same old Roman.

"Where's Kelsey?" I ask, searching the room for my ex-publicist.

Roman surprises me when his expression hardens for a second, eyebrows furrowing in as he scans the room. "She's here somewhere." He rubs the back of his neck, for a second almost appearing worried. "I should go find her. She doesn't love big events like this."

I know he's right. For being in PR for as long as she was, she really hated attending events. Now that she's working as Roman's personal assistant, I can imagine being in this environment might not be her most favorite thing. She was overjoyed when I told her my brother needed a new PA, and she didn't hesitate to take the position. When I told her I would have her back, I meant it. And I'm so glad to still have her in my life as a friend.

Before I can get another word in, Roman saunters off, still

looking slightly worried. I turn to Bethany. "What's going on there?"

"Who knows?" She shrugs, unbothered, as she checks her watch. She's been my friend long enough that she's used to Roman's odd actions every once in a while. "We should get you up there. I said we'd introduce you at exactly nine o'clock."

Bethany grabs my hand and leads me up to the stage, where the DJ hands her a microphone. Bethany gets everyone's attention and thanks them all for coming.

"We have a wonderful evening planned for you all. It means the world to Jersey and our whole team that you all showed up this evening to celebrate her and her new album!" Bethany looks at me, giving me a loving smile as she and the rest of the room clap. "So now, the moment you all have waited for. It's my pleasure to introduce Jersey Matthews to the stage to sing for you tonight!"

I move to center stage, accepting the microphone and scanning the crowd. People cheer my name and hold up their phones as they snap photos or take videos of this moment to share later.

"Well, hi there," I say, my lips curving up. They all cheer again. "I want to thank you all for coming out tonight. This album means a lot to me, and what means even more is that you've stuck with me over the last year during all the changes and the radio silence. Saying thank you is one thing, but I'd like to pay you back by singing a few songs. What do you think about that?"

I laugh when they all cheer again. One of the stage managers hands me a guitar and moves a stool out for me to sit on before positioning the microphone at the proper height. After getting comfortable, I strum a few chords and then look out at the crowd again.

My breath catches.

When I'd agreed to do some live performances of a few songs off the album, I didn't think I'd be holding everyone's attention. I'm a little taken aback at how everyone is zeroed in on me. Of course I've played much larger audiences in much larger venues, but this is the first time I'll be performing *my songs* for anyone other than Mickey and Preston and the few patrons at Red Zone.

For the first time in a long time, everything feels the way it should. I finally get to share my personal words with them. They get to know a part of me that in the past felt so intimate. I never thought those words ingrained in my being were ever worthy of being sung. Now, that part of me knows it deserves to be heard, and I think that's pretty magical.

So I do what I was born to do, and I sing.

As the words and the melody leave me, I scan the crowd, searching for the pair of amber eyes that I know are watching me.

When I find him, my heart skips a beat. The sheer level of pride and love in his expression is overwhelming, like he's never seen anything quite like me before. Holding his gaze, I think in the back of my mind that I've never known success until this moment. It has nothing to do with the division championships, the Super Bowl, or best-selling self-titled albums.

It has nothing to do with any of that, and everything to do with *him*.

Without him, none of it would matter. The life that Hayes and I have built together is the greatest thing I've ever achieved.

Together, we're unstoppable.

The End.

acknowledgments

Thank you to everyone who has been involved with the creating and perfecting of *Everything In Between*. This was my passion project and I could not be happier with how it turned out!

Thank you to my Indie Queens: Alice, Kris, and Tiffany, who have all been so supportive in every possible way. I don't think this job would be half as fun or satisfying without you all! Thank you for the utmost care and attention you showed this book, it wouldn't be what it is without all of your initial input. Thank you for loving Hayes and Jersey as much as I do.

Thank you a million times to my editor, Lacey Braziel. It was truly a privilege to be working with you on this project. I learned so much and had such a great experience honing and perfecting my craft, and I had such a wonderful time getting to know you and yapping about all of our favorite fandoms we have in common! Thank you so much for the love and attention to detail you showed this manuscript. I can't wait to continue working with you on future projects.

Thank you to my wonderful husband who puts up with me when my mind is a million other places in every stage of the writing process. Your support and your patience with me mean the world.

And finally, thank you to Adam (and to the real Adam who inspired him), who miraculously made it to the very last stage of editing before finally being caught. You truly win the gold medal.

Thank you for reading! Onto the next project!

Love, Aria

about the author

Aria Harding is a romance novelist from the Midwest, USA. Aria has been a long-time lover of romance novels and is excited to be a part of the romance book community. Her goal is to write stories that make readers feel as though they are immersed and experiencing the same highs and lows as the characters on the page. Her favorite tropes to write include small town, enemies-to-lovers, second chance and slow burn. Aria always looks forward to connecting with readers so feel free to reach out on social media and have a chat!

Instagram: @ariaharding_author

Chasing Infinity (A Romantic Suspense)

Wonderstruck (A Workplace Billionaire Romance)

Cedar Ridge Series (Small Town Romance)

Book 1: Loathing Ryan (Enemies to Lovers)

Book 2: Liberating Bells (Second Chance Romance)

Book 3: Just Josie (Childhood Lovers / Second Chance)

His Perfect Art Trilogy

Book 1: His Perfect Canvas

www.ingramcontent.com/pod-product-compliance
Lightning Source LLC
Chambersburg PA
CBHW020345010826
48973CB00005B/1279